ANGELICA ELING

CHANGING
Course

A Waverly Cove Romance

Copyright © 2026 by Angelica Eling

ISBN 978-1-971626-01-7

All rights reserved.

No part of this publication may be reproduced, distributed, or transmitted in any form or by any means without prior written permission from the publisher, except for brief quotations in critical reviews and certain other noncommercial uses permitted by copyright law.

This is a work of fiction. Names, characters, places, businesses, events, and incidents are either products of the author's imagination or used in a fictitious manner. Waverly Cove, Maine and all locations within it exist solely in these pages. Any resemblance to actual persons, living or dead, or actual events and places is purely coincidental.

Book Cover by JordanPaigeStudio

For anyone who ever chose the safe path and wondered about the other one.

Disclaimers

Changing Course is a prequel to *Uncharted Waters*, but both novels stand alone. You don't need to have read one to love the other.

I want you to feel safe and comfortable while reading, so here's what to expect in this book:

Kate and Alex's story includes sexual content, scenes of parental pressure and family expectations, academic stress, mentions of food and financial insecurity, and a scene where a character experiences illness.

If any of these things might be difficult for you right now, it's completely okay to set this book aside. Your wellbeing matters more than finishing any story. You can always come back to Waverly Cove when you're ready.

Angelica

Chapter 1

Kate

Fifty-two percent. The red number screamed at me from the top of my latest chemistry quiz, ink slightly smudged where Professor Martinez's hand had dragged across the page. Around me, chairs scraped backward with a screech of metal on linoleum as my classmates surged toward the door. Friday afternoon freedom. Relief. Escape.

I stayed frozen at my lab bench with the benzene rings I'd drawn swimming before me. They were perfect. Six-sided, connected, symmetrical. Little honeycombs arranged in patterns that had been so artful when I'd drawn them. Now the red Xs covering the page ruined the aesthetic.

"Westfield." Dr. Martinez's voice cut through the emptying room. "A word."

My lab partner touched my shoulder as he passed. His mouth was twisted in a grimace that said *better you than me*. I folded the quiz with numb fingers, then unfolded it and started over. Anything to keep my hands busy while my throat closed up.

Dr. Martinez perched on the edge of his desk and waited until the last student filed out. The door clicked shut. I watched through the small window as people moved through September sunshine, free and unburdened.

"This is your third quiz below sixty percent." He pulled off his reading glasses. Without them, exhaustion lined his face. Like he'd had this conversation too many times before.

"I know." The folded quiz paper dampened in my hands. "I've been studying, I swear. Six hours in the library last weekend alone, I went through the entire textbook chapter, I made flashcards..."

"I don't doubt your effort." He rubbed the bridge of his nose where his glasses left red marks. "But Kate, effort and understanding aren't always the same thing."

I nodded absently. The fluorescent lights hummed overhead so loudly that my teeth ached.

"Have you considered that nursing might not be the right fit?"

His words sliced through every careful layer of protection I'd built up. I *had* considered it. Late at night when the formulas swam together like watercolors bleeding past their lines, but hearing them spoken aloud in this sterile lab gave them edges. Made them solid. The butterflies trapped in my stomach suddenly flew free, which only made everything worse because I shouldn't have felt relief.

"Nursing is definitely the right fit." My voice came out higher than normal, almost childlike. I cleared my throat to dislodge the lump forming there. "Healthcare is in my blood. My Dad runs a PT practice, my mom's an ER nurse, and my brother Liam's in med school at B.U. I'm just having trouble with chemistry specifically. Once I get past the pre-reqs, I'll be fine."

Pity softened Dr. Martinez's expression. So much worse than disappointment. "Chemistry isn't just a prerequisite, Kate. It's foundational. Understanding how medications work, how the body processes drugs, how different compounds interact..."

"I know." I interrupted, cheeks flushing hot. "Sorry. I know it's important. I just need to study harder. Or differently. Maybe get a tutor?"

"A tutor might help." He stood, gathering his papers, already moving on. Students like me were a Friday footnote. "There's a list posted in the lobby of the pharmacy building. Some students offer tutoring services. Reasonable rates, usually."

I nodded so vigorously my ponytail bounced. "Yes. Absolutely. I'll check it out today. Right now, actually."

Dr. Martinez paused at the door with his hand on the frame. "Kate. There's no shame in recognizing something isn't the right path. Sometimes the detour leads somewhere better."

Then he was gone, and I was alone in the empty classroom with my 52% and a sense of impending doom.

I pulled my cell out to text something desperate to my best friend, Gemma, and saw a message from my mom, sent this morning before I'd even walked into this disaster.

> MOM
> Hope your quiz goes well, hon!
> Love you.

I could picture her sitting at our kitchen table in Waverly Cove, still in her pajamas but with her scrubs laid out on the chair, typing with her thumbs while she rushed through her coffee before her shift at Coastal Memorial. She'd been so proud when I got into Northeastern's nursing program. She and Dad had told everyone. Neighbors, coworkers, the cashier at Henderson's Hardware, even strangers in line at the Daily Knead bakery. *Our little Katie's following in our footsteps.*

I blinked back tears and shoved the phone in my pocket without responding.

The walk across campus felt like moving underwater. September in Boston wasn't like September back home. The air was heavy with car exhaust and smelled nothing like the ocean. Students rushed past me in both directions, everyone moving with purpose.

I missed the clean bite of salt air. I missed the way autumn snuck into Waverly Cove one branch at a time, maples turning gold and orange. Here, the trees were still a stubborn green. Cracked concrete covered the sidewalks instead of worn brick. Sirens wailed in the distance. A delivery truck beeped in reverse. My mistakes here got recorded in databases and printed on transcripts.

By the time I reached White Hall, my backpack straps had carved grooves into my shoulders and my feet hurt. I'd forgotten to wear socks this morning.

Our room on the eighth floor was barely big enough for two twin beds, two desks, and the accumulated belongings of two girls trying to make a closet feel like home. My side had become an archeological dig of clothes draped over the chair, textbooks stacked in precarious towers, an iPod strangled in its charger cord, and a coffee mug growing something that might qualify as a science experiment if I avoided it for another few days. A massive photo collage covered the wall above my unmade bed: me and Gemma sun-drunk and sand-covered last summer, the entire Westfield clan crammed around me in a graduation cap under a "Class of 2011" banner, my niece covered in more finger paint than the paper she'd been attacking.

I missed them all. The controlled chaos of family dinners, Gemma's summer visits to her grandmother's cottage down by the harbor, even my nosy neighbors.

My roommate, Isa, sat at her desk on her side of the room, surrounded by color-coded notes and textbooks arranged by size. Her scrubs hung wrinkle-free on a hanger hooked over her closet door. She made her bed with hospital corners. Even her pens were perfectly parallel to the edge of her desk. With her flawless caramel skin and pearly white teeth, Isabel Diaz truly was the poster-child for capable nursing student. And I couldn't even resent her for it because she was sweet and kind to boot.

"How'd the quiz go?" She didn't even look up from her notes.

I flopped onto my bed, springs squeaking, and stared at the water stain on the ceiling that looked like an elephant. Or maybe a rabbit. "Like the Titanic meeting the iceberg. Spectacular, tragic, with no hope of righting the ship."

"That bad?" Isa swiveled in her chair and saw my face. "Oh. *That* bad."

"I drew the benzene rings really nicely though." I held up the crumpled quiz without lifting my head from the pillow. "Like, artistically, they were excellent hexagons. Very symmetrical. Worthy of framing, honestly."

"Kate."

"Fifty-two percent."

"Shit." Isa rose and settled on the edge of my bed, careful to avoid the pile of laundry I'd dumped there this morning. She wore leggings and an oversized Northeastern sweatshirt, her dark curly hair pulled back. "What did Martinez say?"

I pressed my palms against my eyes until I saw spots, then pulled them away and blinked at the ceiling. "That I should consider whether nursing is the right fit. And that chemistry isn't just a prerequisite, it's foundational, and if I can't understand it now, how will I ever understand pharmacology..." My throat closed up. "He said there's no shame in recognizing something isn't the right path."

"Okay, but organic chemistry is brutal for everyone. Remember last semester when I had a complete breakdown..."

"You got an A-minus, Isa."

"After studying constantly and consuming enough caffeine to power a small country." She reached over and smoothed out my crumpled quiz paper. "Look, you're really good at the hands-on stuff. Remember in the skills lab when you were the only one who could start the IV on that practice arm? Everyone else kept missing the vein and you just..." She made a quick stabbing motion with her hand. "Boom. First try."

The praise did nothing to silence the whisper: *What if trying isn't enough?*

"Dr. Martinez mentioned tutoring." I rolled onto my side to face her, tucking my hands under my cheek. "Some pharmacy students tutor chemistry, apparently. There's a list posted somewhere."

"That's perfect." Isa lit up immediately. "Pharm students are brilliant at breaking down the complex stuff into actual English. Plus they've taken all the same courses we have, so they know exactly what trips people up."

"You really think it could help?"

"Absolutely. And Kate, come on. You're way too stubborn to let chemistry derail your entire nursing career. You've wanted this since freshman year."

Had I? I tried to trace it back. There was the guidance counselor's office with those awful motivational posters (**Your Future Starts NOW!**), and that time I shadowed Mom at Coastal Memorial and the ER was like this perfectly choreographed dance of people who knew exactly where to go and what to grab and who needed what. But when had I actually decided? Or had everyone just decided for me, and I'd been too busy being a people pleaser to notice?

"Maybe I should check out that list." I pushed up, shaking off the uncomfortable thoughts. Movement was better than thinking. Action was better than doubt. "Martinez said it was in the Pharm building."

"Probably the bulletin board in Ayers Hall. That's where they usually post that stuff. Want me to walk over with you after dinner?"

"Actually..." I grabbed my denim jacket from the floor, shoving my arms through the wrinkled sleeves. "I'm gonna go now. No point sitting around feeling sorry for myself when I could take action, right? Seize the day, and all that."

Isa grinned. Relief smoothed the worry lines between her eyebrows. This was the Kate she knew. Optimistic, bouncing back, already moving toward a solution. "There she is. Text me if you need moral support or someone to vet the tutor for serial killer vibes."

"Will do." I grabbed my backpack, then set it down because I didn't need it, then picked it up again because walking across campus without it felt weird.

I walked fast, weaving through clusters of students, my sneakers squeaking on the walkway. The pharmacy building was across the quad, past the library, right next to the science complex where I'd just failed. Returning to the scene of the crime.

It was easy to find the bulletin board in Ayers Hall right inside the main entrance. My eyes scanned through the layers of flyers promoting study groups, apartments, a mini-fridge for $40 OBO, and about fifteen different spring break trips to Cancun even though it was only September.

The tutoring section was in the bottom right corner. Most looked professionally typed with hourly rates that made my stomach drop. $45/hour. $60/hour. $50/hour for group sessions. My savings from working at my sister-in-law's bakery all summer barely covered textbooks and the occasional coffee.

But then, tucked in the bottom right corner, almost hidden

behind a larger flyer advertising ACT prep, was a simple index card with tidy handwriting:

> CHEMISTRY TUTORING
> General and Organic
> Flexible schedule, reasonable rates
> Focus on conceptual understanding
> Contact Alex Chen

"Conceptual understanding." That phrase grabbed me. Not just memorization, not just formulas. Understanding. Maybe this Alex person knew what it was like to look at chemical structures and see only meaningless shapes.

I pulled out my phone and took a photo of the card, making sure to capture the email details. Through the window beside the bulletin board, students walked past, laughing about something.

The photo on my screen was replaced with a notification that I'd received another message from my mother.

> **MOM**
> How did the quiz go? Dad says hi and wants to know if you need anything from home.

The image formed so clearly: Dad in his office at the clinic, probably between patients, taking a break to ask Mom if she'd heard from me. Mom sneaking her phone out at the nurses' station to check her messages and immediately going into mama bear mode.

> **KATE**
> Fine! Just getting some extra help with chemistry to make sure I really understand everything. Love you both!

I added a heart emoji. Then another one. And a third for good measure. Then felt sick at how fake they looked.

It wasn't exactly a lie. I was going to get help. And I did love them. The rest could wait. The crushing disappointment, the growing certainty that I was forcing myself into a future that didn't fit, the way my stomach twisted every time I thought about my dad telling his patients about his daughter, the nursing student.

Future Kate could deal with all that. Present Kate just needed to make it through today. Then tomorrow. And then the day after that.

I walked back across campus, the sun dropping lower and taking the temperature with it. That New England September shift from afternoon warmth to evening chill. I shoved my hands deeper into my jacket pockets and walked faster.

Back in our room, Isa waited expectantly. "Well? Any promising options?"

I pulled up the grainy photo on my phone and turned it toward her. "Found someone. Now I just have to work up the courage to actually email them."

"Kate Westfield, afraid to talk to someone?" Isa's whole body shook with laughter. "You once convinced that grad student to let us into that fancy donor reception just by smiling and asking nicely."

"That was different. That was charming my way into something fun. This is..." I dropped onto my bed, staring at my phone screen. "This is admitting I need help. That I can't figure it out on my own. That maybe I'm not cut out for..."

"Hey." Isa chastised. "You're not admitting defeat. You're taking charge of the situation. Those are completely different things."

Part of me wanted to believe her. I changed into leggings and an old Waverly Cove Lighthouse 5K t-shirt that still smelled faintly like home. Settling in at my desk and opening my laptop, I nudged aside the stack of chemistry notes I'd made last week.

The blank email stared at me, the cursor blinking accusingly.

```
Hi Alex,

I saw your tutoring card at Ayers Hall.
I'm a sophomore nursing student, and I'm
really struggling with organic chemistry.
My quiz scores have been rough, and I need
to get this under control before I'm too
far behind to catch up.
```

Too desperate. I deleted the last part.

```
I'm a sophomore nursing student taking
organic chemistry, and I'd like to set up
some tutoring sessions if you're still
available. Dr. Martinez recommended
getting extra help, and your card
mentioned conceptual understanding, which
is exactly what I need.
```

Better. More professional. Less drowning.

```
I'm pretty flexible on scheduling, and I'm
a fast learner once things click. I'm
happy to work around your schedule. My
number is below if that is easier than
email.
```

I read it three times and added my name and phone number before sending it.

The whoosh sound felt final. Somewhere on campus, Alex Chen would open his email and see a message from a stranger asking for help. A nursing student who couldn't understand basic chemistry concepts.

I refreshed my email anxiously, as though that would make Alex respond faster. Nothing.

"Kate." Isa didn't look up from her notes. "Stop checking. If he's any good, he'll respond soon. And if he doesn't respond, I'm sure there are other options on that board."

"I know. I'm just..." I closed my laptop, removing the temptation to refresh again. "What if I can't learn this? What if tutoring doesn't help? What if Dr. Martinez is right and I'm just not cut out for..."

"Then you'll figure something else out. You always do." Isa finally turned around. "But you can't future-trip yourself into failure before you've even tried the solution."

She was right. I knew she was right. But sitting here in this dorm room with my 52% and my growing doubts and my parents' pride hanging around my neck, I couldn't help thinking that maybe I wasn't asking Alex Chen to help me understand chemistry.

Maybe I was asking him to help me save everything I was supposed to want to be.

But I'd emailed. I'd taken action. I'd done something instead of just sitting here spiraling.

That had to count for something.

...Right?

Chapter 2

Alex

The graduated cylinder read 47.3 milliliters. I recorded the measurement in my lab notebook with the same careful block letters I'd used since freshman year, then double-checked the number against my calculation. Correct.

Around me, other students rushed through their titrations, eager to finish the assignment and escape into the sunshine streaming through the lab windows. I maintained my usual pace. Precision mattered more than speed. One careless measurement could invalidate an entire experiment.

My phone skittered across the lab bench. The screen showed Māmā, 3:30 PM. Right on schedule.

"One moment." I touched my lab partner David's shoulder. He nodded without looking up from his own pipette. I grabbed my notebook and pen on my way out the door so I could review my notes while I talked.

The hallway outside was quieter and cooler than the classroom. My rubber-soled sneakers squeaked on the polished floor.

"Nǐ hǎo Māmā," I said, automatically switching to Mandarin.

"Alex! How is school today?" Li Mei Chen's voice carried

exhaustion that came from hours standing over a hot stove. The Golden Dragon kitchen geared up for dinner service in the background. Knives on cutting boards. Oil sizzling in woks. The rhythmic chopping of prep work. I could almost smell the garlic and ginger through the phone.

"My law and ethics exam went well. Ninety-four percent."

"Ah, very good. Your father will be happy." A pause filled with more kitchen sounds. "Alex, have you seen Jennifer lately? Mrs. Liu mentioned you haven't called in weeks. But I told her you're both so busy with studies."

I bit my pen cap. The metal clicked against my teeth. Jennifer Liu. The conversation I'd been dancing around since our mutual acknowledgment last semester. We both agreed we worked better as friends than anything else.

"I already have a study partner, Māmā. David and I work well together."

"Yes, yes, David is a good boy. But Jennifer, she needs friends too. Mrs. Liu says pre-med is very hard, very lonely. Maybe you can take her to dinner sometime?"

Through the hallway window, my eyes tracked the stream of students crossing the courtyard below. Couples walked hand in hand toward the dining hall with an ease I observed often but rarely experienced myself. My romantic history consisted of family dinners with Jennifer, whose parents had grown up alongside mine in their village outside Guangzhou.

We'd attempted the dating thing last year to appease our parents. Grabbed dinner a few times. Held hands as we walked down Newbury Street. I bought her a scarf for Christmas that she never wore. When she kissed me outside the movie theater on our fifth date, she angled her face away from the streetlight, and my hands hung at my sides because I couldn't determine where they should go.

Finally, over coffee in the library where I now did my tutoring,

Jennifer set down her cup and met my eyes. "We're great friends, Alex. Maybe that's enough."

Our parents disagreed. The Lius still sent birthday gifts. My mother still asked about Jennifer's classes, her future career, and whether she was eating enough. We remained close friends, despite our failed attempt at romance and the pressure from our parents.

Jennifer texted me a photo from a protest march downtown just last week. She held a sign about affordable housing.

> JENNIFER
>
> My parents think I'm at the library.
>
> Sometimes I wonder if they'd still be proud if they knew the real me.

That message held my attention for a long time before I responded with a thumbs up. I was jealous of her quiet rebellion. The same weight pressed down every time my parents mapped out my future without asking what I wanted, but I'd never been brave enough to step off the path they paved for me.

"I'll keep that in mind." My default response to these suggestions. My free hand absently traced the spiral binding's metal coils.

"Good, good. Your father wants to talk to you."

Static rustled as the phone changed hands.

"Alex." My father's voice came through deep and careful. "Grades still good?"

"Yes, Bàba. On track for the Dean's list again this semester."

"Good. You work hard now to have a good life later. We work at this restaurant so you don't have to, understand? You will become a pharmacist, have respect, and security. Important things."

My free hand formed a fist. Fingernails making crescents in my palm.

"I understand, Bàba."

"Good. And Alex? Jennifer works very hard. She needs a friend like you. Both of you live in Boston now, so there is no excuse not to spend time together."

My shoulder blades prickled. "I'll see what her schedule looks like."

"Good, good. She is a good girl, Alex. Smart, a hard worker, with good family values. You are lucky to have her."

"Maybe." I shifted my weight. "I should get back to lab work."

"Yes, yes. Go study hard. See you for lunch prep on Saturday?"

"Of course."

I ended the call and the hallway ventilation systems hummed in the sudden silence. Through the lab window, David tapped his watch. We needed to finish before the building closed for the evening.

Back at my station, I resumed my process: measure, record, analyze. Each completed step leads toward a predictable outcome. This I understood. Variables I could identify, measure, and manage. Not whatever messy territory my parents' expectations occupied.

"Parents checking in?" David's practiced ease showed in his response. After three years of rooming and studying together, he knew my parents' schedule as well as I did.

"Weekly progress report." I returned each tool to its designated place. "Yours do the same?"

"Every day if I let them." David grinned. "They've started sending me links to dating apps. Apparently, I'm behind schedule on finding a suitable wife."

I stopped organizing my beakers. The look I gave made him laugh.

"Yeah. My dad called yesterday asking when I'm bringing home a nice Korean girl." He piped the solution with steady hands. "Told him Julie's doing great at grad school in California, thanks for asking." He shook his head. "They keep acting like my white girlfriend is somehow going to disappear if they ignore her long enough."

I adjusted my notebook, lining it up with the edge of the counter. David's situation wasn't identical to mine, but the shape felt familiar.

"Do they ever..." I started. The question didn't belong under the bright fluorescent lights of the lab.

"Accept that I might have a different plan?" David finished for me. "Not yet. But I keep showing up anyway."

We finished the homework in companionable silence, my notes filling three pages with detailed observations while David's occupied half a notebook page. Different approaches, same results. Something I found reassuring about our partnership.

As we packed up, I pulled the small stack of tutoring cards from my backpack. Crisp white, with my contact information printed in clean block letters. I made them at the library last week but still wasn't sure about posting them.

"Hey David." I waved the stack in his general direction. "Want to help me post these around campus? Haven't had any takers on my last batch."

David glanced at the cards as he zipped his backpack. "Chemistry tutoring? You explain concepts better than most of our professors." He took three cards. "I'll hang these up in the biology building and maybe the undergraduate library. Lots of pre-meds are struggling there."

"Thanks. I'll handle the pharmacy building and chemistry department." I pocketed the remaining cards. "Though I'm not sure how much time I'll actually have with my course load."

"You'll make time when you see what people will pay for chemistry help." David slung his backpack over his shoulder. "Especially the nursing students. They're drowning in organic chem by October."

I nodded, though working with strangers felt different from helping David understand enzyme kinetics. With him, I knew when silence meant processing rather than confusion. Teaching someone new would require adapting to unfamiliar thought processes.

But my textbook budget was tight, and my parents already worked enough hours to cover tuition. If I could earn enough through tutoring to buy next semester's books and help with lab fees, it would ease some of the financial pressure on my family.

My apartment reflected the same organizational principles as my lab work. Textbooks arranged by subject and height on my desk, class schedules color-coded and pinned to my bulletin board, clothes folded and stored in the small dresser. I'd secured a studio for my final year, leaving behind the shared dorm and the familiarity of rooming with David. The independence and proximity to campus were worth the expense my parents willingly covered, even though staying at their house in Quincy would have been more economical.

Three days after posting the tutoring cards, I'd only received two inquiries. Both freshmen struggling with general chemistry. I'd set up initial consultations for the following week, scheduled around my lab rotations and restaurant shifts.

I sat at my desk checking email before diving into my Friday evening studies. The screen's blue glow washed over my workspace. Professor updates, administrative notifications about Spring registration, a reminder about my pharmacology exam next week. One subject line made me pause: *Chemistry Tutoring?*

Kate Westfield. I opened the email.

```
Hi Alex,

I saw your tutoring card at Ayers Hall.
I'm a sophomore nursing student taking
organic chemistry, and I'd like to set up
some tutoring sessions if you're still
available. Dr. Martinez recommended
getting extra help, and your card
mentioned conceptual understanding, which
is exactly what I need.

I'm pretty flexible on scheduling, and I'm
a fast learner once things click. I'm
happy to work around your schedule.

My number is below if that is easier than
email.

Thanks,
Kate Westfield
(207) 555-1234
```

I read the message twice. The trackpad warmed under my fingertip as I scrolled back to the top, then down again. Nursing student. She'd understand anatomy and physiology basics. But chemistry required spatial thinking about molecules she couldn't see, mathematical relationships that didn't match the concrete memorization of body systems.

The Maine area code caught my eye. I pulled up her profile. Northeastern University, Boston campus. But a 207 number.

Home number, then. Or she'd kept her original phone when she moved for school.

The desk chair creaked as I leaned back. A nursing student

from Maine who needed chemistry help badly enough to spend her Friday night emailing tutors rather than heading to whatever party was happening on campus.

I opened a new message and typed:

```
Hi Kate,

I'd be happy to help with chemistry. I'm
available weekday evenings and weekend
afternoons. Sessions run one to two hours
depending on the material, and my rate is
$15 per hour.

Would you be able to meet on Tuesday
evening at 7 PM? We could use one of the
library study rooms to assess where you're
struggling and develop a plan.

What specific topics in chemistry are
giving you the most trouble?

Alex Chen
617-555-0987
```

After sending the reply, I set my laptop aside and opened my old organic chemistry textbook. The heavy book made a satisfying thump on my desk. I'd need to review general chemistry fundamentals, identify common problem areas, and maybe check my old notes to remember which concepts had given me trouble as an undergraduate. The methodical planning settled my mind, transforming an uncertain social interaction into a series of manageable steps.

I made a note to bring my molecular model kit to our first

session. The plastic spheres and connecting rods had helped me understand three-dimensional structures when formulas alone hadn't clicked.

My laptop chimed. Kate had already responded.

```
Alex,

Tuesday at 7 PM sounds perfect! I'm strug-
gling with molecular structures and bond-
ing. I can understand the concepts when I
read about them, but when I try to work on
problems or predict shapes, I get
confused?! It's like I can see the indi-
vidual pieces but can't fit them together
into the bigger picture.

How will I recognize you at the library???
I'll be the one looking stressed about
chemistry!

Thanks again,

Kate
```

The corners of my mouth twitched upward. Even in written form, her personality came through. Someone who could acknowledge struggle while maintaining optimism. The excessive punctuation suggested enthusiasm, maybe anxiety.

My response was brief.

```
Kate,

The library has study rooms available on
```

```
the second floor. I'm tall with dark hair,
and I'll be wearing glasses. I'll have
chemistry textbooks and molecular models
with me.

See you on Tuesday at 7.

Alex
```

I returned to my textbook, though I couldn't quite focus on the words. Tutoring David or helping Jennifer felt straightforward because I understood their learning patterns through prior interaction. A complete stranger would require more attention to the social cues I sometimes missed.

I flipped through the pages of reaction mechanisms and molecular diagrams, trying to decide what to review first. Structure dictated function in chemistry. If Kate couldn't visualize molecular shapes, she'd struggle with everything that came after. We'd start there. Build a foundation before moving forward.

The apartment was quiet except for the hum of my refrigerator and distant traffic on Huntington Avenue. I made a detailed list of topics to cover, preparing for a tutoring session with a stranger whose enthusiastic triple question marks already suggested someone very different from myself.

Chapter 3

Kate

All of the calculus equations on the whiteboard were giving me a headache. Or maybe that was my failure-induced panic. It was hard to tell at this point. Partial derivatives? Who voluntarily studied partial derivatives? Although, okay, at least one person had sat in this exact study room feeling lost enough to work through an entire problem set on the wall, so maybe I wasn't the most hopeless student to ever occupy this space.

My leg bounced hard enough that my notebook skittered across the table. The study room rivaled a closet for size, and someone had left the heat on too high. Great. Nothing said "competent college student" like sweating before the actual humiliation began.

Alex wasn't late. I was just catastrophically early and had arranged my materials four times already. Blue, black, or red pen? Did it matter? Why had I brought three pens to a tutoring session? What was I planning to do? Color-code my failure?

The door finally swung open at exactly 7pm.

I glanced up. And up. Okay, Alex was *tall*. He wore wire-rimmed glasses and his dark hair stuck up like he'd been running his hands through it. His messenger bag was sliding off his shoulder, but he caught it before adjusting his glasses. The motion left the collar of his dark blue button-down slightly askew.

"Kate?"

I jumped up so fast that the table screeched against the floor. Smooth, Kate, real smooth. "Yes! Alex, right? Hi. Thank you so much for agreeing to this. I seriously thought about bribing you with Needhams from home, but I don't actually know if you like coconut, and also shipping chocolate in this heat seems..." The words tumbled out too fast. Stop rambling before you embarrass yourself, Kate. "Sorry. I talk too much when I'm nervous."

"It's okay." He smiled. "I like Needhams. The coconut is good."

"Oh. Good. Great." We were both standing awkwardly in this tiny room, not sure what to do about it. Shake hands? Sit? I gestured vaguely at the table. "Do you want to..."

"Right. Yes." He took the chair across from me and set his bag down, then seemed to reconsider the position and slid it to the side. The strap caught on the chair arm.

I dropped back into my chair. My blue pen rolled off the table.

We both reached for it at the same time. His hand reached it first, but he pulled back as if the pen might burn him when my hand grazed his. "Sorry, I..."

"No, it's..." I grabbed the pen and knocked my textbook sideways. "Coordination. I have it. Usually."

The corner of his mouth twitched.

He pulled out a notebook from his bag and flipped past several pages covered in handwriting so neat it looked printed, then seemed to think better of it and grabbed a blank sheet instead. "So. Chemistry?"

"Chemistry," I agreed, like we were confirming the existence of the subject. "I'm failing it. Spectacularly. Dr. Martinez actually asked me if I'd considered changing my major, which is basically like asking if I've considered ruining my entire life plan, so that's fun."

Alex blinked owlishly at me with his pen hovering over the page. "What part is... Where should we start?"

I opened my textbook to the chapter that had been making me want to fake my own death for the past week. "This. All of this. Electron configurations, molecular bonding, the part where atoms apparently want to be happy, which honestly–same, but then Dr. Martinez talks about orbitals and hybridization and I just..." I gestured helplessly at the page. "It's like everyone else got a manual and I got a packet of Swedish furniture instructions."

He studied the page. His eyebrows drew together, probably puzzling out how to explain something to someone who clearly wasn't getting it. The study room felt stuffy and hot. Or maybe that was just my face heating up.

"Okay," he said finally. "Let's try... what do you think about when I say molecular orbital?"

I groaned and put my head in my hands. "Truthfully? Okay, you know those subway maps where all the lines cross over each other and go in about a zillion directions? At least those maps tell you 'you are here' and which direction the trains go. This is just... lines. Everywhere. How am I supposed to tell where the electrons can go?"

Silence. I peeked through my fingers.

Alex stared at me, his features giving nothing away. Oh, no. I'd just confirmed his suspicions that I was unteachable. He was probably trying to decide how to escape this tutoring commitment without being rude. Maybe his phone would ring. Maybe he'd pull the fire alarm. Either would be good right now.

"A subway map," he repeated slowly.

"I know it's weird, I just..." I started gathering my things. "Look, if this isn't going to work, I understand. I can find someone else, you don't have to..."

"No, wait." He held up a hand. "That's actually... let me try something." He pulled the blank paper closer and started drawing. Lines, circles, dots. His hand moved across the page with more confidence than he'd had speaking. "What if we actually use the subway map idea?"

I stopped mid-reach for my notebook. "Really?"

"Maybe." He pushed his glasses up. They slid back down. "So if electrons are like passengers, they want the most efficient route, right?"

I leaned forward, cautious. "I mean, passengers make sense. People make sense to me."

"Right. So." He added more lines to his drawing. "Some routes are more popular because they're faster. More direct." He glanced up at me, then back down at the paper. "The electrons fill the lowest energy orbitals first because those are the most efficient routes."

The puzzle pieces in my brain slid into place. "So the orbitals are different train lines? And electrons take the express train first?"

"Exactly." His eyes brightened behind his glasses when he paused again. Then, he seemed to realize he was looking at me and focused back on the drawing. "The express trains fill up first."

I grabbed my red pen and started adding to his diagram. "So if this is the red line, and it fills first, then these electrons would be like morning commuters rushing downtown?"

"Yes, and..." His eyes tracked my pen as it moved across the paper. "You're left-handed."

I paused. "Is that a problem? For chemistry? Did I need to disclose that?"

"No, it's just..." He shook his head slightly. "A lot of visual learners are left-handed. That might be..."

"Visual learner?" I set the pen down. "People usually say I pay attention to everything except what I'm supposed to."

"You just turned molecular orbital theory into a transit system."

He gestured at our drawing. "And you color-coded the energy levels without me saying anything."

The warmth I felt had nothing to do with the overheated study room. "So I'm not completely hopeless at science?"

"No. Just..." He pulled the textbook toward himself. "You need to see it differently."

For the next hour, we worked through problems that had seemed impossible alone in my dorm at two in the morning. It wasn't smooth. I got things wrong. Drew electrons in places they shouldn't go. Mixed up p orbitals and d orbitals because my brain wanted them to be alphabetical.

"Wait, no." Alex leaned over the paper. I got a whiff of laundry detergent and something deliciously masculine. "That electron can't go there. It would be like... like putting a passenger on a train that doesn't exist yet."

"But you said..." The diagram stared back at me, suddenly not as correct as it seemed a moment ago. "Oh. It's in the wrong shell."

"Right, but the logic was good. You just..." He grabbed his own pen and redrew part of the diagram. "Try again?"

He explained it differently, using fewer words this time and more shapes. His glasses kept sliding down his nose. He pushed them up every few minutes, an unconscious gesture that I found myself tracking. When he looked up and found me staring, my face flushed.

"Sorry," he said. "Lost my train of thought."

"It's okay. I lose mine constantly." I tapped my pen against the paper. "So these hybridized orbitals are like... what if the subway built a new express line using parts of different old lines?"

He tilted his head. "That's... actually, yes. They're combining different orbital types to make new configurations."

"Okay." I drew another diagram, more confident now. "So this carbon atom is doing what? Making four new express routes?"

"Yes." He sounded surprised. "That's sp3 hybridization."

"I have no idea what that means, but I'm going to pretend I do and hope it sticks." I grinned at him.

He almost smiled back. I was sure of it this time.

We kept working. The papers between us multiplied, covered with increasingly elaborate subway maps and molecular diagrams. Our handwriting mixed together.

Everything was going well until I accidentally grabbed his hand while blindly reaching for the textbook.

The awkward silence lasted three seconds before I filled it. "Do you do this a lot? Tutoring?"

"Sometimes." He organized his pens into a neat line, creating order from chaos. "I've gotten a few bites on my cards."

"Are they all as hopeless as me?"

"You're not hopeless." He said it to the pens, not to me. "You got that last problem right on the first try."

My gaze dropped to the paper. He was right. I had. "Oh."

"You've been getting them right for a few minutes now." Now he met my eyes. "You're understanding it, not just memorizing steps."

He seemed genuinely surprised and a little proud. Like my success was his success too. The way he said it made me sit taller.

"How did you know to explain it like this?" I asked. "Are you just naturally good at teaching?"

He capped his pen carefully. "I had to figure it out. Chemistry didn't always make sense to me either."

"Really?" I couldn't hide my surprise. "You seem like you probably came out of the womb understanding this stuff."

"No." A shadow crossed his face. "I spent freshman year thinking I'd fail organic chemistry. My parents..." He stopped. He adjusted his pens, though they were already in order. "Failure wasn't an option. So I made it work."

I wanted to ask more, but his tone suggested that door was closed. Instead, I studied him. He had rolled his sleeves up to his elbows, probably because the study room was too hot. His hair stuck up at angles from pushing his hand through it while explaining concepts. The pink on his cheeks might have been the heat or might have been something else.

"Thank you," I said. "For not making me feel stupid."

"You're not stupid." He met my eyes, voice firm. "You just think differently."

His phone chimed from its place on the table. His shoulders tensed as he glanced at the screen.

"I should probably go." He packed up, movements efficient now instead of uncertain. "But this was good. Productive."

"Would you..." The words came out before I could stop them. "Do you want to do this again? I have a quiz next week on molecular geometry, which sounds like something my brain will turn into abstract art."

He paused with his hand on his bag. "Abstract art?"

"You know, where it has some deep meaning but mostly you just feel confused and intimidated?"

The almost-smile was back. "I can work with abstract art."

"Is that a yes?"

"Same time Thursday?"

"Yes. Great. Perfect." I was grinning too wide but couldn't stop. "And Alex? Seriously. Thank you."

He stood at the door, looking back at me. The way he held my gaze felt different than it had an hour ago, like he'd just figured something out. "You're a good student, Kate. You just needed someone to translate it into your language."

Then he was gone, and I sat in the study room alone with our papers spread across the table. I pulled out my phone and took a picture of the whiteboard where we'd drawn our final subway-map molecular orbital hybrid. Just in case I needed to remember that someone had examined my chaotic brain and found something worth working with.

It all made sense here, in this room, with his patient redrawing when I got confused. With his careful pauses before explaining things differently.

Would it still make sense two days from now?

Would he still give me that almost-smile when I compared chemistry to public transportation?

And would it still make my heart race the way it had today?

Chapter 4
Alex

One of the espresso machines in the student union coffee shop screamed through another milk steaming cycle. I'd claimed the corner table ten minutes early, the one where the afternoon light didn't create glare on laptop screens. My molecular model kit sat ready on the table, red oxygen atoms already separated from the white hydrogens.

I'd read the same paragraph about first-pass metabolism three times, but the words weren't sticking. My phone sat next to my textbook with a dark screen. Kate said she'd be here at three.

This was inefficient. I should memorize drug half-lives instead of watching the clock. I forced my eyes back to the page. Hepatic extraction ratio. The formula made sense. Numbers always made sense.

My phone lit up with a text.

> **KATE**
> Running five minutes late! Order me something with enough sugar to fuel a small aircraft and I'll love you forever.

I stared at the message. She didn't mean it literally. People said things like that. Hyperbole was a normal communication pattern. I'd observed this in multiple contexts.

I ordered her a caramel macchiato with an extra shot and black coffee for myself while trying not to overanalyze her choice of words. The student union coffee shop hummed with an undercurrent of overcaffeinated stress. Midterms. Everyone looked desperate.

I organized my notes into three piles: problems Kate had mastered, concepts she still struggled with, and new material for today. Straightening the edges until they lined up. The third pile was smaller than last week. Progress, measurable and quantifiable.

"I'm here!" Kate's voice carried across the room and caught several people's attention. She didn't notice, just dropped into the chair hard enough that our table shook. My coffee sloshed and I caught it before it spilled.

"Sorry, sorry." She breathed fast, cheeks pink from the cold. Hair escaping from her ponytail. "Did I..."

"It's fine." I slid the macchiato across the table.

"You remembered the extra shot." She wrapped her hands around the cup and smiled. "You might be my favorite person right now."

Warmth rushed to my face, and I could feel myself turning red. I busied myself arranging my pens in a line. Black, blue, red. Favorite person. She likely said things like that constantly. To everyone. Data point, not evidence.

"How did your quiz go?" I asked. "The one on substitution reactions."

Her face lit up and she straightened in her chair. "Eighty-one percent. I more than just passed, Alex." She set down her cup too hard and foam sloshed over the rim. "I understood it. I didn't just memorize steps and hope."

"That's good." I pulled napkins from the dispenser and pushed them toward her. "You did the work."

"You provided context." She wiped up the spill, words tumbling faster the way they did when she got excited. "I was sitting there taking the quiz and I could picture your subway map diagrams in my head. The express trains filling up first. It just made sense."

"The analogies were yours," I pointed out. "I just helped organize them."

"Don't do that." She pointed at me with the wadded napkin. "Don't deflect. You're good at this. Teaching. You make impossible things feel possible."

I focused on my coffee, the heat of the cup against my palms. "Teaching isn't the plan."

"Why not?" She leaned forward, elbows on the table. "You're patient. You actually listen when I'm confused instead of just repeating the same thing louder. You..."

"Pharmacy is stable," I cut off that train of thought before it even left the station. "Predictable."

"So is accounting." She pulled out her chemistry notebook, pages now covered in versions of my diagrams in her handwriting. "Doesn't mean you'd enjoy it."

"Some people don't have the luxury of just..." I stopped. Rearranged my pens again even though they were already straight. "The plan doesn't just change."

Kate's hands stilled on her notebook. "You're right," she said finally. "I'm sorry. I didn't mean to assume."

I pulled out the practice problems I'd prepared. Twelve sheets organized by difficulty level. "Let's work on elimination reactions."

The next hour flew by. Kate worked through beta-elimination problems with increasing confidence. Her pencil moved across the page in quick strokes, sketching molecular structures the way other people doodled. Her hands drew my attention. She held her pencil like a paintbrush, hovering over the paper when she was thinking.

"This is where the carbocation forms?" She tapped the paper with her pencil. "Because the leaving group takes both electrons?"

"Right." I leaned closer to see her work. The table was small. Our elbows almost touched. "And why is this carbocation more stable than the other option?"

"More substituted. More alkyl groups donating electron density." Our faces were very close. A small scar marked her eyebrow. Her shampoo smelled like salt air even though we were nowhere near the harbor.

"Like having more friends to lean on during a crisis," she added.

I should say something about the analogy. Something about accuracy. The words stuck somewhere between my brain and my mouth.

"That's..." I leaned back to increase the distance between us. My chair scraped against the floor. "That's right. Good way to think about carbocation stability."

"Thanks." Her smile was smaller than usual. "Sometimes I worry my explanations are too weird."

"They're not weird." I pulled the textbook toward me and flipped to the next section. Something to look at that wasn't Kate's face. "Most students just memorize patterns. Your analogies show you understand the underlying principles."

"Is that why you keep tutoring me?" She did the thing where she looked directly at me. Most people didn't maintain eye contact like that. It made me want to look away, but I didn't. "Because I think differently from your other clients?"

"I don't..." I rearranged the practice problems into a neater stack while I chose my words carefully. "You're the only person I'm currently tutoring."

"Oh." Her eyebrows drew together. "So why..."

"Most people just want help for one exam," I confessed. "You actually want to understand. There's a difference."

Before she could ask another question, my phone alarm sounded. I'd set it for 4:00.

"I should go." I started gathering my notes. "Dinner shift at my parents' restaurant."

"The one in Quincy?" Kate closed her notebook. "I'd love to see it sometime. Family restaurants always feel more..." She paused, like she was looking for the right word. "Alive. Than chains."

Introducing Kate to my parents... The thought twisted my stomach. I wanted her to see it, but I worried about what my parents would think. Worried about what I *wanted* them to think.

"It's not exciting," I said. "Just standard Chinese-American food."

"Food made by people who care is always exciting." Everything disappeared into her bag in seconds. "Plus, I bet you look good in an apron."

Warmth crept up my neck. Kate's expression shifted to surprise.

"I should..." She stood fast enough that her chair tipped backward. "Good luck with your exam tomorrow."

She was halfway across the coffee shop before I remembered to call after her. "Thursday?"

She turned back. "Same time?"

"Same time."

Her grin made my thoughts go sideways.

I gathered my books, giving myself time to catalog what had just happened. Kate thought I'd look good in an apron. She'd said "look good," not "look cute." Different phrasing. Insufficient data to draw conclusions.

People said things like that to friends. I should ask David about normal friend behavior. Except David would immediately make it into something it wasn't. He did that. Made observations and jumped to conclusions without sufficient evidence.

I continued thinking about what Kate had said and how that made me feel the entire trek to Quincy.

The Golden Dragon was in its pre-dinner lull when I arrived. My mother directed waitstaff through opening prep, her voice carrying over the clatter of dishes and silverware. I headed straight to the kitchen, washed my hands, and tied on my apron.

"Alex." My father's voice had that tone that meant Important Discussion. "Help me with dumplings."

I joined him at the prep station. We fell into a familiar rhythm. Roll wrapper, add filling, fold. Three pleats on each side. Except the third pleat never came as tight as Bàba's. His were perfect. Mine were adequate.

We worked in silence for several minutes. My father pinched another dumpling closed with quick, practiced movements. I sometimes wondered if he dreamed about pleated dough.

"Your mother says you..." He paused. Fold, pinch, seal. "She worries you are distracted lately."

"I'm not." I focused on my dumpling. The wrapper was too thick on one side. "My grades are fine."

"Mm." The sound carried decades of skepticism about my definition of fine. "This semester is important. For residency."

I nodded. Set my finished dumpling on the tray. Started another.

"The Lius are coming for dinner." Bàba didn't look up from his assembly line. "Mrs. Liu mentioned you haven't answered Jennifer's messages."

My hands stilled. The dumpling wrapper stuck to my thumb. "I've been busy with..."

"With tutoring." Bàba's tone suggested he'd filed this information under questionable priorities. "Mrs. Liu says Jennifer needs help with organic chemistry also."

The implication was clear. I could help Jennifer. Should help Jennifer. It would serve multiple purposes. Academic support. Family obligation. What my parents called getting to know each other better.

"Jennifer can find her own tutor," I said.

"She's a smart girl. Good family. Pre-med." He gestured with his chin toward the dining room, where Māmā was rearranging table settings. "Your mother likes her."

Of course she did. Jennifer checked every box on my parents' list. First-generation Chinese-American. Excellent grades. Pre-med. Her family owns a bookstore, so she understood long hours and hard work. Practical.

I pictured Jennifer. Then Kate. The scenario sent my stomach into complicated acrobatics. Because I wanted her to fit and didn't know why that mattered.

"Jennifer is very sensible," my father continued. "Focused on her studies. A good daughter."

I finished the dumpling I was working on and reached for another wrapper. "I know."

"Good." He nodded once, like something had been settled. "The Lius will sit at table six."

The front door chimed as the first customers of the evening entered. I wiped my hands and moved to the dining room, straightening my apron and slapping on the smile I'd perfected over years of shifts.

For the next three hours, I took orders, cleared tables, and made small talk with regulars who asked about my studies. Mrs. Yang at table three wanted to know about pharmacy school. Mr.

Wong at table seven asked if I was dating anyone yet. I gave the same answers I always gave. School is good. Classes are challenging. No, not dating anyone.

The Liu family arrived at six. Precisely on time. Jennifer offered a polite smile as her mother and mine exchanged greetings in Mandarin. Māmā's voice rose with enthusiasm. Mrs. Liu mentioned something about how thin I looked. Māmā agreed and immediately headed to the kitchen to tell Bàba to add extra dishes to their order.

"Alex." Jennifer approached while our mothers talked. She held her teacup with both hands, level and steady. "How are classes this semester?"

"Fine. Challenging but manageable." I poured tea for her family's table. Perfect pour, no spills. "How are your studies?"

"Difficult, but I'm maintaining an A minus." She set her teacup down precisely on its saucer. No sound. "My advisor says medical school admissions are getting more competitive. I'm considering adding a minor in biochemistry."

She'd probably calculated the exact GPA boost. I would have done the same.

"That's practical," I said.

Her words lined up in neat rows. Like the dumpling pleats Bàba made in the kitchen. Nothing she said was wrong. Or boring, exactly. Just... expected. Like reading an abstract for a study I'd already seen.

We talked about prerequisites. Study schedules. The new research building. She mentioned a symposium she was attending in March. I nodded at appropriate intervals and refilled teacups.

Nothing about the conversation was bad. Jennifer was intelligent, well-informed, and easy to talk to. She would make an excellent doctor. A considerate partner. A daughter-in-law my parents would be proud of.

But a single interaction with her had never captured my attention for an hour-long commute. I pushed the thought away and focused on the next table's order.

The shift ended at nine. I changed out of my apron, said goodbye to my parents, and headed back toward the T station. The chill in the night air made my breath visible. Forty minutes on the train plus the walk to my apartment. Enough time to review my notes for tomorrow's exam.

Instead, I kept thinking about Jennifer's carefully planned minor and Kate's subway map analogies. How Jennifer talked about organic chemistry like a problem to solve through systematic study. How Kate had looked when that quiz score proved she actually understood instead of just memorizing.

My phone chimed as I turned onto my street.

> **KATE**
> How did the shift go? Did you look cute in your apron???

I stopped walking and stared at the message.

Jennifer would never send a text like that. It was too casual. Too willing to risk sounding inappropriate. Jennifer's messages were polite, informative, and properly punctuated.

Kate's were Kate.

I stood on the sidewalk for thirty seconds trying to plan a response that didn't sound either too formal or too casual.

> **ALEX**
> Standard restaurant apron. Nothing special about it.

Her response came immediately.

> **KATE**
> I'll have to see for myself sometime. 😊

I pictured Jennifer. The way my mother had smiled at her. How Bàba had carefully positioned table six in my section.

> **ALEX**
> You're welcome to visit.

I sent it before I could reconsider.

> **KATE**
> Really??? You'd introduce me to your parents?

Would I? The idea sparked something I couldn't name. Anticipation mixed with anxiety mixed with something else.

> **ALEX**
> I'd like to.

I stared at what I'd typed. Too personal for academic correspondence. But my thumb was already hitting send.

> **KATE**
> Good. Because I already like them from your stories.

Stories? I scrolled back through our text exchanges, looking for evidence. Last week I'd mentioned my father's dumpling technique. On Tuesday, I'd explained why I couldn't meet earlier because of the lunch rush.

When had practical scheduling information become stories?

I unlocked my apartment and dropped my bag by the door. I really should review for tomorrow's exam. Michaelis-Menten equation. Enzyme kinetics. First-pass metabolism.

Instead, I sat on the couch and thought about our tutoring

sessions. How they'd developed a pattern. Kate would arrive five minutes late with her increasingly organized notes. I'd review what we'd covered last time. We'd work through problems until her eyebrows unknitted and she'd lean back with a satisfied smile.

Somewhere in that routine, I'd started looking forward to the moment when concepts clicked for her. Not because she'd mastered another topic. Because her excitement was contagious in ways I couldn't quantify.

I took out my notes. Read the same paragraph three times. My mind was still miles away from my studies.

My parents had warned about distractions. Girls who might derail academic plans. Jennifer Liu represented everything they'd mapped out. Shared cultural understanding. Family approval. Predictable compatibility.

But Jennifer's name wasn't the one stuck in my head. Instead, I kept wondering why Kate had chosen nursing when she thought in visual patterns better suited to something else. Why her question about my tutoring motivation had made me scramble for professional answers when the truth was simpler.

I turned on the TV for background noise. Pulled out some flashcards on half-lives. Clearance rates. Bioavailability. Facts with straightforward answers and predictable relationships.

Much better than trying to figure out what I was supposed to do with this other thing.

This feeling didn't fit into any category I had names for.

I studied until midnight, then gave up and headed to bed. Lay there staring at the ceiling and thinking about coffee cups and subway maps and the way Kate's eyebrows drew together when she concentrated.

Jennifer made sense on paper. But Kate made me want to understand why her brain worked the way it did. Made me curious about things I hadn't thought to be curious about before.

Sleep took a long time to come.

Chapter 5

Kate

Dr. Martinez summoned me to his office after class. I fixated on the whine of the fluorescent light above his desk while he flipped through my quiz because watching his face seemed impossible right now.

"Eighty-nine percent."

The paper on the desk between us had far less red ink this time. My knee bounced against the chair leg, familiar and nervous.

"That's quite an improvement from your fifty-two two months ago." Dr. Martinez settled back, his chair creaking. "I have to say, I'm impressed."

Eighty-nine. Almost an A. When had I stopped thinking in terms of barely-passing and started thinking in almost-As? I couldn't wait to tell Alex. He'd probably give me that small smile, the one that changed his whole face for just a second before he caught himself.

"Your tutor seems to be doing the trick," Dr. Martinez continued.

"He explains things differently. Visual connections instead of just formulas." I pressed my palms against my thighs to stop the knee bounce. It didn't work. "It helps."

"Well, whatever approach you're using, keep it up." He pulled a business card from his desk drawer. The movement was precise and practiced. This wasn't his first time handing these out. "I wanted to discuss an opportunity."

My throat tightened. Opportunities meant expectations. Expectations meant more ways to disappoint people.

"There's a summer clinical position at Children's Hospital." The card slid across his desk. "Twenty hours per week. Highly competitive. Usually reserved for students with consistent high performance." He paused. "But your turnaround demonstrates resilience. Adaptability. The selection committee values that."

The card sat between us. Dr. Priya Banerjee, Academic Advisor, College of Health Sciences. The lettering was embossed, catching the awful fluorescent light.

"You think..." My words came out barely audible. I cleared my throat. "You think I'm ready for that?"

"Your recent performance suggests you can meet challenges when properly supported," he said, tapping the card with one finger. "Dr. Banerjee coordinates the program. I recommend contacting her soon. The application deadline is next Friday."

Next Friday. Eight days to decide about a program that could influence my entire career trajectory. Or at least that's what it felt like in this office with the humming light and the embossed business card that was heavier than any cardstock should.

"Thank you." I stood to make my escape from this unexpected conversation. "I'll contact her."

"Kate?" He was already gathering papers for his next student. "Whatever you decide, you've earned this recognition. Take a moment to acknowledge that."

Students in scrubs and white coats packed the hallway, all moving with determination written across their faces. I'd been trying to look like that for two years now. Maybe the invitation meant I was finally succeeding. Or maybe I'd just gotten better at the performance.

I pulled out my phone and checked the time. Two-fifteen. I had tutoring with Alex at three.

My thumbs moved before I could stop them.

KATE
Got an 89 on my chem quiz!!!! Also, Martinez says I'm ready for a summer clinical program at Children's Hospital?!?

ALEX
That's excellent. Congratulations.

KATE
Can I tell you about it? At tutoring? Or are we strictly chemistry-focused today?

ALEX
We can discuss it. I'm in the library now if you want to come early.

I was already walking that direction. Apparently my feet had decided where we were headed before I'd consciously agreed.

Alex's usual table on the second floor was covered in pharmacy textbooks and color-coded notes. His mouth did that almost-smile thing as I approached. It sent my stomach into complicated acrobatics.

"Eighty-nine." He said it like it meant something. "That's significant progress."

I dropped into the chair across from him. Energy fizzed through my veins, restless and bright. "Almost an A. Martinez thinks I should apply for this summer program. Twenty hours a week at Children's Hospital working with pediatric patients."

"That sounds like exactly what you'd want." Alex closed his textbook, giving me his complete attention. Which always felt like more than it should. Like standing in direct sunlight. "What's the concern?"

"Who said I'm concerned?"

His right eyebrow lifted a fraction.

"Fine." I pulled out Dr. Banerjee's card and started fiddling with it. "It's huge. Career-defining. But it also means committing. Advanced courses in spring, full summer in clinical work. It's all very..." I gestured vaguely. "Certain."

"And certainty bothers you." Not a question. Alex had this ability to see things I hadn't quite articulated yet.

"Maybe? I don't know." My thumb traced the embossed lettering. "A month ago I was failing chemistry and trying not to think about whether nursing was even right. Now there's this opportunity and I should be excited. I am excited. But also..."

"Uncertain," Alex supplied.

"Yeah." I tilted my head back to meet his eyes. "Is that stupid? Being uncertain about something objectively good?"

"No." He leaned back, considering. The afternoon light from the window caught his glasses at an angle. "It's rational to evaluate whether a path aligns with your actual preferences, not just external measures of success."

"Very textbook of you."

"Sorry." That hint of a smile again. "I mean it makes sense to consider whether you want this, not just whether you should want it."

I studied his face. The careful way he chose words. The complete focus he gave when something mattered.

"Do you ever have doubts?" I asked. "About pharmacy? Your whole carefully planned future?"

He was quiet. His fingers tapped against his textbook in a pattern. One-two-three, pause, one-two. "Sometimes. But my situation is different."

"How?"

"My parents have specific expectations." He adjusted his glasses. A tell. He always did that when talking about his family. "Pharmacy is practical. Stable. It provides financial security and professional respect." His voice was level, factual. "Those aren't bad things."

"But do you love it?"

"I don't know if love is the relevant metric." He picked up his pen and rolled it between his fingers. "Sometimes fulfilling obligations is enough. Sometimes that's what being an adult means."

His words sank like a stone. I wanted to argue. To say that surely we should do more than just fulfill obligations. But Alex's face had gone carefully neutral, and I knew that look. It meant the door was closed on this line of questioning.

"Well." I pulled the conversation back. "Martinez gave me until next Friday. Dr. Banerjee is the coordinator."

"Will you meet with her?"

"I should, right? At least learn more about the program." The card sat between my fingers. "Even if I don't apply. I'll try to get an appointment tomorrow. I should probably prepare questions. Make a list. Be organized."

"That sounds practical," Alex acknowledged as he opened his pharmacy notes. "Though knowing you, you'll probably just show up and ask whatever occurs to you in the moment."

"Hey." I wadded up a piece of paper and threw it at him.

He caught it one-handed without even looking up from his notebook. "I didn't say your approach doesn't work. Just that it's characteristically spontaneous."

"Code for chaotic?"

"Code for authentic." He said it simply. Like it was just fact.

I had to look away, blinking against the sudden pressure behind my eyes. Alex saw me. Really saw me. Not the version I tried to present, but the actual messy uncertain me underneath.

"Thank you." My voice came out just above a whisper. "For listening. And for helping me get that eighty-nine."

"You did the work." He pulled out my chemistry textbook from where I'd left it earlier. "Ready to tackle electronegativity trends? I found a better way to explain them."

I should have focused on chemistry and opened my notebook and attended to electron attraction and periodic patterns. But the restless energy from earlier was still there, combined with the warmth of Alex's quiet support and the way he'd called me authentic like it was something he respected.

Before I could think about it, I stood and rounded the table.

Alex's mouth dropped open slightly.

I leaned down and wrapped my arms around his shoulders. "Thank you. Really."

He stilled for half a second. Then his hand came up and patted my back once. The gesture was so Alex. Awkward but genuine. He smelled like laundry detergent and something spicy. Warm. Quietly pleasant.

When I pulled back, I kissed his cheek. Just a quick press of my lips against his face. Friendly and grateful and maybe something more that I wasn't examining too closely.

Alex's eyes widened behind his glasses. His hand lifted to his cheek like he was checking to confirm what had just happened.

"Sorry," I said. Not sorry at all. "Too much?"

"No." His voice came out rough and he cleared his throat. "That's fine. You're welcome."

The color spread up from his collar.

"Your ears are all pink," I told him, settling back into my chair with a grin I couldn't contain.

"They are not." He touched one ear anyway, like he could will it back to normal. "We should focus on chemistry."

"Definitely pink."

"Electronegativity." He opened the textbook with a thunk. "Defined as the tendency of an atom to attract electrons toward itself in a chemical bond."

I was still grinning. The air between us had shifted in the past few minutes. Some invisible line crossed without acknowledging it out loud. Alex was flustered. Because I'd hugged him and kissed his cheek.

That felt like more of a victory than my test score.

"Okay." I tried to match his serious tone and failed completely. "Electronegativity. I'm ready."

His ears were still pink.

"Imagine a game of tug-of-war." His hands moved as he talked. "When two atoms share electrons, they're both pulling on the rope. But some pull harder than others. Fluorine is the strongest player. It always wins. Oxygen is really strong too, nitrogen slightly less. If you look at the periodic table, the strongest players are in the top right corner. The pull gets stronger as you move right across each row and up each column."

I pulled out my notebook and took notes like the dutiful tutee I was. But I was also aware of how Alex's hand moved when he gestured to the periodic table. How his voice steadied as he fell into teaching mode. How he kept sneaking glances at me before snapping his focus back to the textbook.

We studied for an hour. Or rather, Alex tutored and I learned and neither of us mentioned the hug or the kiss or his pink ears. But this new awareness made every accidental brush of our hands feel significant.

"I should go." My brain was overflowing with electron attraction and my notebook was covered in intricate diagrams. "I'm meeting Isa for dinner."

"And I have studying of my own to do." Alex organized his notes with typical precision. "Let me know if you want to discuss it more. The opportunity, I mean. If you need help making a decision."

"I will." I gathered my things slowly. Not quite ready to leave. "Same time next week?"

"Unless you need extra review before the exam." He finally met my eyes. "I could make time if necessary."

"I might take you up on that." I hesitated. "You know you don't have to do all this, right? The extra time, the crazy explanations. You're just supposed to help me pass."

That half-smile was back. "I know."

"So... thanks. For doing it anyway."

"You're welcome." He adjusted his glasses. Not quite meeting my eyes. "It's not exactly a hardship."

I was halfway to the stairwell when he called my name.

"Kate." He stood by the table. Textbooks forgotten. "For what it's worth, I think you're smart to at least talk to Dr. Banerjee. Gather information. You don't have to decide anything today."

"Very practical advice."

"I'm a very practical person."

"You are." I couldn't help myself. "With very pink ears."

I left before he could respond. But I heard what might have been a laugh behind me. Or an exasperated sigh. Hard to tell with Alex.

Either way, I smiled the entire walk back.

Chapter 6

Kate

The next afternoon, I stood outside Dr. Banerjee's office with her business card in one hand and my phone in the other. I'd called that morning asking for an appointment. She'd responded within an hour with a 2pm time slot. Now it was 1:55 and my stomach performed impressive acrobatics.

Her receptionist barely acknowledged me. "She's finishing with her last appointment. Take a seat."

I sat in one of those waiting room chairs designed to be just uncomfortable enough and pulled out my chemistry notes to review. Sitting still made my brain race in directions I didn't want.

Except my notes weren't exactly notes anymore. When had that happened? The molecular diagrams had evolved into elaborate doodles. Electrons had little faces. Chemical bonds were intricate patterns. That benzene ring from last week looked like a mandala. Multiple colors. Shading. Completely unnecessary for passing chemistry.

My pencil case had exploded over the semester. Fine-tip markers. Gel pens in colors nobody needed for science. That pack of brush pens I'd bought "for better diagram clarity." Really I just liked how the ink flowed.

I was failing chemistry while accidentally becoming an artist. Or at least someone who couldn't draw a simple molecule without adding decorative borders.

"Kate Westfield?"

Dr. Banerjee stood in her doorway. She was younger than I'd expected with a practical bob and intelligent eyes. She looked like someone who got things done. "Come in."

Her office smelled like coffee and old books. Family photos shared space with medical journals. A small succulent sat by her computer, its leaves impossibly green against all the institutional beige.

"Dr. Martinez speaks highly of your recent progress." She gestured to the chair. "Please."

I sat. This chair was more comfortable than the waiting room one, which somehow made me more nervous.

"He mentioned the clinical program at Children's Hospital?"

"Yes." She pulled out a folder. Efficient. She probably had three more students waiting. "Working directly with pediatric patients under supervision. May through August. Participants often receive priority consideration for permanent placements."

She spread forms across her desk. Official forms. Important forms. Forms that represented commitment and seriousness and a future in nursing that was becoming more real by the second.

"You'd need to adjust your spring schedule." She pulled out a course catalog already marked with sticky notes. She'd obviously prepared for this meeting, which meant she expected me to say yes. "Advanced Anatomy and Physiology, plus Medical Ethics. Both demanding but manageable if you're willing to work hard."

I nodded and tried to look like someone willing to work. Someone who deserved competitive opportunities. My eyes drifted to my chemistry notes with their elaborate doodles and unnecessary flourishes.

"Kate?" Dr. Banerjee's voice pulled me back. "Is everything alright?"

"Yes. Sorry," I apologized. "It's a lot to process. A month ago I was failing chemistry and now there's this opportunity and I'm not sure I'm ready."

"You've completely turned your organic chemistry grade around. All of your other grades are already very high." She tapped the form. "You're ready."

"But what if..." I stopped. The question was too big.

"What if what?" Not unkind, but not patient either.

"How did you know advising was right for you?"

She paused and set down her pen. "I was in medicine initially. Ten years before I decided I was more interested in teaching and advising than diagnosing. Sometimes our paths change." She glanced at her computer screen. "But that's normal. Everyone has doubts."

"What if they're more than doubts?"

She checked her watch. Still patient, but clearly pressed for time. "Kate, I have an appointment in five minutes. Let me be direct. You have until next Friday to decide. The program is excellent. It would strengthen your resume significantly. But if you're having serious doubts about nursing as a career, that's something to explore with a counselor, not decide in my office."

Right. Of course. She was the program coordinator, not a therapist. I was taking up her valuable time with existential questions when she had a schedule to maintain.

"You're right. I'm sorry." I gathered the forms she'd laid out. "I'll think about it. Thank you."

"The opportunity is there if you want it." She stood. Meeting over. "Just remember that doubt is normal, but so is pushing through challenges. You've proven you can do that."

I left her office with a folder full of forms and a head full of questions multiplying faster than I could process them. The hallway was too bright. Too many people in scrubs looking confident and purposeful while I clutched papers about a future I wasn't sure I wanted.

My feet carried me away without conscious direction. Away from the health sciences building with its glass and steel and medicinal smell. Toward the liberal arts quad where old brick buildings had ivy and character and probably asbestos, but at least they felt less intimidating.

I stopped outside an art supply store I'd passed a hundred times without really seeing. The window display caught me today. Someone had arranged watercolors in a spectrum. Blues fading to greens fading to yellows fading to oranges. Brushes splayed in patterns that reminded me of ferns back home. Paper samples showing different textures that set my fingers itching.

"Just looking," I whispered to no one.

But I was already pushing open the door.

The smell hit me first. Paint and clay and wood and something else I couldn't name. Nothing like the antiseptic chemistry labs or the medicinal health sciences buildings. This smelled like possibility.

A woman emerged from behind the counter. Gray hair with streaks of blue paint. Smock covered in colorful fingerprints. "Looking for anything specific?"

"Just browsing." I touched a paint tube. *Cerulean blue*. Pretty word for pigment and binder. "Actually, I'm thinking about taking an art class. Or I might be. I haven't decided. But if I did, I'd need supplies, right? So I'm looking at what I'd need. Hypothetically."

"First time buying art supplies?"

"Is it that obvious?"

She laughed, but not unkindly. "Just a bit. What kind of class?"

"I'm not entirely sure. An elective during Spring semester maybe. If I decide to. Which I might not." Where was this coming from? And why was I talking so fast? "I'm a nursing major so this would just be an elective. Not a big deal. Just something different."

"Uh huh." She pulled a basket from under the counter. "Watercolors or acrylics?"

"I don't know. What's the difference? Is one easier? I should probably start with easier since I've never done this. Or maybe harder is better? Jump into the deep end? That's a thing people do, right?"

"Watercolor is more forgiving. You can add water if you mess up. Acrylics dry permanent." She pulled tubes off the shelf. "You want forgiving for your first class."

"Forgiving sounds perfect. Very on-brand for me right now." I was definitely talking too much but couldn't stop. "What about brushes? How many brushes does a person need? Is that a stupid question?"

"There are no stupid questions about art supplies." She handed me three brushes. "Round, flat, detail. That's your starter set."

The wooden handles were smooth and warm. Real. The bristles were soft when I touched them. Not like anything I'd held in a nursing lab. Nothing sterile about them at all.

"What if I'm terrible?"

"You'll be terrible for a while." She moved toward paper. Not the inspiring mentor moment I'd hoped for. "That's how learning works. You suck, then you suck less, then eventually you're okay. Sometimes you get good."

"Not super encouraging."

"Do you want encouragement, or do you want honesty?" She

pulled out a sketchbook. Thick paper, spiral bound. "This is student grade. Good enough to learn on, not so expensive you'll be afraid to mess up."

I took the sketchbook. Flipped it open. The pages were cream-colored and blank and full of possibility or failure or probably both. My thumb ran over the paper's texture. Slightly rough. Different from printer paper or notebook paper or glossy textbook pages.

"How much for everything?"

I walked out with a bag of supplies and a receipt that made my checking account cry. Basic watercolors, three brushes, a sketchbook, and a pencil set because she'd convinced me I'd need to sketch before painting. All of it more than I'd planned to spend but less than textbooks cost, so that was something.

The bag felt light in my hand but heavy with implications. I'd just spent money on art supplies. For a class I hadn't even registered for yet.

> **ISABEL**
> Where are you? How did it go with Banarjee?

I checked the time. Three forty-five. Right. Study date. Exam next week. Responsible nursing student things.

> **KATE**
> On my way. Stopped for something. Back in 10.

Isabel was at her desk surrounded by textbooks and color-coded study guides when I entered. Her eyes immediately snapped to the art supply bag.

"Tell me you didn't stress-buy craft supplies." Amused but also slightly concerned. "We don't have room for a quarter-life crisis."

"Not craft supplies. Art supplies." I set the bag on my bed. "I'm thinking about taking an elective next semester."

"Art?" She spun to face me fully. "Kate. You're finally getting your chemistry grades up. Is now really the time for distractions?"

"Just one class." I pulled out the sketchbook and ran my thumb along its edge. The paper felt good. Substantial. "I can still handle nursing courses."

"But why art?" She came to sit on my bed and picked up one of the brushes, testing its weight. "You've been working so hard to prove you belong in the nursing program."

I thought about how to explain it. My pulse jumped when I touched those paints. The immediate rightness of holding a brush. How the art store smell stirred an unfamiliar longing.

"Do you remember when you decided on nursing?" I asked. "How you just knew?"

"Yeah." She set the brush down carefully. "It felt like the right fit. Like this is what I'm supposed to do."

"What if I don't feel that way? About nursing. What if I've never felt that way?"

Isabel leaned back, then forward again, like she was trying to find the right distance for this conversation. But before she could respond, I pulled out my phone. "I need to call Sophie. She'll get it."

My sister answered on the second ring. "Katie girl! What's up? You never call during the week."

"Soph... I did something impulsive." The evidence of my shopping spree still sat in the bag at the end of my bed. "I bought watercolors."

I heard traffic noise came from her end. "Watercolors? Like paint?"

"And brushes and a sketchbook." I pulled them out, arranging them on my comforter while Isabel watched. "I'm thinking about taking an art class next semester."

"Hold on." A car horn blared, followed by some choice words from Sophie. I could almost picture the hand gesture that went with it. "Sorry, I'm walking home from the office. You're taking an art class? That's amazing!"

"Is it? Or is it stupid? I should probably focus on nursing."

"Why?" She sounded distracted. Her breathing came hard like she was walking uphill.

"Because that's what I'm supposed to be doing. What everyone expects."

"Who's everyone?" A pause. "Hang on, crossing the street." More traffic noise. "Okay, I'm back. Everyone who?"

"Mom and Dad. The whole family. Dr. Martinez just offered me this competitive summer internship at Children's Hospital and I'm sitting here buying paint instead of filling out the application."

"Did she say you have to decide right now?" Keys jingling. Door opening. "Sorry, just getting into my apartment. Keep talking."

"Next Friday."

"Okay, so you have time." The sounds of her dropping things. Bag, keys, shoes. "Kate, can I tell you something? Last month when you forgot your chemistry notebook at my place? I looked through it."

My face flushed. "Those were just notes."

"Those were art." She moved around her apartment. "They were beautiful. Intricate and detailed and unnecessary for passing an exam. Which means you weren't doing it for the grade. You were doing it because you wanted to."

My thumb traced the edge of a paint tube. *Alizarin crimson.* Another pretty name for pigment and binder. "What if taking art makes me realize nursing isn't right?"

"Then you'll figure out what is right." Sophie's voice was softer now. Less distracted. "Look, I know our family didn't freak out when I chose social work, but I still felt the weight of it. Like I was disappointing some invisible expectation. But Kate? That weight was mine. I put it there."

"Did Mom and Dad actually say anything when you chose social work?"

"Not what you'd think." She exhaled. "Dad just asked if it made me feel purposeful. And Mom asked if I could do it long-term without resenting it." A pause. "Can you see yourself being a nurse for years without resenting it?"

The question hung in the silence between us. My eyes flitted between the clinical opportunity forms on my desk and the art supplies fanned across my bed.

"I don't know."

"Then maybe one art class is a way to find out." Sophie's voice was gentle. "And Katie? There's no shame in exploring. That's what college is for."

After we hung up, I sat with my phone in my hands. Isabel had gone back to her desk, giving me space but clearly eavesdropping.

"So," she said carefully. "Art class?"

"Maybe." I opened the sketchbook to the first blank page. "I'm going to try drawing something first. See if I even like it."

"Okay." She returned to her textbooks. "Let me know if you want to talk."

The paper was smooth under my fingers. Cream-colored and empty and full of terrifying possibility. I picked up one of my new pencils and drew.

My hand moved almost without thinking, sketching the shape of a face. A strong jawline. The suggestion of glasses. Dark hair that always looked slightly disheveled.

Alex.

I was drawing Alex.

My hand kept moving. The curve of his eyebrow when he got

that skeptical look. The way his mouth quirked when he found something quietly amusing. The precise angles of his face that I'd apparently memorized without meaning to.

The proportions looked wrong. His eyes sat too high, making him look startled instead of thoughtful. The nose was crooked in a way Alex's definitely wasn't.

I erased. Tried again. Worse. Now one eye was bigger than the other and his mouth looked like it belonged on a different person.

"Come on," I muttered, attacking the eyes for the third time.

This was so much harder than decorating chemistry notes. Those worked because they were patterns, not actual people I cared about getting right.

People I cared about.

I stopped. Pencil hovering. Stared at my terrible sketch of Alex with his lopsided eyes and impossible proportions.

When had that happened? When had I started caring about Alex as more than my chemistry tutor? More than the helpful pharmacy student who explained electron configurations with careful patience?

I thought about this afternoon in the library. The way my pulse had sped up when he'd called me authentic. The impulsive hug that had felt completely natural. The kiss on his cheek that I hadn't planned but also hadn't regretted. His pink ears.

My hand moved again, trying to capture that expression he'd had when I'd pulled back. Surprised and pleased and flustered all at once.

But my skills weren't anywhere close. The lines on the page bore only the vaguest resemblance to what I was trying to create. In my mind, it was so clear. The exact shade of brown in his eyes, the way his hands moved when he explained things, precise and purposeful, that quiet smile that transformed his entire face.

But translating vision to paper was impossible. Frustrating.

The gap between what I wanted to create and what actually appeared was enormous.

I flipped to the clean side of the page and started again.

The second attempt was worse. The third, somehow even worse than that.

"Kate?" Isabel's voice made me look up. She'd abandoned her studying and was watching me with concerned curiosity. "What are you drawing?"

"Nothing." I hunched over the sketchbook protectively. "Just practicing."

"Can I see?"

"It's terrible."

"Let me see anyway."

I reluctantly turned the sketchbook around. Isabel's eyes moved over my various failed attempts at capturing Alex's face.

"Is that..." Her eyebrows jumped. "Is that Alex? Your chemistry tutor?"

My cheeks warmed. "I was just trying to draw a face. For practice. Could be anyone."

"Kate." She said my name the way she did when I was clearly lying. "That's definitely Alex. You even got his glasses."

I pulled the sketchbook back and stared at my awful drawing. She was right. Despite the terrible proportions and wrong features, the drawing was unmistakably him. The tilt of his head. The suggestion of careful attention in his posture.

"When did this happen?" Isabel asked gently.

"Nothing happened. We're just studying chemistry."

"You kissed his cheek yesterday."

"How do you..." I stopped. "I texted you about it, didn't I?"

"You sent me seven texts about it." She pulled out her phone and read: "'Kissed Alex on the cheek and his ears turned PINK.' 'Is it weird that I can't stop thinking about his pink ears?' Pink ears pink ears pink ears."

I dropped my face into my hands. "Oh no."

"Oh yes." Isa sat on the edge of my bed. "So. You have feelings for your tutor."

"I don't know." I flopped back onto my pillows. "I didn't mean to. One day he was just my tutor, and then... he wasn't. He's so calm and patient and he explains things in ways that make sense and he never makes me feel stupid even when I mess up. And yesterday when I hugged him, he smelled really good and I just... I wanted to kiss him. So I kissed his cheek. And now I can't stop thinking about it."

"Kate." Isa's voice was careful. "I say this with love. But Alex is your tutor. The person helping you pass chemistry. The class you need to stay in the nursing program. Getting involved with him could complicate things."

"I know."

"So this isn't a good idea." She said it gently but firmly. "You should keep things professional. Focus on passing chemistry and figuring out this whole art versus nursing thing without adding romantic complications."

She was right. I knew she was right. Getting involved with Alex while he was my tutor, while I was trying to figure out my entire future, was terrible timing.

But my hand moved over the sketch anyway. Trying to capture the curve of his smile. The way his eyes crinkled when he found something amusing.

"Kate," Isabel said again. "Are you listening?"

"Yes." I set down the pencil. "You're being practical and protective and completely right about everything."

"But you're not going to listen to me."

"I'm going to try." My voice dropped. "It's just... what if I can't help it? What if it's already too late to keep things professional?"

Isabel was quiet for a long moment. "Do you really like him? Or do you just like that he makes you feel smart and capable?"

The question stopped me cold.

"Both?" I said finally. "He does make me feel capable. But it's more than that. I like how his brain works. How he processes information and finds connections I'd never see. I like his quiet humor and how he gets flustered when I surprise him. I like that he's careful with people's feelings even though he pretends he's just being logical." My terrible sketches sat between us. "And I like that when I'm with him, I can be messy and uncertain and he won't judge me for it. He'll just... help me figure it out."

She squeezed my shoulder. "Just be careful, okay? I don't want to see you get hurt. And I don't want your chemistry grades to tank because you and Alex have some big dramatic falling out."

"We're not going to have a falling out."

"You don't know that."

She was right. I didn't know that. But sitting there with my terrible drawings and my new art supplies and my confusing feelings about Alex, the truth hit me. I was tired of only doing things I was certain about. Tired of playing it safe and following the expected path and never taking risks.

"I'm going to register for the art class," I said suddenly.

Isabel blinked. "Okay. That was a subject change."

"And I'm going to meet with Dr. Banerjee again. Gather more information. Figure out if it's what I actually want." I held her gaze. "And I'm going to keep studying with Alex. Because even if it's complicated, even if it's not practical, I'm not ready to stop seeing him twice a week."

"Well." She returned to her desk. "At least you're being honest about it."

"Is that good?"

"It's something." She opened her nursing textbook. "Now can we please study for the actual chemistry exam you have next week? The one that's not about romantic chemistry?"

I laughed despite everything. "Yeah. Okay. Let me just..." I tore out all my failed attempts at drawing Alex. Crumpled them up. But I couldn't quite bring myself to throw them away. Instead I tucked them in the back of the sketchbook. Evidence of something I was trying to learn. Or evidence of feelings I wasn't ready to examine too closely.

I pulled out my chemistry notes and joined Isabel at our desks. Tried to focus on electronegativity trends and periodic patterns. But my eyes kept drifting to the sketchbook on my bed. To the art supplies that represented one kind of uncertainty. To my phone where Alex's last text still sat unanswered.

> **ALEX**
> Let me know if you need extra review before Thursday.

My thumb hovered over the keyboard.

> **KATE**
> I always need extra review. That's what makes me such a reliable customer.

Delete.

> **KATE**
> Yes please. Also I can't stop thinking about yesterday.

Deleted that even faster.

> **KATE**
> Thursday works.

> **ALEX**
> Of course. Sleep well.

I stashed my phone away and tried to focus on chemistry. The periodic table swam in front of my eyes. Electronegativity trends that I'd finally started understanding blurred together with thoughts about Alex and art classes and clinical programs and all the possible futures branching out from this moment.

"Kate," Isa said without looking up. "You're not actually studying."

"I'm thinking about studying."

"You're thinking about studying with Alex."

"Close enough."

Chapter 7

Alex

The kitchen exhaust fan at The Golden Dragon rattled in the same spot it had for fifteen years, a mechanical wheeze that meant Bàba needed to tighten the mounting screws again. I could feel the heat from the tray I held through the towel. I pivoted past the kitchen door, plates clinking as I headed toward table twelve. The lunch rush would peak in six minutes if the pattern held, and I'd already lost two by checking my phone in the supply closet.

Again.

Kate had texted three times this morning. Quick hellos or single-line updates about family chaos. These were the kind of messages we'd fallen into over the past few weeks. The ones that made me smile at my phone like an idiot while standing in a storage room full of napkins and soy sauce.

I'd been tracking the shift in our communication patterns since the library. Three weeks and four days since she'd kissed my cheek before leaving for fall break. Sample size: two hundred and seventeen text messages. Forty-three phone calls, average duration eighteen minutes. Pattern analysis: significant increase in nonacademic content. Personal anecdotes up forty-seven percent. Shared observations about daily life up sixty-two percent. Messages after nine PM that kept me awake thinking about her laugh instead of pharmacology notes: all of them.

None of which explained the hollow feeling that had settled in my bones when she'd left for Thanksgiving break four days ago.

Steam fogged my glasses as I set down the entrees. I offered refills with muscle memory while my brain stayed two hundred miles north, watching maple candy boil over in a kitchen I'd never seen.

"More tea?" I asked table twelve.

The elderly woman nodded. Her grandson played with chopsticks, making them walk across the paper placemat like tiny legs. I refilled their cups and retreated to the tea station, finally pulling out my phone.

Kate's texts had been sporadic for the first two days of break. Brief apologies about family obligations, promises to call later that never quite materialized. I understood. She'd been away at school for months. Her family had claim to her time. It was reasonable.

It was also the longest stretch we'd gone without real conversation since that first tutoring session in September.

I'd spent Tuesday evening reorganizing my study notes by topic and subtopic when they were already perfectly organized. Wednesday, I'd deep-cleaned my apartment, scrubbing grout with a toothbrush at two in the morning because sleep wouldn't come and my brain kept replaying the soft press of Kate's lips against my cheek. The casual way she'd done it, like kissing me goodbye was natural. Expected. Like we did that sort of thing.

We didn't do that sort of thing.

Except apparently we did now, and I'd been trying to logic my way through what that meant for three weeks while simultaneously pretending I wasn't checking my phone every seven minutes to see if she'd texted.

This morning, though, everything had changed.

> **KATE**
>
> GEMMA'S HERE!!
>
> We're attempting Grammy's maple sugar candy and I can already tell this is going to be a beautiful disaster.
>
> Temperature has to be EXACT though.
>
> You'd probably love supervising us from Boston.
>
> We need adult supervision desperately.

The attached photo showed Kate and a pretty auburn-haired girl standing in a cozy kitchen. It looked like a sugar bomb had detonated. Both wore matching expressions of determined chaos. Kate's hair was pulled back in a messy bun. She had a smudge of something dark on her cheek. She grinned at the camera like the world's most enthusiastic disaster coordinator.

I'd stared at that photo for several seconds before remembering I should have been restocking napkins.

The text had arrived at 9:47 AM. By my count, Kate had sent six more messages in the two hours since, each one progressively more enthusiastic as the maple candy project devolved. Each one making the hollow feeling ease slightly, replaced by something warmer that I refused to examine too closely.

She was talking to me again. Including me in her day. The relief was disproportionate to the situation, which meant I was in deeper than my logical frameworks could handle.

"Alex, table six needs more tea." Māmā's voice cut through the lunch noise. Woks sizzled behind her. Bàba's cleaver hit the cutting board in rapid succession, the rhythm I'd fallen asleep to every night growing up.

I pocketed my phone and grabbed the teapot. Table six. Pour, smile, nod. Ask if they need anything else. The woman wanted more napkins. The man gestured toward the spring rolls cooling on his plate.

"I'll bring fresh ones." I was already moving.

Back in the kitchen, Bàba was preparing an enormous turkey. The Golden Dragon was one of the few Chinese restaurants that acknowledged American holidays. Good for business, Bàba always said. Americans wanted familiar food on Thanksgiving, just prepared by someone else.

"Jennifer's family called." His hands stuffed and trussed the bird with the precision of twenty years doing this exact task. "They want to know if you're available for dinner Saturday."

An alert sounded from my cell phone in my pocket. The sound felt like a lifeline.

I kept my expression neutral. "Saturday dinner?"

"After evening service." Bàba separated the turkey from its backbone with three efficient cuts. "They asked specifically if you would come."

The kitchen fan hummed above us, struggling against the heat from six burners. Māmā appeared in the doorway between prep and dining room. She held a dish towel, folding it into precise thirds. Not saying anything. Just there.

"Saturday," I repeated.

"Jennifer's mother said she's been asking about you." Māmā's hands stilled on the towel. "It would be rude not to go."

The word 'rude' echoed in the kitchen silence. I'd dodged the Liu family's invitations since August. Eventually, avoidance stopped being polite and became an insult.

"I'll check my schedule."

Māmā's eyebrow rose a fraction. We both knew my schedule consisted of classes, studying, and restaurant shifts. Nothing that I couldn't rearrange for an appropriate dinner with an appropriate family and their appropriate daughter who was pursuing an appropriate career in internal medicine.

My phone vibrated again.

"Who keeps texting?" Māmā asked.

"My tutoring student." The half-truth came out smooth. When had I started editing my conversations with my parents? "She has questions about her coursework."

"On Thanksgiving?" Bàba wiped his hands on his apron, leaving dark smears. "Dedicated student."

"She's figuring things out."

Māmā hummed—low, knowing, noncommittal. She returned to the dining room, and I checked my phone.

> **KATE**
> Update: we are FAILING. Maple syrup is everywhere and I mean everywhere. Gemma's making me use a thermometer instead of just eyeballing it like a normal person. Also she's reading the instructions out loud. Send help.

Another photo. This one showed a candy thermometer stuck in a pot of what looked like amber liquid. In the background, someone's hand reached for the stove dial.

> **ALEX**
> What temperature are you aiming for?

> **KATE**
> 235 degrees apparently?? Grammy's recipe just says "soft ball stage" which is not helpful at all. Gemma says that's between 235-240F. How is anyone supposed to remember that??

> **ALEX**
> You write it down.

> **KATE**
> Revolutionary. You should teach classes. "Alex Chen's Method: Just Write It Down"

> **ALEX**
> It works for chemistry.

> **KATE**
> Does it though???

The corner of my mouth lifted. Fair point, given her current grade.

The lunch crowd thinned by three fifteen. I restocked supplies while my parents prepped for evening service, moving through the familiar routine. Nineteen steps from the tea station to the supply closet. The third floorboard from the left creaked under my weight. The storage shelf rattled when I pulled it, meaning we were down to four boxes of chopsticks.

My father's cleaver maintained its steady rhythm. The exhaust fan clicked and wheezed. Somewhere in the prep cooler, a container wasn't sealed properly. The fermented black beans smelled stronger than usual.

The restaurant felt smaller today. Or maybe I was noticing its dimensions for the first time in years. Twelve tables. Forty-eight chairs. One cash register that jammed if you didn't hit the drawer at the right angle. Water stains blooming across the northeast corner of the ceiling where the roof had leaked every March for six years. Bàba kept saying he'd fix it. It was still on the list.

My phone rang as I refilled soy sauce dispensers. Kate's name lit up the screen. An emotion I couldn't categorize fluttered through me. Anticipation, maybe. Or the mild panic of realizing you're looking forward to something more than you should.

I glanced toward the kitchen. My parents were deep in menu

planning, heads bent over Bàba's notebook where he sketched dish ideas in a mix of Chinese characters and phonetic English.

"Hey." I answered before the third ring, then had to dodge sideways as Māmā emerged carrying a crate of bok choy. I retreated to the corner booth. The vinyl seat crackled under my weight. Through the front window, a bus hissed past, and I pressed the phone tighter against my ear.

"Alex! You're on speaker. Settle an argument for us." Kate's voice was barely audible over the din of multiple conversations happening at once. "Dad says you can't make a perfect turkey without a meat thermometer. Mom says it's all about knowing your oven. Scientific opinion please."

"Your father's correct." At least four different voices layered in the background. "Food safety requires specific internal temperatures for poultry."

"HA!" A man's voice boomed. Definitely her father. "The scientist agrees with me, Joanna!"

"Though," I added, because apparently I couldn't leave well enough alone, "your mother's point about oven knowledge suggests years of experience achieving similar results through timing and observation."

The victorious whoop that followed suggested Kate's mother was pleased with this diplomatic revision.

"You just made both my parents happy." Kate's laugh sounded looser than it did in coffee shops. "That's a dangerous skill around this family."

Her words lodged in my chest, immovable. We'd been meeting for weeks, texting constantly, calling late at night to talk about nothing and everything. But this felt different. Her including me in family moments from two hundred miles away, asking my opinion on things that had nothing to do with chemistry. Like the moment in lab when a solution crystallizes. One second it's invisible, the next it's solid.

"Are you busy?" Her tone changed slightly. "I know you're probably working."

The empty restaurant stretched around me. My mother had slipped back into the kitchen. Through the service window, I saw my parents moving through prep, their movements synchronized after so many years working in the same space.

"It's quiet right now. Tell me about the candy disaster."

For the next fifteen minutes, Kate walked me through her grandmother's maple candy recipe. She described the temperature requirements with surprising precision. Explained how the mixture kept changing consistency, how they had to watch for specific visual cues while monitoring the thermometer. She even mentioned something about cold water tests and thread stages.

"You sound like you know what you're doing," I said when she paused.

"Don't sound so shocked. I can follow directions when I want to." A clattering in the background, like pots being moved. "Plus Gemma's here being her usual perfectionist self, making me measure everything twice. She's leveling off measuring cups like we're in a lab."

"How precise?"

"She used a knife to level the brown sugar. A knife, Alex. Like it matters if we're off by a few granules."

I found myself curious about this version of Kate that existed outside our study sessions. The one who measured carefully and paid attention to process when it mattered to her. Who had a perfectionist best friend. This explained some things about her easy acceptance of my approach to our tutoring.

"Alex?" Māmā's voice interrupted. "Can you help with tomorrow's prep?"

"I should go," I told Kate.

"Of course. Thanks for settling the Great Turkey Debate." She paused. "Hey, are you okay? Your texts felt... off earlier."

Kate's messages throughout the day. The sound of her family in the background. The way she included me in moments that had nothing to do with acid-base reactions or organic molecules. All of it had altered my internal framework.

"I'm fine," I said. "Just thinking."

"Dangerous activity for you." Her voice gentled. "Don't overthink everything. Talk later?"

"Yeah."

After hanging up, I stared at my phone. Improved mood. Desire for continued contact. Distraction from routine tasks. All pointing toward a conclusion I'd been avoiding through increasingly elaborate mental gymnastics.

"Alex. Vegetables need chopping." Bàba's voice carried from the kitchen.

I pocketed the phone and headed back, where my parents had spread ingredients across every available surface. The organized chaos of restaurant prep had always felt soothing. Each task building toward a larger goal. Every component necessary and planned.

Today it felt like a distraction from more compelling problems.

I started dicing onions with mechanical precision. The knife hit the cutting board in steady rhythm. Onions, then carrots, then celery. The foundation for tomorrow's stuffing that Americans would order alongside their orange chicken and fried rice.

"Mr. Liu asked about you yesterday," Māmā mentioned.

I kept cutting. Made the carrot pieces uniform. Half-inch dice, the way Bàba taught me when I was twelve.

"Jennifer is planning internal medicine," Māmā continued. She picked up celery, her knife moving faster than mine despite the arthritis in her left hand. "Very stable career. Good for family planning."

Onion fumes stung my eyes. Convenient excuse for any reaction.

My parents' expectations hadn't changed since I was old enough to understand them. Excellent grades. Check. Pharmacy degree in progress. Check. Appropriate marriage to appropriate family. Pending.

A stable life that would justify the decades they'd spent working twelve-hour days at this restaurant. Instead of sleeping. Instead of taking English classes at the community center. Instead of visiting family back in Guangzhou. They'd traded those things for my college fund, for a pharmacy degree that would give me options they'd never had.

Work now. Be happy later. That was the trade, and they expected me to honor it.

Kate texted again as I started the carrots. I gave up any pretense of ignoring my phone in my pocket at this point and propped it on top of the line so I could keep up with the steady flurry of texts from her without interrupting dinner prep.

> **KATE**
> James is showing me his workshop. He builds these incredible boat models. The detail work is INSANE. Look at this!

The attached photo showed miniature wooden vessels in various stages of completion. Each detailed down to tiny cleats and scaled rigging. The craftsmanship was remarkable, the kind of precision that required patience.

> **KATE**
> Want to see them in person sometime? You should come to Waverly Cove. My family would love to meet you.

My knife stopped moving. Carrot pieces scattered across the cutting board.

Kate was inviting me to meet her family. To see her home. To visit this place I'd been picturing through her descriptions for weeks now. To be included in her world beyond coffee shop study sessions and increasingly frequent text conversations.

"Alex, you're making the carrots too small." Bàba's observation pulled me back.

The pieces were no larger than rice grains.

"Sorry. Distracted." I shoved the phone into my pocket quickly, but not fast enough to avoid Māmā's notice.

"By your tutoring student?" Māmā's tone carried volumes.

"She's struggling with some concepts." Technical truth skirting the larger reality that I checked my phone every ten minutes now. That fifteen-minute conversations about candy recipes felt more important than the pharmacology notes I should be reviewing.

"Hmm." My mother's single syllable contained an entire conversation.

I tried applying the logical framework I'd been using for years. Kate was a student. I was her tutor. The relationship had clear parameters and professional boundaries. Visiting her family would blur those boundaries beyond recovery.

Except none of that explained my reaction to seeing her name on my phone. Or why empty restaurants felt lonelier than they used to. Or why I'd been neglecting my lab work to talk about turkey thermometers.

"Some students need more time," I said.

We finished prep in relative silence. Bàba seasoned the turkey. Māmā organized mise en place for tomorrow's service. I completed the vegetable prep and moved on to prepping containers, labeling each with tomorrow's date in permanent marker.

My phone rang again as I finished.

"I should take this," I said, already heading toward the dining room.

"Alex, we still need to..." My father started.

"Five minutes."

I answered in the empty restaurant. Booth three this time. Different vinyl, same crackle.

"Sorry to bother you again." Kate's voice was quieter now. Less background chaos. "I just... are you sure you're okay? I can't stop thinking about your texts earlier. Something felt off."

"I'm fine." The automatic response.

Then reconsidered.

Kate had been honest about her struggles with nursing. About her fear of disappointing her family. About her growing interest in art despite having no plan for how that could work. Maybe I could return the favor. Maybe honesty was worth the discomfort.

"Actually, no. I'm not fine."

"What's wrong?"

"I don't know." The admission felt uncomfortable. Like wearing someone else's clothes. "Everything feels different lately."

"Different how?"

The empty restaurant stretched around me. I thought about the red and gold decorations my parents hung fifteen years ago. The photographs on the wall showing family celebrations and business milestones. Everyone in those photos was smiling. Everyone had made the correct choices that led to appropriate outcomes.

How Māmā's hands were stained from years of industrial soap. How Bàba still struggled with English after three decades because he spent fourteen hours a day in a kitchen instead of a classroom. The apartment they'd lived in for three years that was too small and too cold because they were saving every dollar for my education.

Kate's laugh. Her questions which served no practical purpose but I found intriguing. The way ordinary conversations felt important when she was part of them.

"Like I've been following a plan that makes sense to everyone except me," I said.

Kate was quiet for a moment. In the background, water ran. Someone called her name, distant.

"That sounds lonely," she finally said.

Lonely. I'd never considered myself lonely. I had studies. Family. Clear goals. Structured routines. But sitting in this empty restaurant, thinking about another evening with textbooks while Kate was home making candy disasters with her family, the word fit.

"Yeah." My throat tightened. "It is."

"You know," Kate's voice was careful in a way it usually wasn't, "sometimes plans need adjusting. Things change. That's not failure."

"My parents don't see it that way."

"Your parents love you. They want you to be happy."

"They want me to be successful," I corrected. "Happiness is secondary to security."

They'd traded their comfort for my opportunities. The bargain was clear: I honored their sacrifice by making the choices that justified it.

"What if they don't have to be separate things?" Kate asked. "Success and happiness?"

I didn't have an answer.

In my family's experience, happiness was what you earned after achieving security. You worked hard. Made good choices. Built something stable. Then contentment followed naturally. That was the sequence.

Except I worked hard and made good choices, and instead of

contentment, I felt this restlessness that intensified every time Kate smiled. It was a fundamental flaw in the system nobody had mentioned.

"I should let you get back to your family."

"Alex." Her voice stopped me from hanging up. "Whatever's making you feel different... maybe it's not a problem. Maybe it's just growth. Maybe you're becoming who you're supposed to be instead of who everyone planned."

After she hung up, I stayed in the booth. The vinyl was cold through my jeans. Outside, a car alarm wailed. The paper lantern above table six swayed in the draft from the kitchen door, casting shadows across the wall where my father hung photos of celebrations. My high school graduation. New Years. The day they'd signed the restaurant lease twenty-three years ago.

Everyone smiling. Everyone having made correct choices.

My phone lit up one more time.

> **KATE**
> Have a good dinner shift. Thanks for the turkey expertise. I hope things get easier for you.

I read it three times. Saved the maple candy photos without examining why. Then sat in the dark restaurant, trying to remember the last time I'd looked forward to Monday.

The exhaust fan rattled. The prep cooler hummed. Somewhere, a timer beeped, then silenced as Bàba shut it off.

I pulled up Kate's contact information. My thumb hovered over her name. Over the invitation to visit Waverly Cove, to meet her family, to see the workshop and the candy-making disasters in person. To step outside the boundaries we'd established and into something undefined.

My parents' voices drifted from the kitchen. Māmā saying something about portion sizes. Bàba responding about supplier costs. The same conversation they'd had every week for as long as I could remember. Comfortable. Predictable. Safe.

I locked the phone and sat in the empty restaurant, listening to it breathe around me.

Saturday, the Liu family would expect me for dinner. Jennifer would be polite. We would discuss appropriate topics and build toward appropriate conclusions. I would sit across from her and pretend we were accomplishing something more than checking boxes on a list my parents had drafted before I was old enough to object.

Next week, Kate and I would meet at the coffee shop. She would show me her latest chemistry homework. I would explain concepts she already understood better than she thought. We would talk about topics that had nothing to do with academic requirements. And I would feel this pressure that my logical frameworks couldn't explain or contain.

The paper lantern kept swaying. Red light. Shadow. Red light. Shadow.

I spent the rest of the dinner shift cataloguing these variables and analyzing patterns, trying to logic my way through something that refused to be reduced to equations. Improved mood. Increased distraction. Desire for continued contact. Physical response to her presence. The evidence was overwhelming.

But I couldn't name what I felt. Couldn't organize it into categories or analyze it into submission. Every time I tried to apply logic, tried to restore the previous framework, Kate's voice cut through with her laugh and her questions and her invitation to visit a place where people made candy and built model ships and joked through arguments. A place where happiness and success could exist at the same time.

Māmā emerged from the kitchen.

"Are you coming upstairs?" she asked. "It's late."

"In a minute."

She studied me for a long moment. Then nodded and disappeared toward the back stairs.

Then I sat in the dark, listening to the restaurant hum and rattle around me, trying to recognize the person I was becoming and failing to match him with the person everyone expected me to be.

Chapter 8

Kate

Mom found me in the kitchen Saturday morning, staring at my coffee and a bag of leftover maple candy like they held the secrets of the universe. I'd been sitting at the kitchen table for who knows how long, watching steam curl off my mug and disappear.

"You're awake early." Mom didn't look at me when she said it, just started wiping down the counter in smooth circles even though she'd already cleaned it after breakfast. "Everything okay at school?"

The question had about six levels to it. That's how Mom worked. She'd slip in sideways while you were distracted, and suddenly you'd be explaining things you hadn't meant to say out loud.

"Finals are coming up." I wrapped both hands around my mug even though it was too hot. The burn felt clarifying somehow. "I should probably get back and study."

"Mm." That sound. The one that meant she saw right through me but was willing to wait me out. Five kids had taught her patience. "How's tutoring going? With the pharmacy student?"

My neck flushed. I focused very hard on a coffee ring on the table, a perfect brown circle I could maybe scrub out if I tried hard enough. "It's good. Alex is a really good teacher."

"Alex." Mom said his name like she was testing it out, seeing how it felt. She'd moved on from wiping the counter to reorganizing the fruit bowl, shifting oranges around for no apparent reason. "You know, you've mentioned him quite a bit this weekend."

"Have I?"

"Let's see." She started counting on her fingers, each one a separate indictment. "Alex showed you a new way to think about molecular structures. Alex could settle our turkey debate. Alex thinks you're actually really smart, just learn differently. Then there was something about subways, and..."

"Okay, okay." My face was definitely red now.

"So this Alex," Mom said, way too casual, "he's staying in Quincy for the break?"

"His family has a restaurant." The words were flat. I'd been trying not to think about him spending Thanksgiving alone in an empty library, but now the image was back. Alex at one of those long tables with all his color-coded notes spread out with nobody around. "He's helping them over the holiday."

Mom's hands paused while peeling an orange. "That sounds lonely."

"Yeah." My throat tightened. "Maybe."

For a few seconds the only sound was the refrigerator humming and someone's dog barking three houses down. Mom set the orange down very deliberately and picked up the bag of maple candy I'd made with Gemma. "You know, you made way too much of this. Your roommate's going to be sick of maple by New Year's."

Mom had her scheming face on, the one that usually meant someone was about to get set up on a blind date or volunteered for something.

"Quincy's not that far out of your way back to campus, is it?"

"Mom."

"What?" She was trying for innocent but landing somewhere closer to mischievous. "I'm just saying, it seems a shame to let good maple candy go to waste. And this Alex sounds like he could use something sweet to cheer him up."

"I can't just show up at his family's restaurant. That's..." I gestured vaguely with one hand, trying to find words for why it felt impossible. "That's weird."

"Is it?" Mom pulled out the chair next to me and sat down, still holding the candy bag. "In my experience, food's a pretty universal language. And you've been talking about him all weekend with this little smile."

"I don't—"

"Katie." She tapped my cheek gently. "I haven't seen you light up like that about school in... well, maybe ever. And that includes the time you got to dissect a frog in eighth grade."

"That was cool, though. The way everything connected..." I stopped because she was grinning at me. "It's not like that with Alex."

"What's it like, then?"

I didn't have an answer. Or I had too many answers, all jumbled up like molecules I couldn't quite get to bond right. "I don't know. We just talk. About chemistry and other stuff. He listens better than other people."

"What do you mean?"

"It's like..." I traced one of the coffee rings on the table, around and around. "Like he actually wants to understand how my brain works instead of just telling me I'm doing it wrong."

Mom made a soft humming sound that meant she understood and approved. "Sweetheart, you know Dad and I just want you to be happy, right? Whatever that looks like."

The shift caught me off guard. I'd been expecting more teasing, not this sudden sincerity that made my heart ache. "I know."

"Good." She pressed the candy bag into my hands. "Now, I happen to know there's a 12:15 train that stops in Quincy. Hypothetically."

"You looked up train schedules?"

"Knowledge is power." She kissed the top of my head, and I could smell her lavender hand lotion mixed with the coffee and cinnamon smell that always meant home. "Take the candy, Katie. Life's too short not to follow your instincts once in a while."

So that's how I ended up on the 12:15 train, which turned into a bus connection because of course the T wasn't running direct on a holiday weekend, and I had way too much time to second-guess every decision that had led to this moment. The candy bag sat on my lap like evidence of temporary insanity. But Mom had hugged me hard at the bus station, that fierce Westfield hug that somehow gave permission and protection, and whispered "Trust your instincts" against my hair.

My instincts had gotten me into plenty of trouble before. But they'd led me to Alex in the first place, to those tutoring sessions where I'd finally stopped feeling stupid about chemistry.

The Golden Dragon glowed on a street corner in Quincy like someone had dropped a jewel box in the middle of an ordinary neighborhood. Red lanterns hung over the door, swaying in the November wind. Through the big front windows showcased families crowded around circular tables, chopsticks flashing, steam rising from platters of food. It looked just how Alex had described it, down to the elaborate dragon mural on the back wall.

I stood on the sidewalk for a full minute, holding the maple candy and trying to convince myself this was normal friend behavior. Just bringing candy to someone who'd mentioned being lonely. Totally reasonable. Not at all the result of spending four days replaying phone conversations and remembering the exact way he'd said my name.

When I pushed through the red door, the temperature change was instant. The warm air was loaded with ginger and garlic, sweet and savory all mixed together in a way that made my mouth water. Voices overlapped in English and Mandarin, silverware clinked, a child laughed somewhere toward the back. A place where customers became family.

A woman appeared with menus, her smile professional and welcoming. She had Alex's bone structure, his dark eyes, his mouth. "Table for one?"

"I'm actually... I'm looking for Alex? Alex Chen?" I said it too fast. "I'm a friend. From school."

Her expression smoothed, like a door closing. "Alex is with family tonight. A special dinner." She'd already turned away, dismissing me.

That's when I saw him.

Alex wore a navy suit jacket I'd never seen before. He looked older in it, like someone playing a part. An older man sat to his right. Had to be his father based on the way they both held their shoulders exactly the same. And to Alex's left...

The girl was beautiful in that effortless way some people just are, like they'd been designed by someone who understood aesthetics on a molecular level. Long black hair fell perfectly straight down her back, not a strand out of place. She was laughing at something, her hand resting on Alex's arm. Light and easy, like she'd done it a hundred times before.

Across the table, an older couple beamed at them both.

My brain did this thing where it kept processing information I didn't want to process. Her hand was on his arm. This wasn't casual dinner with friends. This was *the* dinner. The kind with ironed tablecloths and an agenda and everyone's best behavior. The kind that came with expectations.

I should have left. Any reasonable person would have backed straight out that red door and spent the next several years pretending this never happened. But my feet had forgotten how to move and I was still standing there, clutching my bag of maple candy like it was somehow going to explain what I was doing in this restaurant in Quincy on a Saturday evening.

Our eyes met across fifteen feet and two dozen conversations. Surprise first, then confusion. Maybe panic. Then determination. He said something to the table. I couldn't hear it but I saw his father's eyebrows go up. Alex stood so fast his chair scraped loud enough to turn heads.

The girl (Jennifer, it had to be Jennifer) kept her eyes locked on Alex as he weaved through tables toward me. Her expression wasn't what I'd expected. Not anger or possession or even confusion. She looked curious. Her eyebrows rose as she glanced between Alex's retreating back and me frozen by the door. And then (I definitely didn't imagine this) the corner of her mouth quirked up. Just slightly. Like she was impressed, or maybe amused by whatever was unfolding.

Her mother leaned over and whispered something urgent, gesturing at the empty chair where Alex should have been. Jennifer just shrugged and reached for her water glass, deliberately turning her whole body away from both the conversation and her mother's obvious distress. The movement was small but unmistakable. She wasn't playing along.

"Kate." Alex was breathing hard when he reached me, like he'd run a marathon instead of walked across a room. "What are you doing here?"

It stung. A physical sensation like missing a step on stairs. "I wanted to surprise you. You said you were lonely, and I had all this candy from Gemma's, and I thought..." My voice was doing that thing where it raised at the end, turning statements into questions. "I thought maybe you could use something sweet. But this is clearly... I should go."

I turned toward the door and Alex caught my wrist. "Kate, wait. It's complicated."

"Is she your girlfriend?" I couldn't stop myself. My cheeks blazed.

"No." Fast and emphatic. "God, no. Jennifer's a family friend. Our parents have been..." He stopped, jaw working like he was chewing words he didn't want to swallow. He glanced back at the table where five pairs of eyes were definitely watching us. "It's complicated."

"You said that already." I was still holding the stupid candy. It crinkled when my hands tightened around it.

Alex ran his fingers through his hair, messing it up from its careful style. "Our parents think we should be together. They've been pushing us toward this for years, and tonight was supposed to be..." Another glance at the table. "I couldn't say no without causing problems I can't fix."

The restaurant suddenly felt too close, too bright, too full of other people's happiness. Someone walked past with a steaming plate of something and I stepped sideways, bumping into a chair.

"I should go," I said again.

"Kate, please. It's not what you think."

"What do I think, Alex?"

He did an excellent impersonation of a fish. Looked back at the table where his whole carefully constructed life was waiting for him to return and play his part. "I don't know."

And there it was. The truth under all the explanations. He didn't know what I thought because we'd never actually talked about what this was between us. Maybe it wasn't anything. Maybe I'd built something out of study sessions and late-night phone calls that only existed in my head.

"Enjoy your dinner." I pulled the door open. The cold made my eyes water. At least, I told myself it was the cold.

"Kate."

I was already outside, fumbling for my phone with fingers that had gone clumsy and numb. The T schedule blurred when I tried to focus on it. Behind me the restaurant door opened again and I heard Alex's voice.

"Kate, please."

I turned around. He stood on the sidewalk, arms wrapped around himself against the November cold. His hair was a mess now from running his hands through it, and in the yellow streetlight glow he looked younger, uncertain in a way I'd never seen him.

"You're going to freeze," I said.

"I don't care." He took a step toward me. The cold had already turned his cheeks pink. "Jennifer isn't my girlfriend. I've never thought about her that way. But my parents... they have expectations."

"Expectations that include special dinners and suit jackets?"

"Yes."

The simple honesty of it hurt worse than elaborate excuses would have. I could picture it, too. The years of careful orchestration, the subtle and not so subtle pushing, the weight of family obligation pressing down until there was no room left to breathe.

"That sounds really difficult," I said.

"It is."

We stood there while our breath made clouds in the air. Jennifer wasn't watching us through the window. She'd angled her whole chair away from the glass, ignoring her mother's attempts to draw her back into whatever conversation was happening about me at the table. Her parents both looked frustrated with her lack of concern about Alex's prolonged absence. She sat with her chin up, deliberately refusing to engage.

"You should get back to your dinner," I said. "Your parents probably think I'm incredibly rude."

"They think you're..." Alex paused, choosing words. "They think I should be more careful."

"Careful of what?"

"You."

"Me?" I almost laughed except nothing about this was funny. "I can barely pass organic chemistry. What's dangerous about that?"

"Dangerous to their plans."

I thought about my own parents, how Mom had researched train schedules and sent me here with candy and permission to follow my instincts. How Dad worried about my grades but never made me feel like I owed him a specific future. I couldn't imagine navigating feelings under that kind of microscope, every choice filtered through someone else's vision of what my life should look like.

"Alex." I pulled my jacket tighter. My fingers were going numb. "You should go back inside."

"I don't want to."

"But you're going to."

He didn't deny it. The silence was its own answer, and honestly? I couldn't blame him. Family was complex and I barely understood the dynamics of my own, much less his. And I was just... what was I, really? The girl he tutored twice a week for some extra money. The girl who'd shown up uninvited with maple candy like that meant something.

"I'll see you Tuesday," I said, already backing toward the T station entrance.

"Kate."

I stopped but didn't turn around. My throat felt too tight.

"This doesn't change anything. Between us."

But it did. We both knew it. Because now I'd seen the other life he lived, the one where family friends turned into something more with the right parental approval. The one where he wore pressed shirts and played the perfect son and fit into expectations I'd never even considered.

"I know," I lied.

The T station entrance swallowed me. Down the stairs into fluorescent light and the smell of metal and electricity and too many people. A rat investigated a dropped sandwich wrapper on the platform. At least someone was excited about something.

The train was half-empty, that weird evening lull. I found a seat and leaned my forehead against the window, watching my ghost-reflection slide past dark tunnel walls.

Jennifer's hand on Alex's arm. Casual. Comfortable.

Alex in that navy jacket, looking caught. Knowing he'd go back inside.

The train lurched and I grabbed the pole, palm sweaty against cold metal. Across from me a couple shared earbuds, heads tilted together in unconscious synchronization. I looked away.

They'd probably be fine together. Compatible. Same family expectations, same cultural pressures. No confusion about what dinner meant or which world they belonged to.

And I'd still be failing chemistry. Still trying to figure out what major made sense. Still the girl who jumped between ideas too fast.

The train climbed above ground and suddenly there was a dark sky with clouds visible against the city light. I traced patterns the way I used to in the grass behind our house.

My phone chimed. I didn't look.

By the time I got back to campus, I'd reorganized the whole evening into something manageable. I'd misread the situation. Alex was a nice guy helping with chemistry, and I'd somehow turned that into something it wasn't. Classic Kate, making elaborate mental maps out of incomplete information.

Isa was at her desk when I walked in, surrounded by her fortress of color-coded notes and textbooks bristling with sticky tabs. She turned in her chair when I dropped my bag on my bed.

"You're back early." She pushed her reading glasses up into her hair. "Did you come back early for a last minute study session with Alex?"

I shrugged off my jacket and the maple candy fell out of the pocket, landing on the floor with an accusing crinkle. I picked it up and tossed it into the trash. "Actually, I think I'm probably set for chemistry finals. Don't think I need any more tutoring sessions."

Isa's eyebrows shot toward the ceiling. "Really? You were just saying Tuesday how much Alex's sessions were helping."

"Yeah, well." I pulled my laptop out of my bag and opened it just to have something to look at. "I think I've got it figured out now. Might as well save the money, right?"

"Kate."

She'd turned her chair fully toward me, her test prep forgotten. Her eyes drinking in my expression.

"What happened?"

"Nothing happened. I just... I think I'm good on chemistry now."

"You hate chemistry. Last week you said molecular bonding made you want to cry."

"I'm better at it now."

"So you're going to cancel on Alex right before finals?"

"I'm not canceling, I'm just..." My phone vibrated again in my pocket. I pulled it out to silence it and saw two messages on the screen.

> **ALEX**
> Can we talk tomorrow?
> Please?

I stared at them for a long moment. Isa had that expression she got when she was fitting pieces together, the same focus she brought to exam prep questions.

I deleted both messages without responding.

"Kate..."

"I'm tired," I said, which wasn't a lie. Every part of me felt heavy, weighted in a way that had nothing to do with the long train ride back from Waverly Cove. "I'm just going to crash, okay?"

Isa looked like she wanted to push, but she didn't. "Okay," she conceded. "But I'm here if you want to talk."

"I know." I changed into pajamas and climbed into bed even though it was barely eight o'clock, pulling my blanket up over my head like I could block out everything that had happened.

In the dark, I kept seeing Jennifer's hand on Alex's arm. His mother's dismissive expression. The way he'd fit so naturally into that corner table with his family and their expectations.

My phone pinged another time.

I reached out and turned it off completely.

Chapter 9

Alex

I spent the entire T ride calculating scenarios. Testing variables.

Last week, Kate had appeared outside The Golden Dragon and seen Jennifer at the table. Her eyes had widened first, then her mouth had tightened. The whole sequence took maybe two seconds. Like watching a chemical reaction reverse itself.

Three messages sent. Zero responses received.

The crowd thinned as the train approached Quincy. I could have cited pharmacy finals as reason to skip this week's visit, but my parents had called for "a serious discussion." In our family, that phrase could only mean one thing. They knew about Kate.

I emerged from the station into air so cold it made my eyes water. Late November meant the temperature was dropping daily. Three blocks to The Golden Dragon. 547 steps. I'd counted them before without meaning to.

The restaurant's windows glowed red and gold from the same lanterns my mother had picked out fifteen years ago. I'd replaced the bulbs last summer, my father telling me I was doing it wrong the entire time.

The bell over the door announced my arrival.

"Bàba? Māmā?"

My father entered from the kitchen, wiping his hands on a cloth. But he wasn't cooking. No ginger smell. No garlic. Just cleaning solution and the ghost of last night's service. He wasn't cooking, which meant this was worse than I'd calculated.

"Your mother is upstairs. Come." His face was blank. Carefully blank. Years of customer service had taught him how to make his face show nothing.

I followed him through the kitchen to the narrow stairs. We'd lived in the apartment above until I was twelve. Three of us in 600 square feet. Now it was office space and somewhere to rest between shifts. The stairs were steep. Seventeen steps. I'd counted those too.

My mother sat at the small table by the window. Three teacups arranged in a triangle. Teapot centered. Her posture was perfect. Hands folded. She tracked us with her eyes the way a scientist tracks a specimen. I'd learned that look from her.

"Sit," she said. In Mandarin.

English for casual. Mandarin for serious. I took the empty chair, completing our triangle. My father settled into the third position. The geometry was familiar. We'd sat like this when I was choosing colleges. When I'd declared my major. When I'd asked permission to move into my studio instead of commuting.

My mother poured tea. The ritual gave everyone time to prepare. Nobody spoke until all three cups were full. Jasmine. I could identify it by smell alone. We'd served it at the restaurant for fifteen years and I'd probably made a thousand pots of it.

"Mr. Liu called yesterday," my father said. Still Mandarin. "He had questions about the American girl. The one who stopped by the restaurant."

There it was. Direct. No preliminaries.

"Her name is Kate," I said in English. A deliberate choice. "She's my chemistry tutoring student."

My mother's teacup stopped halfway to her mouth. The angle changed maybe five degrees. Most people wouldn't notice. I noticed everything.

"Is that all she is, Lì Xiáng?"

My Chinese name. She only used it for important conversations.

I could construct a story where Kate was just an overeager student. The words assembled themselves in my mind, orderly and logical and false.

"No." I kept my eyes on the tea. Easier than faces. "She's my friend. A good friend."

"A friend who takes the train on Thanksgiving to surprise you?" My father's fingers tightened on his cup. I tracked the movement peripherally. Increased pressure, tendons visible on the back of his hand. "Who interrupts a family dinner with dramatics?"

I took a sip. Gave myself five seconds. The tea was good. My mother always made good tea. "Kate and I have been spending time together outside tutoring. She's important to me."

"Important." My mother repeated the word. Let it sit there. "More important than your future? More important than what we've given you?"

The pressure started in my shoulders. Trapezius muscles, predictable location. Stress always collected there first. My heart rate had increased. Maybe ten percent. I cataloged the responses while trying to formulate an answer that was both true and wouldn't make this worse.

"It's not about comparison," I said, tiptoeing through the minefield of the conversation. "My future and my relationships can coexist."

"Can they?" My father leaned forward. "Pharmacy residencies

don't accept students who can't focus. Dr. Zhang won't offer you placement if you're distracted by girls."

Dr. Zhang. My father's friend. The residency opportunity. The variable I'd known would appear in this equation. I'd been waiting for it.

"My grades haven't dropped," I said. True statement. Verifiable. "I'm still ranked first in my class."

"For now." My mother's voice got softer. That was worse than if she'd raised it. "Lì Xiáng, we know how these things happen. American girls are very free with their affections. Very temporary with their commitments."

My body had an instant physiological response to the perceived insult. Elevated heart rate, heat in my face, tension spreading down my arms. I recognized the symptoms of anger but experiencing them and understanding them were different things.

"You don't know her," I said.

"And you do? After a few months?" My father shook his head. The gesture was small but definitive. "We've known the Liu family for decades. Jennifer understands our culture. Our values. She respects family obligations."

"Kate respects my obligations." I heard my voice get firmer and noted it with interest. "She's smart. Hardworking. Her father's a physical therapist, her mother's an ER nurse. They've built something good in Maine."

"Maine?" My mother scoffed. "Where they catch the lobsters?"

Under different circumstances I might have found that funny. My mother reduced an entire state to its primary export. Instead, I felt myself wanting to defend not just Kate but the whole concept of Maine. Which was illogical. It was just a state. It didn't need defending.

"Yes. Her family are healthcare professionals. They work as hard as you do."

My father set his cup down. The sound was controlled. Everything my father did was controlled. "The difference, son, is that her family was born here. They have all the privileges. They didn't leave everything behind. Didn't work eighteen hours every day so their child could have opportunities."

The immigration narrative. The foundation of every serious conversation we'd ever had. Their journey from Guangdong Province with nothing but determination and my father's family recipes. The early years of poverty. Building the restaurant. The singular focus on my education. I knew this story better than I knew anything. It was the framework of my entire existence.

But Kate's parents had worked those hours too. Just in different contexts. The parallel seemed relevant but I couldn't articulate why without sounding like I was dismissing my parents' history. Which I wasn't. I was just trying to understand why one type of hard work counted more than another.

"I know what you've given up," I said. The words sounded stiff. "I've never forgotten."

"Then you understand why this distraction has to stop." My mother reached across the table. Her hand stopped inches from mine. "You're so close, Lì Xiáng. One semester. Then residency. Then a good position. Then a suitable marriage. The path is clear."

Clear. Yes. The path had always been clear. Drawn before I could walk. Refined as I grew. Presented not as option but as inevitability. And I'd followed it because following it made sense. Because questioning it would hurt them. Because I'd believed that obedience and success were the same destination.

But sitting here watching my mother's hand hovering near mine, my heart rate hadn't decreased. The tension in my shoulders had spread to my neck. My jaw clenched. I cataloged these responses and couldn't make them fit into the familiar equation of filial duty.

"What if I want to choose?" The question spilled out before I'd processed it. "My own path. My own happiness."

My father's jaw set. His eyes flattened. It was like watching concrete harden. "Happiness is what you earn after duty. Not before."

"What if I disagree?"

The silence had weight to it. Physical presence. My parents exchanged one of those married people glances where entire conversations happen without words. When my father spoke again, his voice had lost the patience I was used to. Each word had edges.

"Then you make a choice. This American girl and whatever temporary feelings you have, or the future your mother and I have spent our entire lives building."

"That's not fair." Even as I said it, I heard how it sounded. Petulant. Simplistic.

"Life isn't fair, son. That's the first thing we learned in America." My father leaned forward. I could smell the soap he used. Same soap for as long as I could remember. "If you continue this relationship, we can't support your last semester. And Dr. Zhang will hear that your focus has shifted."

The threat was targeted. Surgical. Without their financial support, I'd need more loans or be forced to move back to Quincy. Without Dr. Zhang's connection, top-tier residencies would be unreachable this late. They'd identified the exact pressure points. I would have respected the strategy if it wasn't being applied to me.

"You'd sabotage my career?" I couldn't keep the disbelief out of my voice.

"We'd save your future from temporary desires," my mother corrected. "Someday you'll thank us."

I stared at my tea. The leaves had unfurled and were drifting in the amber liquid. My heart rate was elevated but steady. My breathing was shallow. Tension in my trapezius, neck, jaw.

There was a question forming, but I couldn't quite reach it. Something about whether happiness you're forced into could even be called happiness. But the thought was incomplete. The data was insufficient.

"I need time to think," I said.

"There's nothing to think about," my father replied. "End this distraction. Focus on your future. Honor our investment."

Their investment. As if I were a portfolio. A return they were waiting to collect.

I studied my mother with her perfect posture. My father with his controlled expression. Two people who had shaped every decision I'd ever made. Who had worked until exhaustion became the baseline. Who loved me with an intensity that left no space for deviation.

"I'll let you know after finals," I said. Stood up. The chair scraped on the linoleum. "I need to study."

My mother's eyebrows drew together. Her mouth opened, then closed. The corners of her lips turned down for maybe half a second before her entire face smoothed to neutrality again. "Lì Xiáng. Alex..."

"I need to study," I repeated. Couldn't process what was on her face. Too much data coming too fast. "We'll talk soon."

I took the stairs down. Counted them without meaning to. Thirteen. But halfway down I stopped. This felt wrong. Like the pressure was building and I couldn't equalize it. I pressed my hand against the wall. I felt the texture of the aging brick under my palm. Cold. I focused on that instead of the pressure. Just needed a moment. Just needed to catalog this sensation and file it away.

Above me, voices. My mother's first, infused with something I couldn't identify through the wall.

"Heng. We need to talk."

I should have kept walking. Given them privacy. But my legs

wouldn't move, and the wall was thin. I didn't want to know what they'd say, but I couldn't make myself leave.

"He's going to ruin everything." My father's voice had an edge I rarely heard. "Twenty-three years, Li Mei. Twenty-three years of eighteen-hour days. He'll throw it away for a girl he barely knows."

"He knows her well enough to defy us." My mother's voice. Still respectful but firmer than she'd been with me. "That tells us something."

"It tells us he's being foolish. Young. Not thinking clearly."

Pause. I counted the seconds. Seven. Eight. Nine.

"What if we're wrong?" My mother again.

"Wrong?" The volume of my father's voice increased. "We gave him everything. Best education. Connections. Opportunities. How are we wrong?"

"Not about the opportunities. About forcing his hand like this. Making him choose."

"We're not forcing. We're showing him reality. If he can't see this girl will ruin his future..."

"What if she doesn't?" My mother interrupted. She never interrupted. "What if we push too hard and lose him?"

More silence. Longer this time. I stayed frozen on the stairs, my hand still on the textured wall, counting my heartbeats.

"I'm afraid, Li Mei."

Three words from my father that I'd never heard before. The data didn't fit any established pattern.

"I know," my mother whispered.

"We left everything for him. Everything. Our families, our language, our home. Worked until my back gave out. Until you couldn't remember sleeping past six. All of it was for him."

Sacrifice. The word they'd used my entire life. The cornerstone of every argument, every guilt-heavy reminder of debt owed. But hearing it now, outside the conversation instead of in it, I processed something new. Not manipulation. Fear. Pure fear.

"What if it's not enough?" My father's voice cracked. The crack was small but I heard it. "What if he fails because of this girl? Loses the residency? Can't get into pharmacy school? What if all our years come to nothing because he fell in love with the wrong person?"

"He won't fail, Heng." My mother's certainty was absolute. "Our son doesn't fail."

"But what if he does? What if we're not there when he falls? What if we pushed him away?"

I pressed my forehead against the wall now. The texture imprinted on my skin. My eyes were burning. Physiological response to strong emotion. Lacrimal glands activating. I cataloged it clinically but couldn't stop it.

They weren't trying to control me. They were terrified. The distinction seemed important but I couldn't process why.

"You're not afraid he'll fail," my mother said. "You're afraid he'll succeed without us. Choose a life we don't understand. A world we didn't build for him."

Long silence.

"Both," my father admitted. "I'm afraid of both. He's our only child, Li Mei. Our only chance. To prove coming here meant something."

"It already means something." My mother's voice. "Look at who he is. Smart. Hard-working. Kind. Exactly who we raised him to be."

"Then why is he choosing this girl over us?"

"Maybe he's choosing himself." My mother paused. Her breathing was audible even through the wall. "The way we never could."

I pulled back from the wall. My forehead tingled from what I guessed was a red mark on it. I touched it. The imprint of texture. The sensation was grounding. Physical. Real.

The conversation continued, but I finally made myself walk

down the stairs into the empty restaurant. The tables were all clean. Chairs stacked. Everything ready for tomorrow's service. I walked through the dining room touching the backs of chairs as I passed. Counted them. The physical count helped. Gave my brain something to do besides try to process what I'd heard.

My parents were scared. Their ultimatum was about fear. They'd built everything on my success and watching me deviate felt like watching their lives collapse. I could understand that intellectually. Could diagram the logic. But understanding it and knowing what to do with it were separate problems.

I pulled out my phone as I walked to the T station. Three messages to Kate, all unanswered. The sample size was small but the pattern was clear. She was avoiding me. Probably smart of her. Probably safer. My life was complicated in ways she hadn't signed up for.

Maybe the logical choice was to let her go. Return to the predetermined path. Stop introducing variables into an equation that my parents solved years ago.

The train arrived at the station. I boarded. Found a seat by the window. The tunnel walls rushed past, too fast to focus on. Just darkness and occasional lights as I tried to calculate what I should do next.

But every calculation kept including Kate. The way she organized chaos. The way she'd asked about my culture with genuine curiosity instead of awkward politeness. The way she'd shown up on Thanksgiving with maple candy because she thought I might be lonely.

The way I felt less alone when she was there.

That last observation couldn't be quantified or verified. But it kept appearing in my data set anyway.

The city gradually appeared outside the window of the train. Buildings. Lights. I leaned my head against the window. The glass rattled my skull. The sensation was uncomfortable but grounding.

My father had said happiness comes after duty. My mother had suggested maybe I was choosing myself. Kate had asked if success counted when you weren't being yourself. Three different frameworks. Three different variables. I couldn't solve the equation with the data I had.

But I also couldn't pretend the equation hadn't changed.

My phone was still in my hand. Kate's contact information on the screen. I could call her. Text her again. Try to explain everything I'd just heard. But I didn't know how to explain it when I hadn't processed it myself.

Type it out anyway. Attempt to organize the data through articulation.

> ALEX
> Kate, I need to

I deleted it. Too vague. Try again.

> ALEX
> I know you're avoiding me. I understand why. But we need to

Delete. Too demanding. Once more.

> ALEX
> My parents know about us. They gave me an ultimatum. I'm supposed to choose between you and my future. But the thing is, I don't think those are actually separate choices anymore. I think maybe

Delete. Too much. Too uncertain. Too many incomplete thoughts.

I shoved the phone back in my pocket.

I'd text her something when my mind was clearer. Maybe I'd never hear from Kate again. Maybe I'd already lost that variable while trying to solve all the others. Maybe that's what happened when you tried to calculate emotions instead of just feeling them.

Chapter 10

Kate

Molecular structures swam across my vision.

I'd been staring at the same page for far too long, tapping my highlighter against the library table in a rhythm that probably annoyed everyone within earshot. Tap tap. Tap tap tap. The benzene ring was a hexagon which made me think of an octagon, like the stop sign outside the library which made me think about how I should probably stop avoiding my problems.

I knew these concepts last week. When Alex explained them.

I flipped back to my notes from last month, the ones full of colored diagrams where I'd redrawn his subway-map analogy for orbital hybridization. Little annotations in margins: "Think Green Line for s-orbital" and "Red Line = p-orbital energy levels." I'd even sketched tiny passengers representing electrons, gave them little faces. One of them had a briefcase.

"That's not going to be on the exam," I whispered to myself, then slammed the textbook shut hard enough that two first-years at the next table jumped.

"Sorry." I mouthed the word, wincing.

Nine days until the chemistry final that would determine whether I could continue in nursing, and my primary study method had just imploded because I'd gone and caught feelings for my tutor who apparently came with family-approved marriage prospects.

I shoved everything into my backpack and the zipper caught on the spiral binding of my notebook. The one that had slowly transformed from molecular diagrams into more art than science over the past month. I yanked it and heard pages tear.

"Shit." I swung the bag over my shoulder and headed for the exit.

Outside, December air slapped me across the face. Finals week campus was like a zombie movie. Students shuffled between buildings with dead eyes, the library behind me glowing like a beacon, every window bright. Two AM study sessions. Three AM breakdowns. Four AM energy drinks. The collective anxiety was practically visible, hanging in the frozen air.

My boots crunched through yesterday's snow. I pulled out my phone and called the one person in Boston who wouldn't tell me I was being dramatic.

"Hey, squirt." Liam picked up on the third ring. Classical music played in the background. He'd been listening to the same focus playlist since high school.

"Are you busy?" My voice sounded weird.

Brief pause. "Just reviewing patient notes. What's wrong?"

"I'm having a chemistry crisis." I stepped around a patch of ice and nearly slipped anyway. "And I need someone to talk me out of dropping out and becoming a professional snow cone vendor."

"In Boston in December. Very practical." A smile colored his voice. "Want to come over? I've got leftover lasagna from that Italian place you like."

"Be there in twenty."

"You look terrible." Liam stepped aside to let me in.

His apartment was exactly what you'd expect from a PT doctoral candidate who'd lived in the same place for three years. Organized but not scary about it. Anatomical drawings framed on the walls next to family photos from home. A small Christmas tree in the corner with the mismatched ornaments Mom had been collecting since the nineties, the ones Liam had insisted on taking his share of. There was the clay handprint I'd made in kindergarten, now a tree ornament, my name misspelled "KAT" in my five-year-old handwriting.

"I'm saving sleep for after finals." I dropped my backpack by the door, kicked off my wet boots. "Or after graduation. Haven't decided."

He disappeared into the kitchen and returned with hot chocolate with extra mini marshmallows floating on top. I took the mug and wrapped both hands around it, letting the heat sink into my frozen fingers.

"So." He settled into his armchair while I curled up on the couch, tucking my feet under me. "Chemistry crisis?"

I took a tentative sip. It was far too hot and nearly scalded my tongue. "I'm going to fail my final."

"You convinced Dad you'd studied for your bio midterm once by memorizing the intro paragraph and talking really fast." Liam raised an eyebrow. "You got a B+."

"That was different. That was high school."

"And you were terrified then too. Called me crying at

midnight, convinced you'd flunk and disappoint everyone." He leaned back. "Then you somehow pulled it together."

"I don't remember calling you."

"You blocked it out. You always do that when you're scared." He said it like he was commenting on the weather. "So what's going on? You've been seeing a tutor, right?"

And that's when it all spilled out. I told him about meeting Alex for tutoring, how he'd made chemistry make sense for the first time ever, how I'd started looking forward to our sessions for reasons that had nothing to do with molecular structures. About the surprise visit to the restaurant. Jennifer Liu with her hand on Alex's arm. His mother's dismissive look. The whole family-approved date setup.

"Wait." Liam held up a hand. "You came back to Boston early, during Thanksgiving break, to bring this guy maple candy?"

"Gemma and I made a lot of it and I thought he might be lonely." I sank deeper into the couch. The cushion wheezed. "It seemed like a good idea."

"Katie." He shook his head. "Remember when you were thirteen and obsessed with Danny Henderson? You suddenly got really into home improvement. Found a new project that needed fixing every week."

"That's not the same."

"You repainted your room three times that summer." He was definitely grinning now. "Three times. Different shades of the same blue. And Danny had to help you pick supplies every single time."

A smile broke through despite everything. "Danny had nice eyes."

"And terrible taste in music. But you pretended to love whatever garbage he was into." He stood and headed for the kitchen. "My point is, you've always been all-in when you care about something. Or someone. It's not a flaw. It's just you."

I pulled the throw pillow onto my lap, found a loose thread and started picking at it. "Being all-in just means I crash harder."

"Yeah, but you also get back up." His voice carried from the kitchen. I heard containers opening and plates clattering. "Remember when you fell off the dock trying to impress James with your diving? Cried for ten minutes, then climbed right back up and did it again."

"I was eight."

"And stubborn even then." Liam returned carrying two plates heaped with pasta and cheesy goodness. The smell of garlic and tomato and cheese made my stomach suddenly remember I'd skipped lunch. "Some things don't change."

I took the plate but didn't dare disturb the perfect layers of pasta and cheese and sauce. A true masterpiece in carbohydrate form. "So I like him. And I'm avoiding him because I saw him with someone his family probably wants him to marry. That's dramatic, right?"

"It is dramatic." Liam dug into his lasagna. "You're a Westfield. We don't do anything halfway. Including self-sabotage when we're scared."

I stabbed at my pasta. The cheese stretched. "I'm not self-sabotaging."

"Katie." He pointed his fork at me. "You threw away your best shot at passing chemistry because you have feelings for your tutor. What do you call that?"

"A strategic retreat."

"Self-sabotage." He took another bite, chewed, swallowed. "Same thing you did when you quit concert band junior year because Laurie Richards was better than you at the flute."

"Laurie Richards had been taking private lessons since she was six."

"And you were good too. But you quit instead of dealing with not being the best." He wasn't being mean about it. Just stating facts. "Pattern, Katie."

I set down my fork. Suddenly not hungry even though the lasagna was delicious. "I don't know what I'm doing, LeeLee. With Alex, with nursing, with any of it. Everyone else has a map and I'm just wandering around hoping I don't walk off a cliff."

Liam was quiet for a moment. Thinking and chewing. Then he set his plate on the coffee table. "Do you remember when I committed to the PhD program instead of going straight into practice?"

"After your master's?"

"It wasn't because I wanted to. Not at first." He leaned forward, elbows on knees. "I had three job offers. One in Portland working with athletes. Good money, practical experience, exactly what you're supposed to want."

"But you chose more school."

"But I chose more school. Even though Mom and Dad couldn't help pay for it. Even though it meant loans I'll be paying off until I'm forty." He smiled a little. "You know what Mom said when I told her?"

I shook my head.

"She said we didn't raise you to follow someone else's map." His voice gentled, reminding me eerily of our Mom. "She said we raised you to draw your own. Then she hugged me and said she was proud I picked the harder path."

"I didn't know that."

"You were in high school dealing with your own drama. And I didn't tell anyone how scared I was." He picked up his plate again. "Here's what I figured out though. The scary choices matter more. The safe path feels good until you realize you're miserable."

My chemistry textbook. The formulas that wouldn't stick. The growing dread every time I thought about clinicals next semester.

The way I'd started drawing in my notebook margins instead of taking notes.

"What if I don't want to be a nurse?"

The words just hung there.

Liam didn't look surprised. Just nodded like I'd confirmed what he'd suspected. "Then don't be a nurse."

"That's it?"

"That's it." He shrugged. "But you still have to pass chemistry. Otherwise your options get narrow real fast."

"That's practical advice, not inspirational advice."

"I'm your brother, not a poster on a guidance counselor's wall." He grinned. "Look, I don't know what you want to do instead. Maybe you don't know either. But I know you need to talk to this Alex guy, get your tutoring back, and pass that final. Then you can figure out the rest."

"Just like that?"

"Just like that." He nudged my plate closer. "Eat your lasagna. You think better when you're not hangry."

I took a bite. The flavors grounded me. Familiar. Comforting. "When did you get so wise?"

"I've always been this wise. You just never listened before." He winked. "Comes with being one of the oldest. We get the wisdom, you guys get the fun."

"That's not how it works."

"Tell Sophie that. She got away with murder because Mom and Dad were too tired by kid three."

We fell into easier territory then. Swapping stories about home. Dad's terrible jokes. Abby's dramatic teenage phase that was still ongoing. Liam didn't fix my problems. Didn't tell me what to do. Just reminded me I wasn't alone in the mess.

When we circled back to chemistry, he pulled out a notepad. "Okay, show me what you're struggling with. Fair warning, I remember maybe sixty percent of undergrad chem."

I dug out my textbook and notes. "It's this whole section on bonding."

"Covalent or ionic?"

"Both. All of it. Everything."

He flipped through my notes, stopping on one of my diagrams. "Is that electron wearing a hat?"

"It helps me remember which one's which."

"That's kind of brilliant." He grabbed a pen. "Okay, let's think about this like the body. Bones and muscles, right? They work together but they're different."

"That's what Alex said. Kind of. His version was better."

"His version involved subway maps, if I recall."

"Yeah."

"So we'll do my version. PT style." He started drawing. "Think of ionic bonds like ligaments. They hold things together but they're more rigid..."

For the next hour, Liam worked through my notes. It wasn't as good as Alex's explanations. The metaphors didn't click the same way. But it helped. Made the concepts less scary. We reviewed three chapters, him drawing diagrams that looked nothing like my textbook but somehow made more sense.

My phone buzzed halfway through. I ignored it until it buzzed again.

"You should check that," Liam said.

"It's probably just Isa asking where I am."

"Check anyway."

I pulled out my phone. Two texts, but not from Isa.

> ALEX
>
> I know you're avoiding me. I understand why.
>
> But if you need help studying for the final, I'm still available. No pressure.

The messages glowed on my screen.

"Is that him?" Liam asked.

"Yeah."

"You going to respond?"

"I don't know." I laid the phone face-down on the couch. "Maybe. Later."

"Katie."

"I know, I know." I picked at the loose thread on the pillow again. "I need to deal with it. But not right now. First I need to figure out if I can even pass this test."

"Fair enough." He turned back to the notes. "So, molecular geometry..."

We studied until my eyes started crossing, until the diagrams blurred together, until I couldn't remember if we were talking about sigma bonds or pi bonds or James Bond. Liam finally closed the textbook around nine-thirty.

"That's enough for tonight. Your brain needs to process."

"But I still don't understand half of it."

"You understand more than you did two hours ago. That's progress." He stood, stretching. "You want to crash here? I can make up the couch."

"No, I should get back. Isa's probably wondering if I died in the library stacks."

At the door, I tugged my boots back on. Wet. Cold. Gross. Liam caught me in a sideways hug while I bent over tying them.

"You're going to be fine, squirt. You always are."

"Even if I decide not to be a nurse?"

"Especially then. Mom and Dad survived me choosing research over practice. And Sophie choosing social work. They'll survive whatever you decide." He squeezed my shoulder. "But you have to decide. Limbo's worse than the wrong choice."

"That's wise again."

"I'm older. It happens." He stepped back. "One more thing

though. This Alex situation? You need to deal with it. Not for the chemistry help, though that would be nice. But because you're going to drive yourself crazy with the what-ifs."

"What if he just wants me for my tutoring money?"

"Then you'll know. And you can move on." He opened the door. Cold air rushed in. "But hiding? That's not you. You've never hidden from anything."

"I hid from Danny Henderson for three months after he found out about the paint."

"You were thirteen. And you asked him to the spring dance anyway."

"He said no."

"But you asked." Liam leaned against the doorframe. "That's the point. You asked."

I stepped out into the cold. "Thanks, LeeLee."

"Anytime, squirt."

The T ride back to campus was mostly empty. Sunday night, finals week, everyone either studying or sleeping or contemplating their life choices. I sat by the window and dark tunnel walls rushed past.

My phone was heavy in my pocket. The two messages from Alex were still unanswered.

> **ALEX**
> I know you're avoiding me. I understand why.

Did he though? Did he understand that I'd shown up with maple candy because I'd missed him? That seeing him at that table with Jennifer had felt like walking into a wall? That I'd spent the last week and a half alternating between angry and sad and convinced I'd made the whole thing up in my head?

> **KATE**
> I need help. Chemistry is kicking my ass and I'm pretty sure I'm going to fail.

Too desperate. Delete.

> **KATE**
> Thanks for offering. Can we meet tomorrow?

Too casual. Like nothing happened. Delete.

> **KATE**
> I miss our study sessions. And also I miss you. Which is probably not appropriate to say to your tutor but I'm saying it anyway because apparently I make terrible decisions when I'm stressed.

Way too much. Delete delete delete.

One impossible thing at a time. First, pass chemistry. Then figure out the Alex situation. Or maybe first figure out the Alex situation so I could pass chemistry. Or maybe just fail chemistry and become a snow cone vendor like I'd told Liam and avoid all my problems forever.

Chapter 11

Alex

The powder in my mortar had reached ideal consistency several minutes ago. I kept grinding anyway, the circular motion providing the illusion of productivity. Kate hadn't responded to my last message. Twelve hours since I'd texted her to offer help preparing for final exams. The read receipt showed she'd seen it at 9:47 PM.

"Chen, you're going to wear a hole in that mortar if you keep grinding."

David had his safety goggles pushed up on his forehead, leaving red indentations across his skin. Dark circles under his eyes testified to our study sessions for the pharmacology final we'd both survived yesterday.

"The particle size needs to be consistent."

"It's been consistent for like five minutes." David capped his solution with the careful movements of someone operating on three hours of sleep. "Unless you're trying to achieve quantum-level uniformity?"

I set the pestle down. The ceramic clicked against the bench and seemed too loud. "Just being thorough."

"Right." David's stool scraped against linoleum as he angled toward me. "So this is about the girl from Thanksgiving?"

My face felt hot. I focused on capping my solution, but my hands fumbled the lid twice before it seated properly. "Kate's not just some girl."

"I know. That's my point."

"It's complicated."

"It always is with relationships."

David started cleaning his workspace, organizing his graduated cylinders by size even though they'd all go in the same bin. "Look, I'm not trying to pry, but you're pale and you've got that twitchy thing happening with your jaw. And you ordered a macchiato earlier when you always get a black coffee."

"Did I?" The cup I'd abandoned on the bench sat cold, a thin film forming on the surface. I couldn't remember buying it.

"Yeah, you did." David fell quiet. Just the sound of glass clinking against metal as he loaded the drying rack. "Want to talk about whatever's eating you, or should I just watch you slowly disintegrate?"

The words I'd been organizing for a week refused to line up in any logical order. Kate had been different since Thanksgiving. We still texted, but the messages were polite inquiries about finals. Brief updates on studying. None of her usual tangents and subtle flirtation.

After she'd shown up at The Golden Dragon and seen me with Jennifer and both our families, the chemistry had changed. The equation didn't balance anymore.

"Kate's been quiet since break," I said finally.

"Oh."

"She used to send three messages when one would do. Now I'm lucky to get single-word responses."

David nodded slowly, still organizing his station even though it was already cleaner than anyone else's. His hands needed something to do when conversations got uncomfortable. I understood the impulse. "Did you two have a fight?"

"No." I blurted. "Not exactly. It's complicated."

That was an understatement. My parents had planned that dinner with the Lius as an elaborate demonstration of what my future should look like. The subtext had been clearer than any data set: Kate was temporary. Jennifer was the correct answer.

"Ah." David set down his last beaker. "Family stuff."

My silence must have been confirmation enough.

"You know," David said, pulling apart a paper towel with unusual fidgeting energy, "when I started dating Julie junior year, my parents had a lot of opinions. Said she was too American, too focused on her career, not serious about family. My mom actually cried. Told me I was breaking her heart."

Julie was David's long-distance girlfriend, currently at grad school in California. An electrical engineering student with several impressive internships already lined up. I'd met her once over video call. Charismatic and confident. A woman who knew exactly where she was going.

"What did you do?"

"Kept dating her." David shrugged. Watching someone so normally precise create chaos with paper shreds was hypnotic. "Turns out parents' opinions don't actually determine your happiness. Revolutionary concept, I know."

My phone chirped. I grabbed it with embarrassing speed.

> MĀMĀ
> Working late tonight. Your father made extra dumplings if you want to come by.

An olive branch. They were trying.

I set down the phone. "Your parents still pay your tuition?"

"Nope. Loans and scholarships." He said it matter-of-factly, sweeping the paper shreds into a small pile. "Which sucks, but it's better than suffocating every time I go home."

But David's parents hadn't left everything behind in another country. David's parents hadn't spent twenty-three years building toward this specific moment. It wasn't the same.

David zipped his backpack with finality. "Listen, I have to catch a flight in four hours. But whatever's going on with your family, with Kate, with all of it? You're allowed to want things for yourself. Even if those things aren't what your parents want."

"It's not that simple."

"It kind of is, though." David slung his bag over one shoulder. "Your parents made their choices. They came here, they built their business, they worked hard. That's their story. You get to have your own."

But that was the problem. My story was supposed to be the epilogue to theirs. The proof that their hard work had all been worth it.

Without that, what was the point of everything they'd given up?

I gathered my things and headed back to my apartment, my phone heavy in my pocket. The December air cut through my jacket like it wasn't there. My hands were numb by the time I reached my building, clumsy on the door handle.

Inside my room, I pulled out my therapeutics textbook and focused on drug interactions and contraindications. The letters rearranged themselves into meaningless patterns. I blinked hard.

The room felt too warm and too cold at the same time. Sweat prickled under my collar while my head throbbed behind my left eye in time with my heartbeat.

I should eat something. I should sleep. I should take care of myself with the same attention I applied to my studies. Instead, I made another cup of instant coffee and returned to my textbook, forcing my brain to absorb information it kept rejecting.

Focus. This was temporary. Just get through finals, and everything would settle into a stable state.

Outside my window, snow was falling again. Thick flakes that caught the light from the street lamps and made the campus look soft. Kate would see snow like this and talk about texture and light, the way artists saw the world instead of scientists. She'd probably try to describe the specific quality of the shadows, using words like "cerulean" and "umber" that meant nothing to my chemistry-trained brain.

Was she watching snow fall wherever she was? Was she thinking about me?

Had I already lost the chance to find out?

I pulled out my phone and typed another message to Kate and saw that David had texted me.

> **DAVID**
> At the airport. Remember what I said about parents' opinions not determining your happiness?

Despite everything, I almost smiled.

> **ALEX**
> Revolutionary concept.

> **DAVID**
> Yeah, well. Think about it.
>
> Also, call Kate.

Such simple advice. So impossible to follow. I wasn't quite brave enough for a call yet, but I thought I might manage something professional. Supportive. The kind of message a tutor would send. Nothing that crossed any lines my parents had drawn in careful red ink across my life.

ALEX
> Professor Martinez mentioned you aced your exam. I'm so proud of you.

The read receipt appeared almost immediately. Then nothing. The three dots that would indicate typing never appeared.

It wasn't until the next morning after my last exam that Kate finally put me out of my misery.

KATE
> Thanks.

One word. A single syllable response to my congratulations.

The letters lost meaning, dissolving into pixels my exhausted brain kept trying to decode for subtext that probably wasn't there. Was the period passive-aggressive? Or just grammatically correct?

She wouldn't be back for weeks, not until the spring semester started. Three weeks of this stalemate. Three weeks of not knowing where we stood or if we still stood anywhere at all.

This was fine. I was fine. This was temporary. Just exhaustion and stress and poor self-care. Nothing that basic biology couldn't resolve with adequate rest and nutrition.

My parents had asked me to choose between my future and Kate. But they'd framed the question wrong. The choice wasn't between success and love. It was between their definition of success and any definition that included happiness.

And I'd been so focused on not disappointing them that I'd forgotten to ask what would disappoint me.

As if she could sense my thoughts, my phone lit up with a text from my mother.

> **MĀMĀ**
>
> Mrs. Liu mentioned Jennifer is also staying on campus. Maybe you two could have dinner since you are not coming home?

And there it was. The gentle pressure that never quite stopped, soft as water wearing down stone. They loved me. They wanted what was best for me. They wanted to give me choices they'd never had.

So why did their love feel like drowning?

Outside, snow kept falling. The campus emptied. And I stayed in my room with my unanswered messages and my untouched textbooks and the growing certainty that I couldn't keep living in the space between who they wanted me to be and who I was becoming.

But knowing that and doing something about it were two different problems entirely.

And right now, I was too tired to solve either one.

Chapter 12

Kate

Some people were natural secret-keepers, the way others were natural athletes or musicians. I was not one of those people.

Secrets scrambled around inside my stomach like live lobsters in a too-small tank. This morning, sitting at Gemma's grandmother's kitchen table, my secret was making a particularly violent escape attempt. I shredded another napkin into confetti while my mother's laugh carried from the living room.

This kitchen had been our headquarters every summer since we were seven. Back then, Nan would set us up with watercolors on the porch while she painted her harbor scenes. Gemma would create careful, precise little landscapes. I would get paint everywhere and love every second of it. Now Gemma was a high school senior, making perfect sugar cookies with the same precision she'd once painted careful sunsets. I was a college sophomore having an existential crisis in the middle of her baking session. Some things changed. Some things didn't.

I'd always been the chaos to her order, the one who splattered paint on Nan's porch while Gemma carefully stayed inside the lines.

"You're doing it again." Gemma lifted a cookie from the baking sheet, not looking at me.

"What?"

"That twitchy thing." She set the cookie on the cooling rack. Picked up another. Her movements were exact. Two finger-widths between each one. "You look like you're about to bolt."

I was mesmerized by the steadiness of her hands. The way she controlled everything, made it perfect. My own fingers had murdered three napkins since I'd sat down.

Through the doorway, Mom gestured wildly with her coffee mug, talking about my wonderful progress in nursing. Nan Prescott nodded along, asked follow-up questions that Mom answered with enthusiasm.

"Kate." Gemma's spatula clinked against the cooling rack. "You've been weird since you got home. Talk to me."

A tray clattered in the living room. Laughter. More questions about my bright future in healthcare.

"I think." My throat closed. I couldn't look at Gemma's face, so I counted the cookies lined up like little soldiers instead. "What if nursing is wrong?"

Gemma's hands stilled. She held a cookie suspended over the rack, not setting it down.

"Wrong how?"

"Wrong like I hate it wrong." The words tumbled faster once they started. "Wrong like I'd rather do anything else. Wrong like maybe I should study art instead and everyone will think I've lost my mind."

She set the cookie down carefully.

"Art."

"I know it sounds—"

"It doesn't sound insane." Gemma turned to face me fully.

"Kate, you've been drawing on everything since we were seven. Last summer you spent three hours making that photo collage for your dorm wall."

"That doesn't mean I should throw away a stable career."

"Says who?"

"Everyone?" I gestured toward the living room, where Mom's voice rose and fell in warm, confident tones. "Common sense? My parents, who built their entire lives around healthcare?"

Gemma reached across the table to still my hand, stopping the napkin destruction. "What does the impractical part of you say?"

I closed my eyes. Tried to find that voice underneath all the logic.

"It says when I'm doodling, time disappears. When I'm in the lab, I'm counting minutes like..." I opened my eyes. "Like a prisoner marking days."

"That seems pretty clear."

"But what if I'm just running away? What if I'm reading everything wrong?" My voice dropped. "What if I disappoint everyone?"

"What if you disappoint yourself?"

The question hit like jumping into January ocean water. Shocking. Breathtaking.

Gemma squeezed my hand. "Also, when did making other people happy and making yourself happy become mutually exclusive?"

"Easy for you to say. Your parents are anthropologists. They probably—"

"My parents are academics who leave me in Waverly Cove every summer so they can pursue their own passions, Kate. They couldn't care less what I major in next year. And even I know you can't keep this from your family forever. You're going to develop stress hives."

I winced. "That obvious?"

"You look nauseous every time someone mentions school." She

pulled her hand back, picked up the spatula again. "Also, you've eaten exactly two bites of cookie. That violates every law of Kate I know."

My phone vibrated against the table. My stomach flipped before I even saw Alex's name.

We'd barely texted since Thanksgiving. Since The Golden Dragon and Jennifer and both families crowded around those pushed-together tables, everyone smiling like they'd orchestrated the whole thing. I'd pulled back. Space, I'd told myself. For both of us.

I'd finally responded when he texted on Christmas, three days ago now.

> **ALEX**
> Merry Christmas.

Maybe it was the holiday spirit, or maybe being surrounded by people I loved reminded me of Alex alone in his studio apartment, the campus empty and quiet around him.

> **KATE**
> Happy Holidays!

Two words and an exclamation point. Safe.

Before, the texts had flowed without thinking. Him sending observations from The Golden Dragon that made me snort-laugh in the library, me complaining about organic chemistry in ways that always circled back to chemistry confusion. He'd respond with actual helpful explanations wrapped in that bone-dry humor where I couldn't tell if he was joking until I'd read it three times.

Now every message sat in my drafts for five minutes before I hit send.

The text that interrupted my conversation with Gemma pinged differently. The flour-dusted phone screen lit up on the counter beside the cooling cookies.

> **ALEX**
> Break good? You good? Everything's good.

I picked up the phone, leaving a white fingerprint on the case. The words were right. Alex-level economical. But they sat wrong in my gut.

> **KATE**
> Everything's good here too. How's your solo study time treating you?

I set the phone down and resumed transferring cookies to the wire rack, but my attention kept snagging on that dark screen. Gemma talked about her plans to visit her cousins in Portland, something about ice skating at Thompson's Point, and I made the right sounds while my thumb rubbed at the dried flour on my phone case.

An hour of cooling cookies and washing mixing bowls and Gemma's voice filling the kitchen.

The phone stayed silent.

When it finally lit up, I grabbed it too fast. I both saw and heard Gemma's sigh, but was too relieved to care.

> **ALEX**
> Books make excellent study partners.

Then, an hour later as we were icing the last cookies:

> **ALEX**
> Though terrible at reminding to eat. Keep forgetting meals exist.

I stared at the screen. Reread both messages. Alex didn't text like this. His messages were precise. Economical. This felt wrong, like seeing a stop sign painted purple.

ALEX

> Do fish get lonely? Asking for a friend.
> The friend is a fish.

"Gemma." I held up my phone. My earlier confession about art was forgotten. "Does this seem weird?"

She leaned over my shoulder, eyebrows climbing. "Is Alex usually this... philosophically concerned about fish?"

"No." My thumb was already finding his number. "Something's wrong."

The phone rang four times before he answered.

"Kate?" His voice sounded thick. Slurred. Like speaking through cotton.

"Alex? Are you okay? That last text—"

"Which text?" Long pause. Distant, like he'd pulled the phone away. "Did I text you? My phone keeps... doing things."

Warning bells clanged in my head. "Alex, you sound terrible."

"Just tired. Been reading about enzymatic reactions for..." Another too long pause. "How long has it been dark?"

I looked out Gemma's window. Late afternoon sun filtered through bare oak branches, making patterns on the floor. "Alex, it's four in the afternoon."

"Really? Time feels... wiggly."

Wiggly. Alex Chen, who used precise scientific terminology for everything, just described time as wiggly.

"Where are you right now?"

"My apartment. I think? Yes. Apartment. The ceiling has that broken fan."

My heart pounded against my ribs. "Are you sick?"

"Maybe? Everything feels floaty."

I was already standing. Chair scraping against tile. "I'm coming back."

"What? Kate, no. You're with your—"

"You sound delirious. I'm getting on the next bus."

"You don't have to—"

"Yes, I do." The certainty surprised me. Whatever distance we'd been maintaining, whatever complications existed, none of that mattered. Not right now. "Stay in your room. Drink water. Don't make any important decisions."

"Okay." His voice was small. Almost child-like. "Kate?"

"Yeah?"

"Thank you."

After I hung up, Gemma pinned me with an analytical expression. One that meant she was connecting the dots I hadn't even noticed yet.

"So. That happened."

"I have to go." Already moving toward the front door. My brain calculated bus schedules, travel time. "He's sick and alone and clearly not thinking straight."

"Kate." Her voice stopped me at the doorway. "I thought you were keeping your distance. After Thanksgiving."

I paused with my hand on the doorframe and one boot tugged on. Thought about how worried I'd felt hearing his voice like that. How all those careful boundaries had evaporated.

"Yeah, well." I looked back at her. "Distance doesn't work so well when someone needs help."

The bus smelled like stale coffee and someone's too-strong perfume. I pressed my forehead against the window, watching Maine blur past. Winter-dead trees. Gray sky. The occasional house with Christmas lights still up.

My leg bounced against the seat. That restless energy I could never quite control got worse when I was worried. The woman across the aisle kept glancing at me, probably wondering if I was high on something.

I pulled out my phone. No new messages. Typed out a text asking if Alex was okay and held my breath until he finally responded in the affirmative.

The bus engine made a constant low rumble. Someone behind me was eating something that smelled like gas station nachos. A kid three rows up kept asking their mom "are we there yet?" in an endless loop.

Nerves made my skin feel tight and itchy, like I was wearing a sweater that had shrunk in the wash.

What if he was really sick? What if he'd gotten worse since we talked? What if I got there and he was—

I shook my head. Pressed my forehead harder against the cold glass. Left a mark on the window that fogged with each breath.

Four hours felt like forty.

The area around campus looked abandoned. Footpaths that usually filled with students lay empty under old snow. Most buildings sat dark and locked. Even the optimistic campus squirrels had disappeared somewhere warmer.

My boots crunched on salt-scattered pavement. My breath puffed white in the air. I texted when I reached his apartment building.

KATE
I'm here. What number are you?

The response took too long.

ALEX
312

The lobby was tomb-quiet. Heated to maybe five degrees warmer than outside. My footsteps echoed on the stairs. Past floors of closed doors and silence. The whole building felt hollow, like everyone had evacuated during some emergency and forgotten to tell me.

Room 312 sat at the end of the third-floor hallway. I knocked, then tried the doorknob and found it unlocked.

"Alex?"

"In here."

His voice led me into a narrow studio that smelled stale. Sickness and closed-up air and something else I couldn't name. The space was neat in that careful way Alex did everything, but looked off. Like someone had tried to maintain order while falling apart.

Alex lay on a narrow bed, fully dressed, looking like he'd been there for days. His hair stuck up at angles that would normally drive him crazy. Unhealthy color painted his cheekbones, too bright against skin that had gone pale.

"You look terrible," I said, dropping my bag.

"What every guy wants to hear from a pretty girl." His attempt at humor came out weak. Each word took visible effort.

I moved closer and took inventory of his apartment. Water bottles were scattered everywhere. Some empty, some full like he'd forgotten they were there. Tissues covered every available surface. Textbooks still open on his desk, notes spread out like he'd been trying to study through whatever this was.

I sat on the edge of his bed. Reached for his forehead without thinking. His skin blazed under my hand.

"You're running a really high fever."

"Not that bad."

"Alex." I left my hand there. His forehead was too hot and too dry. "You texted me about lonely fish."

His eyes closed. When they opened again, he worked hard to focus on my face. "Did I? That's embarrassing."

"It's not embarrassing. It's scary." I looked around the room again. At the evidence of him trying and failing to take care of himself. "How long have you been like this?"

"What day is it?"

"Thursday."

"Then... Monday? Maybe Sunday." He tried to sit up, but swayed and had to grab the wall to steady himself. "The dining hall closed early for break, so I've been—"

"Living on what?"

"Ramen. Some crackers. There's an orange in my mini-fridge that might still be okay."

My nursing instincts kicked in despite my complicated feelings about the field. This wasn't just a cold. This was serious. The kind of sick that required actual medical attention.

"We need to get you to urgent care."

"I don't—"

"You're delirious, you haven't eaten in days, and you're burning up. We're going." I scanned the room for his coat and shoes. "Can you walk?"

"Of course I can walk."

He proved this wildly optimistic by immediately needing to brace himself against the wall. I caught his arm. He radiated heat through his sweatshirt.

"New plan. We're calling a cab. I'm coming with you."

"Kate, you really don't have to—"

I turned to face him, noting the glassy look in his eyes and the too-fast breathing. "Yeah, I do. Come on."

I grabbed his coat from the closet. Helped him into it even though his arms didn't want to cooperate. Found his phone and wallet. Called a cab while he leaned against the wall, eyes closed, looking more fragile than I'd ever seen him.

The urgent care waiting room reeked of bleach and hand sanitizer. Underneath that, something stale. Too many people breathing recycled air for too many hours.

Alex slumped in the plastic chair beside me. The molded seats were designed to be uncomfortable and discourage people from staying too long. He'd pulled his coat tighter around himself even though the room was overheated.

"I'm sorry," he said for the third time since we'd arrived.

"Stop apologizing."

"I wasn't apologizing for being sick. I was apologizing for—" He seemed to lose his train of thought. "What was I apologizing for?"

It hurt seeing him like this. "You don't have to apologize for anything."

"You should be home with your family." He fidgeted in the seat, trying to sit upright. "Not stuck here with me. Babysitting a delirious tutor."

"Alex." I reached for his hand without planning to. It felt natural. "Do you know what I've been doing for the last four days?"

"Being with people you love?"

"I've spent four days being the perfect daughter. Smiling when people ask about nursing. Listening to my mom's telling anyone who would listen about my miraculous nursing turnaround. Acting like I'm not slowly suffocating." I threaded my fingers through his. "This is the first time I've felt useful since the break started."

He gazed at me with fever-bright eyes. "Taking care of sick people makes you feel useful?"

"Taking care of you makes me feel useful."

Something about that distinction mattered, though I couldn't map exactly why. When I imagined myself in nursing scrubs, following protocols with strangers, I couldn't breathe. But sitting here, making sure Alex got help, felt as easy as breathing.

"Alexander Chen?" A nurse called from the doorway.

I helped Alex stand. He reached for my arm automatically, steadying himself. In the exam room, I settled into a guest chair with cracked vinyl upholstery while Alex tried to explain his symptoms.

"I've been tired." He closed his eyes briefly. "And hot. Not temperature hot. Hot like... wait, did I say tired already?"

The nurse had an expression that suggested she'd seen this exact scenario too many times.

"How long has he been like this?"

"Since Monday, maybe Sunday. He's been alone over break. Not eating much. Trying to push through it."

She made efficient notes. "And you are?"

The question hit me like cold water. I opened my mouth. Closed it. We weren't officially anything. We'd barely spoken since Thanksgiving. But looking at Alex slumped in that exam chair, vulnerable and sick and trusting me to help, the truth crystallized.

"His girlfriend." The words flew out before I could stop them. "I'm his girlfriend."

Alex's eyes widened, but he didn't contradict me.

The nurse made another note. "Well, girlfriend, thank you for bringing him in. He looks awful."

"She told me the same thing earlier," Alex managed. A wan smile in my direction that made my heart do complicated things.

After the nurse left to process orders, Alex reached for my hand again.

"Kate."

"I know. We should probably talk about that when you're not running a fever of a thousand degrees."

"I just wanted to say—" He paused, gathering thoughts through the fog. "I like it. When you call yourself that."

The flush on my cheeks rivaled his, but I couldn't blame it on a fever. "Yeah?"

"Yeah."

Forty five minutes and several tests later, we had answers.

"Mononucleosis," the doctor said, reading from her tablet. Her voice clipped, professional. "White blood cell count confirms it. You're dehydrated. Fever of 101.3." She peered at Alex. "When did you last have a full meal?"

Alex studied the exam table. "Tuesday?"

"It's Thursday."

"Then Tuesday."

The doctor made a note. Her stylus tapping against the screen with each mark. "Sleep? Actual sleep, not napping between study sessions."

"Four, maybe five hours a night."

"For how long?"

Alex's silence answered.

The doctor glanced at me. Recognition in that look. The one healthcare workers got when they'd seen the same self-destructive pattern too many times. "Mono often takes hold when your immune system is compromised." She turned back to Alex. "Your body did this to make you stop."

She pulled up something on her tablet. Handed me a printed sheet that smelled like warm toner. "Two weeks minimum of rest. Sleep, fluids, nothing more strenuous than walking to the bathroom. No studying, no work, no pushing through because you feel slightly better."

She fixed Alex with a look. The one that probably worked on every stubborn patient who'd sat in that chair. "If you rupture your spleen trying to prove you're fine, you'll be in the hospital for longer than two weeks. Understand?"

Alex nodded. His expression suggested he was already planning workarounds.

"I'll make sure he rests," I said.

The doctor's expression warmed. "You're the girlfriend?"

The word still felt strange. New. "Yes."

"Then you have my sympathies. College-age men are terrible patients." She stood, tucking her tablet under her arm. "Get him home. Get fluids in him. If his fever goes above 103 or he develops severe abdominal pain, bring him back immediately. Otherwise, follow up with primary care in a week."

After she left, I read through the care instructions. Standard stuff. Rest, hydration, acetaminophen for fever. At the bottom in bold: **No contact sports or heavy lifting. Splenic rupture can occur for up to 8 weeks after infection.**

"I can't be out for two weeks," Alex said.

"You don't have a choice."

"I have a library shift tomorrow—"

"Alex." I cut him off. "You can't even sit upright. You're not working."

For the first time since I'd found him in his room, I saw something in his expression besides fevered confusion. The dawning realization that he couldn't think his way out of this.

"What do I tell my parents?"

The question brought tears to my eyes. Even now, sick and exhausted, he was worried about disappointing them.

"You tell them you're sick. That's all they need to know."

In the cab back to campus, Alex slumped against my shoulder, finally letting exhaustion claim him. His hair tickled my cheek. I caught the faint scent of his shampoo underneath the general sick-person smell. His weight was too warm against my side.

"Kate?"

"Mmm?"

"You called yourself my girlfriend."

My cheeks blushed. "I did. Was that okay?"

"More than okay." His hoarse voice was hard to hear over the engine and road noise. "I've wanted to call you that for weeks. I just didn't think... after Thanksgiving..."

"After Thanksgiving, I got scared." My confession was easier in the dark cab, with Alex too sick to look at me properly. "Seeing you with Jennifer, with both families. What everyone expected. I thought maybe I was just making your life harder."

"You weren't making it harder. You were making it make sense." His weight settled more firmly against me. "Everything else felt like trying to be someone I wasn't. Being with you felt like finally being allowed to just be."

"Then we're both idiots." My voice was barely above a whisper. "Because I was trying to protect you by staying away. And you were trying to be what your parents wanted. We made ourselves miserable trying to do the right thing."

"What's the right thing now?"

I thought about the doctor's words. How stress manifested as physical illness. How Alex's body had forced him to stop pushing toward a version of life that didn't fit.

"I think the right thing is letting yourself rest. Not just physically. From trying to be what everyone else wants." I reached for his hand and found it in the dark. "And maybe let me take care of you for a while."

"I want that." He murmured against my shoulder. "To let someone take care of me. I'm just not good at it."

"Lucky for you, I'm very good at taking care of people I—" I caught myself. The word love hung unspoken in the warm cab air. "People I care about."

He smiled. I felt it more than saw it. "Lucky me."

His eyes were already closing. Breath evening out.

Back in his apartment, I changed his sheets while he showered. The water ran for a long time. When he finally emerged in clean sweatpants and a faded pharmacy school t-shirt, he looked more human. Still exhausted, but cleaner.

I helped him settle into bed. Arranged fresh water bottles within easy reach. Adjusted pillows. Grabbed an extra blanket from the closet because the apartment was still too cold for someone fighting an infection.

The blanket smelled like detergent and dust. I tucked it around him, making sure the edges were secure.

"Kate." He caught my hand as I tucked the corner near his shoulder. "Thank you for knowing how to take care of me."

The words struck me. I thought about my mother, who'd always known when to push and when to comfort. My father, who could tell which kid needed a hug and which needed space. Diane, who'd taught me that feeding people was a language of love. Isa, who'd shown me fierce loyalty disguised as sarcasm.

I hadn't learned to care for people from nursing textbooks. I'd learned it from a family who showed up, paid attention, loved through action and presence.

Maybe that was the problem with nursing. Not the caring itself. But the idea of caring as obligation, as clinical duty, rather than as a choice made from love.

"Get some sleep," I told him. Squeezed his hand. "I'll be here when you wake up."

"You don't have to stay—"

"Alex." I settled into his desk chair. The wooden seat was hard against my legs. "I'm staying."

"What are you going to do while I sleep?"

I looked out the window. The glow of the streetlights filtering through half-closed blinds created patterns of shadow and brightness across the wall. My fingers itched for a pencil.

"I think I'm going to draw."

He smiled. Eyes already drifting closed. "I'd like to see that sometime."

"You will."

Within minutes his breathing evened into a deeper rhythm. True rest, finally. I stayed in the chair, pulled a clean sheet of paper and some pencils from his meticulously organized desk supplies.

I sketched the view from his window. Bare tree branches against winter sky. Frost patterns on glass. The way light changed as afternoon aged into evening.

Yesterday, I'd been suffocating under family expectations in my childhood bedroom. This morning, I'd confessed my art dreams to Gemma. Tonight, I sat vigil over someone I'd claimed as my boyfriend without planning to. Someone whose body had broken down under the pressure of so many expectations.

Bodies told the truth that minds hadn't caught up with yet. Spontaneous words revealed deeper feelings. Someone could choose to care for another person out of love instead of obligation.

I drank in the sight of Alex sleeping. His face was finally peaceful after days of pushing too hard. The doctor's words echoed: *Your body did this to make you stop.*

Maybe we both needed that lesson. To listen when bodies and hearts said stop pretending. To recognize that pushing toward what we thought we should want was destroying what we needed.

I turned back to my sketch. Added details as the room darkened. Outside, the city lay under winter's spell.

Inside, for the first time in weeks, something felt right.

Chapter 13

Alex

Spring semester felt different. Not just because I could finally walk to campus without my legs turning to jelly, or because the January air no longer made me want to crawl back into bed for another twelve hours. Everything felt different because of what had happened during winter break with Kate.

I slid my backpack higher on my shoulder as I walked toward the pharmacy building, still thinking about the conversation we had last week when I was finally on the mend.

"So," she'd said, perched on the edge of my desk chair while I sat on my newly changed sheets, both of us pretending this conversation wasn't long overdue. "Are we going to talk about what happened while I was playing Florence Nightingale?"

I'd just stared at her for a moment, still unable to believe she'd cut her break short and come back to campus when she'd found out I was sick. No one had ever done anything like that for me before.

"When was the last time someone took care of you when you were sick?" she'd asked, her head tilting with genuine curiosity. The question had caught me off guard.

"What do you mean?"

"I mean, when you were a kid and you had the flu, who brought you soup and checked your temperature and made sure you weren't dying of dehydration in your bedroom?"

"I..." I remembered running my hand through my hair, still feeling slightly unsteady despite being mostly recovered. "My parents were usually working. The restaurant doesn't close for sick kids."

The wall she'd been holding crumbled. Her shoulders dropped, and when she met my eyes again, hers were glassy. "So you just... took care of yourself?"

"It wasn't a big deal," I'd told her, feeling strangely defensive about something I'd never questioned before. "I learned to read thermometers pretty early. Medicine bottles have simple instructions."

I could almost see her thinking about her own family. The Westfields she spoke about with such easy affection. The way she described them made them sound like they'd drop everything at the first sign of a sniffle.

"That isn't right," she'd said quietly, in a voice that made me pay attention.

"It was just how things were," I'd explained, falling back on the rationale that had always made sense to me. "They were building something, providing for our family's future. I understood the priorities."

"You were a kid, Alex. Kids shouldn't have to understand adult priorities when they're sick."

No one had ever suggested there was anything wrong with how I'd grown up. It was just how things were in my family. Practical, focused on the future, everyone playing their assigned roles. That my childhood self-reliance might have been lacking something essential had never occurred to me until Kate pointed it out.

The memory made me smile despite the bitter wind cutting across the quad. Kate had a way of addressing things head-on that both terrified and amazed me. No dancing around the subject, no careful analytical approach like I would have used. Just direct, honest Kate, asking the questions I'd been too scared to voice.

What I hadn't been able to articulate then, what I was still trying to process now, was how completely she'd upended everything I thought I knew about relationships. About myself. For three days, Kate had taken care of me with a competence that should have embarrassed me.

I'd always prided myself on not needing anyone. But when mono left me unable to think straight, let alone take care of myself, Kate had stepped in. She'd made sure I took my medication on schedule. Brought me soup that tasted good and water with just enough ice. Changed my sheets when I was too weak to care that I'd been sweating on the same ones for four days.

But it wasn't just practical care. It was the way she'd settled onto my floor with her art supplies, sketching while I slept, humming softly under her breath. How she'd wake me when I needed to eat, never making me feel like an invalid. The way she'd curled up next to me on the narrow single bed that last night, fully clothed and careful not to crowd me, just close enough that I could feel her breathing. I'd never felt so cared for in my life.

"Alex!" David jogged toward me with a pile of textbooks clutched in his arms.

"You're looking human again," he said, falling into step beside me. "Kate finally let you out of quarantine?"

"Hilarious." But I was smiling. I still couldn't believe Kate had figured out from my delirious texts that I was sick and needed help. "I can't believe she came back from Maine early just because I was texting nonsense."

David gave me a sideways look. "So... are you two finally going to figure this out, or do I need to lock you in a lab until you kiss her like some cheesy rom-com?"

My face heated. "We talked."

"And?"

"And we're..." I paused. Chemistry had a precise language for everything. This didn't. What were we exactly? The conversation over break had clarified some things, but we hadn't put labels on anything. "We're seeing where this goes."

David grinned. "About time. You've been moon-eyed over her since October."

Had I been that obvious? Probably. Kate seemed to think so, based on her knowing smile when I'd finally admitted that my feelings had moved far beyond gratitude for a star pupil.

We pushed through the doors of the pharmacy building, headed for a lab that would run until dinnertime.

Kate had Introduction to Studio Art at two, then her nursing fundamentals clinical in the afternoon. She'd been nervous about the art class since she registered last month, full of excitement and anxiety in equal measure.

"What if I'm terrible?" She'd asked, sitting cross-legged on my bed while I was recovering. "What if I only think I like art because I hate chemistry?"

She'd chewed on her bottom lip, a habit she had when she was overthinking.

"What if you're good at it?" I'd countered. "What if you discover something you love?"

The uncertainty in her eyes was heartbreaking. Kate threw herself into everything with such passion, but underneath all that energy, I was recognizing the anxiety that drove it. The need to excel at everything, to make everyone happy, and never disappoint the people she loved. I knew that feeling well.

I received a text from her as David and I climbed the stairs to the second floor.

KATE

First art class in an hour. Trying not to throw up from nerves.

> **ALEX**
> You're going to be amazing. The professor is lucky to have you.

> **KATE**
> How do you know?

> **ALEX**
> Because you see things differently than other people. In the best way.

> **KATE**
> Thank you 🤍
>
> Dinner later? I want to hear about your first day back.

> **ALEX**
> Of course. My treat.

> **KATE**
> We're going Dutch, Chen.

I smiled as I typed back.

> **ALEX**
> Fine. But I'm buying cannolis at Mike's after.

> **KATE**
> Deal.

"Seriously," David said, watching me pocket my phone. "You're disgustingly happy."

I was. That was what kept catching me off guard. I'd spent so much of my life focused on the next goal, the next requirement, the next step in the plan my parents had laid out for me.

But these past few weeks with Kate had shown me what it

felt like to just enjoy the present moment. Even when that present moment included complications I wasn't sure how to handle.

The increasingly tense phone calls from my parents didn't help.

They'd started the week classes resumed. Casual at first, just checking in about my health and the spring semester.

"You sound tired. Is everything alright?" she'd asked on the second call.

"I'm fine, Māmā. Just adjusting to being back."

"Mmm." A pause that felt weighted. "And you stayed on campus the whole break? To study?"

"Yes."

"Even Christmas? You couldn't come home even for Christmas?"

I'd kept my answers vague, not quite lying but not offering the whole truth either. Each call had gone the same way. Her questions getting more pointed, my responses getting shorter. She was gathering information piece by piece, the way she always did. I'd seen her build cases like this my whole life, with restaurant vendors and my teachers and anyone she suspected of holding something back.

By the end of the week, I knew she'd either figured it out or someone had told her. Maybe one of their friends had seen me with Kate somewhere. In a community like ours, information traveled.

Thursday evening, my father called. He never called unless Mom had sent him.

"Lì Xiáng," he said. "We need to talk about this girl."

"Bàba, there's nothing to talk about."

"Your mother is concerned. We told you before the break that this relationship needed to end."

"We're just friends."

"Lì Xiáng." His voice had carried a warning I recognized from childhood. "Don't be flippant. This is serious."

I'd managed to end the call without revealing anything concrete, but I'd known it was only a matter of time before they found proof of what they already suspected.

Last night's call had provided exactly that.

"Alex, you stayed at school when you were sick? Why didn't you call us?"

"I didn't want to worry you. It was just a bug."

A pause. Then, with the careful precision my mother used when she was controlling her anger: "We received something from the insurance company today. A notice about an urgent care visit over winter break."

My stomach dropped. Of course. The insurance company had sent an explanation of benefits. I should have anticipated that.

"Māmā, I told you, I was sick. I visited urgent care because the campus health center is closed over break."

"You listed an emergency contact. Katherine Westfield." Not a question. A statement loaded with implications. "The same girl from Thanksgiving."

There it was. The confirmation they'd been searching for.

"She helped me get to urgent care, that's all."

"That's all?" My mother's voice rose slightly. "You gave this girl permission to make medical decisions for you. You signed her name on official forms. After we explicitly told you before break that this relationship needed to end."

"She was just helping me."

"Did she stay with you?" Still not a question. My mother never asked questions when she already knew the answers. "The form listed a local address. Your address. This girl we told you to stay away from took you to the doctor and stayed with you?"

I closed my eyes, remembering how carefully Kate had filled out those forms, her hand steady while mine shook with fever.

She'd hesitated at the emergency contact line, looking at me with concern.

"I was sick, Māmā. I needed help."

"You could have called us. Instead you called her, Lì Xiáng." My mother switched fully to Mandarin, the way she always did when she was truly upset. "After we made our position clear. After we told you this American girl was not appropriate. After we explained what this would cost you with Dr. Zhang's recommendation. You chose her anyway."

"Māmā, she was just being a friend."

"Friends do not have their names on medical forms as emergency contacts. This is not friendship, Lì Xiáng. This is you directly disobeying us."

She was right. Even if I hadn't corrected the nurse's assumption about the girlfriend label, even if we'd never defined what we were, Kate's presence during those three days had spoken louder than any title could. I'd let her take care of me. Let her become essential.

And my parents had suspected it all week. The insurance form had simply confirmed what they'd already pieced together from my evasive answers and the questions they'd asked around campus.

"I should go, Māmā. I have studying to do."

"Your father wants to speak with you this weekend. In person. We will not discuss this over the phone."

There was an audible click as the call ended.

I stared at my phone, understanding now that they'd been building this case for days. They'd been gathering information with every call, every question, waiting for the proof they knew would come. The insurance form hadn't revealed anything new. It had just given them the documentation they needed to confront me.

"Earth to Alex," David said, snapping his fingers in front of my face. "You're doing that thing where you disappear into your head."

"Sorry." I shook off the memory of my mother's controlled fury and my own recognition that I'd been caught in a lie I'd never quite told. "Just thinking about some stuff I need to handle."

"Family stuff?" David knew about the Jennifer situation. He'd been there for enough awkward encounters to piece together my parents' matchmaking attempts.

"Isn't it always?"

"You know," David said as we approached our classroom, "maybe it's time to stop handling things the way your parents want you to handle them."

Before I could ask what he meant by that, Professor Williams called for everyone to take their seats. But David's words stuck with me through the lecture on drug metabolism and protein binding.

Maybe it was time to stop trying to manage my parents' expectations and start figuring out what I actually wanted.

The answer to that question was becoming clearer every day. I wanted Kate. Not just as a friend or a study partner or someone to spend time with when I was lonely. I wanted her laughter in my room every morning and her terrible jokes during study breaks. I wanted to help her figure out what kind of art made her hands shake with excitement and support her through the nursing classes that drained all the color from her face.

I wanted to build something real with her, even if that meant disappointing the people who'd raised me.

The thought scared me more than any exam I'd ever taken.

After dinner, Kate and I walked toward Mike's Pastry for the cannoli I'd promised. She was still vibrating with energy from her first art class. The air was crisp, but she didn't seem to notice, too caught up in reliving every moment of the afternoon.

"Alex, you should have seen it," she said, walking backwards in front of me so she could face me while she talked. "Dr. Vellacott had us do this exercise where we drew the same object from five different angles, and I've never thought about space and perspective like that before."

Her hands moved as she talked, sketching invisible shapes in the air to illustrate her point. This was the Kate I'd first fallen for, the one who approached everything with so much genuine enthusiasm that it was impossible not to get swept up by her energy.

"And there's this girl in my class, Brixton, who's been painting since she was eight, and her work is incredible, but she was struggling with the perspective exercise and I could help her see it differently. Like, I could visualize the angles in a way that made sense to her."

We'd stopped walking without my realizing it. Kate stood in front of me on the sidewalk, her cheeks flushed from the cold and excitement, her eyes bright with discovery.

"That's amazing," I said, mesmerized by her face in the streetlight. She was glowing.

"Dr. Vellacott said my spatial perception is unusual for a beginner," she continued, stepping closer in her excitement. "She said most people have to be taught how to translate three-dimensional objects to a two-dimensional plane, but it's like my brain already knows how to make that conversion."

Kate was always beautiful, but in this moment, alive with discovery, radiating joy from something that spoke to her soul, she was incandescent.

"And then we did this exercise with charcoal where we had to —" She grabbed my arms suddenly, her hands gripping my jacket sleeves as she tried to contain her excitement. "Alex, what if this is it? What if this is the thing I'm actually supposed to be doing?"

I stared down at her, at the hope and fear and pure happiness warring in her expression, and something in me short-circuited. I've spent my entire life planning, analyzing, calculating every move. But in that moment, watching Kate discover a piece of herself she'd never known existed, I didn't think at all.

I cupped her face in my hands and kissed her.

It was brief. Just the press of my lips against hers, catching her mid-sentence. I felt her quick intake of breath, the momentary stillness of surprise, and then I was pulling back, staring at her with what must have been a shell-shocked expression.

"I..." My brain was buffering, a spinning wheel where my thoughts should be. "I didn't plan that."

Kate blinked at me, her lips parted. Then a slow smile spread across her face. "Alex Chen. Did you just impulsively kiss me in the middle of a rant about charcoal techniques?"

My heart sank. I'd read the moment wrong, picking up signals that weren't there. "I appear to have done exactly that. Sorry, I should have asked first, or..."

"Don't you dare apologize." Kate reached over to take my hand. "That was perfect."

Her words filled me with a mix of embarrassment and exhilaration. "I've never done anything like that before."

"What, kiss someone?"

"Kiss someone without thinking about it for at least a week beforehand."

Kate laughed, the sound bright and delighted. "I'm honored to be your first impulsive kiss."

I met her eyes again, suddenly serious. "You make me want to be impulsive, Kate. You make me want to be... less careful."

Her expression softened. "Is that a good thing or a bad thing?"

"I'm still figuring that out." I squeezed her hand. "But I think it might be the best thing that's ever happened to me."

We found a small table at Mike's, surrounded by the scent of espresso and powdered sugar. Kate ordered a chocolate chip cannoli while I got the traditional pistachio. For a few minutes we just ate, comfortable in the silence that had become natural between us.

"How did the nursing clinical go?" I asked, watching her lick powdered sugar from her thumb.

The brightness in her expression dimmed. "Fine. Good. I mean, it was educational." She nibbled her lip, not meeting my eyes. "We practiced taking vitals and learned about documentation standards."

"But?"

"But what?"

"Kate." I waited until she looked at me. "What aren't you saying?"

She sighed, setting down her pastry. "It's stupid."

"I doubt that."

"I keep waiting for nursing to feel the way art did today. Like, that moment in class when Dr. Vellacott was explaining how light and shadow work together to create form, I got this rush of understanding that made my whole body feel electric. But in nursing..." She shrugged. "I feel like I'm going through the motions. Learning the steps to a dance I don't really want to perform."

"That doesn't sound stupid at all."

"My whole family..."

"Is going to want you to be happy," I finished. "Have you considered that maybe your parents would rather have a daughter who's passionate about her work than one who's miserable in a prestigious career?"

Kate gave me a look that was half gratitude, half exasperation. "When did you become so wise about family relationships?"

"Since I started questioning my family's plan for my life."

The words slipped out before I could stop them, more honest than I'd intended to be.

"Alex," she said carefully, "is everything okay with your parents?"

I could lie. Make something up about normal family pressure; nothing she needed to worry about. It would be easier, cleaner, less complicated for both of us.

Instead, I told her about the phone call.

Kate listened without interrupting. When I finished, she reached across the table to take both my hands.

"This is my fault," she said. "I shouldn't have written my name down as your emergency contact at urgent care. I wasn't thinking about…"

"Hey." I squeezed her hands. "You did nothing wrong. You were taking care of someone you cared about. The problem isn't what you did."

"Then what is it?"

Her fingers were warm beneath mine. "The problem is that I've been lying to my parents about what you mean to me."

"What do I mean to you?"

The question hung between us, loaded with three months of growing feelings and careful boundaries and moments of connection that had changed everything I thought I knew about relationships.

"You mean everything," I confessed. "And that terrifies me."

Kate's breath hitched. "Alex…"

"I know we said we'd see where this goes," I continued, "but I need you to know that for me, this isn't casual. What happened over winter break, the way you took care of me, the way I felt when I thought about you leaving…" I met her eyes. "I'm falling for you, Kate. I think I've been falling for months."

The words settled between us like something physical, changing the weight of the air around our table. Kate stared at me for a long moment, her hands still in mine, and I wondered if I'd pushed too fast, said too much too soon.

Then she smiled, with the same warm, radiant smile that had been breaking down my defenses since October.

"I'm falling for you too," she confessed. "Actually, I think I fell a while ago. I just wasn't brave enough to say it."

The relief that washed over me was so intense I felt dizzy. "So where does that leave us?"

"I think," Kate said, lacing our fingers together, "it leaves us figuring out how to build something real together. Even if it's complicated."

"It's going to be complicated."

"I know." She squeezed my hand. "But Alex, what we have... it's worth fighting for. Isn't it?"

I thought about the way she'd sat by my bed for three days, humming while she sketched. The way she lit up when she talked about art, and the way she made me want to be braver than I'd ever been before. The way she'd looked at me that first day in the library, like I was someone worth knowing instead of just someone who could help her pass chemistry.

"Yeah," I said. "It's worth fighting for."

Kate grinned. "Good. Because I have a feeling we're going to have to roll up our sleeves and..."

As if summoned by her words, my phone rang. My mother's contact photo filled the screen, and I felt Kate's fingers squeeze mine.

"Take it," she said softly. "I'll be right here."

I answered the call, my heart already racing. "Hi, Māmā."

"Lì Xiáng." My father's voice surprised me, with an edge I recognized from the rare occasions when I'd disappointed him as a child. "We need to talk. Your mother and I are driving over this weekend."

My stomach dropped. "Bàba, you don't need to..."

"We do. We have concerns about this girl, about your choices this semester." He paused, and I faintly registered my mother saying something in the background. "We'll be there Saturday at noon. We have some things to discuss."

I set the phone down with hands that weren't quite steady. Kate was watching me with an expression that was equal parts concern and determination.

"So," she said, her voice admirably steady. "I'm about to meet your parents."

"Kate, you don't have to..."

"Yes, I do." She stood up, coming around the table to sit in the chair next to mine instead of across from it. "Alex, we just agreed this was worth fighting for. That includes fighting for each other."

I turned to face her, struck again by how brave she was. How willing to dive headfirst into complicated situations without knowing how they'd turn out.

"My parents can be... intense," I warned. "They have very specific ideas about my future. About who I should be with."

"Are you trying to scare me off?"

"No." The harshness in my voice surprised me. "God, no. I just want you to know what you're walking into."

Kate smiled, reaching up to trace the line of my jaw with her fingertips. "Alex, I walked into your apartment when you had mono and you smelled like you hadn't showered in three days."

"It had actually been four," I admitted.

"Oh. Wow. I really must like you, then." She shook her head and looked into my eyes. "I think I can handle meeting your parents."

Despite everything, I laughed. "You're amazing, you know that?"

"I'm terrified," she admitted. "But I'm also not going anywhere."

I leaned forward, resting my forehead against hers. "I love you," I said, the words feeling natural and right and completely inadequate for what I felt for her.

She melted against me. "I love you too."

And then I kissed her again, deeper this time. This felt so different from our impulsive first kiss. Her hand fisted in my shirt, pulling me closer, and I could taste a hint of powdered sugar as she smiled against my lips.

When we broke apart, that smile expanded into a wide grin. "So," she said, "Saturday should be interesting."

I groaned, burying my face in her neck. "I'm sorry in advance for whatever they say."

"Hey." She pushed me back so she could look at me properly. "Alex, we're going to figure this out. Together. Your parents love you, right? They want you to be happy?"

"In theory."

"And so do I. We'll start there, on common ground." Kate stood up, holding out her hand. "Come on. Let's go back to your apartment and figure out how to explain to two people who don't know me that their son is in love with a nursing student slash starving artist."

I took her hand, letting her pull me to my feet. "When you put it like that, it sounds completely reasonable."

Kate laughed, the sound bright and clear. "Alex Chen, falling in love with me is the least reasonable thing you've ever done."

As we walked into the January evening, her hand steady in mine, I realized she was probably right.

And I was okay with that.

Chapter 14

Alex

We'd walked about half a block from the pastry shop when Kate stopped walking, her hand still in mine.

"You know what?" she said, turning to face me. "Let's go see my brother."

"Your brother?"

"Liam. He lives like, ten minutes away in a remodeled brownstone, near Mass Ave." Kate perked up, like she always did when she got an idea. "I could use some family perspective right now, and honestly? If we're doing this whole 'meeting the parents' thing, maybe you should meet at least one member of my family first."

Meeting Kate's brother spiked my anxiety to a fever pitch. "Kate, I don't know if now is the best time..."

"Alex." She stepped closer, her voice gentle but firm. "Liam's the steadiest person I know. He's in his second year of a doctorate program in physical therapy, he's calm about everything, and he's been my Boston support system since I started college. Plus," she added with a small smile, "he's going to find out about you eventually anyway. Better to get the interrogation over with while I'm there to defend you."

"Interrogation?"

"Protective big brother stuff. Nothing too scary." Kate squeezed my hand. "Trust me, you'll like him. And I think you could use someone who understands family pressure but isn't, you know, emotionally invested in our relationship to talk things through."

She had a point. And something about Kate's confidence in her brother made me curious.

"Okay," I said. "But if he decides he hates me, I'm blaming you."

Kate grinned. "Deal."

We walked through the Back Bay, Kate chattering about Liam's apartment and his program and how he'd be studying when we showed up because he was "pathologically dedicated to his coursework." The air was bitterly cold, but Kate's energy kept me warm, and by the time we stopped in front of a narrow brownstone with bikes chained to the front railings, some of my anxiety had settled into simple nervousness.

Kate led me up two flights of stairs and knocked on a door marked 3B. After a moment, it opened to reveal a tall man with dark hair and the same warm amber eyes as Kate, wearing sweatpants and a BU Physical Therapy t-shirt.

"Kate?" He looked genuinely surprised to see her, then his gaze cut to me with a quick clinical assessment typical of med students. "Everything okay?"

"Everything's fine," Kate said, rising on her toes to hug him. "Liam, this is Alex. Alex, this is my brother Liam."

Liam studied me for a moment longer, then extended his hand. "Alex Chen? The chemistry tutor?"

"That's me." His grip was firm, his palms callused from working with his hands. "Nice to meet you."

"Come in," Liam said, stepping back to let us pass. "Fair warning, I was working on my dissertation, so the place is a disaster."

His small apartment showed careful organization, with an impressive pile of reference books stacked on a coffee table and a skeletal model on the kitchen counter. Everything had its place even when it wasn't currently in that place.

"You want coffee?" Liam asked, already moving toward the kitchen. "I made a pot about an hour ago."

"Please," Kate said, settling onto his couch and pulling me down beside her. "Alex just had a fun phone conversation with his parents."

I shot her a look, but Liam was already turning toward us with three mugs. "Ah. A phone conversation that requires processing with neutral parties?"

"Got it in one."

Liam handed us each a mug and sat in the chair across from the couch, his attention focused on me. "Kate mentioned you're in the pharmacy program. That's a challenging track."

"It has its moments," I said carefully.

"Liam's being polite," Kate interjected. "What he really wants to know is what your intentions are with his sister."

"Kate." Liam looked pained but didn't deny it.

"What? It's true. You're doing that thing where you ask about school and work to figure out if someone's serious about their life choices."

Liam's mouth quirked. "My sister has no filter."

"I know," I said. "It's actually one thing I like about her."

"One thing?"

Kate tensed beside me. This was some kind of test. Not malicious, but evaluative. All the careful ways I could answer ran through my mind, all the diplomatic responses that would make me sound appropriately serious without revealing too much.

I chose honesty.

"She makes me want to be braver," I said. "I've spent my whole life following a very specific plan, making safe choices, avoiding complications. But Kate..." I glanced at her, then at Liam. "She makes me want to take risks for the right reasons."

Liam nodded approvingly. "And what happened on this phone call with your parents?"

Kate reached over to take my hand in a gesture of support her brother immediately clocked.

"They found out Kate helped me when I was sick over break," I said. "The insurance form listed her as my emergency contact. They're coming to Boston this weekend to... address the situation."

"And that's a problem because...?"

I hesitated, unsure how much to reveal about my family's expectations. But Kate squeezed my hand encouragingly.

"Because they have someone else in mind for me," I admitted finally. "Someone who fits better with their plans for my future."

Liam fell quiet, studying both of us over his coffee mug. When he spoke, his voice was thoughtful.

"Let me guess. They've been planning your career path since you were in middle school?"

"Earlier."

"And they've made it clear there's only one acceptable version of success?"

I nodded. His insight surprised me.

Liam set his mug down and leaned back in his chair. "I haven't been where you are. My path's been pretty straightforward. I always wanted PT, my parents supported it, I'm doing exactly what I planned." He glanced at Kate. "But I've seen my siblings navigate this stuff. The gap between what the family expects and what they actually want."

Kate's fingers tightened around mine, her palm warm against my knuckles.

"Sophie spent two years pretending she wanted medical school before she finally admitted she wanted social work," Liam continued. His focus on me was direct and unwavering. "Kate's been in nursing for a semester and a half. I've known since December that it wasn't right for her."

He leaned forward, resting his elbows on his knees. The movement brought him close enough to be heard clearly but far enough to avoid crowding. Had he learned this in medical school or developed it intuitively as the big brother to three younger siblings?

"The Westfields aren't subtle about what we value. Service, healthcare, helping people. It's woven through every family dinner, every story my parents tell about their workdays." A wry smile crossed his face. "But here's the thing: my parents have always been more flexible than any of us gave them credit for. Sophie was terrified to tell them about social work. Turned out they were relieved she'd found something she was passionate about."

Silence stretched between us. Kate's thumb traced small circles against the back of my hand.

"I'm not saying your parents are the same," Liam added. "Different families work differently."

"That's an understatement." The words barely made it past my throat, but they held firm.

"Right. But Saturday, you're going to have to decide something." Liam's voice was steady, certain. "Are you going to keep trying to manage their disappointment by hiding who you are? Or are you going to trust that they love you enough to eventually accept your choices, even if those choices aren't what they wanted?"

Only the radiator ticked, metallic, in the corner.

"Kate has tried to be what everyone needs her to be since she was a kid." Liam studied his coffee mug. "She's exhausting herself trying to make everyone happy. You know what I told her last semester when she stopped by before her final organic chemistry exam?"

"Liam." Kate's voice dropped to barely more than a whisper.

Liam's calm authority carried warmth. "I told her she can't live her whole life afraid of disappointing people. That sometimes disappointing people is the price of being honest." His gaze met mine and held. "Your parents are going to be disappointed on Saturday. No way around that. The question is whether you're going to apologize for existing outside their plan, or whether you're going to stand by your choices."

He lifted his mug, took a long sip, set it down.

"I'm the steady one in this family. Never rocked a boat in my life." He traced the rim of his mug with one finger. "What I wanted and parental expectations happened to align, but watching my siblings struggle with it taught me something: the people who love you will come around. It might take time. It might be messy. But if they really love you, they'll figure out how to accept that you're not who they thought you'd be."

His gaze moved from Kate to me. "And the person sitting next to you? She's worth whatever comes on Saturday. I can promise you that."

Kate's expression filled with pride at her brother's words. Her hand gripped mine like she had no intention of letting go.

"She is." My throat constricted around the words. "Worth fighting for."

Liam smiled, the expression reaching his eyes, like he'd already known my answer.

"Then you already know what you need to do. You just have to be brave enough to do it."

We talked for the next hour. Kate told Liam about her art class while he leaned forward with questions that revealed he'd clocked her interests long before she'd recognized them herself.

"You know Mom has an entire box of your drawings in the attic," Liam said. "Everything from those maps you made of Waverly Cove when you were seven to the sketches you did on napkins at Christmas dinners."

"She does?"

"Kate, she's been saving them for years. She won't be surprised that you want to study art. She's going to be relieved you finally admitted it to yourself."

Kate processed this, realizing that her family had been waiting for her to catch up to what they'd already seen.

When we finally stood to leave, Liam walked us to the door.

"You should bring Alex home for spring break," he said, looking between us. "Let him see where you come from. Meet the rest of the family. We can take the kayaks out."

Kate's eyes widened. "Liam..."

"What? You're smitten with each other." His tone was casual, but his eyes were keen. "I can see it from here. And if you're going to face his family this weekend, seems fair that he should meet yours eventually."

"We haven't really talked about..." Kate started.

"I'd like that," I said, surprising myself. "If you think your parents wouldn't mind."

Liam laughed. "Are you kidding? They'll probably feed you until you can't move and send you home with enough leftovers for a month. That's how Westfields show love."

As we left his building, Liam called after us. "Alex?"

I turned back.

"Saturday's going to be hard," he said. "But don't let them convince you that love is a luxury you can't afford. Sometimes it's the only thing worth having."

Walking back toward campus, Kate had gone quiet.

"You okay?" I asked.

"Yeah. Just thinking about what Liam said." She bumped her shoulder against mine. "He likes you, you know."

"How can you tell?"

"He invited you kayaking. That's Liam's happy place. He never invites anyone to go with him because it 'disturbs his peace' or whatever." Kate stopped walking and turned to face me. "Alex, are you really okay with coming to Maine? Because my family is... a lot. In the best way, but still a lot."

Liam's steady presence came to mind. The way he'd offered perspective without pretending to have all the answers. If Kate's family was anything like her brother, I wanted to meet them. He'd even had us exchange phone numbers as I was leaving in case I needed a friendly ear to process anything.

"I'm more than okay with it," I said. "Actually, after Saturday with my parents, Maine might be exactly what we need."

Kate smiled, a radiant expression that made my heart grow three sizes. "Good. We're probably going to need all the family support we can get."

A text arrived from Liam as we walked.

> LIAM
> Take care of her. And remember: Saturday's going to be hard, but you already know what matters most. Trust that.

I showed the message to Kate, who grinned.

"See? Told you he likes you."

Maybe everything would be okay. I had Kate. And apparently, I had Liam too. And on Saturday, I was going to have to be brave enough to tell my parents that sometimes the life they wanted for me and the life I wanted for myself weren't the same thing.

The thought still scared me. But standing there with Kate's hand in mine, I was ready to face it.

Chapter 15

Kate

For the next three days, panic grew despite my efforts to quell it at the thought of meeting Alex's parents for the first time.

Spoiler alert: I failed.

By Saturday morning, rejected outfits buried my bed. Layer upon layer of clothing choices, each representing a different strategy for making Alex's parents hate me less than they already did.

"You're overthinking this," Isa said, sprawled across her perfectly made bed, watching my fashion crisis unfold. "Just wear something normal."

"Define normal." I pulled a navy cardigan over a simple white blouse, then immediately removed it. "Is this 'I respect your culture' normal or 'I'm dating your son but I'm very wholesome' normal or 'Please don't hate me' normal?"

"Those aren't types of normal." Isa rolled her eyes. "Those are types of anxiety."

She wasn't wrong. The Chen parents were coming to campus for a "discussion" about my relationship with their son. Alex had warned me they wouldn't be pleased, but his stoic expression when he mentioned their impending visit had told me more than his words. This wasn't just displeasure. This was life-altering for him.

I settled on a modest knee-length sweater dress with three-quarter sleeves in a soft blue. Professional enough for a job interview, conservative enough for church, and just casual enough to pretend this wasn't the most terrifying Saturday morning of my life.

My stomach twisted as I applied minimal makeup. Painting a realistic still life in art class last week had been easier than keeping my eyeliner steady this morning.

"You look fine." Isa gave me the once-over when I turned to her for approval. "Very respectable New England girl."

"Is that good or bad?"

"It's just who you are." She shrugged. "No point pretending to be someone else. They'll figure it out eventually. For the record, this level of stress is why I never take my abuela up on any of her offers to set me up with a 'Good Dominican Boy' from the neighborhood."

I was just about to ask what being a "Good Dominican Boy" entailed when I was interrupted by my phone.

ALEX

They just called. They're parking now. Meeting at the campus center in 15.

KATE

On my way. It's going to be fine.

A blatant lie, but what else do you say when someone's parents are driving two hours round trip to explain why you're an unsuitable girlfriend?

The ten-minute walk across campus gave me too much time to

rehearse a mental script that would inevitably abandon me the moment I needed it. Boston in early February competed for Worst Weather Champion. The wind sliced between buildings to find every gap in my warm wool coat. Strangely, the physical discomfort helped. Hard to catastrophize about meeting the parents when your face might freeze off before you arrive.

Alex stood ramrod straight by the campus center entrance. Even from fifty feet away, tension was visible in his shoulders.

When he saw me approaching, he exhaled as though he'd been holding his breath for hours.

"They're inside," he said, his voice low as I reached him. "At a table near the coffee counter."

"How are you doing?" I asked, resisting the urge to take his hand. Public displays of affection seemed inappropriate, given the circumstances.

"I'm..." He started, then exhaled slowly. "Let's just get through this."

"I read an article about Chinese family expectations last night." I wanted to swallow the words back down. "Not that one article makes me an expert, obviously. I just wanted to understand."

"Kate." Alex interrupted gently. "Just be yourself. That's all I want." He hesitated, then added, "Just let me handle the conversation flow, okay? There are protocols."

Protocols. Right. Meeting your boyfriend's parents needs an instruction manual.

We entered the building. Warm air enveloped us along with the familiar scent of coffee and the ambient noise of weekend student activity. Alex scanned the space, then nodded toward a corner table where an impeccably dressed couple sat with perfect posture, neither touching their water glasses.

Mr. and Mrs. Chen looked just as I'd remembered from our brief encounter at The Golden Dragon, yet somehow more formidable in this context. His father sat rigidly straight, his wire-rimmed glasses and close-cropped salt-and-pepper hair accentuating the stern expression on his face. His mother wore elegance like a second skin, her purple sweater set perfectly pressed, her dark hair showing only the slightest silver threads at the temples.

Alex straightened his shoulders as we walked toward them, and I mirrored his posture. My heartbeat drowned out the coffee shop's ambient noise.

"Bàba, Māmā," Alex greeted them in Mandarin, then switched to English. "This is Kate Westfield." He turned to me. "Kate, these are my parents, Heng and Li Mei Chen."

I extended my hand the way my father had taught me when I was twelve. Firm grip, eye contact, warm smile. "It's very nice to meet you both, Mr. and Mrs. Chen."

Mrs. Chen took my hand first. Her grip claimed rather than greeted. "Hello, Kate." Her gaze moved from my face to my dress, my shoes, back to my face. She hadn't blinked yet.

Mr. Chen's handshake was brief and businesslike. "Miss Westfield." Just two words, but they contained a universe of unspoken judgement.

"Please, sit," Mrs. Chen said, gesturing to the empty chairs across from them.

I slid into the seat, hyperaware of my posture, the position of my hands, and whether my expression looked respectful or terrified or some ghastly combination of both. Alex sat beside me, close enough that warmth radiated from his arm, but not touching.

Silence stretched between us before Mrs. Chen spoke.

"Alex tells us you are studying nursing." Her tone was polite, conversational even, but this was the most important job interview of my life.

"Yes, I'm in my sophomore year." I nodded, grateful for the softball question. "My mother is an ER nurse, and I've always admired her."

"A respectable profession," Mr. Chen acknowledged with a slight nod. "And your father?"

"He's a physical therapist. He owns a practice in Maine."

"So your family understands professional commitment," Mrs. Chen observed. "That is good."

I wasn't sure whether this was going well. Their expressions remained neutral, giving nothing away. I glanced at Alex, who sat with the same rigid control, though his fingers tapped against his leg under the table. His nervous tell.

"Alex has been helping me with chemistry," I offered. "He's an excellent tutor."

"Yes, we know about the tutoring," Mr. Chen said, his tone making it clear he knew it had evolved into something more. "Alex has always been academically gifted. He has a promising future in pharmacy."

The emphasis on "future" wasn't subtle. I swallowed.

"He does," I agreed. "He explains concepts better than any of my professors."

"Alex has many responsibilities," Mrs. Chen said, folding her hands on the table. "His studies, his residency, his work at our restaurant when needed. He is very busy with his proper priorities."

The temperature of the conversation seemed to drop ten degrees with that single word: "proper."

"I understand that," I said carefully. "I admire how dedicated he is."

"Then you understand why distractions are problematic at this crucial time in his education," Mr. Chen stated flatly.

And there it was. I was a "distraction."

Alex tensed beside me. "Bàba—"

"It is not disrespectful to state facts, son," Mr. Chen continued. "Your mother and I have given everything to provide you with opportunities in America. The restaurant, our long hours, sending you to good schools. This is all for your future success."

The stories Alex had told me came alive in my mind. His mother arriving at the restaurant in darkness, her breath fogging in the pre-dawn cold as she unlocked the door at six. The rhythmic chop of her knife prepping vegetables for lunch service that wouldn't start for hours. His father's scarred, capable hands moving with the precision of decades as he folded dumplings the way his own father had taught him, each pleat a small act of inheritance. The cramped apartment above the restaurant where they'd lived those first five years, every surface covered with textbooks Alex had bought secondhand, every dollar that didn't go to rent or ingredients tucked away for his future.

"We want only the best for you, Alex," Mrs. Chen added. Her expression softened slightly. "You know this."

"I know that," Alex said, his voice controlled but with an undercurrent of tension I'd never heard before. "But Kate isn't a distraction. She's important to me."

My hand ached to reach for his under the table. This wasn't about my comfort. This was his battle.

"You are young," Mrs. Chen said gently. "There will be time for relationships after you establish your career." She turned to me, her expression not unkind but unyielding. "Kate, you seem like a nice girl. But you must understand, in our culture, timing is everything. We must build the foundation before the house."

"With respect, Mrs. Chen," I said, impressing myself with how steady my voice sounded, "I don't believe caring about someone interferes with building a strong foundation. If anything, support from the right person can make that foundation stronger."

Mrs. Chen's eyebrows rose. My words had surprised her.

"American thinking," Mr. Chen said dismissively. "Very individualistic. Our culture values family obligation and proper order of priorities."

The way he spat "American" made it sound like a character flaw.

"My family believes in hard work and commitment too," I countered, feeling a flash of defensiveness on behalf of my parents. "They've built their careers through years of dedication."

"Then they should understand our position," Mrs. Chen said. She paused, studying me more carefully. "Tell me, Kate. What do your parents think about you dating someone while you are still in school? Do they approve of divided attention during such an important time?"

The question surprised me. She was trying to understand rather than just reject.

"They trust me to manage my priorities," I said carefully. "They raised me to work hard and be responsible for my choices."

Mrs. Chen nodded, processing. "And you believe you can balance both? Your studies and this relationship?"

"Yes," I said. "I do."

Mrs. Chen exhaled through her nose—not quite a sigh, but close.

"And what about when he must decide about residencies?" she continued. "What about when Alex must choose between opportunities in different cities? What about his responsibilities to family?"

The question told me this wasn't just about academic distraction. This was about Jennifer Liu and the hopes and expectations I couldn't fulfill.

"We have invested everything in your future, son," Mr. Chen said, leaning forward slightly. "Everything. We did not come to America for you to throw away opportunities on temporary feelings."

"They're not temporary," Alex said, so quietly I almost didn't hear him.

The silence that followed was deafening. Mr. Chen's expression hardened, while Mrs. Chen fussed with her water glass.

"I think," Mrs. Chen finally said, addressing me directly, "you seem like a kind person. But you must understand our concern. Alex is our only child. All our hopes rest with him."

The statement settled over us. All their hopes. All they'd given up. The entire reason they had come to America, worked brutal hours, and built a life from nothing. It was all concentrated in the young man sitting beside me.

"I understand," I admitted. "And I respect how much you've done for Alex. I really do." I took a breath. "But I also care about him. Not his potential or his future earnings or his status. Just him."

Mrs. Chen studied me for a long moment, her expression unreadable. Mr. Chen's jaw tightened.

"Lì Xiáng," Mr. Chen said, switching to Mandarin. The words that followed were incomprehensible to me, but the finality in his tone was unmistakable.

Alex responded in Mandarin, his voice calm but firm. The exchange continued for several excruciating minutes, with Mrs. Chen occasionally adding quieter comments. I sat stock-still, invisible despite being the clear subject of their discussion.

Finally, Alex switched back to English. "We should continue this conversation another time," he bit out. "Kate and I both have studying to do."

Mr. Chen's expression could have frozen Boston Harbor. "We did not drive all this way for such a brief discussion."

"I know, Bàba. But I think we all need time to reflect." Alex stood, a clear sign the meeting was over, whether or not his parents approved. I followed his lead, gathering my coat from the back of the chair.

"It was nice meeting you both," I said politely, despite the suffocating tension. My mother would have been proud of my manners, if nothing else.

Mrs. Chen inclined her head. Mr. Chen said nothing, his steely gaze fixed on his son.

"I'll walk you to your car," Alex told his parents, then turned to me. "I'll call you later."

The dismissal stung. He needed space to handle this without an audience. I nodded, attempted a smile that became a grimace as the Chen family walked away. Alex's back was as rigid as a flagpole.

I stood alone at the campus center while students continued with their Saturday, not realizing that someone had just judged me unsuitable as a girlfriend.

My phone vibrated against my thigh.

> ISA
> How'd it go?

A response formed in my mind, trying not to sound pathetic or dramatic.

> KATE
> About as well as meeting people who think you're ruining their son's life could go.

I stepped outside into the February cold, which now seemed fitting for my mood. The wind had picked up, carrying occasional snowflakes that melted on contact with my overheated cheeks. As I walked toward campus, what had just happened replayed in my mind.

The Chens weren't cartoon villains. They were parents who had given everything for their son and had specific ideas about how his life should unfold to honor what they'd built for him. In some ways, I understood their perspective better than I wanted to admit.

Hadn't my parents done the same for my education? Didn't they have expectations about my nursing career? The parallel made my stomach twist uncomfortably.

But a difference existed. My parents might be disappointed if I changed course, but they wouldn't present it as a betrayal of their life's purpose. They wouldn't make their love conditional on my career choices.

Would they?

The question haunted me as I trudged across campus, snow beginning to fall more steadily around me. I'd never tested those boundaries. I'd always been reliable Kate. Following the expected path, making the safe choices. Maybe I wasn't so different from Alex after all.

My phone rang, startling me from my thoughts. Alex's name flashed on the screen.

"Hey," I answered, pressing the phone to my ear. "That was fast."

"I'm sorry." His voice was strained. "That was uncomfortable."

"It's okay." The lie was instant, reflexive. "Are you alright?"

"No," he admitted. "Can I come over later? I don't want to talk about this over the phone."

My stomach dropped. Was this the breakup visit? Had his parents issued an ultimatum I hadn't understood through the language barrier?

"Of course," I said, trying to keep my voice steady. "I'm heading to my dorm now."

"I'll be in touch soon." He paused. "And Kate? I'm really sorry about all of this."

The call ended, leaving me standing in the thickening snowfall, ice crystals catching in my eyelashes.

I resumed walking, faster now, my mind racing with possibilities. Would Alex choose his family's expectations over our relationship? Could I blame him if he did? What would I do if faced with a similar choice?

The questions spiraled, relentless as the falling snow, offering no answers, only the cold certainty that nothing about this situation would be simple.

Chapter 16

Alex

Silence accompanied us to my parents' car, snow falling around us. The parking garage echoed like a tomb, our footsteps bouncing off concrete walls.

"Lì Xiáng," my father said when we reached their sedan, his hand resting on the driver's door without opening it. "You understand what is at stake here."

"I know you're scared," I said gently.

My father's eyes flashed. "We are practical. We are protecting you from making a mistake that will cost you everything."

"Heng." My mother touched his arm softly.

But he shook his head, turning to face me head-on. He looked tired, more than I'd ever seen. The lines around his eyes had deepened since Thanksgiving. His shoulders, always so strong, seemed to carry an invisible weight.

"You think we are being unreasonable," he said, his voice rough. "You think we do not understand love, that we are cold and traditional and stuck in old ways."

"Bàba, I didn't say—"

"You don't have to say it. It's written on your face." He removed his glasses, pressed his fingers against the bridge of his nose. When he spoke again, his voice had lost its edge. "You know what I was doing when I was your age, Lì Xiáng?"

I shook my head.

"I was washing dishes in a restaurant basement in Guangzhou, trying to save enough money to take the qualifying exams for culinary school. Working sixteen-hour days, sleeping on a cot in the storage room." He replaced his glasses. "Your mother worked in a textile factory, her hands bleeding from the machines, saving every yuan for her future. We had nothing. No family support, no safety net, nothing but our own work."

He'd told versions of this story before, but the way he told it now sounded raw.

"When we came to America, we had two suitcases and three hundred dollars," he continued. "We slept in the restaurant kitchen for the first two months because we could not afford an apartment. Your mother was pregnant with you, sick every morning, but she still worked the lunch shift. She would vomit in the bathroom, wash her face, and serve customers with a smile."

My mother refused to meet my gaze.

"We did not do this because we are cruel people who want to control your life," my father said, his voice tight. "We did this so you would never have to sleep in a kitchen. So you would never have to choose between buying food and paying for school. So you would have opportunities we could only dream about."

"I know that, Bàba—"

"No." He cut me off. His hands were shaking. "You know it is like a story I tell. You don't know it here." He pounded his fist against his breastbone. "You don't know what it feels like to be terrified every single day that it will all fall apart. That one mistake, one distraction, one wrong choice will destroy everything you built."

The parking garage was silent except for the wind whistling through the concrete pillars.

"When you were eight years old," my father said quietly, "the restaurant almost failed. The papers published a bad review and customers stopped coming. We could not make rent. I had to borrow money from people I swore I would never ask. Men who charge interest that ruins families. Your mother and I, we did not sleep for weeks. We worked until our hands bled, trying to save what we built."

"I remember. You were never home that summer."

"We fought to make sure you still had a home to return to." My father's voice broke. "And when we finally saved the restaurant, when we finally paid back every dollar we owed, I promised myself that you would never face that kind of fear. That all our work would give you security. Safety. A future where you never have to beg for money or sleep in kitchens or wonder if one bad day will destroy your life."

He turned to look at the campus buildings visible through the garage opening, snow falling past the concrete frame.

"And now you are telling me you want to risk it all for a girl you met four months ago."

"It's not—"

"Lì Xiáng." My mother spoke for the first time, her voice soft but firm. "Your father is not explaining this well, but what he is trying to say is..." She paused, choosing her words carefully. "We are terrified. Not of Kate. Not really. We are terrified of what happens if you fail."

"I won't fail."

"But what if you do?" My father's voice broke. "What if you are so distracted by this relationship that your grades slip? What if you don't get into a good residency program? What if you end up like us, working seventy hours a week just to survive, watching your children go without things they need?"

He gripped the car door handle, knuckles white.

"I cannot watch that happen to you," he said. "I cannot watch you throw away everything we built. It would break me, Lì Xiáng. It would mean everything we suffered was for nothing."

The confession settled between us in the cold air. My father, who never showed weakness, who never admitted fear, stood before me with tears in his eyes.

"I love you," he said roughly. "More than I know how to say. And that is why we are here. Not to control you. Not to be cruel. Because we are terrified of losing you to a mistake we could have prevented."

My mother moved closer to him, taking his hand. They stood together, two people who had built a life from nothing, who had given up everything they knew so I could have opportunities they'd never imagined. And they were terrified.

"I understand," I said. "I do, Bàba. But I'm not going to fail. And Kate isn't a distraction. She's..."

"She is important to you," my mother finished gently. She was quiet for a moment, then switched to English. "What does she like to do? Kate."

The shift surprised me. "She... she loves art. Painting. She's kind to everyone. She remembers the names of people in the dining hall, asks about their families."

My mother nodded slowly, absorbing this. "Does she work hard?"

"Very hard. That's how we met, because she was so determined to succeed at chemistry."

Another nod. My father stood rigid beside her, frustrated by this detour but silent.

Then my mother switched back to Mandarin. "But Lì Xiáng, love is not enough when you are young and still building your foundation. Love cannot pay rent. Love cannot guarantee your future."

My father's voice hardened, all emotion draining from it as he switched into the practical mode I knew too well. "If you continue this relationship, we will stop paying your tuition and living expenses immediately. You will need to figure out loans, work, whatever you must do. But that is not all."

He paused, making sure I understood. "Dr. Zhang has been holding a residency position for you at Mass General. He did this as a favor to us, because of our friendship, because he believes in our family. If you choose this girl over your future, I will tell him we can no longer vouch for your focus and dedication. He will give that position to someone else."

My mother's hand tightened on his arm, but she didn't dare contradict him. She never had and never would.

"These are not threats, Lì Xiáng," my father continued. "These are consequences. You are asking us to watch you throw away your future. We cannot do that. We cannot help you destroy yourself."

He opened the car door. The conversation was over in his mind.

"We should go," my mother said. "We all need time to think about this." Tears gathered in her eyes. "Lì Xiáng, we are not saying you can never have love. We are saying now is not the time. Can you understand the difference?"

I didn't answer. Couldn't answer. Because the difference between "never" and "not now" seemed meaningless when the girl I loved was walking away through the snow, thinking I was about to choose my parents over her.

They got into the car. My father started the engine but didn't shift it in gear immediately. Through the window, he pressed his forehead against the steering wheel, my mother's hand on his shoulder.

Then they drove away, leaving me standing in the cold garage, my heart split between the parents who had given me everything and the girl who made me feel like I could be more than the sum of their dreams.

Chapter 17

Kate

I sat on my bed, phone in hand, debating whether to text Alex or give him space. It had been far too long since his call. My dress pinched at the ribs with each breath. I'd chosen it this morning feeling hopeful. Now the zipper dug into my side, a reminder of how wrong everything had gone.

Isa sat at her desk pretending to study, but every few minutes her gaze flicked toward me. She'd been there when I returned, had taken one look at my face and offered to "hunt down those judgmental assholes and give them a piece of her mind." I'd declined, but her fierce loyalty had started the tears all over again.

"He'll text," Isa said finally, breaking the silence. "Or call. Or show up. Alex isn't the type to just ghost you."

"What if his parents convinced him?" The question barely made it past the lump in my throat. "What if they're right? What if I am just a distraction that's going to ruin his life?"

"Kate." Isa spun her chair around. "Stop. You are not ruining anything. His parents are scared, and scared people lash out. It doesn't make them right."

I pulled my knees up and wrapped my arms around them.

"You didn't see his mother's face. Like I was something dirty he'd stepped in."

"Then his mother has terrible judgment." Isa's voice was firm. "Because you're amazing. And if Alex can't see that..."

A knock on the door cut her off. We both froze.

"That's probably just Maya from next door," I said, even as my pulse jumped. "She borrowed my notes."

But when I opened the door, Alex stood in the hallway with snow melting in his dark hair, looking exhausted.

"Hi," he said.

"Hi." I stepped back to let him in, searching his face, trying to prepare myself for whatever was coming. "You're soaked."

"It's snowing harder." He brushed at his jacket as though that would dry it. "I walked for a bit. Needed to clear my head."

Isa grabbed her laptop and textbooks before I could make eye contact. "I'm going to the library. Text me when it's safe to come back." She squeezed my shoulder on her way out, giving Alex a look that could have stripped paint.

The door clicked shut behind her. Alex and I stood in the space between the beds, not quite looking at each other. The radiator clanked, the muffled bass line from someone's music down the hall, my breathing too loud in the sudden stillness.

Say something, I told myself. But what? What do you say when you're waiting to find out if your entire relationship is about to implode?

"So," I said finally, forcing the word past the tightness in my throat. "That went well."

He laughed—broken and hollow. "Kate, I'm so sorry."

"You don't have to apologize for your parents." The words left my mouth, and I wasn't sure I believed them. Weren't we all responsible for the people we brought into each other's lives?

"I do, actually. They were..." He ran a hand through his damp hair. His fingers were trembling. "They were themselves. Just more intense than usual."

I sat on my bed, hugging my knees to again. The position had become familiar, my default when the world felt too big and overwhelming. "They're scared."

"What?"

"Your parents. They're terrified." I squeezed my knees tighter, feeling a slight pull in my hamstrings. "They didn't drive an hour in a snowstorm to be mean. They came because they're afraid you're going to throw away everything they built for you."

Alex stared at me as if I'd just divined this from a crystal ball. "How did you...?"

"Because I would worry about that too, if I were them." I rested my chin on my knees, muffling my voice. "They gave up everything. Their home, their language, probably their families. Everything they knew and everyone they loved. And they did it all for you. For your future. And now here I am, some random American girl who they think is going to derail all of that."

"You're not random." Alex moved closer, his voice dropping to that soft, intense tone he used when he was trying to make me understand something important. "And you're not derailing anything."

"But they don't know that." I lifted my head. "All they know is that you were on track, following the plan, doing everything right. You were being the perfect son, the perfect student. And then I showed up with my chemistry struggles and my art dreams, and suddenly you're talking about things they never planned for. Of course they're freaking out."

Alex sat beside me on the bed, close enough that our shoulders touched. The dampness from his jacket seeped through my sleeve, cold against my skin, grounding me in the moment. "My father cried."

I blinked. "What?"

"In the parking garage. After you left." He stared at his hands like they held answers he couldn't quite read. "I've never seen him cry. Not once in my entire life. Not when my grandfather died. Not when they almost lost the first restaurant to a bad review. Not ever. But today he cried because he's terrified I'm going to fail and end up like them. Working brutal hours, never having security, always one bad day away from losing everything."

I'd met his parents for less than an hour, but I could picture it. Alex's controlled, reserved father breaking down in a parking garage, years of composure crumbling under the weight of his fear for his son.

"Alex..." I didn't know what else to say. What do you say when someone's entire world is fracturing?

"He said loving you isn't enough. That love can't pay rent or guarantee my future. That he and my mother loved each other and look where it got them. Eighteen-hour days, never quite making ends meet, always struggling." His voice had gone flat in a way that scared me. "And maybe he's right."

The words stung. I inhaled slowly, trying to think past the sudden tightness in my throat, past the voice in my head screaming that I'd known this was coming, that it was inevitable.

"So what are you saying?" My stomach knotted even though I wasn't sure I wanted the answer.

"I don't know." He turned to face me. Exhaustion and love and fear all tangled together in his eyes. "I care for you, Kate. That's not a question. That's the one thing I'm absolutely certain about. But I also love them. And I can't..." His voice broke, and he had to stop to swallow the emotion. "I can't make them understand that you're not a threat to everything they've built."

Part of me wanted to argue, to insist that we could make them understand, that love was enough, that everything would work out. But I'd seen his mother's face. I'd heard the edge in his father's voice even when he spoke English, the barely restrained panic underneath the politeness. Words or wishes wouldn't convince them.

"So what's our next move?" I asked.

Silence hovered between us, heavy with everything we weren't saying. Outside, snow hit the window in soft patters, the wind picking up. The storm intensified.

"I need to prove to them I can do both," he said finally. "That I can be the son they need me to be and also be with you."

"And if you can't prove it?"

"Then..." He couldn't finish the sentence.

I reached for his hand, threading my fingers through his. His palm was cold from the walk, but his grip tightened, almost desperate. "Then we figure it out together. One day at a time."

The words sounded naive even as they left my mouth. Like something from a greeting card or a rom-com, too simple for the complexity we were facing. But what else was there? Grand declarations? Promises we couldn't keep? Sometimes the only option was to take the next step and hope the ground held.

He squeezed my hand so hard it almost hurt, like he was afraid I might disappear if he loosened his grip. "I don't want to lose you."

"You won't," I said, with more confidence than I felt. The lie tasted bitter on my tongue, but I forced it out anyway because one of us had to believe we could survive this. "We'll make this work."

"How?"

"I don't know yet," I admitted. "But we're both pretty smart. We'll figure something out."

The words felt inadequate, too small for the size of the problem we were facing. But Alex pulled me closer, wrapping his arms around me, and I pressed my face against his shoulder, breathing in the scent of snow and his detergent and something uniquely him. His jacket hung damp and cold, but underneath warmth radiated, his pulse racing against my cheek.

For a long moment, we just held each other. Tension hummed

through his body, his breathing not quite steady. My mind kept replaying the scene in the campus center. His mother's cold dismissal, his father's calculated politeness, the way they'd switched to Mandarin like I wasn't even there.

"My mother asked about you," Alex said into my hair, his voice tentative.

I pulled back. "What?"

"After you left. She asked what you like to do, what makes you happy." He pulled back just enough to meet my eyes. "She's never asked about anyone other than Jennifer before."

My pulse jumped. "What does that mean?"

"I think..." He hesitated, working through the implications, analyzing the data like one of his chemistry problems. "I think it means she's trying. In her own way. She's not ready to accept this, but she's not completely closed off either."

It wasn't much. A few questions about my character, my habits. But in the context of everything else that had happened, it felt significant. Like a door that had slammed shut was now ajar.

"We can work with that," I said, and this time I meant it. This time it didn't feel like naive optimism but like an actual plan, a thread we could follow through the maze.

Alex smiled, tired but genuine. His face transformed, chasing some of the exhaustion from his features. "You're really not giving up on this, are you?"

"On you? Never." I scooted closer, close enough to see the flecks of gold in his dark eyes, the way his pupils dilated in the dim light of my dorm room. "Your parents are terrified of losing everything they built. But I'm terrified of losing you. So we're all scared. We just have to decide if being scared is enough reason to give up."

"It's not," Alex said firmly, and there was conviction in his voice I hadn't heard before.

"No," I agreed. "It's really not."

I leaned in and pressed a kiss to the corner of his mouth, soft and lingering. The moment my lips touched his skin, the air in the room seemed to electrify. He exhaled, the tension in his shoulders easing. When I pulled back, his hand cupped my jaw, holding me there.

"Stay," I whispered, the word barely more than a breath. "We don't have to figure everything out tonight. Just... stay."

He nodded, releasing a breath he'd been holding. I grabbed his damp jacket and draped it over my desk chair to dry. When I turned, he watched me with an intensity that made me aware of every inch of space between us. Not analytical this time, not that careful observation he usually did. This was different. Hungrier.

"Kate," he said, and there was vulnerability and want in his voice.

I crossed back to him, hyperaware of how the snow continued to fall outside, muffling the rest of the world. "Yeah?"

Instead of answering, he reached up and cupped my face in his hands, thumbs tracing my cheekbones. When he kissed me, it felt different from all the other times. The tentative first kiss in the hospital, the sweet ones outside my dorm, the quick stolen moments between classes. This kiss was deeper. More certain.

More like a beginning than a question.

His lips were soft and warm, and when he tilted his head to deepen the kiss, I made a small sound in the back of my throat. My hands moved to his shoulders, then up into his still-damp hair, and I felt him shiver at the touch.

"Are you sure this is what you want? That I'm what you want?" I whispered against his mouth, even though my pulse was racing so hard I was sure he could feel it.

"Yes," he breathed, pulling me closer until I was practically in his lap, our bodies pressed together from shoulder to hip. "More than anything."

His hands moved from my face to my waist, tentative but wanting, and I felt the heat of his palms through the fabric of my dress. One of his hands slid up my back, fingers tracing the line of my spine, and I arched into the touch instinctively.

We broke apart for air, both breathing hard, and I took in his appearance. His hair was disheveled from my fingers, his lips swollen, his pupils blown wide. He looked undone in a way I'd never seen before, and knowing that I had done that, that I could affect him this way was empowering.

"Alex," I said, and need threaded through my voice.

"Kate." He said my name like a prayer, like a promise, and then he was kissing me again, deeper this time, more insistent. His hands slid into my hair, tugging gently, and a sound escaped me—desperate and wanting.

I pulled him closer, needing to feel his warmth, his solidity, the proof that despite everything that had happened today, despite his parents' ultimatum and all the uncertainty ahead, this was real. We were real.

His hands slid to the hem of my dress, fingers slipping beneath to trace patterns on my bare skin, and the world narrowed to just this. His mouth on mine, his touch leaving trails of fire, the way we fit together like we were designed for exactly this moment.

Everything else faded. The fear, the doubt, the impossible situation with his parents. Right now, in this moment, only we existed.

Chapter 18

Alex

We broke apart, both breathing hard. Kate's eyes had darkened, questioning. Her lips, swollen from kissing, her cheeks flushed. I couldn't look away.

"Is this okay?" she whispered.

The responsible part of my brain, the part that always thought five steps ahead, knew we should slow down. Both of our emotions were raw. Her roommate could return. This was moving too fast.

But for once, I didn't want to be responsible. I didn't want to think about my parents' ultimatum, or cultural expectations, or the carefully planned future that was currently crumbling around me. I wanted to feel instead of think, to experience instead of analyze.

"Yes." The certainty in my voice surprised me. "More than okay."

Kate's smile was equal parts shy and mischievous. Her fingers found the top button of my shirt, hovering there. "You'll tell me if it's too much?"

My nod made the first button slip from her grasp. She laughed, nervous but genuine, and tried again.

"Join the club," I said when our fingers tangled together attempting to help.

The sound of our laughter broke something open between us. When she finally pushed my shirt apart, her hands rested on my chest. My pulse raced beneath her palms.

"You're shaking," she observed softly.

"Cold or nerves. Probably both." The admission felt easier than I'd expected.

Kate's thumbs traced gentle circles on my skin, warmth following each touch. "We can stop whenever you want."

I swallowed. "I don't want to stop. This is just very new for me."

"I know." Her hands continued their exploration, tentative and wondering, as if memorizing the contours of my stomach and shoulders. "We'll figure it out together."

I reached for the hem of her dress, pausing there.

"Yes," she breathed.

Together, we navigated the fabric over her head, though it seemed determined to resist. When it finally slid free, Kate's hair was staticky and disheveled.

"Well, that was elegant," she joked.

"Perfect." I meant it. She sat before me in simple cotton underwear, her cheeks flushed, her hair a mess, looking nothing like polished magazine images. Real and vulnerable and breathtakingly beautiful.

Kate reached behind to unhook her bra, but her hands fumbled. "This is actually harder from this angle. Can you...?"

"I have no idea how those work," I admitted. "I understand the basic mechanics of a clasp, but the practical application..."

She twisted to give me better access, laughing. "Just pinch the two sides together and pull."

After three failed attempts, Kate reached back and covered my hands with hers, guiding the motion. The clasp released. When the garment fell away, coherent thought abandoned me.

"I think my brain just short-circuited."

"Most guys just say 'wow,'" Kate teased, though her arms crossed slightly to cover her cleavage.

"Don't." I gently pulled her arms away. "You're beautiful. I'm just trying to remember how to form words."

Her smile was both shy and pleased. She took my hands and placed them on her waist. "You're fine. Just explore. There's no wrong answer."

My fingers trembled as they traced her skin. She was softer than I'd imagined, warmer. When my thumbs accidentally brushed the underside of her breasts, her breath hitched and I mumbled an apology.

"That was good," Kate exhaled. "You don't have to apologize for everything, Alex."

"Overthinking?"

"Catastrophically."

She leaned forward, pressing her forehead against mine. "How about we make a rule? No more apologies unless something actually goes wrong. Deal?"

"Deal."

We made our way to the bed through awkward maneuvers. I knocked my head on her desk lamp; she caught her foot in her backpack strap. We half-fell onto the mattress.

"Smooth," Kate said, breathless.

"I'm usually much better coordinated."

"Textbook perfect would be boring." She shifted so we were face to face, and I became hyperaware of every point where our bodies touched. Her legs tangled with mine, the press of her breasts against me, the warmth of her breath on my neck.

"Kate, I have absolutely no idea what I'm doing," I confessed. "I understand the mechanics in theory, but..."

She placed a finger against my lips. "I'm not expecting some kind of Olympic performance. This isn't an exam you can study for."

"But I want it to be good for you."

"It will be good because it's us." She brushed her thumb across my knuckles. "Just focus on what feels right."

Her hand slid down to the waistband of my pants, pausing.

"Yes." I answered the unspoken question.

She worked the button free, then the zipper. When her hand slipped beneath the waistband of my boxers, my entire body jerked and I made an undignified sound somewhere between a gasp and a whimper.

"Oh, I like that sound," Kate purred, her eyes dark.

Her touch was tentative at first, exploratory. I focused on breathing as the sensations threatened to overwhelm rational thought.

"This might be over embarrassingly fast," I managed.

Kate smiled, pressed a kiss to my jaw. "Then we'll have an excuse to do it again."

I reached for her then, my hand trembling as it slid over her hip, then inward. When my fingers grazed the delicate fabric of her underwear, she inhaled sharply.

"Keep going."

I traced the edge of the fabric. Kate shifted, giving me better access, then guided my hand more firmly against her. Even through the thin cotton, heat radiated from her core.

"Here," she murmured, helping me slide her underwear down. The fabric caught on her foot, and we both laughed as she kicked it free, sending it flying across the room.

When my fingers found bare skin, Kate made a sound I felt in my bones. I explored carefully, mapping this unfamiliar territory, paying attention to her reactions. When I touched a particular spot, her breath caught and her hips arched.

"There?"

"Yes. Just like that."

I continued the motion, her face revealing everything she was feeling as I cataloged each response. Her eyes had fallen closed, her lips parted, small sounds escaping her throat.

"I want to taste you." My voice was full of gravel and want.

Kate's eyes flew open. "You don't have to—"

"I want to. I just need guidance."

She reclined against the pillows. "Start slow. Pay attention to how I respond. And Alex? Stop worrying about doing it right."

I kissed my way down her body, each press of my lips tentative. When I reached her thighs, Kate's hand threaded through my hair, not directing, just present. She made a soft encouraging sound.

"A little lighter," she murmured after my first clumsy attempt. "And maybe... yes, like that."

I adjusted, following her cues. When I found a rhythm that made her hips lift off the bed, pride warred with nervousness.

After several minutes, she tugged gently at my hair. "Come here."

I kissed my way up. Kate pulled me into a deep kiss, unconcerned with tasting herself on my lips.

She reached down to slide my boxers off. They caught on my hips, ending up inside-out and tangled around one ankle.

"Significantly less romantic than I imagined," I said.

Kate laughed. "Real. Better than some choreographed fantasy."

Lying together skin to skin, a new wave of panic struck. "Kate, I need to tell you something."

She waited.

"I've never..." The precise scientific language I relied on failed me. "This would be my first time."

Kate's expression softened. "I kind of figured that out already."

"Does it bother you?"

"That you've waited for something meaningful? No." She took my hands in hers. "It makes me feel special."

I exhaled. "My parents had very strict expectations. No dating until university, and even then, only with approved matches."

"My first time was with my high school boyfriend," Kate offered. "It was fine. Nice, even. But we were together for convenience, not because we deeply connected." She paused. "There was one guy last year. Just once."

Her honesty calmed my nerves a bit, but not nearly enough.

"I'm nervous."

"We don't have to—"

I kissed her. "I want this. With you. I just might need guidance."

Kate smiled. "We'll figure it out together."

She grabbed a scrunchie and placed it on the doorknob outside, then locked the door. The click echoed in the quiet room.

Kate turned to me, then paused. "Wait. Do we need..." She gestured vaguely.

My brain, which had focused entirely on the idea that this beautiful woman was about to have sex with me, suddenly remembered basic biology. "Oh. Yes. I don't have a, uh, I didn't think—"

"I have some." Kate crossed to her desk and opened the bottom drawer. She pulled out an actual bouquet. Made of condoms. Arranged with ribbons.

I stared at it.

"Gemma gave it to me as a joke when I left for college," Kate said, her cheeks pink. "Said I needed to be 'prepared for all life's adventures.' I've been hiding it in my desk for two years."

"There are at least a dozen varieties in there."

"I know. Glow-in-the-dark. Flavored. One claims to heat up, which seems optimistic." She plucked the most normal-looking one from the arrangement. "You think you know someone, and then they give you novelty condoms shaped like roses."

I laughed. "Your best friend gave you a condom bouquet."

"My best friend has no boundaries." Kate returned to the bed, tossing the packet on the nightstand. "But at least she's practical?"

"Gemma gave you glow-in-the-dark condoms and you're calling her practical."

"She also gave me the normal ones." Kate kissed me. "Now stop thinking about my weird friend and focus on me."

When she positioned herself above me, straddling my hips, desire pierced the anxiety. "What if this is over really fast? Or what if I can't... what if my body doesn't cooperate?"

Kate cupped my face. "Alex, breathe. If it's fast, we'll try again later. If something doesn't work right away, we'll figure it out."

"I just want—"

"It already is good," she assured me. "Because it's you and me, and we trust each other."

She reached between us, her hand wrapping around me. My hips gave a jerky thrust.

"Breathe," Kate reminded me, amused and fond.

She positioned herself, sank slowly. My hands tightened on her hips. I couldn't catch my breath. She paused, waiting until I nodded before moving again.

"I don't know," I said when she asked if I was okay. "This is a lot. In a good way. I think."

Kate smiled, staying still. "Take your time."

The process unfolded slower than expected, less smooth. We adjusted angles several times. At one point she shifted and I slipped out entirely.

Kate reached down to guide me again without comment. When she finally took me in completely, we both stilled. Heat. Fullness. Her breath against my neck.

"I'm trying to remember how to form words," I admitted. "And also trying very hard not to move because if I do, this might be over immediately."

She laughed, breathless. "Maybe that's okay for the first time."

Kate moved then, finding her pace. Every shift of her hips sent sensations cascading through me.

"Stay with me," Kate said. "Don't disappear into your head."

"There's a lot to process. Multiple sensory inputs, physical responses, emotional significance. Every nerve ending in my body is firing simultaneously."

She leaned in to kiss me. "Just feel, Alex. Stop analyzing. Just be here with me."

I focused on sensation rather than cataloging it. The heat of her body, the pressure where we joined, the way her breath hitched. My hands explored as she moved—the curve of her spine, the dip of her waist, the soft skin of her thighs.

But coordination was difficult. When Kate moved in one direction, I tried to match her and threw off our rhythm. We crashed together. She sucked in air through her teeth.

"I'm fine," she said before I could ask. "Just... maybe let me lead for now? Until you get a feel for it?"

Frustration built alongside pleasure. Kate adjusted our position. The new angle made my hips jerk.

"That was good," she breathed. "Do that again."

I replicated the motion with questionable success.

"You're learning," Kate said gently. "Your imperfection makes this better. More real."

She pressed her forehead against mine. "Stop trying to perform. Just let it happen. Trust your body to know what to do."

I took a shaky breath, released my need for competent execution. Kate's eyes held mine as we moved together. I stopped thinking about technique and let my body answer hers. When she made soft sounds, I paid attention to what movement had caused them.

The pressure built, coiling low in my belly. Kate tensed above me, her movements becoming less controlled.

"Kate, I'm going to..."

"Let go," she whispered into my hair.

My release was waves of pleasure so intense it bordered on overwhelming. Sounds escaped me, my hands gripping her waist probably too tightly, my body arching up into hers.

When awareness returned, Kate was still above me, breathing hard, her face flushed. She hadn't finished. At least I didn't think she had.

"You didn't—"

"That was beautiful," she said firmly. "Watching you lose control was beyond hot."

I tightened my hands on her waist as she moved. "Wait. Show me. I want to finish what we started."

Kate's expression softened. "Alex—"

"Please. I need to know I can give you this too."

She studied my face, then nodded. She guided my hand between us, showing me the rhythm and pressure she needed.

When she finally tensed and shuddered, her head falling back, satisfaction trickled through my exhaustion. Watching her come apart, knowing I had done that despite my inexperience, felt perhaps more meaningful than my own release.

She collapsed against me, both of us panting, our skin damp with sweat. I held her close, marveling at how perfectly we fit together.

"What are you thinking?" Kate asked after our breathing had slowed, her fingers drawing lazy patterns on my skin.

The question deserved thought. "That I understand now why my parents tried to prevent this before marriage."

Kate propped herself up, concern crossing her features.

"Not because it's wrong," I clarified quickly. "But because it creates a connection that makes decision-making much more complicated. When you've shared this kind of vulnerability with someone, objectivity goes out the window."

Kate laughed, her whole body vibrating against me. "Only you would analyze what just happened in terms of decision-making efficiency."

"Old habits."

"And what does your analysis conclude?"

"That I love you," I said simply. "All our pieces fit together into something whole."

Kate's arms tightened around me. "I love you too. All your pieces. Including the awkward fumbling."

"There was quite a bit of that."

"Made it memorable. This was us."

I took care of the condom and returned to lie beside her, pulling her against me where she fit as if designed for that exact space. Her head rested on my shoulder, her breath warm against my skin.

"What happens now?" she asked after a comfortable silence. "With your parents, I mean."

Reality intruded, though its presence felt more manageable.

"I don't know. This is unknown territory."

"Will they actually cut you off?"

"Possibly. More likely they'll employ strategic pressure first. Limited contact. Disappointed silence. Appeals to filial duty." I paused. "My father mentioned withdrawing my living expenses and the pharmacy residency program I've been working toward."

"That's not a threat. That's emotional blackmail."

"It's one of his principles. Follow-through is the foundation of proper parenting."

Kate was quiet for a long moment. "I don't want to be the reason you lose everything you've worked for."

I turned to face her. "You're not taking anything from me. I'm making a choice. For the first time in my life, I'm actually choosing instead of just following the path laid out for me."

"But what if—"

"No what-ifs," I said firmly. "I want to finish my pharmacy program because I genuinely love the field, even if it was initially my parents' suggestion. I want to maintain a relationship with my parents if possible. I love them, despite everything. But I also want you. You help me see the world differently. You make me brave enough to question, to explore, to choose."

Her smile was like sunrise. She leaned in to press a soft kiss on my lips.

"For the record," she said, "I want you too. The real you, not the perfect son or the brilliant student. The complicated, thoughtful, occasionally frustrating man who somehow makes chemistry tutoring the highlight of my week."

"So we face whatever comes next together?"

"Together," Kate confirmed, settling back against me.

We lapsed into comfortable silence. The consequences of today's confrontation with my parents would come, bringing challenges I couldn't yet predict.

But for the first time in my life, the uncertainty didn't feel like a failure of preparation. It felt like possibility was open-ended and full of potential.

I'd spent my whole life following my parents' plan. The right schools, the right major, the right path. But Kate made me wonder what I'd been optimizing for. Whose version of success I'd been chasing.

And somehow, lying there with Kate Westfield's head on my chest and her hand over my heart, that revelation felt less like disappointment and more like the first step toward becoming myself.

Chapter 19

Kate

The nursing student in me knew the technical term was 'metacarpophalangeal joint.' The artist in me knew it was the place where the hand became something more.

My charcoal-smudged fingers rested against the easel as Professor Vellacott circled our drawing stations. Her silver bangles jingled with each step. The sound had grown as familiar as my own breathing since I started Introduction to Studio Art. Like a timer ticking down. Or counting up. I wasn't sure which.

"Remember." Professor Vellacott stopped near the center of the room. Her crisp British accent made even the mundane sound important. "You're not drawing hands. You're drawing the space around the hands. The negative defines the positive."

The space around things.

My charcoal scratched against paper. The rough texture caught and released. Caught and released. I'd been thinking about negative space a lot. Not just in drawings.

Like the space between who I was supposed to be and who I was becoming.

The space between my family's dreams for my career and the ones forming in my head without permission.

The space between nursing textbooks and sketch pads.

Spaces that once seemed manageable. Narrow enough to straddle. Now they gaped wide enough to fall through.

"Westfield."

Professor Vellacott stood beside my easel, head tilted, silver hair catching the afternoon light through the tall studio windows. Her gaze fixed on my sketch the way a surgeon might examine an X-ray.

My breath hitched.

"Interesting work." She tapped my drawing with one ring-laden finger. The metal clicked against paper. "You have strong instincts. Your understanding of anatomy shows here." Another tap. "The tension in these tendons. How the light falls across the knuckles. You've studied the structure."

I waited. A 'but' always followed.

"But you're still drawing what you know rather than what you see." She tilted her head the other way. "There's a difference between technical accuracy and artistic vision. You'll need to develop both if you want to pursue this seriously."

Heat crept up my neck and cheeks. Other students glanced over. Brixton from the corner station. Marcus by the window. All of them watching to see what the nursing student would say.

"I'm working on it."

"I can see that." Professor Vellacott moved closer. Her perfume smelled like something expensive and European. "Keep pushing yourself beyond the clinical. Learn to trust your eye, not just your brain." She paused with her hand on my easel. "You're in nursing, correct?"

I nodded. My throat closed.

"Interesting combination."

She walked away. Left me standing there with charcoal dust

on my fingers and questions swirling through my head like paint dropped in water. Dispersing. Bleeding into everything.

Six hours later, I stood in Pediatric Clinical Rotation establishing an IV line in a child-sized training mannequin. The silicone arm felt nothing like real skin. Too smooth. Too cool. But my hands knew what to do anyway.

I slid the needle in at the proper angle. Secured the catheter. Checked the flow. The saline dripped at exactly the right rate.

My instructor made a note on her clipboard. The pen scratched across paper. That satisfying sound of approval being documented.

"Excellent technique, Ms. Westfield." She clicked her pen. "Your placement is textbook."

My classmates glanced over. Admiration. Envy. The usual cocktail when your last name carried weight in the medical community. Being a Westfield came with certain expectations. Healthcare was supposed to be in my blood. In my bones. In my destiny.

I should have felt proud. Accomplished. Something.

Instead, my hands felt empty. Like I was holding the tools but missing the reason to use them.

My phone vibrated against my thigh. Three short bursts. Alex, without question. He always checked in between part-time jobs now. Ever since his parents cut him off. Ever since he chose me over their money and their plans and their version of his future.

Guilt ate at me again. Three weeks had passed since he'd lost everything, and I still stood here in scrubs playing the part of nurse.

"Ms. Westfield, would you show the group?" My instructor's

voice pulled me back. "Your venipuncture technique is what everyone should aim for."

I nodded. Moved to the front of the room. My sneakers squeaked against the linoleum. I went through the motions. Showed them the angle. The depth. The way to check for proper catheter placement. My body knew every step of the choreography through some bizarre combination of repetition and genetics.

The daughter of an ER nurse and a physical therapist. Sister to Liam, who was making a name for himself in Boston PT circles. This should have been my calling. My path. My inevitable future.

So why did it feel like I was reciting lines from a script I'd never agreed to memorize?

As I finished to approving nods, that voice in my head whispered again. The one that had been getting louder since January. *Maybe skill wasn't the issue at all.*

"You're catastrophizing." Alex's voice filtered through my phone speaker, calm as always. Like he was explaining a chemical reaction instead of my entire life crisis.

I paced my dorm room. Stepped over sketch pads. Around nursing textbooks. The floor was a minefield of competing futures.

"I know that." I flopped onto my bed. The ceiling above held sketches I'd taped up over the past month. Hands reaching. Faces turning. The Boston skyline catching dawn light. When had I hung up so many? "But there's this guilt about being capable at something and not wanting to do it. Like I'm wasting some genetic healthcare superpower. Like I could save lives but I want to draw pretty pictures instead."

"Kate."

"Meanwhile, I'm in clinical rotations feeling like I'm wearing someone else's scrubs. Just going through the motions." I sighed as I took in my ceiling gallery again. "But in the art studio, I forget to check the time. I forget to eat lunch. Sometimes I even forget my own name, which is concerning from a neurological standpoint."

"That sounds like passion to me."

"Or a concerning inability to regulate my blood sugar." I turned on my side. My mattress springs creaked. "My parents and Liam are all in healthcare. It's the family legacy. Like every Kennedy going into politics or every Walton running Walmart. They've been joking about me being a nurse since I was five and slapping bandages on everyone's scraped knees. I had a little medical kit I carried everywhere. Pretty sure I tried to give my teddy bear a tuberculosis vaccination."

"That doesn't mean it's who you are."

I closed my eyes. Let his words settle. Alex had risked everything to stand up to his parents. He was working three campus jobs to replace lost financial support. He understood family pressure better than anyone I knew.

"I'm going home for spring break next week." The thought formed and exited my mouth in the same nanosecond. Which is how most of my important life decisions happened. Brain to mouth in point-five seconds. "I should tell them. About art. About you. Everything."

Alex didn't respond immediately. He'd be adjusting his glasses right now. Buying himself time to translate emotion into words that made sense.

"Are you sure?" he asked finally.

"No." I laughed shakily. "But I'm tired of hiding the two best parts of my life."

More silence, just the sound of his steady breathing through the line. He'd be sitting at his desk, surrounded by pharmacy textbooks and notes in his precise handwriting.

"I think that's brave," he said.

"Says the guy who defied generations of cultural expectations and lost his parents' support."

"That's different."

"It's not." I sat up and my back cracked in three places. The bottom vertebra, the middle, and the one just below my shoulder blades. "Your parents gave you an impossible choice and you chose what was right for you. My parents have never even had to give me a choice. I've been doing their choosing for them. Assuming I know what they want without ever asking."

"Kate."

"I'm calling my mom. Right now." The words tumbled out fast and sure.

"Wait. Now? It's almost eleven."

"She'll be up. Mom's always doing paperwork for Dad's practice until midnight. Sometimes later." I paced from my window to my desk. Three steps one way. Three steps back. "Besides, if I wait, I'll lose my nerve. Then I'll spend another four months drawing hands in secret like some kind of artistic double agent."

"Do you want me to stay on the line?"

"No. This is something I need to do alone." I took a breath. My lungs expanded. Contracted. Normal respiratory function. "But thank you. For asking."

"Text me after?"

"I promise. Unless I spontaneously combust from familial disappointment, in which case, please water my plants and tell everyone I loved them."

He laughed. Soft and warm. The sound turned my insides to something resembling overcooked oatmeal. "You'll be fine. Stop spiraling and call your mom."

I ended the call and pressed my mom's contact before I could create a pros and cons list. Those things were the death of spontaneity and the birth of eternal procrastination. Besides, I already knew the pros and cons. I had memorized them weeks ago.

She answered on the third ring.

"Katie? Is everything okay?" Concern colored her voice. The late hour plus my history of only calling for good news or actual emergencies. Most college students texted proof of life. I was no exception.

"Everything's fine, Mom." I paused. My mouth dried out. "No. That's not true. I need to tell you something and I've dragged my feet because I thought you'd be disappointed but I can't keep pretending anymore and I just—"

"Honey, slow down." Her voice anchored me—solid, present, mom-shaped. "Take a breath and try again. Whatever it is, it will be okay."

I inhaled and closed my eyes. "I don't think I want to be a nurse anymore."

The silence that followed lasted maybe four seconds but felt like four hours.

"Oh." Another pause. She shifted. Her chair creaked. "Okay. That's a big decision."

Her tone stayed neutral. Too neutral. Like she took someone's blood pressure and didn't want to alert them that it was dangerously high until she confirmed the reading.

My stomach plummeted. "You're disappointed."

"I'm not disappointed, Katie. I'm just..." She sighed. The sound crackled through the phone. "I'm processing. And I'm worried."

"About what?"

"Well, you're halfway through your prerequisites. That's significant time and money to walk away from." Her pen clicked. Open. Closed. Open. Closed. Her nervous habit. "And nursing is stable. Reliable. There will always be jobs. Always be a demand. What are you planning to do instead?"

"Art," I squeaked out. The word was barely audible, like it was apologizing for existing. "I've been taking a studio class and Professor Vellacott thinks I have potential if I keep working at it."

"Art." Mom repeated it, testing its weight. "Katie, I'm not trying to discourage you. But have you thought about what that means? How you'll support yourself? The art world is incredibly competitive. Even talented people struggle to make a living."

"I know that." My voice rose. "I'm not naive."

"I didn't say you were naive. I'm being honest about the realities." Her voice softened in a way that somehow made everything worse. "Your father and I have always encouraged you to follow your interests. But we also want you to take care of yourself. To have security."

"Like you did?" I flung the accusation defensively without thinking about it.

"What's that supposed to mean?"

I took a breath. My heart hammered against my ribs. Too fast. Too hard. "You're an ER nurse, Mom. You work weekends and holidays and night shifts. Is that what you always wanted?"

The silence stretched uncomfortably far. Her pen stopped clicking.

"That's complicated," she said at last.

"How?"

The pause lasted longer. Her breathing carried through the line. Her chair creaked as she changed positions.

"When I was your age, I wanted to be a music therapist." Her voice sounded distant. Like she was looking at something beyond her office walls. Beyond our house. Beyond Waverly Cove itself. "I played piano, if you can believe it. Classical, mostly. Chopin. Debussy. I was pretty darn good."

I sat up straighter and my mattress springs protested. "You never told me that."

"It's not something I think about much anymore."

She'd be sitting at Dad's desk now. Probably surrounded by insurance forms and patient files. The lamp casting yellow light across her tired face.

"My parents thought it was a lovely hobby but not a stable career." Her voice stayed far away. "They encouraged me to do something more practical. Nursing was a solid compromise. Helping people, steady income, always in demand. All true things."

"But?"

"But some nights in nursing school I'd come home to play until my fingers hurt. I'd wonder what my life would have been if I'd been brave enough to try." She paused and I heard her swallow. "I don't regret nursing, Katie. I've helped so many people. I'm good at what I do. But a small part of me always wondered. What if."

I blinked against the sudden tears forming in my eyes. "Mom."

"I haven't played in years." Her voice still carried that distance. "We don't even have a piano anymore. I sold it when Abby was born and we needed to convert the study into a bedroom. I told myself it was practical. That we needed the space. But the truth is I stopped playing long before that. It became easier not to be reminded of what I'd given up."

I didn't know what to say. My whole life. And I'd never known this about her.

"So when you tell me you don't want to be a nurse," she continued, "part of me worries you're making a mistake that will lead to financial struggle and instability. Regret." She took a shaky breath. "But another part of me doesn't want you to wake up down the road and wonder what if. The part that remembers what it feels like to love something so much you lose track of time."

"I'm scared too." I admitted. "I'm terrified I'm throwing away a guaranteed career for something with no guarantees at all."

"That's the thing about passion, though." She let out a small laugh. It sounded sad. Worn. "It doesn't come with guarantees. But neither does safety. I chose the practical path and I still have regrets."

We sat in silence. She was two hundred miles away but somehow right there.

"What do you think I should do?" I asked.

"I think that's a decision only you can make." She paused. "But I'll support you either way. Even if I'm worried. Even if I'm scared for you. That's what parents do. We worry and support you at the same time. Sometimes in the same breath."

"What about Dad?"

"Your father will share my concerns about stability. He's practical like that. Built a whole practice on it." She paused. "But he loves you, Katie. We both do. That doesn't change based on your major."

That sounded like Dad. Concern first. Feelings second. Support always.

"There's something else." My heart pounded faster. "I'm seeing someone. Alex Chen. He's in pharmacy school."

"The tutoring friend you helped over Christmas? The maple candy guy?"

"Yeah. It's more than that now. It's become serious."

"Okay." Her voice had warmed. Switched to mom-hearing-about-a-boy mode. "Tell me about him."

So I did. I told her about Alex's steadiness. His terrible dad jokes that made me groan and laugh at the same time. The way he viewed the world as an equation he could solve with patience and precision. I told her about his parents' disapproval. Their ultimatum. His lost financial support. The pharmacy residency opportunity that had evaporated because he wouldn't end things with me.

"He stood up to his family for you?" Mom asked when I finished.

"And for himself." I picked at a loose thread on my comforter. "For the right to make his own choices."

"He sounds brave."

"He is."

"Then I'd like to meet him. Bring him home for spring break if he's willing to face the Westfield interrogation."

I laughed. Tension eased from my shoulders. "It won't be too bad?"

"Oh, it'll be terrible." The smile in her voice was audible. "Your father will ask about his intentions and his five-year plan. Liam will pull up his academic record somehow. Diane will feed him until he can't move and Sophie will ask invasive questions about his family tree. Abby will probably interrogate him about his star sign. Normal Westfield stuff."

"You're not helping."

"But we'll love him because you love him. That's how this works." She paused. "Katie, I can't promise not to worry about your career choice. I will worry. Probably a lot. Probably too much. But I don't want you living with the what-ifs that I have. If art makes you forget to eat, forget your own name, that means something."

"Even if it's not practical?"

"Especially if it's not practical. Practical is overrated." There was a definite smile in her voice now. "Though I'd feel better if you at least minored in something with clearer job prospects. Hedge your bets a little."

"I can do that." The pressure behind my eyes eased, and colors looked brighter somehow. "Thank you, Mom. For telling me about the piano."

"Thank you for being brave enough to tell me the truth instead of switching majors and hoping we wouldn't notice."

"I considered that strategy."

"I know you did. You're my daughter, after all." Affection infused her words. "Now go call that boy of yours and tell him he's invited to Maine. Fair warning, if you think meeting his parents was tough, wait until he meets your siblings. Nothing but the best for their little sister."

After we hung up, I didn't move. Just lay there with my

sketches overhead and nursing textbooks digging into my side. The conversation hadn't gone how I'd expected. Mom was worried. Scared for me. But she'd also told me about a piano I'd never known existed. About what-ifs that still hurt after decades. She didn't want me collecting my own.

I reached for my phone and texted Alex.

KATE

That was harder than I thought. She's worried. But she told me something she's never told anyone. And you're officially invited for spring break. Prepare yourself.

ALEX

Proud of you. And I've already survived my parents. How bad can yours be?

I laughed, and the tight band around my ribs finally loosened. My sketchbook lay open on the floor where I'd dropped it earlier. I picked it up and turned to a blank page, then started drawing without thinking.

My mother's hands curved over piano keys she'd never let me see her play.

The charcoal moved. My hands knew what to do.

Chapter 20

Alex

I'd never been greeted by so many people at once.

The Westfield family home was a white colonial on Shoreline Road with black shutters and a front porch that wrapped around two sides. Three cars filled the driveway. Two more lined the curb. Kate had warned me her family was large, but she hadn't mentioned they all just decided to come home for Spring break. I'm sure it was just a coincidence that Kate happened to be bringing her boyfriend home.

The front door opened before we even reached it.

"You must be Alex." A tall man with broad shoulders extended his hand. Silver hair, lines around his Westfield-brown eyes, and a grip firm enough to feel like a test. "I'm Kate's dad, Robert. Everyone calls me Bob. Welcome to Waverly Cove."

I shook his hand. Matched his pressure. Released at the socially appropriate three-second mark.

"Thank you for having me."

A woman appeared beside Bob. Same warm eyes as Kate. Same chaotic brunette bun. Laugh lines bracketing her wide smile. "I'm Jo, Kate's mom."

Jo bypassed the handshake entirely and pulled me into a tight hug.

My shoulders locked. Every muscle from my neck to my lower back contracted like I'd been dropped in ice water. Physical contact with strangers ranked somewhere between public speaking and dental procedures on my comfort scale. My mother reserved hugs for Chinese New Year and report cards with perfect marks.

Jo stepped back, still smiling. If she felt my full-body recoil, she gave no indication.

"We've heard so much about you," she gushed. "It's wonderful to finally meet you."

"Thank you for having me," I repeated, clinging to the script of social niceties that served as my emergency protocol for unexpected human contact.

"Come in, come in." Bob ushered us inside. The foyer smelled like bread baking and something savory. "Kate can show you where to stash your bag."

Kate's fingers interlaced with mine. Her palm was warm. Mine was clammy. I'd been cataloging potential parental objections for the entire four-hour bus ride from Boston. Pharmacy student instead of doctor. Family rebel who'd defied his parents. Academic distraction for their daughter. I'd revised my defense arguments six times by Portsmouth.

We'd taken maybe five steps into the house when a woman emerged from the kitchen wearing a flour-dusted apron. Pregnant. Third trimester based on the size and position of her abdomen. Kate had warned me, but seeing it in person made the data more concrete.

"You're here!" The woman's delight seemed genuine. Excessive, but genuine. "I'm Diane. James's wife." She gestured to a tall man who appeared behind her. He shared Kate's dark hair and angular features. "That's James, Kate's oldest brother. And this little one," she turned to reveal a small girl hiding behind her legs, "is Rosie. And this one," she rested a hand on her rounded stomach, "doesn't have a name yet, but she's making her presence known. Pretty sure she's going to be one heck of a soccer player, or maybe a Rockette."

The small girl studied me for a long moment with a skeptical expression. Then she retreated further behind her mother's legs.

"She's shy with new people," Diane explained.

"Wise to be cautious of strange men, Miss Rosie," I said. "I know I am."

James laughed, surprised but genuine.

"He speaks," James said, the corner of his mouth lifting. "Kate warned us you weren't much of a talker."

"Only until he's comfortable," Kate admitted. "Then he has opinions on everything."

More people appeared. I catalogued them as they were introduced. Sophie, Kate's sister. Taylor, Sophie's fiancée. Abby, the youngest sister. Liam I'd already met in Boston. Each introduction was free from the assessment criteria I'd prepared for. No one asked about my GPA. My career trajectory. My family's financial status. The absence of evaluation left me disoriented, like conducting an experiment without a control group.

Kate tugged me through the crowd. "Let me show you where we'll be staying."

She led me upstairs. Thirteen steps. The banister was smooth under my palm, worn from years of hands sliding along the wood. At the top, a hallway extended in both directions. Family photos covered the walls in mismatched frames. Kate turned left and opened a door on the right.

"This used to be Liam's room," she explained. "Now it's the official guest room."

The room ran small. Blue walls. White trim. A patchwork quilt on the bed, handmade from the look of the uneven stitching.

One window overlooking the backyard. A wooden dresser with brass pulls. A lamp on the nightstand with a ceramic lighthouse base.

I set my bag down like it contained volatile compounds.

"Your family is not what I expected."

Kate tilted her head. "What did you expect?"

"Interrogation. Background checks." I ran a hand through my hair and immediately regretted the resulting disorder. "My parents would have conducted a thorough investigation by now. Credit check. Analysis of long-term earning potential. Probably contacted my undergraduate references."

Kate laughed and stepped closer. Her shampoo's scent comforted me. "They trust me. And they know how important you are to me."

Trust without verification. Acceptance without qualification. Foreign concepts that I couldn't quite process yet.

"Dinner's in an hour," Kate said. "Want a quick tour before everyone bombards you with conversation?"

I nodded. Kate led me back downstairs, fingers still interlaced with mine. She pointed out family photos as we walked and explained inside jokes I didn't understand yet. Kate as a gap-toothed child holding a fish half her size. The five Westfield siblings crowded onto a dock, sun-browned and grinning. James and Diane's wedding. Sophie and Taylor's engagement. A slightly younger Jo and Bob holding an infant I assumed was Rosie.

My parents curated photos. Formal portraits in matching frames. The Westfield walls held candid moments in frames made from driftwood and painted macaroni. Each one held a story that Kate narrated with obvious affection.

"This is from the summer I broke my arm falling off the lighthouse trail." She pointed to a photo of herself with a bright blue cast covered in signatures. "Dad was so calm. Mom freaked out, which never happens because she's an ER nurse."

"You broke your arm falling off a cliff?"

"I was twelve and showing off." She laughed. "But the lighthouse trail has guardrails now." For some reason, she looked proud about that.

The tour ended in the kitchen. Jo was directing traffic with the ease of an ER nurse running a trauma bay. Diane kneaded bread dough at the counter. Her hands pressed and folded. Pressed and folded. The rhythm was meditative. Abby chopped vegetables at the island. Taylor and Sophie set the table, moving in synchronized patterns that suggested years of practice.

"Alex, do you cook?" Jo asked.

"Yes. My parents own a restaurant. I grew up in the kitchen."

"Perfect." Jo handed me a knife and gestured to a pile of potatoes on the cutting board. "You're on potato duty."

My breathing eased for the first time since we'd arrived.

I picked up the knife. Tested the weight. Good balance. Sharpened enough. I started peeling. My knife found a rhythm. Uniform cuts. Consistent thickness. Conversations flowed around me, but I didn't have to participate. Just had to process potatoes into even pieces suitable for roasting.

No one commented on my technique. No one corrected my work. Kate moved between helping her mother and checking on me. Her hand would brush my shoulder as she passed. A casual touch that sent small electric currents through my nervous system.

At one point, Diane paused her bread kneading. One hand found her lower back. The other moved to her belly where movement rippled beneath her shirt.

"You okay?" James asked immediately.

"Just the usual." Diane shifted her weight. "Baby's dancing on my sciatic nerve."

"Let me finish the bread." Sophie washed her hands. Soap and water. Proper technique. "You should sit."

"I'm fine." But Diane let herself be guided to a chair at the table anyway.

"The bakery, a toddler, and growing another human," Jo said. Matter-of-fact but affectionate. "The doctor says everything's perfect. You just need to pace yourself."

"I know, I know." Diane settled into the chair with visible relief.

The immediate support registered. The absence of criticism. The way they cared without diminishing Diane's autonomy. Data points that contradicted everything I knew about family dynamics.

Dinner was chaos.

Multiple conversations happening simultaneously. Mismatched plates passed in random patterns. People reaching across each other for serving dishes without ceremony or apology. At The Golden Dragon, meals followed strict protocols. Designated serving order. Appropriate topics curated for mealtime discussion. Even at home, dinner was orderly. Quiet.

This was neither.

Kate's family debated local politics. Shared hospital stories my parents would never discuss in mixed company. Liam imitated their grandmother's accent. Diane threw a roll at him. It bounced off his shoulder and landed in his water glass. Laughter erupted. Jo snuck food onto Bob's plate while correcting everyone's medical terminology.

I answered direct questions. Mostly I observed. Strategies emerged. Patterns clarified.

"So, Alex." Bob's voice cut through a momentary lull in the chaos. "Kate tells us you're finishing your pharmacy program soon."

I nodded, braced for the interrogation I'd been expecting since we arrived.

"That's impressive," Bob continued. "Pharmacy's a solid field. Jo's cousin Mark is a pharmacist down in Portland."

"And he makes a killer haddock chowder," Jo added. "More medicinal than anything he dispenses at the hospital. That's his real claim to fame."

I waited for the follow-up questions. Career trajectory. Salary expectations. Whether pharmacy was competitive enough compared to medicine. They didn't come.

"How are you handling the financial situation?" Liam asked. "Kate mentioned your parents withdrew support."

Direct. Blunt. My family would have considered the question rude. But Liam's tone held no judgment. Just curiosity.

"I applied for emergency financial aid," I answered, setting my fork down. "And I've picked up two jobs on campus in addition to my tutoring. Library circulation desk and assisting in the lab. It should be enough to finish the semester."

Bob nodded. "Smart thinking. And after graduation?"

"I'm applying for several residency programs. Melrose Wakefield is my top choice." I paused as I chose honesty over pride. "It's not as prestigious as the one my father arranged. But it would be a solid program."

"I hear that Melrose has an excellent program," Jo said. "Coastal Memorial has a robust pharmacy department, too, and I'd be happy to put in a good word there."

"Thank you." I waited for the critique. The subtle indicators that my revised plans were inadequate. Instead, Bob simply nodded.

"You've landed on your feet. That's impressive."

The table fell silent for a moment. Then Bob glanced at Kate with a curious look on his face.

"Kate mentioned she's thinking about switching to art."

Kate's hand found mine under the table.

"She has genuine talent," I said carefully. "Her spatial

reasoning is exceptional. The way she visualizes three-dimensional structures—"

"Oh, we know she's talented." Bob interrupted, but not unkindly. "We've been watching her turn every notebook into an art project since middle school." He took a breath. His fingers drummed once against the table. "I just want to make sure she's thought it through. The practical side of things."

Kate stiffened beside me. "Daddy—"

"I'm not saying don't do it." Bob held up a hand. "I'm saying I've seen plenty of talented people struggle to make a living. Health insurance. Retirement planning. Steady income. Those things matter." He shifted his focus to Kate. "You know we'll support whatever you choose. But I'd be lying if I said I wasn't worried about the financial reality."

Here was the parental concern I'd expected for myself. Redirected toward Kate instead.

"That's fair," Kate said finally. "I'm worried about that too."

"But you're still going to do it?" Bob asked.

"I think I have to. I can't spend the rest of my life wondering *what if*." Kate shot a glance at Joanna, who simply smiled knowingly at her daughter.

Bob studied his daughter for a long while. Then he nodded. "Then we'll figure it out. Together." He glanced at me with the hint of a smile. "At least you're dating someone who can get you discounted ibuprofen for all those starving artist headaches."

Scattered laughter broke the tension. Jo reached over and squeezed Bob's hand. Some unspoken understanding passed between them. The conversation moved on, but Kate's grip on my hand remained tight for several more minutes.

Dessert followed. A picture-perfect apple pie that Diane had somehow made between everything else she managed. The family lingered at the table. Coffee appeared. Tea. Conversations splintered into smaller groups. Diane excused herself to take Rosie to the bathroom. Jo and Bob disappeared into the kitchen with armfuls of dishes despite multiple offers to help.

"Game night," Abby announced to the room. "Living room. Five minutes. No excuses."

Kate caught my expression. "It's tradition," she explained. "Every time the family's together. Someone always suggests cards."

"Someone being Abby," Liam clarified as he pushed back from the table. "Every single time."

"Because I always win," Abby called, already heading toward the living room.

By the time Kate and I made it to the living room, cards were already spread across the coffee table. The family arranged themselves on couches and chairs, still holding coffee cups and dessert plates.

"Want to join?" Kate asked me. "Fair warning, Abby cheats."

"I count cards," Abby corrected without looking up from her shuffling. "It's not cheating if it's skill. Not my fault the rest of you play based on vibes."

"I'd like to watch first," I said.

Kate nodded and led me to the couch beside Liam, who explained the game. Something involving traded cards and point calculations. Two rounds passed. Strategies emerged. Interaction patterns clarified. No one threw cards in frustration. No one accused others of playing incorrectly. Even when Bob won the second round triumphantly, the complaints from the others held no real resentment.

During the third round, Jo declared herself "too tired for this nonsense" and headed upstairs with Bob. Diane followed shortly after, carrying a drowsy Rosie on her hip. James disappeared into the kitchen.

"Finally," Abby said, shuffling the deck. "Now we can play for real stakes."

"We're not playing poker again," Sophie said firmly. "You cleaned us all out last Christmas."

"That's because you all telegraph your hands." Her shuffle showed practice. Skill. "Taylor literally bites her lip when she's bluffing."

"I do not." Taylor bit her lip.

James pointed from the kitchen doorway. "You just did it."

The laughter grew easier now. Less performative. I'd been observing for hours. James spoke rarely but with intention. Liam diffused tension before it escalated. Sophie and Taylor communicated in half-sentences. Abby challenged every rule. Kate bridged all of them, translating between personalities with the fluency of a middle child.

"Alex's turn to deal," Kate announced. She slid the deck toward me.

I accepted it. The deck of cards showed wear. Soft edges. The weight felt comfortable in my hands.

"What are we playing?"

"Hearts," Liam said. "Unless you know something better."

I considered this. "I know a variation. Chemistry Hearts. Similar rules, but with penalty modifications based on suit sequences."

"Nerd alert." Abby grinned. "I'm in. Explain."

As I outlined the rules, I realized that they weren't just tolerating my participation anymore. They leaned forward. Asked clarifying questions. Showed genuine interest. Kate's hand found my thigh under the table. Squeezed once, and I shivered.

We played three rounds. Abby won the first through aggressive play that reminded me of Kate's impulsiveness. James won the second by staying so quiet everyone forgot to watch his hand. The third round devolved into chaos when Taylor and Sophie got into a heated debate.

"You said you didn't have any hearts left!" Sophie accused.

"I said I didn't have many hearts left," Taylor corrected. "Many is subjective."

"Many is not subjective. Many is—" Sophie turned to me. "Alex, back me up here. Many is a quantifiable term."

Trapped between scientific accuracy and relationship preservation.

"Many is technically subjective without defined parameters," I said carefully. "However, in context, it implies—"

"He's saying I'm right," Taylor interrupted.

"He's saying you're both wrong," James translated. The corner of his mouth twitched. "Diplomatically."

Kate laughed a full belly laugh, head tipping back. "Welcome to Westfield family game night, Alex. Where the rules are made up and the points don't matter because someone always argues about semantics until we give up and eat cookies instead."

"We have cookies?" Abby asked, abandoning her hand immediately.

"Diane made snickerdoodles before you got here," Liam said. "They're in the owl jar."

The migration to the kitchen was immediate. I hung back, still processing the rapid social dynamics. But Kate tugged me along.

"Come on. If you don't move fast, Abby eats them all."

"I have a high metabolism," Abby called. Already extracting cookies from a ceramic owl-shaped jar. "And I'm still growing."

"You haven't grown in three years," Sophie said.

"Spiritually. Emotionally. In wisdom."

"In audacity," Liam corrected. He took two cookies and handed one to me without asking if I wanted it.

We arranged ourselves around the kitchen island. Perched on stools. Leaned against counters. Kate hopped up to sit on the counter itself and pulled me to stand between her knees. Her casual physical affection still caught me off guard, but I was learning to accept it rather than analyze it.

"So Alex." Sophie's tone suggested an agenda. "Kate mentioned you're working multiple jobs now. That's got to be exhausting."

"It's manageable."

"Translation: it sucks but he's too proud to admit it." Kate played with my collar. Warmth from her fingers spread against my collarbone.

"Must be hard," James offered. "Doing it without family support."

I took a breath and chose honesty over deflection. "It's different from what I expected."

"Different how?" Sophie asked. Her directness reminded me of Kate but with a more contemplative quality.

"More freedom." I worked through the thought slowly. "More consequences, but also more choice. I spent my whole life following a predetermined path. Now I'm improvising."

"And how's that working out for you?" Taylor asked. Genuine curiosity in her voice.

I locked eyes with Kate and found her already studying me. Those expressive brown eyes saw more than I sometimes wanted to reveal.

"It's scary."

"That's growth," Sophie said. "Scary usually means you're doing something right."

"Or something monumentally stupid," Abby added. "But sometimes those are the same thing."

"Profound," Liam said dryly. "You should write fortune cookies."

"I would write the best fortune cookies. 'Your lucky numbers are: none. Life is chaos. Have a nice day.'"

The inclusive laughter warmed me. I relaxed further. The

tension I'd been carrying since Boston dissipated like precipitate in solution.

"Okay, real talk though." Abby pointed her half-eaten cookie at me. "You're good for Kate. She's been different since she met you. In a good way."

"Abby—" Kate's cheeks flushed.

"What? I'm being nice. I can be nice."

"It's true," Sophie agreed. "You're happier. More yourself."

Kate's fingers tightened in my shirt. "That's not just because of Alex—"

"It's partly because of Alex," Liam said. "Nothing wrong with that. Relationships do that. Help you figure out who you actually are."

James nodded. His silent validation somehow carried more weight than any of the lengthy speeches.

"Well." Taylor raised her glass of milk. "To Alex. For being the chemistry nerd who accidentally helped Katie find art."

"To Alex," the others echoed.

I stood there surrounded by Kate's siblings, accepting their toast with a mixture of discomfort and something unfamiliar. Kate leaned her forehead against mine and pitched her voice low.

"Told you they'd like you."

Later, after Sophie and Taylor had retreated to their room and Abby had disappeared upstairs, I stood alone in the kitchen with James and Liam. Kate had gone to find her phone charger and promised to return soon.

The kitchen had gone quiet. Just the hum of the refrigerator. The tick of a clock somewhere. James leaned against the counter. Liam sat at the island.

"So," Liam began. He exchanged a glance with James. "We wanted to have a talk."

My threat-detection system activated. I ran through every interaction I'd had with Kate since arriving. Had I violated some unspoken Westfield family code? Overlooked a Maine-specific relationship protocol?

"This is the part where we're supposed to warn you about breaking our little sister's heart," James said.

"Tell you we know how to dispose of a body where it'll never be found," Liam added. Cheerfully. "That sort of thing."

My mouth was a desert. "I see."

"The problem is," James continued, "Kate would absolutely murder us if she knew we were doing this."

"Slowly," Liam agreed. "With extreme prejudice."

"And then lecture our corpses about female autonomy and the problematic nature of treating women as property to be defended by male relatives."

I recalibrated my understanding. "So this isn't actually a threatening conversation?"

"Oh no, it absolutely is," Liam said. Grinning now. "We're just acknowledging the inherent absurdity of the ritual while participating in it anyway."

"Meta-threatening," James clarified. "Very postmodern."

I relaxed slightly and chose my next words carefully. "I appreciate your commitment to tradition while maintaining self-awareness about its problematic aspects."

Both brothers barked a genuine laugh.

"He really talks like that all the time," Liam said to James. "I thought Kate was exaggerating."

"Look, Alex." James set his coffee mug down. The ceramic clicked against granite. "The truth is, we haven't seen Kate this happy in maybe ever. Whatever you're doing, it's working."

"She's always been trying to please everyone," Liam added. His tone was more serious now. "Katie chose nursing because it was the family thing. Even though anyone with eyes could see she was always drawing instead of studying. You're the first person who seems to actually care what she wants instead of what she thinks everyone else wants from her."

"I didn't do anything special." I meant it. "I just paid attention to what came naturally to her."

The brothers exchanged another look. Years of brotherhood compressed in one glance.

"That is special," James stressed. "Not every guy would do that."

"So consider this less of a threat and more of a thank you," Liam concluded. "With maybe just a tiny threat sprinkled in for tradition's sake."

"I would expect nothing less."

"And hey." James stood. "When my second daughter arrives this summer, we're having a gathering. Small. Just family. You should come back for it."

The assumption of my continued presence caught me off guard. My parents calculated social invitations like business transactions. Here, they offered them with the same casual ease as passing salt.

"I'd like that."

"Good." James clapped my shoulder. The pressure was intentional. Conveyed masculine approval without causing discomfort. "Because Kate's already promised to help Diane with the baby for a week, and she'll be unbearable if you're not here too."

Kate appeared in the doorway. "Talking about me?"

"Always," Liam said. "It's our favorite hobby."

"How long have you been standing there?" I asked.

"Long enough to know I need to rescue you." Kate held out her hand. "Come on. Before they start showing you my baby pictures."

"We were getting to those next," Liam confirmed.

"There's one where she tried to give herself a tattoo with permanent marker," James added. "Age three. Very artistic."

"Traitors." But Kate was smiling. She tugged me toward the door. "Ignore them. They peaked in high school."

"We absolutely did not," Liam called after us.

"Debatable," James said to him.

Upstairs, Kate shook her head as we entered the guest room. "I apologize for my brothers. They think they're funny."

"They are, though."

"Don't encourage them." She started changing for bed. "What did they actually say?"

"That they'd murder me if I hurt you. But they were very self-aware about it."

"Oh, very meta."

"Exactly."

Kate laughed, climbing into bed. "That's very them. Did they at least approve?"

"I think so. It's hard to tell with the layers of irony."

"Welcome to my family." She patted the space beside her. "Come on. Tomorrow's another day of Westfield chaos. You'll need sleep to survive it."

I got ready for bed and slid under the quilt beside her. Kate immediately curled into my side, fitting there like she'd always belonged.

"Alex?"

"Mm?"

"You did good today."

"I mostly just stood there."

"Exactly. Perfect execution." Her voice carried drowsiness. "Night."

"Goodnight."

She fell asleep within minutes. I lay there a bit longer, listening to the house. The wind outside. The distant creak of settling wood. The sound of Kate's breathing beside me.

Tomorrow would bring more of this. More family. More noise. More overwhelming acceptance.

I was almost looking forward to it.

Chapter 21

Alex

On the second day of our visit to Waverly Cove, Kate suggested we walk into town. The mid-March air promised eventual warmth, but snow still clung to shadowed corners where the sun hadn't reached. Kate had borrowed one of Liam's old scarves for me. Thick wool, smelling faintly of cedar and salt air. She wore her father's coat, so big on her that she had to roll the sleeves up twice.

"Ready?" Her breath was visible in the cold.

I nodded, following her out the front door.

The Westfield house sat quiet behind us. Everyone was sleeping in after the late night, even Rosie, who James had warned usually woke before dawn. The streets were empty except for a neighbor clearing their driveway, the scrape of shovel on pavement the only sound besides our footsteps.

Kate pointed out landmarks as we walked. The path to the eastern headland with its lighthouse, currently closed for the season. The turnoff to what she called "the secret beach," only accessible at low tide. We slowed as we approached a cottage with blue shutters and a front porch swing wrapped in plastic for winter.

"That's where we spent most summers," Kate said, pausing at the gate. "Gemma's grandmother would make us sandwiches and we'd disappear until dinner. Mom used to joke that she should just move my bed there. I only got Gemma for summers and holidays. I never wanted to miss a minute with her."

A younger Kate took shape in my mind. Sun-browned and wild-haired, running between the two houses like she owned the whole town. It wasn't difficult to picture.

Kate touched the gate without opening it, studying the porch swing. "See that? Her grandmother has it painted every spring. Always the exact same shade of blue because Gemma can't handle any variation. Even at eight, she was like that. Everything had to be exactly right." Her smile turned fond but tinged with concern.

"You worry about her," I observed.

"She worries about everything being perfect. I worry about her worrying." Kate's hand dropped from the gate. "Sometimes I think she's going to exhaust herself trying to control things she can't actually control."

She turned away from the cottage and we continued walking. The town itself was small enough to hold in my palm. Weathered storefronts with salt-worn paint lined the main street, buildings that had withstood decades of New England winters. Everything stood closed this early on a Sunday morning, but Kate narrated anyway. The hardware store where she'd bought her first toolbox. The bookshop that sold only local Maine authors. The diner where the high school kids congregated after football games.

"And this is Diane's bakery." Kate stopped in front of a sign that read The Daily Knead. Display cases and a chalkboard menu were visible through the dark windows. "Best cinnamon rolls on the coast. She makes them with cardamom."

"Cardamom?"

"I know. Sounds weird. But it works." Kate pressed her hands against the glass, peering inside. "I'm sure she'll make some for breakfast this morning. Fair warning. They're addictive."

We walked further down the street. A maritime supply shop that appeared to double as a fishing tackle store. A small gallery with watercolors in the window of seascapes and lighthouses, the kind tourists bought.

"Nan's paintings used to be in there," Kate said, following my gaze. "Before she got too old to keep up with the gallery's consignment schedule. Now she just paints for herself."

"Nan?"

"Gemma's grandmother." Kate's expression softened. "I think a lot of my interest in art probably comes from all the time I've spent at her house."

We turned down a side street toward the water. The harbor opened up before us with boats covered in blue tarps, docks stretching into gray water, and the smell of salt and seaweed strong enough to taste.

Kate led me to a small dock extending into the harbor. The wood had weathered smooth, the railing cold under my palms. Water lapped against the pilings with a rhythm that reminded me of breathing. Steady. Inevitable.

"What do you think?" Kate asked, her breath visible in the cooling air.

"It's beautiful." I meant it. "I see why you love it here."

"It's more than just the place." Kate leaned against the railing, looking out over the water. "It's the people. Everyone knows everyone, but not in a suffocating way. It's—"

"A community," I supplied. "An actual functioning one."

Kate nodded. "Exactly. When James and Diane got married, the whole town helped with the wedding. When Gemma's grandmother broke her hip last year, there was a rotation of people bringing meals and checking on her. It's just how things work here."

The relationships my parents maintained sprung to mind. Carefully bounded. Transactional. The fish vendor who saved the best catch for the restaurant. The family who supplied specialty ingredients. Mutual benefit rather than unconditional support.

"Your family is very different from mine," I mused quietly.

Kate's hand found mine on the railing. Our fingers interlaced, her palm warm despite the cold. "Different doesn't mean better."

But in some ways, it did. The absence of performance metrics. The lack of conditions on belonging. The simple acceptance of me as I was, not as someone I should be.

We stood there for a while, watching boats bob on their moorings. The sun climbed higher, turning the water from gray to silver to something almost blue. A few gulls circled overhead, their cries harsh and lonely.

"We should head back," Kate said eventually. "Before they send a search party."

The walk back was quieter. My hands were numb despite my pockets. My nose felt frozen. But the tension inside me had eased during the walk. The rhythm of footsteps. The quiet moments between Kate's stories. The simplicity of just existing beside her without feeling like our relationship was something to hide.

When we reached the house, warmth and noise spilled out as Kate opened the door. Voices from the kitchen. The smell of coffee and something baking. Laughter.

"There you are," Jo called from the kitchen. "Perfect timing. Diane just popped cinnamon rolls in the oven."

"Told you," Kate whispered, grinning.

The kitchen overflowed with people again. James sat at the

table with Rosie on his lap, reading her a book about sea animals. Diane stood at the counter whipping up icing. Sophie and Taylor shared a chair, Taylor's arm around Sophie's shoulders. Bob fumbled with the coffee maker, hair still mussed from sleep.

"Good walk?" Bob asked, handing me a mug without asking if I wanted one.

"Yes. Thank you."

"Kate give you the whole tour? Lighthouse, secret beach, Gemma's house, the dock?"

"All of it," Kate confirmed. She grabbed her own mug, adding cream and sugar until it was nearly white.

"Did she tell you about the time she fell off that dock?" Liam asked, appearing in the doorway.

"I didn't fall. I was pushed."

"By who?"

"By you, actually."

"Lies and slander." But Liam was grinning. "Though in my defense, Sophie did dare me to."

The family settled into breakfast with the same chaotic energy as dinner. Overlapping conversations. Food passed without ceremony. Rosie managed to get syrup in her hair. James quietly cleaned it up while Diane cut her cinnamon roll into smaller pieces.

I sat between Kate and Liam, answering questions occasionally but mostly just observing. The way Bob's hand found Jo's shoulder as he passed behind her chair. How Sophie and Taylor communicated in shared glances. The ease with which this family existed together, no performance required.

After breakfast, the family scattered. James disappeared into the workshop with his dad. Sophie and Taylor headed out for a walk around the harbor. Diane gathered a still-sleepy Rosie and their things. "We should get this one home for a proper nap," she said to James. "Before she gets too wound up."

"I'll walk you out," James said, already reaching for Rosie's coat.

Liam retreated to the den with his laptop to study.

"I'm going to sketch a bit," Kate said, kissing my cheek. "There's this corner in the living room with perfect light. You okay on your own for a while?"

"I'll survive."

She squeezed my hand once, then headed for the living room, sketchbook already in hand.

I helped Jo clear the table. Brought dishes to the sink. Started loading the dishwasher with the methodical precision I'd learned in my parents' restaurant.

"You don't have to do that," Jo said, but she didn't stop me.

"I don't mind."

We worked in comfortable silence. Jo washing serving dishes. Me drying. The kitchen windows showed bare trees, brown grass, patches of snow clinging to shadows.

"Alex?" Jo's voice was careful. "Can I ask you something?"

My shoulders tensed automatically. "Of course."

"How are you holding up? With everything that happened with your parents?"

The question caught me off guard. "I'm managing," I said automatically.

Jo set down the pan she'd been washing and turned to face me fully. "That's what Kate says too. 'I'm managing.' 'It's fine.' But managing isn't the same as being okay."

I set the dish towel down and focused on my hands instead of her face. "It's... complicated."

"Most important things are."

The kitchen had gone quiet except for water dripping from the faucet. Somewhere in the house, Kate was sketching. James was building boat models with Bob. Life continued around us while I stood there trying to find words for feelings I hadn't fully processed myself.

"I know logically that what they did was wrong," I said finally. "That choosing Kate was the right decision." I paused before forcing myself to continue. "But there's still this part of me that wants to call them. To tell them about your family. About how James taught me about boat motors yesterday and Kate showed me the town this morning. About how Bob listened to Kate when she talked about switching to art." I swallowed hard around the wave of emotion. "They'd never understand it," I continued. "But I still want to tell them. I keep thinking about things I want to share with them, and then remembering that I can't. That they chose their conditions over me."

Jo was quiet for a long moment. When she spoke, her voice was soft. "That sounds like grief."

"They're not dead."

"No. But you're grieving what you thought you had. What you wanted them to be." She dried her hands on a towel, then leaned casually on the counter. "And that's allowed, Alex. You don't have to pretend it doesn't hurt."

My defenses cracked open just enough to let the truth out. "It's strange," I said, voice rough. "To be welcomed so easily here. After everything. Your family doesn't know me. You've known me for three days. But you treat me like I belong. Like there's no question about it."

"That's because there isn't," Jo said simply. "You make Kate happy. That's enough for us."

"But what if I'm not—" I stopped and gathered my thoughts. "What if I can't be what she needs? What if my parents were right and I'm too focused on my own goals to be good for her?"

"Are you too focused on your own goals?"

Recent months flashed through my mind. Changing my plans to accommodate Kate's schedule. Defending her choice to switch majors. Coming here despite my discomfort with large family gatherings.

"No."

"Then your parents were wrong." Jo's voice was firm now. "Love isn't about abandoning yourself for someone else. It's about growing together. Making room for each other without erasing who you are." She paused. "Kate's father and I don't always agree on things. I wanted the kids to stay closer to home for college. He thought they should experience the world. But we figured it out. We made room for both of us to be right."

"My parents have expectations," I said. "To marry someone they chose. To live according to their plan."

"And that isn't what you want."

"No."

"Then you made the right choice." Jo stepped closer and rested her hand on my arm. A simple gesture that communicated warmth and acceptance. "It's okay to miss them anyway. To wish they were different. To grieve for the relationship you had before."

The words hit a buried place. What I'd been trying to keep locked away since December.

"I miss having parents who fit the role," I said quietly. "Even if they never actually did."

"I know." Jo's eyes were warm and understanding in a way that was almost hard to swallow. "And I'm so sorry you had to make that choice. But for what it's worth? You're always welcome here. Family doesn't end with blood."

I nodded. Couldn't quite speak.

Jo squeezed my arm once, then turned back to the dishes to give me space to collect myself. To breathe through whatever I was feeling as I processed our discussion.

"Thank you," I managed after a minute.

"Nothing to thank me for." She handed me another plate to dry. "Just telling the truth."

We finished the dishes in silence. Slowly, I was learning what family could look like when it worked.

When we were done, Jo dried her hands and turned to me with a small smile. "Now, I believe the boys wanted to show you the workshop. Fair warning—James will talk your ear off about wood grains if you let him."

"I don't mind."

"Good. Because he's been excited about having someone new to show off to all week."

She patted my shoulder as she left the kitchen. And I stood there for a moment, letting the conversation settle. Letting myself acknowledge what I'd been avoiding.

Grief didn't need death to be valid. Loss didn't need to be final to hurt.

And maybe, I was learning how to live with both.

The afternoon passed in comfortable rhythms. James and Bob showed me the workshop—a converted corner of the garage that smelled of sawdust and varnish, lined with tools hung in precise order. James explained the difference between white oak and red oak while Bob demonstrated dovetail joints. I understood perhaps a third of what they said, but their enthusiasm was infectious.

Later, I found Kate in the living room, curled in the window seat with her sketchbook. Afternoon light streamed across her work. I recognized quick studies of the harbor view, the boats at their moorings rendered in charcoal. I settled on the couch with a book I'd brought, content to exist in the same space while she drew and I read. Every so often she'd glance up, catch my eye, smile before returning to her work.

Liam emerged from the den around three, declaring he needed coffee and human interaction or he'd forget how to speak in anything other than medical jargon. We spent twenty minutes in the kitchen while he made elaborate pour-over coffee and explained his thesis on pain management with the same intense focus I recognized in myself when discussing pharmacology.

By the time James and Diane returned for dinner bearing a casserole that filled the house with the scent of cheese and herbs, I felt woven into the fabric of the day. Not a guest being entertained, but someone who simply belonged.

Later that evening, I found myself wedged beside Kate on the couch, close enough that our thighs touched through my jeans and her leggings. She'd abandoned her sketching the moment Sophie suggested a movie. Now *The Princess Bride* played on the TV, apparently a Westfield family favorite that everyone could quote by heart.

Liam was enthusiastically doing so along with the priest on screen, down to the terrible accent.

"Every. Single. Time," Abby said without looking away from the screen.

Kate shifted beside me, adjusting her position so her head rested against my shoulder. Her hand found mine, fingers threading together in a familiar pattern. Normal couple behavior. Nothing unusual.

Except then her thumb started tracing slow circles on my palm.

The movement was small. Intentional. The kind of touch that seemed innocent but sent sensation up my arm and into my chest. I tried to focus on the TV, where they were storming the castle. Kate's thumb continued its exploration. Across my palm. Along the thin skin of my wrist where my pulse beat. Back again. Each circuit methodical.

I glanced down at her. She was watching the screen, face

perfectly neutral, like she wasn't currently cataloging every point where our bodies connected.

"You okay?" she whispered. Her breath was warm against my neck.

"Fine."

Her thumb continued. On screen, Westley was confronting Prince Humperdinck. The family was rapt, even though they'd all seen this dozens of times. Kate's hand slipped free from mine, found my knee instead. Rested there. Her pinky finger traced the seam of my jeans.

"Last night was nice," she murmured.

"It was."

"I like sleeping next to you." Her hand moved higher on my leg. Not dramatically. Just enough that the pressure registered through denim.

"Kate—"

"Shhh." She pressed one finger to my lips. Her nail was short, practical, with a tiny ridge I could feel against my mouth. She was grinning now. "Pay attention. We're just getting to the good part."

But she didn't move her other hand. And when she shifted position again, pressing closer against my side, her breast brushed my arm through the thin cotton of her shirt.

I couldn't have told you a single thing that happened for the rest of the movie.

The credits rolled to the sound of Liam's exaggerated sniffling.

"Gets me every time," he said, wiping dramatically at his eyes. "True love conquers all."

"You're a sap," Abby told him.

"Romantic," he corrected. "I'm a romantic."

Diane stood, gathering the blanket Rosie had been wrapped

in. The girl was boneless with sleep against James's shoulder. "We should get this one home to bed," she said quietly.

James rose carefully, cradling Rosie against his chest. "See you tomorrow?" he asked the room generally.

"Brunch," Jo confirmed. "Eleven-ish."

Sophie and Taylor stood next, Taylor's hand finding the small of Sophie's back in a gesture so automatic it seemed unconscious.

"Night, everyone," Sophie said. She looked at me, then at Kate's hand still resting on my thigh, and smiled. Not mockingly. Just knowing. "Sleep well."

Taylor winked.

My face heated. Kate laughed quietly beside me.

"Ignore them," she said, standing and stretching. Her sweater rode up, showing skin above the waistband of her leggings. The curve of her hip. "They think they're hilarious."

Liam appeared in the kitchen doorway, laptop tucked under one arm. "Hey Alex, just so you know—" He tapped his headphones. "Noise-canceling. I won't hear a thing from the den tonight. Just saying."

"Liam," Kate said, but she was still laughing.

"What? I'm being helpful." He disappeared down the hall, calling back, "Have a good night!"

Abby stood, stretching. "You two are adorable," she said. "And for what it's worth, Mom and Dad sleep with a white noise machine." She paused at the base of the stairs. "Not that you need to know that. But just in case you were wondering."

She was gone before I could formulate a response.

Kate held out her hand. "Coming?"

I took it. Let her pull me to my feet. The living room felt suddenly empty without everyone else, quieter except for the ticking of the grandfather clock by the front door and the distant sound of water running upstairs. My palms were damp. Had been since that moment on the couch when her thumb started its circuit.

We climbed the stairs together, her hand warm and dry in mine. At the landing, she paused. Turned to face me in the dim hallway. The nightlight by the bathroom cast yellow light across half her face, left the other half in shadow. She was backlit, her hair glowing amber at the edges.

"Alex?" Her voice dropped lower. "Just so we're clear... I want more than just sleeping tonight."

My mouth had gone completely dry. "Your parents—"

"—put us in the same room," she finished. "On purpose. They're not naive. And I'm not asking for anything you're not ready for." She stepped closer. Her hand came up to cup my jaw, thumb brushing the corner of my mouth. "But I've been thinking about you all day. About us. About last night and how much I wanted to do more than just cuddle."

"Oh."

"Yeah." Her smile was gentle but held heat. "Oh."

She kissed me. Soft at first, then deeper when I responded, her mouth warm and tasting faintly of the mint tea she'd had after dinner. When she pulled back, we were both breathing harder.

She continued down the hall to the guest room. I followed, trying to remember the square root of seven hundred twenty-nine to distract myself from the way her hips moved when she walked. Twenty-seven. The answer was twenty-seven. That calculation did absolutely nothing to help.

By the time we reached the door, my hands were shaking.

Kate noticed. Of course she did. She always noticed.

"Hey." She stopped before opening the door. Squeezed my hand. Her palm was warm, steadying. "We don't have to do anything you're not comfortable with. We can still just sleep if you want."

"I want to." The words came out too fast. "I'm just—your family is right here. Your father shook my hand today. Your mother hugged me. They've been nothing but welcoming, and now I'm standing outside their guest room about to—"

Kate kissed me again. When she pulled back, her expression was soft.

"Breathe," she said.

I breathed. The hallway smelled like old wood and lemon furniture polish. Somewhere downstairs, the refrigerator hummed to life with a mechanical shudder.

"Come inside," Kate said. "We'll figure it out together."

She opened the door and I followed her in, cataloging every sound—the latch clicking into place, her footsteps on the hardwood, the rustle of sheets as she sat on the bed. The moonlight streaming through the window turned everything silver and shadow.

Kate reached for the lamp on the nightstand. Yellow light spilled across the quilt, warm after the cool moonlight.

"Better?" she asked.

I nodded, but I couldn't quite find words yet.

She patted the space beside her on the bed. "Come here."

I crossed the room. Sat beside her on the quilt that smelled like lavender fabric softener. Kate's hand found mine again, and this time when her thumb traced patterns on my palm, I understood exactly what she was asking.

"Last chance to change your mind," she whispered. "I mean it. No pressure."

I turned to look at her. Really look. Her hair was messy from where she'd been leaning against me during the movie. Her lips were slightly swollen from kissing. She was watching me with patience and want in equal measure, willing to wait however long I needed.

"I don't want to change my mind," I said. "I'm just trying to—" I gestured vaguely. "Calculate the optimal approach to this situation given the variables of family proximity and questionable sound-proofing and the fact that your father could probably break me in half if—"

Kate laughed. Soft. Affectionate. She leaned in and kissed the words right out of my mouth.

"Stop calculating," she whispered against my lips. "For once in your life, Alex Chen, stop thinking."

"I don't know how to do that."

"I know." She kissed me again. Her mouth warm and soft and distracting enough that I stopped listing reasons why this was a terrible idea. When she pulled back, I followed her, not ready to stop. "It's one of my favorite things about you."

Kate leaned back, drawing me with her. We sank into the quilt together, careful, testing the springs. The mattress was softer than mine in Boston, gave more under our combined weight. The quilt smelled like lavender and lemon. The detergent Jo used.

"Still with me?" Kate whispered against my lips. Her breath was warm.

"Yes." My hands found the hem of her sweater, the soft cotton worn thin from washing. Paused there. "Is this okay?"

"Very okay."

She helped me pull it over her head. The fabric caught on her hair, making it stand up with static electricity. She laughed, breathless, as she tried to smooth it down.

I caught her hands. Pressed a kiss to each palm, feeling the calluses she'd developed from holding paintbrushes. "Leave it. I like it messy."

"You like nothing messy."

"I like you messy."

Kate's smile was brilliant even in the dim moonlight. She reached for my shirt, fingers working at buttons that suddenly seemed too small, too numerous. I helped, our hands tangling together until we were both laughing quietly, heads bent close.

"We're still terrible at this," she giggled.

"We'll improve with practice."

"Is that a promise?"

I kissed her instead of answering, lowered her back onto the quilt. The bed frame gave a small creak of metal on wood and I froze completely.

"It's an old house," Kate said gently. "Everything creaks."

But now I was intensely aware of every sound. The wind rattling the window pane. Footsteps in the hallway. Water running through pipes somewhere in the walls. A door closing. The distant tick of a clock. The house itself seemed to be listening, full of ears.

Kate's hand found my face, turned me to look at her. "Hey. Stay here. With me."

I focused on her. On the way moonlight caught in her eyes and turned them luminous. The slight flush on her cheeks, spreading down her neck. The curve of her collarbone where my hand rested, where her pulse beat fast.

This was Kate. The girl who'd come back from Maine early because I was sick. Who'd nursed me through mono even though I'd been insufferable about it. Who'd stood up to her family about changing majors. Who decided I was worth choosing even when my own parents had walked away.

"I'm here," I said.

She pulled me down into another kiss. This one slower. More deliberate. I let myself sink into it, let the worry recede enough to focus on the present moment. On learning the map of her. The places that made her breath catch—the curve where her neck met her shoulder. The places that made her arch toward me—just below her ribs. The sounds she tried to muffle against my shoulder when I found particularly sensitive spots.

My hands traced the line of her ribs, feeling each one. The dip of her waist. The flare of her hip. She arched into my touch, then immediately stilled, eyes going wide.

"I want you," she whispered.

We both froze. Listened. My heart hammered so loud I was certain it would wake the house. But there was nothing except the normal sounds. Wind. Pipes. The settling of old wood.

"Maybe we should—" I started.

"Be creative?" Kate's smile turned wicked. "Less movement?"

I considered the physics. The geometry. The angles. "That's actually very challenging."

"You like challenges."

She wasn't wrong.

We rearranged ourselves carefully. Kate ended up half on top of me, which minimized the stress on the bed frame but created entirely new problems with my ability to think clearly. Her weight felt perfect. Real in a way that eclipsed everything else.

Her mouth found mine again and again, kisses punctuated by whispered fragments.

"Is this okay?"

"Yes. More than okay."

"Your hands...there...yes—"

"Kate, you need to be quieter."

"You need to stop doing that thing with your—" Her breath caught. "Oh."

I pressed my hand gently over her mouth, felt her smile against my palm. She bit down softly. Not hard. Just enough to feel, enough to send heat straight through me. Her eyes were bright with mischief and want and deeper feeling.

This was completely new territory for me. The constant awareness of potential discovery making every touch feel stolen, precious. The way Kate's natural expressiveness warred with the need for quiet, turning every sound she did make into something that felt like victory and vulnerability at once.

I was learning her differently than I had that first time. This wasn't about overcoming nervousness about the act itself. This was about trust. About vulnerability. About caring more about her pleasure, her comfort, her joy than my own embarrassment or fear of discovery.

Kate's breathing quickened and became shallow. Her fingers dug into my shoulders and left crescents I'd feel tomorrow. I kissed her deeply, swallowed the sounds she was trying to make, felt her body tighten and tighten and then release. She pressed her face into the curve of my neck as she fell apart, and I held her through it, one hand stroking her hair, the other pressed against her back. Whispered things I'd never said to anyone. That she was beautiful. That I'd never felt like this. That I was terrified and sure at the same time.

When she finally relaxed against me, boneless and warm, she pressed a kiss to my jaw. Her breath still coming fast.

"Your turn," she whispered.

"You don't have to—"

"I want to." Her hand slid lower, found me through my jeans. "Unless you really don't want me to?"

The question was genuine despite her current position, despite the heat in her eyes. This was Kate. Always checking. Always taking care of me, even in moments like this.

"I want you to," I managed, voice rough. "But I don't know how quiet I can be."

"Then we'll just have to make sure you're very, very quiet." Her smile was wicked and tender at the same time, a combination only she could manage. "I have some ideas about that."

She kissed her way down my body. Torturously slow. Every kiss intentional, mapped like she was memorizing me. The hollow of my throat. The center of my chest. Lower. I gripped the quilt in both fists, focusing on staying absolutely silent as she worked her way down, and her fingers found the button of my jeans.

When her mouth finally reached its destination, I bit down on my own hand to keep from making a sound. Hard enough to taste copper.

Kate was learning me the way I'd learned her. Patient when I tensed. Attentive to every reaction, every intake of breath. Responsive to the smallest signals—the way my hand tightened in her hair, the way my hips jerked despite my best efforts to stay still. And the bed frame, miraculously, blessedly, stayed silent.

After we both snuck out to get cleaned up, we lay tangled together in the moonlight. Her heartbeat pulsed against my ribs. I inhaled deeply, savoring the scent of her.

"See?" she whispered eventually. "Nobody heard anything."

"Liam winked at me."

She stilled. "What?"

"Earlier. On the way back from the bathroom. He winked."

Kate propped herself up on one elbow to look at me. "That doesn't mean anything. Liam winks at everyone. It's his thing. He winked at the mailman yesterday."

"It felt meaningful."

"You're paranoid." But she was grinning now, eyes bright with amusement. "Though I admit the soundproofing in this house is questionable at best."

We lay quiet for a moment. The house settling around us with creaks and sighs. Somewhere downstairs, a clock chimed midnight. Twelve clear notes that seemed to hover in the air.

"Alex?" Kate's voice turned serious.

"Mm?"

"Thank you for coming here with me. I know meeting families is terrifying, especially after everything with your parents. But it means a lot to me. That you're here."

I pressed a kiss to her hair, breathed in the scent of her. "There's nowhere else I'd rather be."

"Liar." But her voice was warm with affection. "You'd rather be in a quiet lab with proper soundproofing and no one around for miles."

"Okay, yes. But this is a very close second."

She chuckled quietly against my chest. The sound vibrated through both of us, made me tighten my arms around her.

"I love you," I said. The words flowed easier here, in the dark, with her warmth against me and the house quiet around us. "I know I don't say it enough."

"You show it," she said. "That counts."

"I want to say it too."

She tilted her head up to look at me, eyes searching mine. "Then say it."

"I love you," I said again. The truth of it was solid and sure.

Kate's eyes brightened. She kissed me softly. "I love you too. Even when you're overthinking creaky bed frames and structural acoustics."

"Especially then."

"Especially then," she agreed.

We fell asleep like that. Wrapped around each other in the guest room of her childhood home, in the house full of people who'd welcomed me without conditions or expectations. And if I dreamed about chemistry equations and sound dampening materials, that was my own business.

The next morning arrived with pale light filtering through the guest room window and the smell of coffee drifting up from the kitchen. Kate was already awake, propped on one elbow watching me with a soft expression.

"Morning," she whispered.

"Morning."

"Sleep okay?"

"Better than okay."

She smiled, leaned down to kiss me. "We should probably get up. Mom's making pancakes."

The morning passed quickly. Breakfast with the family—Bob reading the Sunday paper, Jo humming while she cooked, Liam half-asleep at the table with his coffee. James and Diane arrived with Rosie around ten, and the house filled with noise again. Kate showed me more of the town, we helped clean up after lunch, and suddenly it was time to leave.

When Jo hugged me goodbye, I was more prepared and managed not to completely freeze. I actually leaned into it this time and let myself accept the gesture for what it was.

Bob shook my hand. "You're welcome anytime, Alex. And I mean that."

"Thank you. For everything."

Liam winked again in a way that confirmed all of my fears about the soundproofness of guest room walls, but I'd decided last night not to analyze everything so much.

Even Rosie escaped the protection of her father's legs and gave mine a squeeze goodbye, her small arms barely reaching around my knee.

Kate said her goodbyes with the ease of someone who knew she'd be back soon. Hugged everyone. Made promises to call. Reminded Diane to call the minute she went into labor.

As the bus carried us back to Boston, Kate fell asleep against the window almost immediately. The exhaustion of the visit catching up with her. The landscape changed from rural to suburban to urban as the Maine coastline gave way to New Hampshire, then Massachusetts.

I'd arrived in Waverly Cove carrying years of carefully constructed barriers. Between obligation and desire. Between parental expectations and personal fulfillment. Between intellectual understanding and emotional experience.

I was returning with many of those barriers dismantled. Not by force but by gentle persistence. Kate's family had shown me what unconditional acceptance looked like. Even Bob's honest concern about Kate's art career had made that support feel more real, not less.

Jo's words in the kitchen echoed. About grief being valid even when loss wasn't final. About family not ending with blood.

My parents and what I'd lost. What I was gaining instead.

Kate stirred beside me as we passed the Boston city limits sign.

"Welcome back," I said softly.

She smiled, eyes still half-closed. Reached over to rest her hand on my thigh. "Did you have a good spring break?"

The question was simple. The answer was complex. Layered with implications I was still processing. Meaningful conversations in the kitchen. Waking to find her watching me with tenderness. Bob's worried but accepting face. Jo's words in the kitchen. The way love and concern could coexist without canceling each other out.

"The best," I said simply. Covered her hand with mine.

She interlaced her fingers with mine as the bus turned toward South Station. We carried Waverly Cove with us. A foundation for whatever happened next.

Chapter 22

Kate

I stood outside Professor Vellacott's office with my hand hovering over the doorknob. Behind this door was my future. My actual future, not the one I'd been trying to force myself into like a pair of shoes two sizes too small.

Deep breath. The art department hallway smelled like linseed oil and turpentine and possibility. Knock.

"Come in."

Professor Vellacott sat behind a desk buried under organized chaos. Stacks of papers. Art books with paint-smudged covers. What looked like a half-finished clay sculpture of a hand. The office walls displayed student work alongside her own watercolors. A living gallery. My fingers itched for a brush, the pencil, anything.

"Kate." Reading glasses had slipped halfway down her nose. Silver frames with small stones embedded in the corners. "Right on time."

"I brought my paperwork." I pulled out the completed major change forms. Each line filled in with my neatest handwriting. "I also have my portfolio. It's not much yet, but—"

My hands hesitated. The desk was so cluttered. What if the key to my entire future got lost under sketches and half-drunk coffee cups?

"Sit." She gestured to a chair across from her desk.

I handed over my portfolio as I sat. Sketches. Watercolor attempts. The hand studies that had earned her earlier praise. My right knee started bouncing. The wooden chair creaked with the rhythm.

What if she changed her mind? What if my work from last month was a fluke and everything since then was garbage? What if I'd imagined I had talent because I wanted it so badly?

"You've done more work since I last saw these." She paused at a detailed study of intertwined hands. Alex's hands, though I hadn't labeled them. The way his long fingers curled protectively around mine had fascinated me for hours while I got the shading right. "These are quite good."

"I've been practicing whenever I can."

She closed the portfolio and turned her attention fully to me. Her eyes were keen. Assessing. "Why the change from nursing? Your advisor mentioned you were performing well in all of your classes this semester."

This was the question I'd prepared for. Had rehearsed answers in the shower, on the bus, while brushing my teeth. But what emerged was the naked truth.

"Because when I'm in clinicals, I'm counting minutes until I can leave." I leaned forward. The chair creaked again. "When I'm drawing, I lose track of hours. I'm technically competent at nursing, but art makes me feel alive. It's the difference between performing the steps of a dance routine correctly and feeling the music."

The professor's face stayed neutral. But a slight upward tilt at the corner of her mouth caught my attention.

"Well." She picked up a pen. Signed her name across the forms with a flourish. Three bold strokes. "The department is pleased to have you, Miss Westfield. Your paperwork is in order. We'll need to discuss your course schedule for next semester, but that can wait until next week."

Just like that.

Years of expectation. Months of anxiety. And it came down to a signature and a smile.

"Thank you." I had no idea why I was suddenly breathless.

"Don't thank me." She returned the forms. Warmth still radiated from the paper. "Just make art that matters to you. That's all I ask."

I floated out of her office.

Art major. The words tasted different than 'nursing student' ever had. Less antiseptic. More vibrant. Like the difference between hospital fluorescent lights and real sunshine.

I crossed the quad. I basked in the Spring warmth on my face and the smell of fresh-cut grass. The guilt about leaving nursing had dissolved after Mom's confession about her piano. Now that my major change was official, the remaining doubts scattered like dandelion seeds in wind.

I was so absorbed in this lightness that I walked straight into Dr. Martinez.

"Miss Westfield!" He stepped back, holding his coffee cup protectively. "Nearly lost my caffeine there."

My face heated. "Dr. Martinez! I'm so sorry, I wasn't—"

"Clearly." But he was smiling. That grandfatherly expression I'd seen when he'd first suggested nursing might not be my path. "You look like you're walking on air. Good news?"

I clutched the signed paperwork so tightly that the corners dug into my palm. "I just officially changed my major. To art."

I braced for impact. What if he thought I was running away from something hard? What if he saw it as giving up?

But Dr. Martinez's smile widened. "Art. That makes perfect sense, actually."

"It does?"

"Kate, I've been teaching chemistry for thirty-two years. You know what I've learned?" He adjusted his coffee cup, settling into professor mode with the ease of someone who'd given this speech before. "The students who struggle most aren't the ones who lack intelligence. They're the ones trying to force themselves into the wrong shape."

I didn't know what to say to that.

"Those benzene rings you drew on your first quiz?" he continued. "Technically incorrect. But beautiful. You have an artist's eye, not a chemist's mind. There's no shame in that. In fact, there's honor in recognizing it."

"I thought you'd think I was taking the easy way out."

"Easy?" Dr. Martinez laughed, warm and genuine. "My daughter is a professional violinist. When she told me she was leaving pre-med to pursue music, I was terrified for her. Absolutely terrified." He paused. "But watching her perform now? She's exactly where she should be. Sometimes the brave choice is the one that looks like surrender."

He shifted his leather satchel higher on his shoulder. "I pushed you because you were clearly capable of more than you were giving chemistry. But I also saw someone working against their nature. Art will let you work with it instead."

"Thank you." I meant it more than two words could convey. "For pushing me. For helping me see that detour you mentioned."

"You found your own way." He glanced at his watch. "Now, I have office hours in five minutes, and you look like you have places to be. Congratulations, Miss Westfield. I expect great things from you."

He walked past, then paused and looked back.

"And Kate? When you have your first gallery showing, send me an invitation. I'd like to see what you create when you're not fighting your own instincts."

He disappeared into the science building. I clutched my signed forms a little tighter. Dr. Martinez had been the first person to question whether nursing was my path. Now he was among the first to celebrate my finding the right one.

Full circle. But moving forward instead of back.

I pulled out my phone. Checked the time. Alex should be finishing his pharmacy lab now.

KATE
On my way. P.S. I'm officially an art major next semester!

ALEX
Proud of you. 💜 See you in 10.

Those words stung my eyes.

He was proud of me for following my passion. Meanwhile his own carefully planned path had become a minefield of financial obstacles and professional setbacks. While I got to pursue dreams, he was drowning.

I tried not to worry about Alex's situation as I headed toward the pharmacy building, but my brain had other ideas. He was always so tired now. He'd been working the library closing shift last night. Then opening at the campus lab this morning. Three jobs meant his schedule looked like a Tetris game designed by someone who hated him.

I found him outside the pharmacy building. Leaning against the brick wall. Backpack at his feet. Phone pressed to his ear.

The tension showed in every line of him. His shoulders were up near his ears. He rubbed his forehead with his free hand.

"I understand," he was saying. Voice carefully controlled. Flat. "Thank you for letting me know."

He ended the call. Stood there staring at his phone like it might spontaneously combust.

"Hey." I approached slowly. "Everything okay?"

His face spoke of exhaustion that went beyond physical tiredness. The kind that settled in your bones when the world kept taking pieces and offering nothing back.

"I was returning a call from Dr. Zhang's office." His voice was too even. "The residency position is officially no longer available."

My stomach dropped. We'd known this was coming since his father made that phone call weeks ago. But hearing it confirmed felt like watching a door slam shut. Locked. Sealed with concrete.

"Alex, I'm so sorry."

"It's done." He picked up his backpack with careful deliberation. "I have other programs I'm applying to. It's fine."

But it wasn't fine.

Dr. Zhang's program had been prestigious. Competitive. The kind of opportunity that opened doors throughout a career. The other programs he'd mentioned were respectable but nowhere near the same caliber. And they were all across the country. Cities where neither of us had connections or support.

"When did they call?"

"This afternoon. Right after I got my exam back." He started walking and I fell into step beside him. "I got a 78."

I did the mental math fast. Alex didn't get 78s. Alex got 95s and occasionally complained they weren't 98s. A 78 meant something was seriously wrong.

"You were working until two in the morning at the library." I kept my voice careful. "Then you had that early shift at the lab. When did you sleep?"

"I caught a few hours." He rubbed his eyes. "It's manageable."

"Alex, a 78 is not manageable for you. That's going to pull

down your GPA right when you need strong grades for these other residency applications."

"I'm aware." The words cut deep. He paused. Took a breath. "Sorry. I'm trying to figure out how to reduce my hours without going further into debt. The emergency aid covers about forty percent of what I need. My jobs cover another forty-five. That leaves me short about fifteen percent every month, which I've been covering with a credit card."

I'd known things were tight. But hearing the actual numbers was something else entirely.

He was working himself into the ground and still falling short.

"What about the library position? Could you drop that one and pick up more hours at the lab instead since it pays better?"

"The lab can't give me more hours. Rules about student worker limits." He rolled his shoulder, working out the stiffness. "And I need the library job because it's the only one where I can sometimes study during slow periods. Tutoring and the lab both require constant attention."

We reached a bench near the student center. I pulled him to sit. He looked like he might fall over otherwise.

"Have you eaten today?"

He thought about it. Too long. "Coffee counts, right?"

I pulled out my meal card. "I'm getting you food. Wait here."

"Kate, I can—"

"Wait. Here." I used my camp counselor voice. The one that meant business. "I'll be right back."

Ten minutes later, I returned with a loaded sandwich, fruit, and another coffee. Alex accepted the food with a look that made my heart ache. He ate fast. Mechanical. Like someone who'd forgotten food was supposed to taste good.

"Better?" I asked when he'd finished.

"Yeah. Thanks." He crumpled the wrapper into a neat ball. "I needed that."

"When's your next shift?"

"I'm tutoring four to nine. Then I'm supposed to work the closing shift at the library, but I'm thinking of calling in. I need to start on the residency applications."

I pulled out my phone and opened my calendar. "What if we blocked out dedicated study time for the next two weeks? No work during those hours. Focusing on your exams and applications. You could cut back the library shifts to three days instead of five."

"That would put me more in the red financially."

"Then we work around it." I started making notes. "My meal plan resets next week with more points than I can use. That's food covered. What else?"

"Kate—"

"What else?" I pressed. "Transportation? Books? What are your other expenses beyond rent and utilities?"

He quieted. That calculating expression I knew so well crossed his face. When Alex was quiet like this, he was running numbers. Analyzing variables. Looking for the logical solution.

"If I could cut the library during the week, I could focus on keeping my lab and tutoring shifts. Those pay better anyway." He pulled out his laptop. Opened a spreadsheet that made my non-numerical brain hurt. "With your meal plan covering food, I'd be short about two hundred a month. I could cover that with the credit card, but the interest..."

"Or." The idea formed as I spoke. "What if you didn't have to pay rent for a couple months? Your apartment is month-to-month, right?"

"Yeah, but I need a place to live here in Boston until I know where my residency will take me."

"What if you gave notice for May first? Gave yourself a breather until residency starts? Liam has that pull-out couch in his apartment. I'm sure he'd be happy to let you crash there and split utilities or something." The words tumbled faster as the plan took shape. "You could stay there temporarily. Store your stuff. That's two months of rent saved, which would more than cover your shortfall."

Emotions flashed across Alex's face too fast to track.

"You want me to move in with your brother." Each word was surgical. Deathly calm.

"I'm suggesting a practical solution to a financial problem." I leaned forward. "You're killing yourself trying to work three jobs while maintaining your grades. Something has to give, and it shouldn't be your education. You're so close to the finish line. Liam's place is closer to campus anyway, and—"

"Kate." He put his laptop away with deliberate care. "I appreciate what you're trying to do. But it won't work."

"But Liam is never home and I'm sure he'd appreciate the help covering utilities. You need a place to stay. It's mutually beneficial."

"No." His voice flattened. "It's your family taking pity on me."

My pulse quickened. "That's not fair. You're in an impossible situation that isn't your fault. Your parents created this mess. Why should you suffer because of some outdated—"

"It's not outdated." His jaw tightened. "In my family, a man doesn't rely on his girlfriend's family. It's shameful."

"Well, maybe your culture's expectations are unreasonable!" We were dangerously close to shouting at one another. "Maybe they're setting you up to fail!"

The silence that followed felt like glass breaking.

Alex stared at me. His expression shuttered. Closed off. Locked down.

"I need to get to work." He stood, spine rigid, shoulders locked. "Thank you for lunch."

"Alex, wait—"

But he was already walking away. Holding everything in place with sheer force of will.

I'd pushed too hard. Said too much. And a gulf opened between us where moments ago there'd been nothing.

I sat on the bench after he left.

The paperwork sat in my lap. My official art major declaration. The ink still smelled fresh.

I'd gotten what I wanted. Alex was about to lose everything he'd spent four years building, but I didn't have much time to dwell on it because Isa's text came through before my thoughts could spiral.

> **ISA**
> Dinner? Heard you had big news!

> **KATE**
> Not hungry. Raincheck?

> **ISA**
> You ok?

> **KATE**
> Not really. Think I just screwed up with Alex.

> **ISA**
> Coming to find you. Where are you?

I gave her my location. Students moved across campus with the confidence of people whose lives were proceeding according to plan. Had I ever felt that way? Maybe freshman year, before chemistry destroyed my nursing dreams and I met a pharmacy student whose dedication both inspired and terrified me.

Isabel appeared fifteen minutes later with two macchiatos and determination in her eyes.

"Spill." She handed me a cup and sat beside me.

I told her everything. The failed exam. The lost residency. My suggestion about staying with Liam. His reaction to my comment about his culture.

"Ouch." She winced. "You really stepped in it."

"I know," I groaned, wrapping my hands around my coffee cup. The warmth didn't help. "I was trying to help."

"By making him a charity case." She said it carefully, but the words still stung. "Kate, I love you, but you have a habit of solving problems on autopilot and missing the emotional complications."

"It *is* logical, though. He's working himself into the ground for pride."

"It's not pride." Isabel turned to face me. "Think about it from his perspective. His parents already think he's making a mistake by choosing you. If he moves in with your brother because he can't afford his own place, it proves their point. That he can't take care of himself. That being with you means needing rescue from your family."

I hadn't thought of it that way.

In my mind, I'd offered practical support. But to Alex, accepting might mean confirming every fear his parents had about our relationship.

"So what do I do?" Surely a talented nursing student like Isabel Diaz knew what to prescribe for a case of temporary insanity.

"You apologize for dismissing his emotions. Then you ask what he needs from you, instead of assuming you know." She squeezed my shoulder. "And you give him space to figure out his own solutions, even if they're not the ones you'd choose."

The advice made sense. But accepting it felt like watching someone drown when you had a life preserver in your hands and they refused to take it.

"What if his solution is to break up with me?" I voiced the fear that had been lurking since he walked away. "What if he decides I'm not worth all this?"

"Then you deal with that if it happens." Isabel's voice was firm. "But Kate, that boy is crazy about you. This is a hard moment. Don't make it harder by forcing solutions he's not ready for."

I spent the rest of the afternoon in my studio space. Professor Vellacott wanted studies of natural forms. Leaves. Shells. The curve of driftwood.

My hands kept returning to the same subject. Bridges.

Bridges under construction, rebar exposed. Bridges spanning gaps that made my stomach drop. My subconscious wasn't being subtle.

Around six, my musings were interrupted by a text message.

> **ALEX**
> Can we talk? I'm at the library until 9 but could take a break.

My heart jumped, rattling against my ribs.

> **KATE**
> On my way. Bringing sustenance.

I found him on the library's third floor, tucked into a corner study carrel. Surrounded by textbooks. Exhaustion lined his face. Drawn. The fluorescent lights made the shadows under his eyes look bruised.

He accepted the brownie and tea I placed beside him with a small nod.

"Hey." I slid into the chair across from him.

"Hey." The strain around his eyes was worse than this afternoon. "Thanks for this."

"I'm sorry." I blurted before I lost my nerve. "I was trying to help, but I completely dismissed your feelings. And I said something thoughtless about your culture."

He studied his coffee cup. "I overreacted too. You meant to be generous. I turned it into something else."

"No. Isabel helped me see that I was wrong." My sweaty palms pressed against my thighs. The denim scraped rough under my touch. "I was being too logical and practical. I tried to fix your problem without thinking about what that meant for you. How your parents would see it. How you'd see yourself."

"What did Isabel say?" A slight smile tugged at his mouth despite everything.

"That I have a habit of solving problems impulsively and missing the emotional complications. Which is accurate and also annoying to hear out loud." I reached across the table. Palm up. An invitation.

He placed his hand in mine. His thumb traced a small circle on the back of my hand. His gaze dropped to our joined hands, then back up. He opened his mouth, like he was running calculations on the exact right way to phrase what he needed.

"Could you..." He trailed off and took a deep breath before starting again. "Would it be weird if I asked you to hold me for a minute?"

Six months ago, he'd barely let me hug him goodbye. Three months ago, he'd stiffened whenever I reached for him in public. Now he was asking. Clearly. For what he needed.

"Not weird at all." I stood, tugging him up with me.

We were tucked in the back corner of the stacks at nearly 8pm. I doubted many students haunted this part of the library. If they did, they were likely more focused on whatever eleventh-hour Hail Mary cram session they were here for than anything Alex and I were doing.

I wrapped my arms around him and he pulled me close, his face pressed against my hair. His whole body exhaled.

"Thank you," he murmured against my temple.

"For what?"

"For not making me find the words for why I need this."

My arms tightened around him. His hands splayed across my back, anchoring me against him. We stood like that for a long moment. His heartbeat steady against my cheek. The scent of his detergent mixing with library dust and printer toner.

When I tilted my head back to look at him, that constant self-regulation had loosened. His shoulders weren't squared. His breathing wasn't steady.

"Kate."

"Alex?"

Instead of answering, he kissed me. My fingers curled into his shirt. His hand cupped the back of my neck. The kiss turned urgent. Weeks of stress and fear and fighting poured into it, everything we both understood but couldn't say.

I backed against the bookshelf. A few books rattled on the shelves but held. Alex's forehead pressed against mine as we broke apart, both breathing harder than we should be in a library.

"Sorry," he whispered. "I didn't mean to..."

"Don't apologize." I caught his face between my hands. "I'm so proud of you for asking for what you need. Do you know how far you've come?"

He tried to read the truth of it on my face. "It's easier with you. Knowing what I need. Being able to say it."

"Good." I pressed a quick kiss to his jaw. Then another to his lips. My hands lingered on his arms before I made myself step back. "But maybe we should study before we get kicked out of here."

"Probably wise." His mouth curved up at one corner, then the other. The smile transformed his tired face. "Though for the record, that was significantly better than a study session."

"High praise indeed."

We settled back into our study spot. The fluorescent lights hummed overhead. Someone sneezed three aisles over. Alex reached for my hand without looking, his fingers threading through mine while his other hand took notes.

I pulled out my sketchbook and he opened his textbook. The pages rustled as he settled in.

I sketched while he studied. Quick lines, roughing out the shapes of what might become figures, but I had nothing planned. My charcoal smudged at the edges.

After a while, Alex shifted closer. His shoulder pressed against mine, solid and warm. I leaned into him, letting my head rest there. He turned pages with his free hand, the other still holding mine.

Chapter 23

Alex

I shelved a heavy medical reference book with a thud that echoed through the empty library.

Five and a half years of perfect attendance. Immaculate lab notes. Midnight study sessions. All of it should have culminated in the Zhang residency. Instead, I was working my third job of the week, re-shelving books at the campus library until midnight for minimum wage.

The computer chimed with an email notification.

I clicked to open it. Already knew what I'd find.

```
Dear Mr. Chen,

Thank you for your interest in the Merck
Pharmaceutical internship program. After
careful consideration, we regret to inform
you that we have moved forward with other
candidates.
```

> We encourage you to apply earlier next year...

Next year. As if I had that luxury.

I deleted the message. Clicked out of the window. The library's harsh white light cast shadows across empty study tables. Nearly midnight during the week before finals. Even the most dedicated students had retreated to their dorms.

Ten more books on my cart. Nine. Eight. The rhythm of shelving usually helped. Tonight each movement felt like cataloging small failures. Seven. Six. Five. My reflection in the dark window showed a gaunt face I barely recognized. Four. Three. I'd lost at least fifteen pounds. Dark circles pooled beneath my eyes like bruises. Two. One.

"Chen, you can clock out now." Marissa called from her office. "I'll lock up."

"Thanks. See you tomorrow."

My voice was as worn thin as I felt, despite my gratitude for the early reprieve.

The spring air hit me as I pushed through the library doors. Almost warm after hours in climate control. Campus stood still, most windows dark except for the occasional glow of a late-night studier. Three months ago, I would have been one of them. Organized notes spread across my desk. Confidence in my future solid as concrete.

Now I was taking the long walk back to my apartment. Hoping the activity would clear my head before I attempted to study for my own finals.

A text from Kate was already waiting for me when I pulled out my cell to check in with her.

> **KATE**
> Just finished a new painting! Professor V says it might make the student showcase. Can't wait to show you tomorrow! Love you 🤍

I smiled despite myself. Kate's enthusiasm was contagious even through text.

> **ALEX**
> Looking forward to seeing it. Love you too.

The contrast between our situations was not lost on me.

While my carefully constructed future crumbled, Kate was flourishing. Her decision to switch from nursing to art had been seamless. Her family supportive both emotionally and financially. The Westfields had even offered to help with her summer program tuition. A fact she'd mentioned casually, as if parental support was the most natural thing in the world.

I didn't begrudge her happiness. Seeing Kate find her true calling was one of the few bright spots in my current existence. But the gap between our experiences widened daily. Her family's unwavering support versus my parents' continued silence. Her exciting new opportunities versus my dwindling options.

By the time I reached my apartment, the hour neared one in the morning.

I flipped on the lights. The space grew increasingly spartan. I'd sold my gaming console last month to cover my cell phone bill. Stocked my pantry with ramen and oatmeal. My desk was bare except for textbooks and pharmacy notes. This tiny shoebox of a studio now seemed a far cry from the well-appointed dorm rooms I'd maintained throughout college.

My stomach growled. Hollow. Insistent. I'd skipped dinner again. The coffee and granola bar from nine hours ago wasn't sustaining me anymore.

I opened the cupboard and counted the remaining packets of instant ramen. Three left. Rent was due in a week. I was still $180 short even after this week's paychecks. The ramen would need to last.

I closed the cupboard. Reached for a glass of water instead.

Sleep would dull the hunger.

But sleep would have to wait while I forced myself to the desk. I had another final in two days. A paper due tomorrow. Graduation application documents to complete. My eyes blurred as I opened my textbook. I pushed through. Reviewed absorption rates and half-lives until the words swam on the page.

My alarm blared at six.

My cheek peeled off a diagram of hepatic clearance. The page lay wrinkled and damp with drool. I'd fallen asleep at my desk again.

The shower ran scalding. Water needled my skin. My scalp. The back of my neck. Steam filled the bathroom until the mirror fogged over completely.

When I wiped it clear, a stranger looked back. Thinner. Paler. Tension lines around the eyes and mouth that hadn't been there in September.

I turned away from the mirror and let the fog obscure the evidence of my failure.

The campus career center opened at eight.

I'd scheduled this appointment weeks ago. Back when I thought Ms. Peterson's pharmaceutical industry connections might solve my residency problem.

Her wall clock read 8:03. Three minutes in her waiting area felt like thirty. Her desk overflowed with industry magazines and pharmaceutical company stress balls. Small plastic pills and capsules stamped with corporate logos.

"Alex Chen." She scanned my file. "Pharmacy program, 3.98 GPA, graduating next month with a PharmD. Impressive record."

"Thank you." I straightened in my chair. Weight pulled at my shoulders.

"So what brings you in today? With your credentials, I'd expect you to have your post-graduation plans locked down."

I laid it all out. The withdrawn family support. The blocked Zhang residency. The string of rejections from programs that had filled their spots in January.

Ms. Peterson pursed her lips as I explained my plight. She set down my file. Folded her hands on top of it. "This is unusual timing. Most competitive residency programs finalize their selections in January or February. April is very late in the cycle. Graduation is only six weeks away."

"I understand that." I kept my voice level. "But my circumstances changed unexpectedly. I'm hoping there might be openings. Last-minute cancellations."

She typed something into her computer. Brow furrowed. "Without recent internships, current letters of recommendation, or comparable experience, the top residency programs will be challenging." She said it carefully. "You might need to adjust your expectations."

Adjust your expectations.

The phrase landed like a physical blow.

My entire life was built on expectations. My parents' expectations that I would succeed. My own expectations that hard work guaranteed results. Adjusting meant failure.

"What about hospital pharmacy positions? Retail?" My voice sounded foreign to my own ears.

"Those are certainly options." She clicked her mouse. "They don't require residency, though the career trajectory is different. Let me print some information for you."

I left her office fifteen minutes later with a folder of "alternative career paths" and a feeling I couldn't name. The campus was full of end-of-semester energy. Students lounged on the quad. Laughing about summer plans. Graduation parties. I walked through them like a ghost.

My lab shift started at ten.

For four hours, I prepared compound medications. Measured precise dosages. Documented batch numbers and expiration dates with the methodical care the work demanded. The work required focus for triple-checking calculations and following protocols exactly. But my hands knew the motions well enough that my mind wandered to the unfinished document on my laptop outlining my five-year plan. My path was no longer clear.

By three o'clock, I was back on campus for an afternoon class. Then a quick dinner alone in the dining hall. At five, I was due at Kate's studio.

Despite my exhaustion, seeing her was the one bright point. Her art studio had become a sanctuary of sorts. Temporary reprieve from the crushing weight on my shoulders.

The studio was in the basement of the Fine Arts building. A maze of partitioned spaces. Kate's area was easy to spot. Vibrant canvases against industrial walls. Pinned photographs covering a corkboard.

"Alex!" Kate's face lit up when she saw me. Paint smudged her cheek. A streak of burnt umber that matched her eyes. She dropped her brush and wrapped her arms around me, unconcerned about transferring paint to my clothes. "I've been dying to show you this piece."

Her enthusiasm melted the frozen thing inside me. I squeezed her back. The world was perfect in her arms.

"Let's see this showcase-worthy painting."

She pulled me to a large canvas propped on an easel. "I've been working on this for three weeks. Staying late every night to get the light right. Professor Vellacott said I'm finally starting to understand how to layer colors properly. See how the transparency builds depth here?" She pointed to the water in the foreground. "That took me so many tries before I figured out the right balance of pigment to medium."

The painting was arresting. A coastal scene that captured both Waverly Cove's physical features and its emotional resonance. She'd translated her hometown's essence onto canvas. Gave memories form. But more than that, technical precision showed in every brushstroke. The careful attention to color theory. The deliberate composition choices. It was hard to believe that her skills had progressed so far so quickly.

"It's beautiful." I meant it. "You've captured the place completely. Your feelings about Waverly Cove come through. And the technical execution... You've really developed your skills."

"You really think so?" She studied my face. Seeking my opinion despite her professor's praise. "I know art isn't your thing."

"Just because I don't create it doesn't mean I can't appreciate it." My cheeks felt stiff. The smile wouldn't quite take. "You've found something you're good at. You've worked so hard. I'm proud of you."

Kate hugged me again. Pulled back with paint smudges now on my jacket sleeve. "That means a lot coming from you. I've been in the studio until midnight most nights this week trying to perfect the technique." She held up her fingers. Stained blue and ochre in the creases. "Look at this. It won't come off."

"Chemistry to art in three months." I managed a more natural smile this time. "Fast transformation."

"Right?" She gestured around her studio space, knocking over a jar of brushes. Caught it before it spilled. "It feels right in a way nursing never did."

I nodded. "When does the showcase happen?"

"Beginning of June. Oh!" She wiped her hands on a cloth already stiff with dried paint. Grabbed her phone. "Mom called earlier. They're covering the entire summer program. All of it. Dad said art supplies cost less than nursing textbooks, so they're actually saving money."

She laughed.

I tried to join her.

My phone lit up as my mother's name appeared on the screen. It was her first outreach in weeks.

> MĀMĀ
> When is graduation?

No greeting. No congratulations. But she was asking. That had to mean something.

"Who's that?" Kate asked. My expression must have changed.

"My mother." My thumb hovered over the message. "First time she's reached out since everything."

Kate set down her paintbrush. Wiped her hands on her jeans. "What does she say?"

"She wants to know when graduation is." I swallowed. Hated the flicker of hope I couldn't quite extinguish. "Maybe they're—"

> MĀMĀ
> I need to know when to remove you from our insurance.

The second message landed like a fist to the sternum. Not coming to celebrate. Just calculating the exact date they could cut me loose from the family plan.

"Alex?" She spoke carefully. "What is it?"

"They're not coming." The words scraped out. "She needs to know when I'm officially off their insurance."

Kate's face fell. She reached for my hand. Her fingers still warm from holding paintbrushes. "I'm so sorry, Alex."

I pulled away. Typed a terse response with the date and time. The screen blurred as I hit send.

"Six years of work, and all she cares about is the policy expiration date." I shoved the phone deep into my pocket. As if I could bury the disappointment along with it. "Forget it. What time will you finish up here? I should head to my library shift."

"I'll wrap up in about an hour." Her voice stayed careful. "Want me to bring dinner to your place later? You look exhausted."

The concern in her voice should have been comforting. Instead, it grated against my nerves. One more way I was failing. "I'll be back around midnight."

"I'll be there." She stood on tiptoe to kiss my cheek. "With actual food, not whatever sad freeze dried dinner you were planning."

I managed a nod and left. My steps echoed in the empty hallway. The contrast between Kate's bright paint-filled space and my stark reality felt like moving between different worlds. Her future expanded. Mine contracted.

The entire library shift blurred together. Scanning books. Restocking shelves. Answering the same question about printer access codes multiple times.

When I finally made it back to my apartment, the hall clock read 12:27am.

Kate sat cross-legged outside my door. A bag of takeout beside her. She stood when she saw me. Brushed off her jeans. "Did they keep you late again?"

"Inventory." I jammed my key into the lock. It stuck. I wiggled it and the mechanism finally gave way.

The apartment smelled stale. I hit the light switch. Kate followed me in, and the space seemed to shrink. Textbooks stacked on the coffee table. The desk. The floor beside my bed. Dust coated the windowsill thick enough to draw in. The walls were bare except for a single pharmacy program calendar. Months out of date.

Kate set the takeout bag on the kitchen counter and started opening containers.

"I brought Thai from that place you like." Her voice was too bright. "The one with the yummy green curry."

"Thanks." I dropped my backpack and sank onto the couch. Too tired to feign enthusiasm.

Kate busied herself finding plates and utensils. Chatting about her day. Her upcoming final projects. A funny text from her sister Abby. Her voice filled the empty corners of my apartment. But instead of bringing warmth, each word seemed to highlight the growing distance between us.

"I thought maybe this weekend we could look at summer options." She set a plate of food in front of me. "Mom said you're welcome to stay in Waverly Cove. It would save on rent. Maybe she could hook you up with something at the Coastal Memorial pharmacy there for the summer."

The suggestion was well-intentioned. Practical. Generous. It should have been a relief.

Instead, it was the last crack in my already fractured composure.

"So I should give up on Boston opportunities and move to your parents' house?" I bit the words out so tightly that my teeth barely unclenched. "Become the charity project of the Westfield family?"

Kate froze, fork halfway to her mouth. "What? No, that's not—"

"Not what you meant?" I stood, unable to remain still with the pressure building inside me. "Then what did you mean, Kate? That I should abandon everything I've worked for and follow you to Maine?"

"Alex, I'm trying to help. You're working three jobs and barely sleeping. I'm worried about you."

"I don't need your worry. I need to fix my career." The apartment was too small for pacing, but my feet moved anyway. Five steps. Turn. Five steps back. "Not all of us can change life plans as easily as changing TV channels. Some of us have to consider consequences."

Kate set down her plate, face flushing. "You think I casually decided to change my entire future? That it was easy?"

"Wasn't it? Your family supported you instantly. They're paying for your summer program, for god's sake. You have no idea what it's like to lose everything you've worked for."

"That's not fair." Kate stood now too. Her voice rising to match mine. "I struggled for months before making that decision. I was terrified to tell my family. And I've been working my ass off in that studio every single night to prove I made the right choice. You think technical mastery happens overnight?"

"But they embraced it immediately, didn't they? Meanwhile, I haven't spoken to my parents in months because I chose you." The words cut like knives. "I lost my residency. My financial support. Possibly my entire career."

"So this is my fault now?" Kate's eyes glistened, but her voice gained strength. "I never asked you to choose between me and your family."

"You didn't have to ask. Your existence in my life was enough."

As soon as the words left my mouth, I knew I'd crossed a line.

Kate flinched like I'd physically struck her.

"Do you regret it?" she whispered. "Being with me?"

The rational part of my brain screamed at me to stop. To apologize. To explain that my anger wasn't really directed at her. But exhaustion and frustration had overridden my usual self-control.

"Right now, I regret a lot of things." I turned away. Couldn't look at the hurt blooming across her face. "Maybe I should have stuck with the plan my parents had for me. At least then I'd have a future."

Neither of us moved.

The refrigerator hummed. A car passed outside. Headlights swept across the wall.

Kate's expression hardened. When she spoke, each word had a harsh edge. "You want to talk about consequences?"

I turned to face her.

"You want to know what I think?" She stepped closer. Her eyes bright with angry tears. "I think you're terrified. Not of losing your career. Of having to build something yourself instead of following the path your parents laid out for you."

"That's not—"

"Yes, it is." Her voice rose. "You're so busy mourning your perfect plan you can't see the opportunities right in front of you. Ms. Peterson gave you alternatives. You have options for working in a pharmacy. But you'd rather wallow in failure than adapt, because adapting means admitting your parents' plan wasn't the only valid one."

"You don't understand—"

"No, YOU don't understand." She grabbed her jacket, movements jerky with anger. "I changed my entire life plan. I walked away from everything I thought I was supposed to be. And you know what the scariest part was? Not disappointing my family. It was realizing I'd wasted two years trying to be someone I wasn't because I was too afraid to try something new."

She moved toward the door. Then spun back around.

"You're doing the same thing. Clinging to a plan that's already failed instead of making a new one. And you're making me the villain in your story because it's easier than admitting you're scared."

"Kate—"

"I'm not a liability to your future, Alex. I'm the person who stood by you when you made the hardest choice of your life. But I won't be your punching bag while you figure out whether chasing your own dreams is worth the cost."

Her hand was on the doorknob.

This time when she paused, her voice was deadly calm.

"When you decide whether building a life with me is what you want, we can talk. Until then, I'll give you the space you need to figure it out."

She walked out.

The door closed with a click that somehow hurt more than a slam would have.

The apartment was deathly still.

No rustling takeout bags. No Kate moving through the space making it feel less like a cell.

My legs gave out. I sat on the couch. Then slid down until my elbows rested on my knees. Pressed the heels of my hands against my eyes until I saw stars.

You're terrified of building something yourself.

My throat burned.

Six years of college. Six years following a plan my father drew up when I was fourteen. Study pharmacy. Accelerated doctorate.

Internship with Zhang. Marry someone appropriate. All those years, and I'd never once asked myself what I wanted.

The textbooks stacked on my coffee table blurred. Pharmacology. Therapeutics. Clinical practice guidelines. I'd memorized thousands of pages. Could recite drug interactions in my sleep.

But I couldn't answer the simplest question: what did I want my life to look like?

My phone sat on the cushion beside me. Kate's contact was still on the screen from when she'd texted earlier. Before I'd made her the enemy because facing myself was too hard.

The takeout containers sat abandoned on the counter. The food growing colder by the minute. Another well-intentioned gesture I'd thrown back in her face.

For the first time, I asked myself: was the plan I was pursuing worth the cost? If success meant sacrificing love and happiness, what was I achieving anyway?

The thought was terrifying. A complete restructuring of the principles that had guided me since childhood.

Without that, who was I?

I had no answer. All I had was an empty apartment. A cold meal. The echo of Kate's anger mixing with her hurt. And the knowledge that I'd destroyed the one thing that had made any of this feel worthwhile.

The worst part?

She was right. About all of it.

Chapter 24

Kate

My unfinished painting stared at me. I stared back. We'd been locked in this standoff all afternoon and my brush still hovered an inch away, paint drying on the bristles.

Around me, the art studio hummed with energy. Palette knives scraped against canvas. Someone sighed, followed by the snap of charcoal breaking. Three other students had claimed refuge here during finals week, each lost in their own work.

A drop of ultramarine blue landed near my paint-spattered sneaker as my hand shook.

The studio smelled astringent. Turpentine fumes coated the back of my nostrils. Late afternoon light slanted through the tall windows, dust floating lazy through the beams. I'd come here to capture that light, that suspension. But every time my brush got close to the canvas, the jagged wrongness that had taken up residence in my stomach stopped me.

"Breathe," I whispered. "Just start."

I dragged the brush across the white. This wasn't the graceful composition I'd planned when I mixed my palette an hour ago. But it matched the feeling. Visceral and raw.

Not all of us can change life plans as easily as flipping TV channels.

Alex's words hung there as I pulled another slash of blue across the canvas. Mixed black into my palette. The colors smeared together like a bruise. My wrist worked on its own, finding the angles of his face that night. The exhaustion carved beneath his eyes. The tight set of his jaw, muscle jumping in his cheek.

Seven days. We'd barely spoken in seven days. Terse texts like items on a to-do list. *Studying for finals. Good luck with yours.* No mention of what he'd said. No acknowledgment of how I'd left his apartment and cried the whole walk back to my dorm.

Across the studio, someone turned up their music. Classical strings that built and built without resolution. The melody scraped against my frayed nerves.

I added more paint, my movements growing less controlled. The composition took shape despite my resistance. Or maybe because of it. Dark masses pulling away from each other. Spaces between them that felt like wounds.

"That's intense."

I startled and the brush skidded, leaving a streak I hadn't planned. Professor Vellacott stood beside me with her silver-streaked hair in its usual messy bun and paint smudges on her forearm. Her critical eyes took in my chaotic composition.

"Sorry," I mumbled. "It's not working. I'll start over."

"Don't you dare." She touched my shoulder, warm through my thin t-shirt. "Honest emotion lives here. That's rare. Follow it through. See where it leads."

She moved on to another student. I stared at what I'd created. The dark masses. The violent energy. It looked like a storm. Like grief. Like the opposite of every beautiful thing I'd been trying to create for months.

I smeared crimson onto my palette and let the red bleed into darker colors. When I added it to the canvas, it transformed everything. Deep red pulsing like the hurt beneath my ribs. Like everything I hadn't been able to say.

Alex hadn't meant it. I knew he hadn't. He was drowning. Working three jobs while watching his future crumble because he'd chosen me over his parents' support. Of course he'd lashed out at someone safe. Someone who wouldn't leave even when he was falling apart.

But knowing that didn't make his words hurt less. Didn't erase how they'd reached the most vulnerable part of me.

I'd spent months second-guessing my choice to change majors. Lying awake worrying I was being selfish. Wondering if my family's easy acceptance meant they thought I couldn't handle nursing after all. Every conversation with my academic advisor, every withdrawn class, every new art course pulling me further from the path I'd planned since I was sixteen.

And Alex had made it sound so casual. So easy.

Like flipping TV channels.

I scraped at the canvas with my palette knife, creating texture. The crimson caught the light differently now. Sometimes bright as fresh blood. Sometimes dark as old scars.

The student with the classical music turned it down. In the new silence, radiators clanked. Someone's phone rang in a backpack across the room. The world kept going while everything inside me felt suspended.

I stepped back from the canvas. The paint glistened wet in some places, dried matte in others. Edges smudged where I hadn't waited for layers to set. The composition lurched to one side, unbalanced. But those harsh angles and bruised colors captured what the past week had felt like.

The pain showed there. The anger beneath all my careful understanding. And deeper still, the fear that Alex might be right. That I chased new passions without thinking through consequences. That commitment looked different than what I'd believed.

The brush trembled. I set it down before another drop of paint could fall.

I tried adding yellow to the edges. Light breaking through the storm. It didn't work. Too cheerful. Too easy. Like slapping a smile on a scream. I scraped it off before it could dry.

Just like me. Flipping life plans like TV channels.

I scrubbed my eyes with the back of my wrist, not caring about the paint I smeared across my cheek. I blinked rapidly. I'd been so careful not to cry this week. Not to let anyone see. But here, surrounded by the intense focus of other artists lost in their own worlds, I couldn't hold it back.

The tears fell hot and fast.

I let them.

"You need food," Isa announced that evening, dropping her backpack on my bed with a thud. The desk lamp wobbled. "Actual food, not whatever pencil you've been nibbling between art studio sessions."

I glanced up from my sketchbook. Loose lines sprawled across the page, searching for something less literal than the bridge I kept failing to capture. Isa stood in my doorway, arms crossed. The scent of coconut leave-in conditioner and coffee drifted in with her, cutting through the stale air I'd been breathing for days.

"I'm not hungry," I whined.

My stomach betrayed me with a growl loud enough that Isa laughed.

"Yeah, clearly." She pulled takeout containers from her bag. The tantalizing aroma of pad thai hit me like a memory of normal life. "Chicken pad thai. Extra lime. And I'm not leaving until you eat at least half and tell me what fresh hell you've been putting yourself through this time."

The tangy, spicy smell made my mouth water. I pushed aside the sketchbook and accepted the container she thrust at me.

"Thanks." I twisted noodles around my fork, watching them glisten with oil and crushed peanuts. "Sorry I've been—"

"A ghost? A zombie? Pick your undead creature." Isa settled cross-legged on my bed, opening her own container. "You've been ignoring texts, missing meals, and I'm pretty sure you wore that same shirt yesterday."

I glanced down at my paint-splattered button down. "It's my studio shirt."

"It's also the shirt you slept in, if the wrinkles are any indication." She pointed her fork at me. "Kate. Talk to me."

We ate in silence for a few minutes. The familiar comfort of Isa's presence unwound the tightness in my shoulders.

"The bridge I was painting didn't work," I said finally, gesturing at my sketchbook. "I keep trying to create this connection between different worlds, but it keeps turning into chaos. Storms and gaps and everything falling apart."

Isa chewed on both her noodles and my confession. "Maybe because relationships aren't neat architectural structures. They're messy. They break. Sometimes they're more gap than bridge."

"Professor Vellacott said to follow the chaos. See where it leads."

"Smart woman." Isa set down her food. "So what happened with Alex? The truth, please, not the 'everything's fine' version you texted me."

The noodles turned to paste in my mouth. I forced myself to swallow. "He said I change my life plans as easily as flipping TV channels. Like deciding to pursue art instead of nursing was some casual choice. Not something that kept me up nights for months."

Isa winced. "Ouch. That's harsh."

"He implied I didn't understand commitment. That I shouldn't have changed majors." The hurt rose fresh, burning the back of my throat. "As if I don't know what it means to work for something. To disappoint people who thought they knew what your life would look like."

"He's stressed out of his mind, Kate. Working three jobs, barely sleeping."

"I know that." The words snapped out and I immediately regretted them. "Sorry. I know. That's why I've been giving him space. But it's been a week, finals are almost here, and he hasn't—" My palm pressed to my mouth, keeping my lips from trembling, keeping a sob from breaking free.

"And you miss him," Isa said softly.

I nodded, not trusting my voice.

"You were trying to help, right? When you suggested he come to Waverly Cove this summer."

"I was trying to solve his problems again," I groaned. "Save on rent, help at my family's bakery, give him space to breathe. I thought it was being supportive. But to him it probably felt like I was trying to fix him."

"Maybe," Isa said carefully. "You know how guys can be about pride, especially when they're struggling. And from what you've told me about his family, independence means everything to him right now. Accepting help might feel like admitting defeat."

I picked at my food, even though I had lost my appetite. The noodles had gone cold, congealing. "So what do I do?"

"What does your gut tell you?"

"To talk to him. To fix this." I gestured at my sketchbook, at the failed compositions scattered across my desk. "To figure out how to build the connection right."

Isa smiled. "There's your answer."

"But what if he doesn't want to talk to me?" The fear I'd been holding back for a week leaked out. "What if he meant what he said? What if he's decided I'm not worth all the trouble I've caused?"

"Kate." Isa leaned forward, catching my gaze. "That boy looks at you like you hung the moon and painted all the stars to match. One fight doesn't erase months of whatever you two have built. It just means you're both human."

Hope flickered. Fragile but persistent. "I'll find him tomorrow. After his library shift."

"Good." Isa nudged the takeout container closer. "Now eat your noodles before I force-feed you like you're one of my little siblings."

I managed a smile and took another bite. The pad thai still tasted good, even cold.

By the next afternoon, I was determined to fix the awkwardness between me and Alex. He would be at the campus center around three. He always studied there between his morning lab shift and evening library hours. Second floor near the economics offices where fewer people gathered and the fluorescent lights were marginally less soul-crushing.

My sneakers scuffed against concrete as I rehearsed. *I'm sorry about last week. I know you're under immense pressure. I wasn't trying to solve your problems or minimize what you're going through. I want to support you. We'll figure this out together.*

I spotted him at a corner table near the windows. He wore the gray hoodie I'd given him for his birthday. The one he said helped him think. His hair stuck up on one side like he'd been running his hands through it.

Halfway across the floor, I was already choosing what to say first. *I'm sorry* or *Can we talk?* Or maybe *I miss you.*

Then I registered the second person at the table.

Jennifer sat across from him. Glossy black hair falling in a perfect sheet over one shoulder. She wore a cream cashmere sweater that probably cost more than my textbooks. Polished in a way I never managed, especially after a week of living in my studio clothes.

I should have stopped. I should have turned and texted him later. But my feet carried me closer even as my brain screamed warnings.

Jennifer leaned forward across the table, saying something with intense focus. Reached out and placed her hand over Alex's where it rested on his notebook.

I froze mid-step.

The gesture looked natural. Comfortable. Her pale hand covering his darker one, fingers curving around his in a way that spoke of familiarity. Of history. Of easy intimacy between two people who'd known each other since childhood. Who understood each other's worlds without translation.

My stomach dropped.

Alex bowed his head. His shoulders were tight. He didn't pull his hand away. He just sat there, looking at their joined hands like he was trying to solve an equation that wouldn't balance.

Around us, the campus center continued its normal rhythm. Keyboards clicking. Someone's music bleeding through inadequate headphones. The hiss of the espresso machine downstairs. But in that corner by the windows, just Alex and Jennifer remained, their hands together on the table, and me standing there like an idiot, realizing I'd walked into something I wasn't supposed to see.

The moment couldn't have lasted more than a few seconds. But it was enough to register the cold wrongness growing beneath my ribs.

Then Alex looked up.

His eyes met mine across the space between us. His face paled. The hand under Jennifer's jerked away so fast he knocked his water bottle over. It hit the floor with a hollow clatter that cut through the ambient noise. The parallel to all those months ago at The Golden Dragon was so ironic that I barked out a laugh.

"Kate." His voice was strangled. His eyes widened.

Jennifer turned to see what had startled him. Surprise and relief crossed her face when she saw me standing there.

I made my legs move forward. Made myself keep walking even though every instinct screamed to run. To get out before I fell apart in front of them. Before the tears forming behind my eyes could fall where they'd see.

"Hi." My voice sounded so steady that I was proud. I tucked my trembling hands into my jacket pockets and extended one to Jennifer, who looked startled but recovered fast. She stood with fluid grace to meet me. "We weren't properly introduced last time. I'm Kate Westfield."

Jennifer shook my hand. Her palm was soft and cool. "Jennifer Liu. Alex and I were just—"

"Catching up." I withdrew my hand. My heart hammered in my throat. "I can see that."

The silence that followed felt heavy and wrong. Alex had risen to his feet. His water bottle lay abandoned on the floor. His notebook splayed open with pen marks bleeding across chemistry equations. He looked exhausted. Hollow-eyed and pale beneath his tan. The gray hoodie hung on him like armor that had stopped working.

"Kate, this isn't—" he started.

"Jennifer, would you mind if I talked to Alex alone for a minute?" I kept my voice level. Controlled. Channeling every ounce of Westfield resilience my family had ever modeled.

She glanced between us. Whatever she saw decided for her.

"Of course. I should get back to campus anyway. I have a study group."

She gathered her things with efficient movements. Phone, planner, an expensive-looking thermos. Then she paused beside Alex, resting her hand on his shoulder in another gesture that looked too natural. Too familiar. "Think about what I said, okay?"

He nodded without looking at her. His eyes stayed fixed on my face like he was trying to read words written there in a language he didn't quite know.

After Jennifer left, I sank into the chair she'd vacated. Still warm from her body. The heat felt like an accusation. Around us, students continued their normal routines, oblivious.

"That looked cozy."

Alex flinched back from the unspoken accusation. "Kate, that conversation wasn't what it looked like."

"It looked like two people who understand each other. Talking honestly about tough choices." I forced myself to meet his eyes. "It looked like she was comforting you. And you let her."

"She's an old friend. Her parents have been calling my parents, trying to—" He broke off, running his hands through his already-disheveled hair. "It's complicated."

"I'm sure it is." The hurt I'd been processing through paint and canvas all week bubbled up. Refused to stay contained in artistic expression. "Seven days, Alex. We've barely spoken in seven days. Terse texts that felt like checking boxes. And when I finally work up the courage to come find you, you're here with her. Holding hands."

"We weren't holding hands." His voice rose. Defensive. "She reached across the table and—"

"And you didn't pull away." I leaned forward. "Not until you saw me."

The truth of that hung between us. His face paled even

further. He scrambled for words to explain. To make it make sense. But what explanation could there be?

"How much did you hear?" he asked.

A laugh caught in my throat. "I didn't hear anything. I saw. And that told me everything I needed to know."

"That's not fair." Alex leaned forward, urgent. "Jennifer understands things you can't about my family situation, but that doesn't mean—"

"That's the problem, isn't it?" I didn't realize I had shouted it until a few students nearby glanced over. I took a few calming breaths so I could lower my voice to a more appropriate level. "There will always be things about your world I can't understand. Cultural contexts I'm missing. Family dynamics I can't grasp no matter how hard I try."

"Kate, please." He reached for my hand across the table, but I pulled back, tucking my hands in my lap. His fingers landed on the wood instead, inches from mine. The gap might as well have been miles. "I need you. Not someone who fits into neat boxes my parents drew ages ago."

For a moment, I wavered. His brown eyes pleaded with me. The same eyes that had watched me paint with such wonder. That had crinkled at the corners when I'd made terrible chemistry puns during our first tutoring sessions. The same eyes that had looked at me like I was something precious. Something worth fighting for.

Then I remembered his words from last week. *Not all of us can change life plans as easily as flipping TV channels.*

I remembered the casual way Jennifer had touched his shoulder. The natural comfort between them.

I remembered the exhaustion in his voice during that fight, when he'd said he was tired of fighting everyone.

"I think we need to take a break." The words felt foreign. Like speaking a language I'd just learned and wasn't sure I was pronouncing right. But once spoken, I couldn't take them back.

"Until after finals. Until graduation. We both need space to figure out what we really want. What we can sustain."

"No." There was a hint of panic in his tone and expression now. A slight mania. "Kate, don't do this. Don't use one moment out of context to—"

"It's not one moment." I stood and grabbed my bag. "Last week happened. You're exhausting yourself trying to hold everything together. And maybe you need someone who doesn't add to the complication. Someone who makes your life easier instead of harder."

"That's not what I want." He stood too, desperation edging his voice. "I don't want easier. I want you."

"Right now, you need someone who understands your world without you having to explain it." I had to force the next words out. "And right now, I need to be sure that what we have is worth all the fighting. For both of us."

His face crumpled before he caught himself and slid his mask of control back into place. The one he wore when he was protecting himself from hurt. "So that's it? One misunderstanding and you're walking away?"

"I'm not walking away. I'm giving us both space to be certain." I took a step back, creating physical distance to match the emotional gulf. "Good luck on your finals, Alex."

I made my way down the stairs, through the campus center's overheated lobby, and out into the spring sunshine that now felt too bright. Too cheerful.

Pink blossoms fell from the trees, drifting down like pink snow. One landed on my sneaker and stayed there for a moment before the wind carried it away.

Beautiful and temporary. Like everything else.

Chapter 25

Alex

The student center hummed with activity as seniors picked up graduation packages. Excited chatter was punctuated by occasional high-pitched squeals when friends spotted each other across the room. I stood in line, watching others compare cap sizes and pose for photos while my mind kept returning to Kate. It had been nearly two weeks since she'd asked for space. Days of her face replaying on a loop. The way she'd looked when she'd turned away from me and Jennifer outside the student center. Not anger. I could have handled her anger. It was the hurt and resignation in her expression that haunted my thoughts.

"Chen, Alexander," I told the volunteer when I reached the table.

An older woman with gray hair sprayed into architectural rigidity checked her list. "Pharmacy, honors. Congratulations, young man." Her smile revealed too many teeth, the automatic brightness of someone who'd delivered the same line two hundred times today. "How many guests should we expect?"

Two weeks ago, the answer would have been three for my

parents and Kate. But my parents had withdrawn their financial support the day I'd chosen Kate over Jennifer. And Kate...

"Uncertain at this time," I replied.

"Well, we need a headcount for seating." Her pen hovered over the form, drops of ink gathering at the tip. "Write down your best guess, honey."

Around me, other students marked numbers with confidence: five, seven, twelve. Family members who would fill those chairs, take photos, celebrate. A father lifted his daughter's cap high in the air while her mother angled her phone to capture the moment. The daughter laughed, reaching for the cap, her other hand pressed against her father's shoulder for balance.

"Three," I said finally.

She nodded and handed me a stack of three tickets. The seats would exist whether anyone filled them or not. At least this way they'd be theoretical possibilities rather than confirmed absences.

I examined the small cellophane package as I moved away from the table. The gold sash caught the fluorescent light. Pharmacy graduates wore gold to represent the value of medicine, according to the information packet. But the symbolism rang hollow when I thought about my father's friend withdrawing his recommendation letter, about how quickly professional value could evaporate when personal choices didn't align with expectations.

The mail room sat empty, most students having abandoned campus communications now that summer break loomed beyond finals. I twisted the small metal dial on my assigned box, muscle memory guiding the familiar combination. Two envelopes waited inside, both bearing formal letterheads.

I pulled them out and leaned against the cool metal wall.

My hands trembled when I broke the seal on the first envelope. Not emotion. Just the physiological consequence of four-hour sleep averages sustained over fourteen days. Caffeine metabolism had its limits, and I'd exceeded mine sometime around day ten.

> CONGRATULATIONS ON YOUR UPCOMING GRADUATION!
>
> WE'D LOVE TO WELCOME YOU INTO OUR PHARMACY PROGRAM. DR. ZHANG SPEAKS HIGHLY OF YOUR POTENTIAL.
>
> LET'S DISCUSS YOUR FUTURE WITH US...

I stopped at the second sentence. Read it again. Dr. Zhang. My father's friend, the one who'd withdrawn his letter of endorsement when I'd chosen Kate over the arrangement with Jennifer.

Except this letter came from Western Massachusetts Medical Center, where Dr. Zhang held no affiliations.

I opened the second envelope from Providence Medical Center, scanning past the polite opening.

> MR. CHEN,
>
> YOUR APPLICATION TO OUR RESIDENCY PROGRAM SHOWS EXCEPTIONAL PROMISE.
>
> WE'D LIKE TO SCHEDULE AN INTERVIEW AT YOUR EARLIEST CONVENIENCE...

These weren't the top-tier programs I'd once targeted. But they were solid opportunities that hadn't existed yesterday morning when I'd checked my application status. Someone had advocated for me recently enough to shift outcomes.

I pulled out my phone before the logic could catch up with the impulse.

"Jen? It's Alex. Are you free to meet?"

The coffee shop Jennifer suggested sat three blocks from campus, wood-paneled walls and leather chairs creating an atmosphere of established professionalism. Nothing like the bright, chaotic spaces where Kate and I had studied together. Where she'd filled margins with tiny sketches while I'd explained electron configuration, where our knees had touched under small tables and neither of us had moved away.

I ordered water instead of coffee, conscious of the $127.43 in my checking account as of this morning. Rent was due in eight days. I'd been running the numbers obsessively, trying different calculation methods as if algebra could somehow make $127.43 cover $850 plus utilities plus food.

Jennifer arrived in pressed slacks and a white blouse, hair pulled back in a sleek ponytail. She ordered tea and settled across from me with economical movements.

"I'm glad you called," she said, stirring honey into her cup. "I've been worried about you since our conversation last week."

I placed my graduation package on the chair beside me and pulled out the two letters, sliding them across the table. "Two residency offers arrived this morning. Programs that had already rejected me."

She read them both. When she finished, she smiled. "That's wonderful, Alex."

"Did you speak to Dr. Zhang on my behalf?"

"My father did." She took a sip, the porcelain cup making a soft clink against the saucer. "He and Dr. Zhang play golf every month."

"Why would your father help me?" My fingers tightened on the water glass. "I declined the match our parents arranged. I chose Kate."

Jennifer set down her cup. For the first time since I'd known her, the professional composure slipped. "Because I asked him to."

She paused, arranging her words with the same precision she brought to lab work. "When our parents first introduced us, I was willing to see where it went. You're brilliant, we understand each other's culture, our families approved. All the right boxes checked."

I waited, the coffee grinder whirring behind the counter.

"We tried it," she continued, "and decided we were better as friends. I figured my parents would eventually accept we weren't a good fit and find another suitable match, and I was happy to wait. Then I met Mark at a campus blood drive last year. He was writing a piece for the school paper about donation rates. Kept asking questions while I was trying to focus on not sticking myself."

The corner of her mouth lifted. "He made me laugh about phlebotomy techniques. Such a small thing. But suddenly I couldn't imagine spending my life with someone who didn't make me want to debate medical journalism ethics at two in the morning."

Jennifer had changed over the past year. The way she'd politely but firmly declined her parents' dinner invitations, how she'd stopped responding immediately to their calls. I'd attributed it to academic pressure, not active resistance.

"Your parents wanted you to marry me." A statement, not a question.

"They wanted me to marry you. Or someone like you." She looked at me. "Pre-approved, compatible, safe. I told them about Mark after our third date. They were furious. Threatened to cut me off, same as yours did to you."

Her voice dropped lower, conscious of the few other patrons

scattered through the shop. "But I watched what happened to my older brother when he married the woman they chose. He's successful, stable, and absolutely miserable. I refused to follow that path."

A timer dinged behind the counter. Someone laughed at a nearby table. Normal sounds in a normal coffee shop where people made normal choices that didn't rupture family structures.

"But your parents changed their minds," I said. "They accepted Mark."

"Eventually. It took time." Jennifer's fingers traced the rim of her cup, following the delicate curve. "My father struggled most. Then Mark won a regional reporting award last month. My father read his pieces about local government corruption and started asking questions about investigative journalism. Mark was patient, respectful, never pushed. Gradually, my father realized this man I'd chosen had his own achievements. Not a distraction from my future, but someone building it alongside me."

That explained the shift when we'd met at the registrar's office. The day Kate had seen us together. Jennifer had carried herself differently, more confident in her choices, less apologetic about defying expectations.

"So you're helping me because..."

"Because I know what it's like to love someone your parents don't understand." She leaned forward slightly. "And because you did it, Alex. You chose Kate even though it cost you everything."

She took a breath. "When our parents' arrangement fell through, I felt guilty. But also relieved. There was no chemistry between us. Just... compatibility. I learned that compatibility without chemistry is just a nicer word for settling."

I processed this reorganization of data, adjusting my understanding of Jennifer from passive participant to active resistor. She'd been fighting her own battle for years while I'd been too focused on my own situation to notice the parallels.

"You're still pursuing medical school," I observed. "You're still following your parents' path in that regard."

"I'm becoming a doctor because I want to be one." She straightened in her chair. "And I'm dating a journalism major my parents initially rejected. My father didn't change his mind until Mark won that award. Success is a language our parents understand, Alex. But here's what took me years to learn. We can define success on our own terms. We just have to be patient enough to let them catch up."

The scent of coffee beans saturated the air as a barista ground a fresh batch. Rich, bitter, almost overwhelming.

"I didn't realize you felt that way," I said. "That you could pursue both."

"Both family and self?" Jennifer's eyes held amusement mixed with understanding. "Our generation doesn't have to choose between them, Alex. We create the middle path. It's harder than either extreme, and it takes longer, but it's possible."

Kate's face surfaced in my mind. The way she'd sat cross-legged on my dorm floor during my mono, bringing soup and ginger tea without being asked. How she'd listened when I'd tried to explain filial piety, cultural obligation, the weight of being an only son. How I'd thrown her family's support in her face like it was weakness, like their unconditional love somehow counted for less than my struggle.

The unfairness of it crystallized. Not abstract knowledge anymore. Concrete fact.

"Kate saw me with you that day," I said. "Outside the student center. She misunderstood what we were discussing."

Jennifer nodded slowly. "I suspected as much from her expression when she turned away. I would have explained if she'd given me the chance, that we were talking, that I was offering support as someone who understood the pressure."

"She thought I was reconsidering. Choosing cultural compatibility over what we had."

"Were you?" Her voice stayed quiet, but the question demanded an answer.

I thought about that moment with Jennifer, how I'd been venting about the impossible calculus of making everyone happy. She'd understood certain aspects of my situation that Kate couldn't, because she'd lived them. Understood them from shared experience.

"No," I said finally. "I was venting. You understood things Kate couldn't."

"Because my parents raised me with similar expectations." Jennifer leaned back in her chair. "But Alex, Kate was trying to understand. She asked questions, made effort, stayed even when you were difficult about it. That matters. That's the real work."

I ran my finger along the edge of my graduation package, then made a decision. Removed the three tickets and placed them on the table between us.

"Would you like to come to my graduation? I wrote down three guests when they asked for a count."

Jennifer's eyes widened slightly. "Wouldn't you rather save those for Kate? Or your parents?"

"Kate asked for space. And my parents..." I let the sentence hang unfinished. "I'd rather not have empty seats with my name on them."

She picked up the tickets, studying them carefully before tucking them into her purse. "I can't come, Alex. Mark and I will be in New York this weekend so he can look at housing for his graduate program at Columbia."

"Then why take them?"

She raised an eyebrow. "Let's call it a contingency plan."

We spent the next twenty minutes discussing the residency opportunities. Jennifer offered practical advice about interview preparation, what questions to expect, how to frame my academic performance despite the personal challenges. But as we prepared to leave, a question I'd been avoiding surfaced on its own.

"When does the Providence residency start?"

"July first, I believe. Most of them do."

Six weeks. Six weeks to somehow make $127.43 stretch to cover rent, utilities, food. The library position ended at graduation. Tutoring income had dried up when finals started. I'd been so focused on securing a residency offer that I hadn't calculated the logistics of survival in the gap between.

Jennifer studied my face. "Alex, are you okay financially until then?"

The concern in her voice made the situation more concrete, harder to abstract away with optimistic projections.

"I'll figure it out."

"That's not an answer."

If I was very careful, if I ate almost nothing and walked everywhere and hoped my landlord didn't enforce late fees, maybe three weeks. Four if I got creative about calories per dollar. The residency would pay enough to live on once it started, but the first paycheck wouldn't arrive until mid-July at the earliest.

"I have some savings," I said.

Her mouth tightened, but she was too polite to push. "If you need help..."

"I'll be fine." Pride, apparently, had a cost I couldn't quite calculate. "Thank you for asking."

She left with a gentle reminder to email her if I needed anything. I remained at the table, watching through the window as she crossed the street toward the T station. The coffee shop was emptying, afternoon crowd giving way to early dinner preparations. Students streamed past outside, laughing and making plans for the evening.

I'd been so focused on the binary choice, my parents' approval or Kate, that I'd missed the possibility of a third option. Not compromise, which implied sacrificing what mattered. But synthesis. Creating a path that honored both parts of myself.

The question was whether Kate would still be interested in that synthesis. Whether I'd burned that bridge so thoroughly that no amount of realization could rebuild it.

And whether I could afford to pursue any kind of future when I couldn't afford next month's rent.

Chapter 26

Alex

My apartment felt lonelier than usual that night. My exams finished last week, all with top marks. The achievement felt strangely inconsequential. I was at a loss for what to do after six years of pushing toward a goal. I focused my nervous energy on packing, organizing my possessions into labeled boxes with the same methodical attention I'd once applied to studying. Books: chemistry, pharmacology, organic synthesis. Clothes: professional, casual, winter. Kitchen: minimal, rarely used except for the weeks when Kate had—

I stopped, holding a mug she'd left behind. Dark blue ceramic with a small chip on the handle. She'd been drinking tea from it the night before my midterms, feet tucked under her on my couch while I practiced synthesis problems.

"You're going to ace this," she'd said with absolute confidence. "Your brain is basically a chemistry textbook that learned to walk."

I set the mug aside, unable to pack it with the others headed for donation.

My phone rang, startling me. David's name flashed on the screen.

"You busy?" he asked without preamble.

"Packing."

"Stop packing. I'm bringing pizza. And you're going to eat it and talk to me like a human being instead of the emotionally stunted robot thing you've got going on lately."

"I'm fine."

"You're definitely not fine. I can hear it in your voice. That weird flat thing you do when you're pretending everything's okay." He paused. "Pepperoni or veggie?"

"I don't—"

"Pepperoni it is. Be there in thirty. And I'm picking up beer too. Don't even try to tell me you're too busy."

He hung up before I could protest further.

David arrived exactly a half hour later carrying a large pizza box and a six-pack of beer. He surveyed my apartment with a critical eye.

"Jesus, Alex. You've organized your boxes by content type and labeled them with a color-coding system." He set the pizza on my small kitchen table. "This is deeply concerning behavior."

"It's efficient."

"It's a cry for help disguised as a filing system." He opened the pizza box. The smell of melted cheese and pepperoni filled my apartment. "Sit. Eat. Tell me why you look like you haven't slept in a week."

"I've been sleeping." Four hours a night wasn't technically insomnia. It was just suboptimal sleep hygiene.

David gave me a look that suggested he wasn't buying my technical evasions. He grabbed two plates from my bare cabinets and loaded them with pizza slices. Then he opened the nearly empty drawer and registered the sparse contents as he grabbed the bottle opener. His eyes swept the apartment again, this time with different attention.

"When's the last time you grocery shopped?" His tone carefully casual.

"I've been eating."

"That's not what I asked." He handed me a plate. "You've got like three things in your fridge. And they're all condiments."

"I've been busy packing."

"Right." David took a large bite of pizza, chewed thoughtfully. "So here's the thing. I got off the phone with my cousin Callie. She's the one who graduated last year? Moved straight on to her residency at Mass General?"

I waited.

"She said the first paycheck didn't hit until like six weeks after she started. Something about pay periods and processing." He took another bite, not quite meeting my eyes. "I was thinking about that, and about how you lost your library job, and about how you probably haven't been tutoring much during finals..."

The observation was too accurate to be coincidental. David had been doing his own calculations.

"I'll figure it out."

"You know what your problem is?" He finally addressed me directly.

"I suspect you're about to tell me regardless of my answer."

"You're trying to solve emotional problems with logic. And also financial problems with pride." He handed me a beer. "You can't spreadsheet your way out of heartbreak or poverty, man."

I took the beer because refusing would only prolong the conversation. "I'm not trying to spreadsheet anything."

"Really? Because I bet you've got a budget breakdown somewhere that shows exactly how long you can survive on ramen and stubbornness."

He wasn't wrong. The calculations were in my notebook, written three nights ago at two in the morning when sleep proved impossible and anxiety demanded concrete numbers.

CURRENT FUNDS:
Bank balance: $1,247.23

EXPENSES:
Rent: $1,025
Utilities (estimated): $100
Food: $100
Transit Card: $70
Emergency buffer: $100

SHORTFALL:
By June 1: approximately $148
By July 1: approximately $1,542

The math was unforgiving.

"I don't have a budget breakdown," I lied.

"You absolutely have a budget breakdown." David took another slice. "But that's not the most important thing we need to talk about. Though we're coming back to it, because I have thoughts about your financially suicidal decision-making."

"What's more important than my impending homelessness?"

"The Kate thing." He set down his pizza. "What happened? Because from where I'm sitting, you had a fight, Jennifer showed up being helpful in that annoyingly perfect way she has, and Kate saw you two together and jumped to conclusions."

"She didn't jump. I pushed her." I set down my beer without drinking more. "I told her that not all of us can change life plans without a thought. That she shouldn't have changed majors."

David stopped mid-chew. "You said what?"

"I was exhausted and stressed and working three jobs and watching my parents cut me off and she was trying to solve it by offering me space in her brother's apartment like that wouldn't be humiliating—" The words tumbled out faster than I could organize them. "And she was talking about Waverly Cove and moving in with Liam and none of it addressed the problem which is that I can't accept charity and I can't fail and I can't—"

"Breathe," David interrupted. "Jesus, Alex. That's impressively terrible."

I took a breath, forcing myself to slow down. "It wasn't even true. It was frustration. I was jealous that her family made everything easy for her while mine cut me off. But that wasn't her fault."

"No, it definitely wasn't." His voice carried disappointment. "So what now? You give up?"

"She asked for space. I'm respecting that."

"You're hiding." David grabbed another slice, pointing it at me for emphasis. "There's a difference between respecting boundaries and using them as an excuse to not fight for what you want."

"What I want doesn't matter if I hurt her in the process of wanting it."

"That's the dumbest thing you've said tonight, and you've said some pretty dumb things." He chewed thoughtfully. "Look, I get it. You're scared. You already lost your family over this relationship. If you put yourself out there and Kate still doesn't want you back, then what? You've lost everything for nothing."

The accuracy of his observation was uncomfortably precise.

"When did you become a therapist?"

"I took one psychology elective. I think that qualifies me to analyze my emotionally constipated best friend." He grinned, but it faded quickly. "Alex, man, do you still love her?"

"Yes." The response didn't require any calculation.

"Does she make you happy? Like, genuinely happy, not 'this aligns with my five-year plan' happy?"

Kate in her studio surfaced in my mind. Paint smudged on her cheek, explaining color theory with the same passion I used for chemical bonds. The way she'd nursed me through mono despite my protests, learning to read my silences as clearly as my words.

How her family had welcomed me to Waverly Cove like I wasn't the son who'd disappointed his own parents. How she'd looked hurt and confused when I'd thrown her family's support in her face as if it were somehow a weakness rather than a gift.

"She makes me more than the sum of my achievements."

"Then stop organizing your feelings into boxes and do something about it." David stood, crossing to my desk where my laptop sat closed. "Come on. Where are these residency programs?"

"What are you doing?"

"Research. Your favorite activity." He opened my laptop, which helpfully still had my residency spreadsheet pulled up. Of course it did. "Providence and Western Mass. Okay. Western Mass is better ranked?"

"Without a doubt. Better research opportunities, higher match rate for fellowships, stronger connections to pharmaceutical companies, more prestigious faculty—" I joined him at the desk, unable to resist the pull of data analysis.

"But Providence is closer to Boston." David was already pulling up Google Maps. "Hour drive. That's nothing."

"Geography isn't the issue."

"Shut up and let me work." He opened a new tab, typing rapidly. "RISD. Rhode Island School of Design. You know what that is?"

"A prestigious art school?"

"A prestigious art school with gallery partnerships throughout Providence." He clicked through several pages. "Look at this. The city has an entire arts district. Multiple galleries. Artist co-ops. A museum."

"Kate's studying at Northeastern."

"Kate could study art anywhere. She could transfer, or do a summer intensive program, or teach, or a million other things artists do." David pulled up more tabs, building a visual argument across my screen. "But you need an accredited pharmacy residency program with availability for this year. So the question isn't where Kate could go. It's where you can both build careers."

He showed me possibilities I'd been too narrow-minded to see. Gallery density in Providence. Artist communities. The Newport Art Museum partnership. All within reasonable proximity to Providence Memorial Hospital.

"Jennifer said I could find a middle path."

"Jennifer's right. Annoyingly." David minimized the browser windows and turned to face me. "Look, your parents might never fully accept Kate. That sucks. But you can build a life that leaves space for them to change their minds while still being with the person you love. A life where you're both pursuing your passions, not just surviving them."

I studied the closed laptop, thinking of the painting Kate had been working on before everything fell apart. The way she'd seen past the surface to the softer parts beneath. How she'd tried to understand my cultural obligations even when I hadn't helped her understand.

Jennifer's words: *We create the middle path.*

"I haven't responded to either offer yet."

"So respond." David grabbed his beer. "Choose the place where you can have both. Career and life. Pharmacy and art. Chemistry and Kate."

"That's terrible wordplay."

"It's inspirational wordplay." He grinned, but then his expression turned more serious. "But Alex, real talk for a second. About the money situation."

"I said I'll figure it out."

"Yeah, and I'm saying you don't have to figure it out alone." He leaned against my desk, arms crossed. "My parents are paying for my apartment through August. I've got a single room, but the couch pulls out. You could crash there until your residency starts. No rent, split utilities and food."

Pride flared immediately. "I can't—"

"Before you say you can't accept help or whatever bullshit you're about to spout, let me remind you that you let me copy your organic chem notes for an entire semester when I was recovering from ACL surgery sophomore year. You tutored me through physical chemistry for free. You've bought my dinner dozens of times over the past four years." He held up a hand to stop my protest. "I'm not offering charity, Chen. I'm offering friendship. There's a difference."

The offer was tempting enough to be dangerous. Six weeks of not worrying about rent would solve the immediate crisis. But accepting help still tasted like admitting defeat.

"I'm also a terrible roommate," David continued. "I leave dishes in the sink, I play video games too loud, and Julie and I are kind of annoying with how cute we are together on video calls. So really, you'd be doing me a favor by having someone around."

Despite everything, I almost smiled. "How are things with Julie?"

"Good. Really good." He shrugged, but genuine warmth showed in his expression. "She laughs at my terrible jokes, which is my love language. We're not like, serious serious yet, but it's getting there. Which is part of why I'm being pushy about this Kate thing. You deserve to have good too."

David wasn't the supportive friend dispensing perfect advice. He was someone building his own life, figuring out his own relationship, dealing with his own uncertainties. And he was offering to share his space anyway.

"I don't know what to say."

"Say yes. Say thank you. Say literally anything except 'I'll figure it out.'" David grabbed another slice of pizza. "Come on, Chen. You're graduating in next week. Make one decision that isn't about being the perfect son or the perfect student or the perfectly self-sufficient martyr. Make one that's about being happy."

Happy. I'd spent six years optimizing for achievement instead of happiness, which in retrospect represented a significant planning oversight. My mother at the restaurant surfaced in my mind. The small nod she'd given me when I told her about Kate. Not approval, exactly. But not complete rejection either. Jennifer's father helping me despite my rejection of their arrangement. David showing up with pizza and a pull-out couch because he knew I'd be alone in my apartment, mentally filing my emotions into categories instead of processing them.

Kate, somewhere on campus, probably painting through her own confusion while I sat here pretending organization could solve heartbreak and poverty simultaneously.

"Okay." The word came out rough.

David's eyebrows rose. "Okay meaning...?"

"Okay I'll stay on your couch. Until the residency starts." The words still sounded strange but right. "And okay I'll respond to Providence. And okay I'll... I'll try to talk to Kate. After graduation. Give her the space she asked for, but not forever."

"Holy shit, did you accept help and commit to emotional vulnerability in the same conversation?" David grabbed his beer and held it up. "This calls for a toast. To making decisions that aren't logical, but happy."

I raised my own beer, the bottle cold against my palm. "To middle paths."

"And to not being homeless," David added with a grin. "Also important."

We drank, and for the first time in two weeks, the hollowness inside diminished slightly. The pizza was good, the beer was cold, and my best friend had offered me exactly what I needed without making it taste like failure to accept.

After David left, I reopened my laptop. The residency spreadsheet stared back at me, waiting for updates. I created a new tab labeled "Providence Research" and methodically documented everything we'd found.

And underneath all the data, a single question I'd been avoiding: *What if I could have both?*

The Western Mass program was objectively superior by every metric I'd previously used to evaluate opportunities. But maybe I'd been using the wrong metrics all along. The data was pointing me toward what mattered beyond rankings and prestige. A place where both Kate and I could pursue our passions. Where success could be measured in more than career advancement. Where I could prove to my parents that choosing love didn't mean abandoning ambition.

I opened my email and drafted a response to Providence Memorial Hospital, my fingers steady on the keys for the first time in weeks.

```
Dear Dr. Morse,

Thank you for your interest in my applica-
tion. I would be honored to interview for
your residency program.

I'm particularly drawn to Providence Memo-
rial's community focus and your partner-
ships with local healthcare initiatives. I
believe the program's emphasis on patient-
centered care aligns well with my goals as
a pharmacist.

I'm available for an interview at your
earliest convenience. Please let me know
what dates and times work best for your
team.
```

```
Sincerely,

Alexander Chen
```

I read it over again before hitting send, then immediately pulled up my budget spreadsheet and added a new line:

Housing - David's couch: $0
Utilities (split): ~$50
Food (split): ~$50

    The numbers finally balanced. It wasn't perfect, but it was enough to breathe.

    Tomorrow I would continue packing. I would prepare for graduation. But tonight, I allowed myself to consider a different kind of future. One where accepting help wasn't failure, but the first step toward synthesis.

Three days before graduation, I found myself standing outside The Golden Dragon at eight in the evening. The dinner rush was ending, the last few customers paying their bills and heading out into the warm spring night. Through the window, my father tallied receipts at the front desk.

    I almost turned around multiple times before finally pushing through the door.

    The bell chimed, catching my father's attention. For a moment, neither of us moved.

    "We're closing soon." His voice neutral in Mandarin.

    "I know. I..." I switched to English, then back to Mandarin, unsure which language could better convey what I needed to say. "I wanted to tell you something."

My father set down his pen. "I got a residency position. In Providence. I start in July."

It wasn't how I'd pictured telling anyone, but at least the words were out in the open now.

"Providence." He repeated the word carefully, as if testing its weight. "The residency program there is... adequate?"

Coming from my father, adequate was practically effusive praise.

"It's a good program. Good clinical experience. Strong community connections. And..." I hesitated, "and it's close to opportunities for Kate. If she's still willing to consider a future that includes me."

My father's expression remained carefully neutral, but something shifted in his gaze.

"You're still pursuing this relationship."

"I am." I met his gaze directly. "She's the one who's tried hardest to understand what this," I gestured between us, "what all of this means to me."

He was quiet for a long moment. When he spoke, his voice was softer. "Your mother worries about you. She thinks you're not eating properly."

"I'll be okay. My friend David is letting me stay with him until residency starts. So I'll have a place to live, and food, and—"

"Your friend is helping you?"

I nodded, bracing for criticism about accepting handouts. Instead, my father's expression did something complicated. Sadness, surprise, and satisfaction washed rapidly across his features.

"That's good. A man needs friends who support him when family cannot."

The statement landed heavily, though I wasn't entirely sure how to interpret it.

"Come." He surprised me by gesturing toward the back. "We made extra dumplings. We should not waste food."

I followed him through the kitchen, where my mother glanced up from her workstation with visible surprise as we passed, to the small back office that had served as my after-school study space for years. My father pulled out two chairs and retrieved a container of dumplings from the small fridge he kept for family meals.

We ate in silence for several minutes. The dumplings tasted exactly as I remembered: perfectly balanced flavors, the wrapper thin but not fragile. My father's recipe, perfected over decades of practice.

"Your mother worries." He finally broke the silence, still speaking Mandarin. "She thinks you're too thin. That you're not sleeping enough."

"I'm managing."

He gave me a look that suggested he didn't believe me. "This Providence program. They have good placement rates for fellowships?"

"About seventy percent. Lower than Western Mass, but still respectable."

"And you chose Providence because...?"

Because it's near art galleries and teaching opportunities for Kate. Because it's close enough to visit her family in Maine and maybe, eventually, close enough for you to visit if you ever decide to. Because I'm trying to build a life instead of a career. Because Jennifer taught me that middle paths exist if you're patient enough to walk them.

"The community focus appeals to me. And the clinical exposure is excellent. Plus the cost of living is lower than Boston, which will help me save money during the residency."

My father nodded, accepting this explanation. "Dr. Zhang spoke well of your work. He said you have..." He paused, searching for the right word. "Dedication."

"I thought Dr. Zhang was no longer willing to recommend me."

"Dr. Zhang understands family loyalty. He also understands that sometimes..." My father set down his chopsticks. "Sometimes children must make their own choices. Even when parents believe those choices are... unwise."

It was the closest thing to understanding I'd heard from him since the fight.

"I didn't choose Kate to hurt you. I chose her because I love her. Because she makes me want to be more than successful. She makes me want to be happy."

My father was silent for a long moment. When he spoke, his voice carried emotion I wasn't expecting.

"Your mother and I, we came to this country with nothing. Everything we built took years." He gestured around the small office, encompassing the restaurant beyond. "We wanted our son to have opportunities we never had. To not have to struggle the way we did."

"I know."

"But perhaps..." He paused, picking up his chopsticks again but not eating. "Perhaps we focused too much on security and forgot about happiness. Your mother's parents arranged our marriage. We were fortunate that we grew to love each other over time. But not everyone is so lucky."

I stared at my father, uncertain how to process this admission.

"I am proud of your achievements." He continued, still not looking at me. "Your grades, your honors, your acceptance to pharmacy programs. These things matter. They prove you took advantage of the opportunities we gave you. But your mother, she says..." He switched to English suddenly. "She says I am too focused on the practical. That I forget my son is also a person, not a future."

"Bàba—"

"I do not agree with your choice." His voice firm, switching back to Mandarin. "This girl, this Kate, she is not what we hoped for you. But Jennifer's father, he tells me his daughter also chose differently. Against their wishes. And she is happy now. Still successful, but happy." He swallowed hard. "Maybe our generation, we do not understand everything about this world you live in."

It wasn't acceptance. It wasn't approval. But it was acknowledgment, and that was more than I'd dared hope for.

"I'm still going to Providence. I'm still going to pursue this relationship if Kate will have me back."

"I understand." My father stood, gathering the empty container. "But you will still call your mother. She worries."

"I'll call."

He paused at the door of the office, his back to me. "The graduation. We will... consider attending."

Then he was gone, leaving me alone with the echoes of the most honest conversation we'd had in months.

I sat there for several more minutes, processing what had happened. The first foundation stone of that middle path Jennifer had mentioned. The beginning of a bridge that might someday span the distance between my parents' expectations and my own choices.

My mother appeared in the doorway, holding another container. "Take this." Her voice brisk in Mandarin. "You're too skinny."

"Māmā, I'm fine—"

"You're too skinny." She pressed the container into my hands with finality. Soup, from the weight of it. "And you look tired. You're sleeping enough?"

"Yes." The lie seemed necessary.

Her eyes narrowed, but she didn't argue further. Instead, she reached out and adjusted my collar with quick, efficient movements.

"This girl, Kate. She is cooking for you?"

The question caught me off guard. "We're... we had a fight. We're taking space."

"Mmm." My mother's expression was inscrutable. "Space is good sometimes. Helps you see clearly. But too much space, and people forget why they were together." She gave my arm a single awkward pat. "Don't be stupid about this, Lì Xiáng. If she makes you happy, you fix it."

Then she was gone too, leaving me holding a container of soup and wondering when my parents had become capable of surprising me.

Chapter 27

Kate

I was alone in the campus art studio at midnight, surrounded by scattered reference photos and empty coffee cups. My graduation gift for Alex was nearly complete. What started as a simple painting weeks ago, when we'd first fought, had evolved into something more complex.

The canvas held two figures on opposite sides, but instead of the literal bridge I'd initially planned, the negative space between them now swirled with abstract patterns of molecules that gradually transformed into loose brushstrokes of blues, golds, and deep reds. Chemistry dissolving into art. Order into emotion.

Except it wasn't dissolving smoothly. Not yet, anyway.

The molecular structures on the left side remained crisp, precise, almost rigid in their scientific accuracy. The artistic brushstrokes on the right were loose and expressive, but they stopped abruptly where they should have begun to blend. Between them, the transition zone was muddy and uncertain. The line where the forms merged looked forced and awkward.

"Just one more hour," I muttered to the empty room, staring at the muddled middle section. "Then maybe you'll actually look like something besides a relationship crisis rendered in paint."

I'd worked on that transition for several nights now, trying to find the right balance. Every time I thought I had it, the paint looked too literal. Too neat. Too finished, when nothing about us felt finished.

Maybe that was the point.

I didn't realize how long I'd been lost in thought until I received a concerned message from my roommate.

> **ISA**
> It's midnight. Either you're coming back or you've fallen face-first into a paint palette. Please confirm life signs.

I smiled.

> **KATE**
> Still breathing. Mostly fumes though.

> **ISA**
> You've been there every night this week. The painting isn't going to paint itself, but it also won't run away.

I stepped back, tilting my head. The piece was technically unfinished. The dissonance in the middle, those awkward transitions where chemistry and art didn't quite mesh yet, was honest. That was us. Still figuring it out, still learning each other's languages.

I added a single stroke where the molecular patterns reached toward the artistic side. Not connecting fully, just reaching. A gesture of possibility rather than resolution.

> **KATE**
> I'm alive. Need to finish Alex's gift. Don't wait up.

> **ISA**
> You sure this is a good idea after everything?

No, I wasn't sure of anything anymore. Not after our fight where Alex had essentially said I couldn't understand his struggles because I'd had an "easy" path changing majors. Not after weeks of silence that felt like breathing underwater.

But yesterday, I'd found an envelope in my campus mailbox. Alex's graduation tickets with a note paper-clipped to them:

> *He wanted to invite you himself but thought you wouldn't come. I've seen how he looks at you. Please go in my place. He needs someone there who truly cares.*
>
> *-Jennifer*

I'd stared at Jennifer's note for a full minute. The fact she was advocating for me meant the rigid walls I'd imagined around Alex's world might have some flexibility I hadn't seen.

Maybe I was just assuming the worst, like I had with my parents' reaction to changing my major.

I texted back.

> **KATE**
> Working on plan B too. Will explain tomorrow.

I pulled out my other, smaller canvas. Opening my laptop, I scrolled through photos until I found what I needed. A selfie I'd texted my mom of me holding the maple candy during my disastrous first visit to The Golden Dragon. The restaurant's distinctive red and gold façade glowing in the evening light, the Chinese characters above the door bold against the deep blue twilight.

"Please let this work," I whispered, mixing a rich cadmium red. "Or at least let it not make everything worse."

Three hours later, with paint-stained fingers and eyes burning from exhaustion, I had two finished pieces. One finished piece, technically, and one intentionally unfinished. The main painting with its unresolved tension in the middle, molecules and brushstrokes that didn't quite merge yet, and the small, luminous painting of The Golden Dragon restaurant. The second wasn't my usual style. More realistic and detailed, every brush stroke deliberate. I'd worked from reference photos but added golden sunset light that transformed the modest restaurant into something almost magical.

As I carefully placed both paintings on the drying rack, Professor Vellacott's words from last week's critique echoed: "Art doesn't always build bridges. Sometimes it just helps us see the other shore more clearly."

Tomorrow, I would find out if she was right.

The T rumbled beneath me as I headed toward Quincy, both paintings carefully wrapped and nestled in my portfolio case. Outside the window, Boston scrolled by. Brick buildings, narrow streets, glimpses of the harbor between buildings. I'd rehearsed what I wanted to say at least fifty times since dawn, each version sounding more desperate than the last.

"*Hi, Mr. and Mrs. Chen. Remember me? The girl who ruined your son's perfect future? I brought art!*"

Definitely not that one.

"*I understand your cultural expectations and respect your sacri-*

fices. I would like to discuss potential compromise solutions regarding your son's romantic future."

Too much like a business negotiation.

"Please come to Alex's graduation. He loves you. Also, surprise, I still love him even though we're technically not speaking right now."

Closer, but still not right.

A young woman across from me glanced up from her phone, probably wondering why I was muttering to myself. I offered an apologetic smile and focused on my breathing instead.

The train lurched into the station. My stomach followed suit. I'd been here exactly once before. That awful night I'd found Alex having dinner with Jennifer and both their families. Now, in daylight, the neighborhood revealed details I'd missed during my tearful retreat.

Chinese characters adorned storefronts alongside English translations. Roasted ducks hung in restaurant windows. Elderly men played chess in a small park while children darted around them. A woman arranged fresh vegetables at a market stand, calling out prices in rapid-fire Mandarin.

This was Alex's world. Or part of it, anyway. The cultural tapestry his parents had woven for him, the community that shaped his earliest understanding of belonging.

As I approached The Golden Dragon, I pictured my last visit here. Seeing Alex with Jennifer. The confusion on his face when I confronted him. The cold sidewalk beneath my feet as I fled back to campus. I felt so foolish for my reaction and all the unnecessary stress it caused both of us, but who knows where Alex and my relationship would be now if I hadn't taken that first impulsive step.

Now, standing before the familiar red door with its golden dragon handle, I considered turning around. This was presumptuous, intrusive, possibly even disrespectful. Who was I to insert myself into this family's business? Maybe Alex had been right. Maybe I couldn't understand the weight of cultural expectations because my own family had supported my choices so readily.

A small sign in the window read **OPEN 12-10** in both English and Chinese characters. It was barely 9 AM.

"You can do this," I whispered, clutching my portfolio case. "Just be respectful, be honest, and try not to make an absolute fool of yourself. Two out of three would be great at this point."

Before courage could desert me completely, I pushed the door open. A small bell jangled.

Mrs. Chen emerged from the kitchen, wiping her hands on a cloth. When she saw me, she froze. Her grip tightened on the cloth.

"I'm sorry to interrupt." My carefully rehearsed speech evaporated, words tumbling out quickly. "I was hoping I can speak with you and Mr. Chen. About Alex. About tomorrow."

Her eyes narrowed. "The restaurant is not open."

"I know. I'm not here for food." I took a deep breath. "Please. Five minutes."

She studied me for a long moment. Then she called toward the kitchen in Mandarin.

Mr. Chen appeared, his expression hardening when he saw me. He wore a crisp white shirt, his posture perfectly straight.

"You," he said accusingly. "Why are you here?"

I straightened my shoulders, suddenly conscious of my paint-stained fingernails and the wrinkles in my dress from the T ride. "Alex graduates tomorrow. I thought... I hoped... you might consider attending."

"We have nothing to discuss." Mr. Chen's voice was flat. "The restaurant is open tomorrow. Saturdays are very busy."

"The ceremony is at eleven," I persisted. "The restaurant doesn't open until noon."

Mrs. Chen glanced at her husband, then back at me. Her

expression held less certainty than her husband's immediate dismissal.

"Alex knows we are not coming," she said quietly.

"He doesn't expect you to," I confirmed. "But it would mean everything if you did."

Mr. Chen said something pointed in Mandarin. Mrs. Chen responded in calmer tones. A brief exchange followed that I couldn't understand. I stood there, catching my breath, feeling like I'd walked into the middle of a foreign film without subtitles.

Finally, Mr. Chen turned to me. "You do not understand. Alex made his choice. He chose you, not family duty."

"That's not true." Both of them looked surprised at my objection, so I moderated my tone. "I mean... Alex respects you both enormously. He talks about your how hard you've worked to give him opportunities constantly."

"Then why throw away an opportunity?" Mrs. Chen asked. Her voice held genuine confusion. "The pharmacy career we worked for. A good match with a good family. Security."

This was the heart of it. Not that Alex had chosen me, but that he'd deviated from their carefully constructed plan.

"May I sit? Please. I'm not leaving until you hear me out."

Mrs. Chen's eyebrows rose. Mr. Chen's expression darkened, but he gestured stiffly toward a nearby table. "Five minutes."

I sat carefully, setting my portfolio case beside me. They remained standing, a united front across the table. For a moment, I was being interviewed for a job I was woefully unqualified for.

"Your son graduates with honors tomorrow because of your dedication," I started. "Everything he's accomplished is because you gave him the foundation, the work ethic, the opportunities. He knows that better than anyone."

Mr. Chen's expression didn't change, but he was obviously listening.

"Alex worked three jobs this semester after losing your

support," I continued. "Library assistant until midnight, pharmacy lab in the mornings, tutoring between classes. He's exhausted, but he's still determined to become a pharmacist, to make you proud."

Mrs. Chen's eyes widened. She glanced at her husband.

"He works three jobs?" she asked quietly.

I nodded. "He doesn't complain. He... does what needs to be done. Just like you taught him."

"Why do you care?" Mr. Chen's voice was blunt. "You are temporary. His education is permanent."

The dismissal stung, but I understood the calculation behind it. In their view, I was a fleeting distraction from Alex's true path.

"I care because Alex deserves to have his family there tomorrow," I said steadily. "I understand I'm not what you wanted for him. I can't replace the daughter-in-law you imagined." I met his gaze directly. "But I do love your son, and I will honor your family if you give me the chance."

Mrs. Chen's posture seemed less rigid now. She said something to her husband in Mandarin, her tone thoughtful this time rather than argumentative. He responded firmly, but she countered with words that made him pause.

The Mandarin words were opaque to me, but the emotional undercurrents were not. Concern, frustration, conflicting loyalties. And in Mr. Chen's voice, perhaps a thread of uncertainty where before there had been only conviction.

"May I show you something?" I carefully opened my portfolio case, withdrawing the smaller wrapped canvas. My hands trembled as I unwrapped it, revealing the painting of The Golden Dragon restaurant at sunset, the light catching on the red and gold details, the restaurant name rendered in both English and Chinese characters.

Mrs. Chen moved closer, studying the painting with an intensity I hadn't expected.

"I painted this," I explained. "Alex has told me about this place.

How you built it from nothing after coming to America, how it represents everything you've accomplished here."

I set it carefully on the table. "I wanted to understand what matters to Alex, and this place matters. Your sacrifices matter."

Mr. Chen's stern expression wavered as he leaned forward to examine the painting. Fine lines creased the corners of his eyes and there was a slight stoop to his shoulders that his perfect posture couldn't quite disguise.

"You did this?" Mrs. Chen asked, touching the canvas lightly, her fingertip hovering over the Chinese characters I'd so carefully copied.

"Yes. I'm an art major now. I used to be in nursing, but..." I trailed off, realizing this probably wasn't helping my case. "Art helps me understand things words can't express."

"Why did you paint our restaurant?" Mr. Chen asked. "Why not... Alex?"

The question surprised me with its insight. "Because this restaurant isn't just a building. It's your life's work. It's the foundation you built for Alex. It matters to him, so it matters to me."

Mrs. Chen picked up the painting, leaning in to study it.

"You got the characters right," she said to me. "That is not easy for an American."

"I practiced," I admitted. "A lot. I wanted to be respectful."

"This restaurant is important to this family," Mr. Chen said, his tone still formal but slightly less cold. "It was many years of hard work."

"I know," I said quietly. "Alex is proud of what you've built. He doesn't want to throw that away. He just wants to find his own path too."

Mr. Chen shook his head, but it seemed more weary than angry now. "American children always want their 'own path.' In our culture, children honor their parents."

"In my family," I said carefully, "my parents believe the greatest honor is seeing their children happy. Different families show respect in different ways."

Mr. Chen's jaw tightened. Mrs. Chen's eyes narrowed. Neither spoke. I'd hit a nerve.

"My father was the first in his family to go to college," I continued quickly. "He and my mom worked double shifts for years to send all five of us kids to school. My older brother became a fisherman instead of getting a degree. They were disappointed at first, but now they're proud of his business. I'm not saying our way is right and yours is wrong. I'm just... I'm trying to understand what Alex is carrying."

Mrs. Chen studied me with renewed interest, the wariness in her expression mixing with recognition, maybe. "Your family... they support art instead of nursing?"

I nodded. "They wanted me to be happy more than they wanted me to follow their plan. But it took time. They were scared at first. They worried I was making a mistake." I paused. "That doesn't mean I don't understand how much harder it is for Alex to disappoint you. How much it hurts him to feel he's let you down."

Mr. Chen spoke in Mandarin, the words stretching longer than before. Mrs. Chen's thumb traced the painting's frame as she answered. He said something else. She gestured toward the canvas. He shook his head.

Finally, Mrs. Chen turned to me. "Why did you come here? What do you want from us?"

The directness of the question caught me off guard. "I want... I want Alex to have his family at his graduation. That's all. Even if things don't work out between us, he deserves that."

"You would do this even if he does not choose you?" Mrs. Chen asked, her expression genuinely curious now.

"Yes." No hesitation. "Because he loves you both, and you worked so hard to make tomorrow possible. That matters more than whether I'm part of his future."

Mrs. Chen set the painting down carefully on the counter.

"I should go." I stood, sensing I'd pushed as far as I could. "Thank you for listening. That's more than I had any right to ask for."

As I turned toward the door, Mrs. Chen called after me. "The ceremony is at eleven?"

I looked back, a spark of hope flickering cautiously. "Yes. Northeastern University main auditorium."

She nodded once. Barely perceptible. Not a promise, but not a refusal either. Mr. Chen's expression remained unreadable, his arms crossed, but he hadn't shut down the possibility completely.

"Take the painting," I said, gesturing to the canvas Mrs. Chen had set down. "It's for you. For your restaurant. A graduation gift."

Mrs. Chen looked surprised. "A graduation gift? For us?"

"I have another for Alex," I explained, patting my portfolio case. "This one is for both of you. For everything you did to help Alex become the amazing person he is today."

Mrs. Chen and Mr. Chen exchanged another glance. Then Mrs. Chen picked up the painting again, holding it more carefully now.

"Thank you," she said quietly. "You are very... thoughtful."

I wasn't sure if that was approval or just politeness, but it was more than I'd expected. I left two tickets on the hostess stand as I walked out.

The May sunshine warmed my cheeks as I stepped outside. My shoulders loosened and I breathed easier. I had no idea if I'd made any difference at all, but for the first time in days, the spring in my step was back.

Back on campus, I wandered through the gardens, my portfolio still clutched tightly. The emotional intensity of facing the Chens had left me drained but somehow less heavy. Whether they showed up tomorrow or not, I'd tried. I'd seen their world more clearly, even if only a glimpse.

I found a bench beneath a flowering crabapple tree and sat, finally allowing the tension to release from my shoulders. Students streamed past, laughing and talking about summer plans, oblivious to the small drama unfolding in my mind.

ISA
> Mission accomplished?

KATE
> Maybe. Will know tomorrow at 11, I guess!

ISA
> Did you have lunch? I'm at the dining hall.

I hadn't eaten since the bagel I'd nervously nibbled before the train ride to Quincy.

KATE
> On my way.

As I walked toward the dining hall, I spotted a familiar figure coming across the quad. Jennifer Liu, her posture perfect, hair sleek in a way mine never managed no matter how many products I used. She spoke with a professor, nodding seriously at whatever he was saying.

I hesitated, then changed course. Jennifer politely excused herself from the conversation.

"Kate," she said, her voice neutral but not unfriendly. "I didn't expect to see you here."

"I wanted to thank you," I said. "For the tickets. For the note."

She adjusted her bag on her shoulder. "You're welcome. Though I'm not sure Alex would thank either of us."

"Why did you do it?" The question had been bothering me since I received her note. "I thought... I assumed you and Alex..."

Jennifer's laugh was unexpectedly warm. "That we were destined for an arranged marriage? Our parents certainly thought so." She shook her head. "Alex and I tried dating sophomore year. We make excellent friends and terrible lovers."

My cheeks blazed. "I didn't mean—"

"It's fine," she said, with a small smile. "Look, Alex and I understand each other. We both have parents with expectations. The difference is, I've learned to navigate them without drowning. Alex is still figuring that out."

"I saw his parents this morning," I confessed.

Jennifer's eyebrows shot up. "You went to The Golden Dragon? Bold move. How did that go?"

"I'm not sure. I gave them a painting. Mrs. Chen seemed less hostile by the end?"

"Li Mei is more flexible than her husband," Jennifer nodded. "She's protective, but she ultimately wants Alex to be happy. Heng is more traditional. Li Mei is the one who convinced Heng to let Alex move to a studio near Northeastern instead of staying closer to home. She pushes back more than people realize."

The casual way Jennifer used their first names reminded me of the gap between our experiences with Alex's family. But the information was valuable. Mrs. Chen had fought for Alex's choices before.

"I invited them to graduation," I said. "I don't know if they'll come."

Jennifer studied me for a moment. "You really do care about him."

It wasn't a question, but I answered anyway. "Yes. I do."

"Then don't give up on him," she said simply. "Alex needs

someone who sees him beyond the perfect student and dutiful son. That was never going to be me." She glanced at her watch. "I have to go. Good luck tomorrow."

Jennifer walked away, her confidence unshakable. A strange mix of gratitude and envy swirled through me. She had found a way to balance her parents' expectations with her own desires. Maybe she was right about Mrs. Chen too.

I texted Isa as I continued toward the dining hall.

> KATE
>
> Well that was weird. Jennifer and I are besties now I think?
>
> ISA
>
> The plot thickens. I ordered you a sandwich. Hurry before I eat it.

That evening, I carefully wrapped Alex's painting. The abstract molecular shapes that didn't quite dissolve into artistic expression yet looked right now. Honest in their incompleteness. Not a literal bridge between us, but a visual representation of how we'd influenced each other. Chemistry into art. Logic into emotion. Two people whose differences created something new in the space between them, even if that space wasn't fully resolved yet.

"Please let this work," I whispered to the silent room.

My phone chimed with a text from Mom:

> MOM
>
> Good luck tomorrow honey. Dad and I are so proud of you.

I smiled, though something ached beneath it—how easily my parents had accepted my new path. How different things might have been if they'd responded like the Chens.

KATE

> Thanks Mom. Give everyone a hug from me.

For the first time in weeks, I fell asleep easily.

The campus was a flurry of graduation energy. Proud families taking photos, seniors in caps and gowns hugging friends, younger students enjoying the festive atmosphere before heading home for summer break.

I stood at the edge of the quad, scanning the crowd for any sign of Alex or his parents. My gift was wrapped and tucked safely in my bag.

"Any luck?" Isa appeared beside me, looking uncharacteristically dressed up in a floral sundress.

"Not yet." I chewed my lower lip. "Maybe this was stupid. Maybe I made everything worse."

"Or maybe you showed two stubborn people that their son is loved." Isa squeezed my shoulder. "Either way, you tried. That counts for something."

"Does it though?" Other families around us embraced their graduates, took photos, celebrated together. "What if Alex doesn't even want me here?"

"Then Jennifer wouldn't have given you her invitation," Isa said practically. "Come on, let's find seats. The ceremony starts soon."

Inside, we found seats midway back, perfect for watching the procession. Isa kept up a running commentary about people's mortarboard decorations to distract me, but my gaze remained fixed on the entrance.

"They're not coming, are they?" I whispered as the ceremony was about to begin.

Isa squeezed my hand. "We're here. That's what matters now."

It had to count for something.

Chapter 28

Alex

Graduation morning arrived with little fanfare. I'd been awake since 4:30, my brain refusing to cooperate with standard sleep patterns.

By 9:17 AM, I'd already showered, shaved, and adjusted my tie fourteen times. The charcoal gray suit I'd purchased from the thrift shop for residency interviews hung perfectly, its conservative cut selected after extensive research into professional attire that conveyed competence without overreach.

A flurry of texts had poured in on the Westfield family group chat. I hadn't realized Kate had added me to it.

> JO
> Congratulations, Alex! We're all so proud of you.

Sophie had sent emojis: graduation caps, party poppers, and a random lobster that made no sense but was quintessentially her.

> ABBY
> Don't trip on stage or say anything weird if you have to give a speech.

Then David had texted separately.

> **DAVID**
> See you after the ceremony, roomie. We did it!

The family I'd briefly belonged to still acknowledged me. My best friend would be there. This should have felt like enough.

It didn't.

I stood in my bathroom now, royal blue doctoral hood and gold sash draped over the towel rack.

This wasn't how today was supposed to unfold. In the original plan, the one I'd formulated years ago, my parents would drive in from Quincy. My mother would be straightening my already straight tie. My father would offer rare verbal approval.

In the revised plan, the one that had evolved over the past months, Kate would be here with her camera, making me laugh about the graduation regalia. She would whoop and holler when my name was called.

Instead, I stood alone.

My phone chimed again.

> **DAVID**
> You better not be combing your tassel or something equally ridiculous.

> **ALEX**
> No combing. Just wondering if there's a precise angle for optimal tassel placement.

> **DAVID**
> You're hopeless. See ya at graduation lunch.

I picked up the graduation regalia package one final time, checking that everything was in order. Tassel positioned correctly.

Honor cords arranged by significance. Name card for the announcer tucked into my pocket with just enough visible to grab quickly.

As I locked my apartment door, I allowed myself one moment of honesty. "This isn't how this day was supposed to be," I said aloud to the empty hallway.

Then I straightened my shoulders and walked to campus, where I would cross the stage to receive my degree. The seats reserved for my guests would remain empty, unless some spectacularly confused strangers decided to claim them.

But maybe something unexpected would happen.

And if not, I'd have a fancy piece of paper with my name on it to remind me that I'd accomplished something, even if I'd lost something equally valuable along the way.

The pharmacy graduates formed a line in order of GPA. I stood fourth toward the front. Daphne Sparks had beaten me by 0.02 points. Around me, classmates celebrated. Someone's water bottle smelled distinctly of vodka.

"Chen! You ready to finally escape the organic chem torture sessions?" Mike Polanski's hand landed on my shoulder. His regalia hung askew, tassel dangling at a precarious angle.

"Definitely." I smiled—the perfected version: corners up, teeth visible, duration: 2.3 seconds. "Though I hear MCAT prep students are actually worse."

"Thank god we're done with that. Residency next, then world domination, right?"

I nodded. Explaining that I had no idea where I was going next because my five-year plan had imploded was too many words for graduation small talk.

The processional music began. Left, right, left, right. I counted the steps between graduates. Eighteen inches. Consistent spacing. Focus on the rhythm, not the empty seats.

But as we entered the auditorium, my eyes moved automatically across the sections. Years of restaurant work had trained me to assess a room without conscious thought.

The auditorium was alive with excited chatter. Parents held smartphones above the crowd, snapping pictures. The air conditioners struggled against the May heat and the body warmth of a thousand guests. Perfumes, cologne, and the musty velvet of rarely-used graduation gowns mingled in the air.

Then I saw her.

Center section, fifth row. Kate wore a blue dress the same shade as my hood. Her dark curls fell loose around her shoulders instead of pulled back in her usual messy bun. Her roommate Isabel sat with her, presumably for emotional support.

Our eyes met.

My left foot forgot which direction it was supposed to travel. The graduate behind me made a sound that suggested imminent collision. I corrected course and forced my legs to remember their function.

Kate had come.

Despite everything. She'd come.

Then I saw the figure at the back of the auditorium.

My mother stood against the wall, separate from the other families. She wore her good silk dress, the green one with the subtle brocade that she only wore for Lunar New Year and other important occasions. Her hands were folded in front of her. Her back was straight.

She was here.

My foot caught on nothing at all. I stumbled but kept walking. My rhythmic steps had become a conscious effort instead of automatic.

Both of them. They'd both chosen to come.

The rest of the processional happened around me. My brain catalogued variables: Kate's presence, my mother's appearance, and the empty seat where my father should have been.

The diploma in my hand weighed less than I'd expected for something that represented six years of work. The leather case was cool and smooth against my palm, embossed with the university seal.

I moved through the crowd, shaking hands with professors, nodding at congratulations, scanning for Kate while trying not to look like I was scanning.

The cacophony of the post-ceremony celebration surrounded me. Camera shutters clicking, parents calling out names, the dean's voice still echoing through the loudspeakers. Someone popped a bottle of champagne nearby, the cork hitting the ceiling with a distinct thunk, followed by surprised laughter and hurried apologies to the facility staff.

"Not bad, Chen."

David appeared at my elbow, delivering what passed for a hug in our friendship: one firm shoulder clap and a nod.

"We did it."

"We did it." He held up his camera. "I've got photographic evidence of this historic occasion. Including the 7 seconds where you looked genuinely emotional."

"Delete that immediately."

"Not a chance." The corner of his mouth twitched. "So... what now?"

Before I could formulate an answer, Kate moved through the crowd toward us. She carried something wrapped in brown paper.

"Incoming." David's voice was quiet. "I'll catch you at the restaurant."

He vanished with impressive speed.

Kate stood in front of me, holding out the package with both hands.

"Congratulations." Her voice was soft. "Doctor Chen."

My fingers brushed hers as I took the package. "You came."

"Of course I came." She tucked hair behind her ear on the left side—always the left when nervous. "Your accomplishments matter to me. Even when we're fighting."

"Kate, about what I said—"

"Open it first." She nodded at the package. "Please."

I unwrapped the paper with the same care I'd use for lab samples. The painting inside showed two figures on opposite sides of a divide. On the left, I recognized my own careful hand. Benzene rings, carbon chains, the molecular structures I'd once sketched for her on coffee shop napkins. On the right, her brushstrokes exploded into color. And across the center, the two merged. Science transforming into art. My language becoming hers, hers becoming mine.

My throat closed.

"It's us. Different languages for seeing the same world."

I looked up from the painting. Chemistry had given me formulas for reaction rates and equilibrium constants. Nothing in my studies had prepared me for this.

I exhaled slowly. "I saw my mother."

"Alex, I know. I saw her too."

"How did you—"

"I visited The Golden Dragon yesterday." Her hands fidgeted with her purse strap. "I wanted them to know what they'd be missing if they didn't come today."

I stared at her. "You visited my parents?"

"I painted their restaurant." She said it like it was obvious. Like walking into the place where I'd been effectively disowned and offering them a painting was a logical next step. "I wanted them to know I see what matters to you. That I respect it."

Over Kate's shoulder, my mother approached. Kate followed my gaze and surprise crossed her face.

"I should go." Kate whispered, following my gaze. "This is your moment with her."

My hand caught her wrist. "Stay."

My mother stopped in front of us. Her expression gave away nothing.

"Congratulations, son." She spoke in English, formal and precise. "We are proud."

My fingers tightened around Kate's wrist. "Thank you for coming, Mom." I paused, measuring the risk. "You remember Kate."

My mother's eyes cut to Kate. I knew that look. The same one she used when selecting produce at the Asian market.

"Good to see you again." Her voice was careful. "Your painting of the restaurant is very accurate."

Kate's surprise mirrored my own. She recovered faster than I did. "Thank you. I wanted to capture the warmth of it."

My mother's face softened around her eyes, the kind I remembered from childhood moments when I'd done something unexpectedly right.

She reached into her purse and withdrew a red envelope. "From Bàba and me. For graduation."

I took it with my free hand, still holding onto Kate. I knew without looking that it contained the customary $888 for good luck, and I had to blink hard to clear my vision. "Will you join us for lunch?"

My mother shook her head. "I need to help with the lunch shift. Saturday is busy." She paused. "Perhaps dinner. Another day."

She nodded once at Kate in acknowledgment. Then she walked away.

I exhaled.

"That was..." I started.

"A first step." Kate's voice was quiet. "Small, but significant."

I let go of her wrist, only to take her hand properly. My fingers found the spaces between hers. "Kate, I need to explain about Jennifer."

"She gave me your graduation tickets. And told me you'd want me here instead of her."

"She did?"

"She seems to understand you pretty well."

"Not as well as you do." I studied the painting in my hands. My world and hers, overlapping. "No one sees me the way you do."

Around us, families embraced. Cameras flashed. Graduates threw their caps and nearly hit professors. Our moment felt separate from all of it.

"Can we go somewhere?" I asked. "And talk?"

Kate squeezed my hand. "I know just the place."

The campus garden between the science building and the art department was neutral territory. Kate led me to a bench beneath a flowering dogwood, and I sat down in my absurdly formal regalia, setting her painting carefully beside me.

I took off my cap. The tassel I'd adjusted several times this morning hung crooked now. I left it that way.

The garden hummed with life. Bees moved methodically between late spring blooms. A cardinal flashed red against the green leaves. The scent of freshly cut grass mingled with the sweet perfume of flowering dogwood, and beneath it all, the earthy smell of soil warming in the afternoon sun.

"I'm sorry." Start with the most important part. "What I said about you changing majors like flipping TV channels. I was wrong. I know it took courage to follow your path."

Kate traced invisible patterns on the bench between us. "And I'm sorry I made it sound simple. Letting my family help you. I wasn't seeing the complexity."

"I was jealous." The word felt foreign in my mouth. Messy. Imprecise. "Your family accepted your change. Mine..."

"Cut you off."

"But my mother came today." I studied Kate's face. "Because of you. Why would you do that? After I pushed you away?"

"Because I never wanted you to choose between worlds, Alex." Her hand crept toward mine on the bench between us. "I wanted to help connect them, somehow."

The garden path curved around us, students in graduation finery passing by with their families. The breeze carried fragments of their conversations.

"I never should have implied your art wasn't as important as pharmacy. Or that you had it easier."

"Different challenges. Not easier ones. I might not have lost family support, but I had to take a leap into the unknown."

The distant celebration sounds drifted across campus. I reached for her hand, needing the anchor.

"What happens now?" The question encompassed more than just this afternoon.

Kate started to say something, but I tightened my grip on her hand.

"I need to tell you something first." I took a breath. "I accepted a residency offer in Providence."

Her eyes widened. "You... what?"

"Western Mass General had the better program. Higher ranking, more research opportunities, better chance at a fellowship afterward." The analytical part of my brain had catalogued all the pros and cons in a spreadsheet that I'd revised countless times. "On paper, it was the obvious choice."

"Alex—"

"But Providence has partnerships with RISD and the Newport Art Museum." My words picked up speed. "The gallery scene there is actually remarkable for a city its size. There are three artist co-ops within a two-mile radius of the hospital. The rent is comparable to Boston, maybe slightly lower. There's a community college with continuing education art classes if you wanted to teach. And the commute to potential gallery shows in Boston is only about fifty minutes."

Kate stared at me. "You researched all of this?"

"I made a spreadsheet." Of course I had. "With columns for gallery density, average artist income, cost of living, proximity to art supply stores, and—" I caught her expression, one eye arched in silent judgement. "I might have gotten slightly obsessive about the data."

"Slightly." Her voice was soft.

"The point is, I chose Providence because it's a place where both our careers can exist. Where I can do my residency and you can build your art practice. Where we can..." I paused, suddenly aware of how presumptuous this sounded. "Assuming you want to. Build something. Together."

"You made this choice before we even reconciled." Kate's voice was slow, processing.

"I made it right after our fight." I looked down at our joined hands. "When I realized I'd rather adjust my five-year plan than lose you. Again."

Kate leaned her forehead against mine. "Tell me more about Providence. About how you see it working."

The question was practical, grounding. I appreciated it more than she knew.

"The residency is at Rhode Island Hospital. I'd work eighty-hour weeks, especially the first year." I didn't sugarcoat it. "But there's an apartment building on Benefit Street that's within walking distance of both the hospital and RISD's museum. You could convert the second bedroom into a studio. It has north-facing windows, optimal for painting light."

"You've already viewed apartments?"

"I've toured three. Virtually." The admission felt embarrassing. "The Fox Point neighborhood has a farmers market on Saturdays. You could sell prints there, build a local client base while submitting to galleries."

Kate smiled. "And where do you fit into this detailed vision? Besides working eighty-hour weeks."

"Year one would be rough," I admitted. "But there's a coffee shop halfway between the hospital and the apartment where we could meet for breakfast before shifts. Year two gets better. There's more predictable hours. By year three, I'd have enough schedule control to actually attend your gallery openings."

She traced my jawline with her fingertip. "You're already thinking about year three?"

"I think about everything in multi-year increments. It's a problem."

"It's not, though." Her eyes stayed locked on mine. "Not anymore. Because now you're planning for us, not just yourself."

I took a breath. "I know it won't be easy. The residency is brutal. My parents aren't suddenly going to embrace everything. I'm sure your family is worried about me taking you away from Maine."

"I noticed you didn't include my family's issues in your spreadsheet analysis."

"Column J, tab 2. Family integration challenges, ranked by intensity and frequency."

Kate laughed. "Of course you did."

"The point is, I know there's still a lot to work through. I know

I haven't magically fixed my issues." This was harder to say. "The way I pull back when I'm stressed. The way I get lost in work. The way I categorize emotions instead of feeling them."

"And I know I still barrel into situations without thinking. Rush decisions. Make sweeping assumptions about what's best for everyone." Kate squeezed my hand. "We're works in progress."

"But I want to progress. With you." I pulled the tassel on my cap straight, then deliberately messed it up again. A small act of rebellion against my need for order. "Even if I'm still learning how."

Kate pulled back enough to meet my eyes. "Yes."

"Yes?"

"Yes, I want to try Providence. Yes, I want to build something with you." She smiled through tears. "Yes to your obsessive spreadsheets and your research about gallery density and your complete inability to make major life choices without multiple columns of data."

I might have smiled then. "I should probably mention the spreadsheet also has a tab for potential apartment locations, cross-referenced with commute times to both the hospital and the nearest art supply store."

"Of course it does." Kate kissed me, soft and brief. "You're ridiculous."

"You like it."

"I really do."

I checked my watch. "I'm supposed to be meeting David for a celebratory lunch at 2. We have approximately ten minutes before he orders everything on the appetizer menu."

"Well." Kate's fingers traced a line up my arm, slow and deliberate. "Your apartment's close, isn't it?"

My brain, which had been functioning at its usual analytical capacity, suddenly forgot how to process information. "My apartment."

"We could text David that we're running late."

"Kate." Desire roughened my voice. "Are you sure?"

She answered by kissing me.

Not the tentative kiss from earlier. This one was deliberate, her hand sliding to the back of my neck, pulling me closer. When she pulled back, we were both breathing harder.

"I'm sure." Her whisper was warm against my mouth. "I've missed you, Alex."

I stood, pulling her with me, the painting gathered in one hand while the other held hers. "My apartment. Now."

We barely made it through the door.

I set the painting down, propping it safely against the stack of moving boxes. Then Kate was in my arms, her fingers working at the graduation regalia I was still wearing.

"This has too many components." She struggled with the hood clasp.

"Doctoral regalia typically consists of—" I started, then stopped when her hand found skin beneath my shirt. "Okay, we can skip the detailed explanation."

She laughed, breathless.

I walked her backward toward the bedroom, shedding the regalia as we moved. The hood landed on a box. My cap hit the floor at an angle that would have bothered me this morning. Right now, I couldn't bring myself to care.

Kate's blue dress had a zipper. I found it, my hands less steady than they should be. She helped, reaching back to guide the zipper down, and then the dress pooled at her feet.

"Alex." She touched my face, making me look at her. "Stay with me. Don't disappear into your head."

I kissed her, trying to communicate everything I couldn't quite articulate. How I'd missed this. Not just the physical connection, but the way she grounded me.

We tumbled onto the bed, my carefully packed moving boxes forgotten. Her hands were everywhere, relearning the map of my body. My mouth traced the line of her neck, her collarbone, lower. She made a sound that sliced straight through me.

"I'm sorry." The words murmured against her skin. "For pushing you away. For making you feel like you weren't enough."

"Show me." Her fingers threaded through my hair. "Show me I'm enough."

So I did.

I took my time, wanting to memorize every sound she made, every place that made her breath catch. Kate wasn't patient. She never had been. Soon, she was pulling me up, pulling me closer, wrapping herself around me.

"I love you." I whispered against her collarbone as we moved together, easier than ever had before. "I love you."

"I love you too." Her breath was warm against my ear.

The careful control I maintained in every other aspect of my life dissolved. There was just Kate. Her hands, her mouth, the heat of her skin against mine, the way her body responded to every touch.

When we finished, we lay tangled together in the afternoon light filtering through the window. Fingers traced idle patterns on my skin as her heartbeat slowed, matching mine.

"We're very late now."

"David will survive."

"He's probably ordered the entire menu out of spite."

Kate propped herself up on one elbow, her hair falling around us. "Worth it?"

I tucked a strand behind her ear. "Definitely worth it."

She smiled, then reached for her phone on the nightstand. "I should probably text him though. Before he sends a search party."

She typed, then set the phone aside. "What did you say?"

"That we're running late and to order without us." She settled back against me. "He responded with about fifteen eye-roll emojis."

"Sounds about right."

We lay quiet for a moment, the significance of the day settling around us. Graduation. My mother's appearance. Kate's return. All the pieces of my carefully ordered life rearranging themselves into something I hadn't planned but maybe needed more.

"You know what's strange?" I asked softly.

"Hmm?"

"All this time, I thought my parents were the ones who couldn't change. But maybe it was me too. Maybe I was so busy charting the exact right course that I couldn't see when it was time to adjust."

Kate lifted her head to look at me. "We're all works in progress."

"Some more than others."

We walked together toward the restaurant where David waited, our steps falling into sync.

My mother had skipped her shift at the restaurant to come. Kate had come. The path ahead wasn't clear or straight. There would be more misunderstandings, more family tensions, more balancing acts between worlds. But as we crossed campus in the spring afternoon, I finally looked forward to the future.

"One step at a time?" Kate asked.

I squeezed her hand. "One day at a time."

The story was still being written. Chemistry and art. Tradition and change. Where I came from and where I was going.

With Kate.

Epilogue

Kate

Purple paint streaked across Chloe's cheek and threatened to catch the wayward hairs escaping her blonde ponytail. She attacked the paper with seven-year-old abandon that only exists until an adult forces you to color between the lines.

"Miss Kate, look!" She shoved her painting at me. Overlapping colors that might've been a sunset. Or a dragon. "I mixed red and blue like you said, but it made purple, not green!"

"Red and blue *do* make purple." I crouched beside her workspace. The art room at the local summer camp always smelled of acrylic paints and sweaty kids. "You need blue and yellow for green."

Her eyes widened. She snatched a fresh sheet of paper, squeezing paint straight from the bottles onto the page before I could suggest moderation.

My phone skittered across the table.

> **ALEX**
> Done at 6 today. Your place or mine?

Two years of this question. We kept separate apartments. His studio was three blocks from Rhode Island Hospital, my one-bedroom near RISD's campus with north-facing windows. His parents approved of this arrangement. For all they knew, we had a traditional courtship with appropriate boundaries.

He'd slept at his place maybe four nights in the past month.

KATE

Mine. I'll actually cook something with vegetables.

ALEX

Ambitious. I like it.

Also I want to talk about something tonight.

Want to talk.

He'd been so careful lately. Watchful. Like he was working up to something. And last week when David's engagement photos filled my feed, he'd gone quiet beside me as I scrolled, studying my face with an intensity that made my stomach drop.

Was this finally it?

"Miss Kate, it's *still* not green!"

Chloe had created a brown swamp creature. "You get brown when you mix all the colors." I grabbed a clean sheet. "Fresh start?"

By five-thirty, I'd taught three kids color theory, prevented a paint war, and explained that sharing brushes wouldn't contaminate artistic vision. My shirt still showed the evidence. Green on one shoulder, blue fingerprints on my pant leg where Marcus grabbed me reaching for paper towels.

I'd graduated a few weeks ago with my Bachelor's in Art, but I was still working at the local summer arts program to supplement the meager commissions I earned as a fledgling painter.

I loved it. Every chaotic second.

The walk home took fifteen minutes through the shining sun of early June in Providence. Perfect weather before summer humidity hit, students still lingering instead of fleeing for break. I walked past empanada vendors, coffee carts, and the old guy with an accordion outside the RISD Museum. I dropped two dollars in his case. He nodded mid-song without pausing the tinny melody.

My apartment occupied the third floor of a converted Victorian. Hardwood, crown molding, and a shabby-elegant charm where you had to jiggle the bathroom doorknob just right and the radiators fought with the pipes all winter.

The corner of the living room was my studio. Canvases were everywhere. Finished pieces for gallery submission, commissions in progress at various stages. My easel by the window to catch the best light, paint supplies on a thrifted rolling cart held together by copious amounts of duct tape.

I'd worked on emotional landscapes for months. Abstract pieces trying to capture feelings words couldn't touch. The current canvas was a wash of blues and grays with hints of yellow dancing like sunlight on water. Waverly Cove on a summer day when everything felt exactly right.

I studied it, deciding whether the shadows needed more depth. Just as I was about to grab a brush and start adding to the painting, I heard a message alert from my phone.

> **ALEX**
> Running late. Insurance authorization disaster. 6:30?

> **KATE**
> No rush. Haven't started cooking anyway.
>
> You okay?

> **ALEX**
> Fine. Bureaucracy.

I headed for the kitchen. Cooking had become meditation these past few years, how I centered after managing creative chaos. Tonight I planned salmon with roasted vegetables. Simple and good. The kind of dinner that said 'I'm taking care of us' without three hours of prep after a long day.

Thirty minutes later, the salmon was done and the vegetables were perfectly roasted. I plated everything with more care than necessary, arranging colors like a composition. Yellow peppers, orange carrots, deep pink salmon, bright green zucchini.

A key turned in the lock just as I was lighting two candles on the table... just in case.

Alex looked considerably better than he had for the entire brutal first-year rotation. Second year meant better hours and more predictable schedules, so we could actually eat dinner together on weekdays. His hair still stuck up in the back, probably from pulling at it during some pharmaceutical emergency, but his eyes were clear and his smile was genuine when he saw the set table.

"This looks amazing." He set down a bottle of wine and crossed to kiss me. "You're amazing. Have I mentioned that today?"

"Not since six AM when you left." I leaned into him, breathing coffee and hospital soap and home. "How was the insurance disaster?"

"Resolved. After forty-five minutes of hold music and three representatives." He pulled back to study me. "How was camp today?"

"Chaotic. Creative. One kid discovered that mixing all colors makes brown and was devastated." I moved to pour wine while he washed his hands. "But they're learning. Getting better every week."

"Like someone else I know."

I glanced over my shoulder. "Meaning?"

"Your show last month sold three pieces. Even the piece you were fretting about turned out beautifully. You're doing it, Kate. Building the career you wanted."

His praise still made me blush. I hoped it always would.

We ate, conversation flowing through the day. A difficult prescription case. A grant application for the arts education program. Weekend plans. Hiking if the weather held, visiting my parents if it didn't.

It wasn't until we'd cleared the table and moved to the couch with glasses of wine did Alex shift into something more serious.

"So." He set down his glass. "I wanted to talk about something."

My stomach dropped. Here it was. The conversation he'd mentioned. Would he really finally ask, or was I building this all up in my head? Reading too much into his recent behavior?

I set down my glass and turned to face him, sitting on my hands to still their shaking. "Okay."

He took a breath. The kind that meant careful thinking, logical frameworks, organized thoughts. "I've been thinking about the future. What comes after residency."

"That's almost three months away." Which he obviously knew, but my mouth needed something to do. I was proud of it for not yelling 'ask me already!' and making me look like a fool if that wasn't where this conversation was headed.

"Right. And I've had fellowship offers. Boston, Philadelphia, New York."

I had that lobster-scrambling-in-a-tank feeling in my stomach again. Alex was brilliant. Any hospital would be lucky to have him. Boston I could handle, but Philadelphia? New York? Even further from my family? I would follow him anywhere, but I just assumed he'd never ask me to.

"But I've been thinking about what I want." He ran a hand through his hair, making it stick up more. "Not what looks best on a CV or what program ranks highest. What would make me happy."

"What would make you happy?" My brain struggled to keep up.

"There's a position opening in Waverly Cove." Quick, like he'd been holding the words. "At Shoreline Pharmacy. The owner's retiring. They need a new lead pharmacist. It's not prestigious. Won't advance my career. But it's..."

"Home." Warmth and hope bloomed—sudden and bright. "You want to move to Waverly Cove."

"I want to move wherever you want to be." He reached for my hands. "But I thought... maybe Waverly Cove makes sense. You've been talking about wanting a bigger studio space. Your family's there. James and Diane, Sophie and Taylor are working to open the brewery, and Abby's student teaching. And I know you miss Maine."

I stared at him. "You want to move to Waverly Cove. Work at Shoreline Pharmacy. Where Mrs. Jeffers corners people about her bunions."

"What is it with that town and Mrs. Jeffers' bunions?" A smile tugged at the corner of his lips. "Your dad's receptionist mentioned them last Christmas at the holiday party."

"Alex, that's..." I stopped, organizing my thoughts. "That's a huge step down career-wise. No research. No prestigious hospital connections. Just a small-town pharmacy."

"Just a community that needs a good pharmacist." He squeezed my hands. "And a place where the woman I love could make a living with her art without constantly worrying about rent."

The woman I love. The words still made my heart skip after two years together.

"Your parents will have opinions." Understatement of the century.

"They'll adjust." He smiled. "Eventually. Meanwhile, I'll be building the life I want."

I studied his face. The warmth in his eyes, the slight nervousness in his shoulders, how his thumb traced circles on my hand. He meant it. He wanted this.

"When would this start?"

"September first. Right after residency." He paused. "I told them I needed to discuss it with you before giving a final answer."

I could picture it. Moving back to Maine. Living in Waverly Cove. Being near family. Having Alex there, not visiting on weekends when schedules allowed but present in daily life.

But a thought nagged at me. The way he'd presented this. Carefully, logically, laying out practical considerations. Job secured, timeline established. Everything organized.

"Did you practice this conversation?" I asked suddenly.

His ears turned pink. "I may have rehearsed the key points."

"Key points."

God, I loved him. This brilliant, careful man, planning for our future and getting flustered when I called him on it.

And that's when my mouth made a decision my brain hadn't approved.

"Marry me."

The words erupted before I could stop them. Before thinking about timing or proper etiquette or anything. Just impulsive and completely sincere.

Alex froze. "What?"

"Marry me." My heartbeat thundered in my ears. "You're planning our whole future. Jobs, houses, space for my studio. Choosing a life that makes sense for both of us instead of just the most impressive option. So let's make it official. Let's get married, Alex."

His expression darkened before smoothing into careful neutrality.

"Kate..."

"I know it's impulsive. I know you probably had a timeline and this isn't how you imagined it. But I don't want to wait for the perfect moment or right time or whatever we're supposed to wait for." Words tumbled over each other. I could barely speak fast enough to let them all out. "I love you. I want to build a life with you. And I want to do it officially, legally, in a way that tells everyone including your parents this is real and permanent and..."

"Kate." His voice was quiet.

I stopped mid-spiral. "What?"

He reached into his pocket and pulled out a small velvet box.

My jaw hit the floor. "Is that..."

"I was going to propose." He opened the box, revealing a rose gold ring.

My artist's eye drank in every detail, even while my mind raced to catch up with what was happening. The band was delicate but sturdy, with five tiny stones set flush into the metal. No prongs to snag on canvas or collect paint. They ran in an asymmetrical cluster rather than a straight line: peachy morganite flanked by teal sapphire, amber citrine, lavender tanzanite, and bright peridot. It was utterly non-traditional, and so specifically me that my vision blurred immediately.

"That's what this conversation is about. I was going to present the practical considerations first. Job, housing, financial stability. Then ask you properly."

"You're proposing?"

"I had more of a speech prepared." He was trying not to smile now. "Very organized. Hit all the key emotional beats."

"Of course you had a speech."

"I've been carrying this ring for two months." He pulled it from the box, held it between us. "Waiting for the right moment. When we'd have time to celebrate. When I could properly explain my reasoning."

"Your reasoning." Then I laughed. "Alex Chen, you made a spreadsheet about proposing, didn't you?"

"There may have been a spreadsheet." His ears were definitely red now. "With columns for optimal timing, emotional readiness indicators, and a tab with various contingency plans depending on your response."

"Contingency plans?"

"You're unpredictable. I had to prepare for multiple scenarios." Fully smiling now. "Though I hadn't accounted for you proposing first."

"I ruined your plan." Half-laughing, half-crying, completely overwhelmed. "I'm sorry. My mouth is a volcano and everything comes out before my brain catches up."

"I know." He cupped my face with his free hand, thumb brushing away a tear I hadn't realized fell. "It's one of the things I love about you. You're spontaneous and impulsive and brave enough to say things I'd spend months obsessing over."

"So what do we do now? Do you give your speech? Do I finish proposing? Is there protocol for simultaneous proposals?"

"I don't think there's established protocol." He held up the ring. "But since I designed this, and yes, there was a comparison matrix for jewelers, maybe we could meet in the middle?"

"How do we meet in the middle of a proposal?"

"Like this." He shifted, kneeling on the floor beside the couch, still holding the ring. "Katherine Westfield, you proposed approximately five minutes ago. I'd like to counter-propose. Will you marry me?"

My heart might crack open from fullness. "That's not a counter-proposal. That's just a regular proposal."

"Will you marry me?" he asked again, patient and steady.

"Yes," I cried, tear-soaked and joyful. "Yes, obviously, that's what I was trying to tell you before you pulled out the ring and made me feel like an idiot for—"

He kissed me, silencing whatever rambling excuse I was about to give. When we broke apart, he slipped the ring onto my finger. Perfect fit. Of course. He'd probably measured my other rings and consulted jewelers and done extensive research on sizing.

I admired how candlelight caught the stones. I loved that Alex knew me well enough not to buy some diamond monstrosity that would get ruined when I was painting. "All that careful preparation for nothing."

"I disagree." He settled back on the couch, pulling me against him. "I got to see you propose first. That's better than any scenario I'd planned."

"Even the ones in your spreadsheet?"

"Especially those." His arms tightened around me. "Because they were all about me doing it right. But this was us figuring it out together. Messy and imperfect and honest."

I turned to kiss him properly. His mouth opened under mine, and the kiss deepened. When I pulled back, his pupils were dark and his breathing had changed.

"So we're doing this," I asked, soft and wondering. "Moving to Waverly Cove. Getting married."

"Apparently so." His hand slid up my spine, warm through my shirt.

"Your parents are going to have so many opinions."

"Undoubtedly." His lips found my neck, pressing kisses along my pulse point. Heat gathered low in my belly.

"My mom's going to want to plan everything immediately."

"I'd expect nothing less." His teeth grazed my earlobe and I shivered.

"And we need to tell everyone." I breathed. "Siblings, your parents, Gemma... oh god, Gemma's going to cry and claim she knew this would happen."

"She did know." He pulled back to look at me, his hand cupping my face. "She and Isa were secret conspirators on your ring design."

Just when I thought I couldn't love this man any more, he goes and asks my closest friends in the world for help designing the perfect ring. "You asked Isa and Gemma?"

"I needed input from people who actually know you." His thumb traced my bottom lip. "Your parents know as well. I asked their permission."

"And yours?" The worry slipped out.

His smile turned soft. "My mother cried. My father shook my hand and said I chose well." He paused. "It took time, but they see what I see now. They know how happy you make me."

Of course he'd asked for their blessing too. Ever the dutiful son, but this time following his heart and his duty in the same direction.

I kissed him again. His hands slid under my shirt, fingers splaying across my lower back. Two years together and his touch still made my nerve endings sing.

"When do we tell everyone else?" I murmured against his mouth.

"Later." His hands moved higher, tracing the line of my spine. "Much later."

"Alex Chen, are you suggesting we celebrate our engagement before making phone calls?"

"I'm suggesting," he said, pulling me onto his lap so I straddled him, "that we have the rest of our lives to tell people. But right now, I'd like to enjoy having my fiancée all to myself."

Fiancée. The word sent a sudden thrill through me.

I rolled my hips experimentally. He hardened beneath me. His hands tightened on my waist, an intake of breath.

"Kate..."

"Yes?" I did it again, slower this time, his face fascinating to watch.

"You're being a menace." But his hands were already working at the buttons of my shirt.

"You love it when I'm a menace."

"I love you." He pulled my shirt open, his palms sliding over my ribs. "Menace or not."

I tugged at his sweater and he helped me pull it over his head. Two years, and I still loved mapping the planes of his chest and the lean muscle of his shoulders. My hands knew every line of him now. Where to press to make him gasp, where to trail my fingers to make him shiver.

His mouth found my collarbone, then lower. When his lips closed over my breast through my bra, I arched into him with a soft sound.

"Bedroom."

"Good idea."

We stumbled down the short hallway, hands never leaving each other. He pressed me against the doorframe, kissing me deeply while his fingers worked at my bra clasp. It sprung free easily. He'd grown much better at that over the years.

My knees hit the edge of the mattress and I pulled him down with me. We landed in a tangle of limbs, laughing breathlessly before the laughter dissolved into more kissing. His weight pressed me into the bed, solid and familiar and exactly right.

"I love you."

"I love you too." He shifted to kiss down my neck, my shoulder, the valley between my breasts. "My chaotic, impulsive, beautiful fiancée."

"Who proposed before you could."

"Who proposed before I could." He smiled against my skin. "Ruining my constructed plan."

"You're not really upset about that."

"I'm not upset at all." He hooked his fingers in my waistband, looking up at me. "May I?"

After two years, he still asked. Still checked in. It made me melt every time.

"Please."

He pulled my pants and underwear down in one smooth motion. His hands traced back up my legs, thumbs brushing the sensitive skin of my inner thighs.

"You're overdressed." I tugged at his belt.

He stood to remove his pants, and I took the opportunity to admire him. Lean muscle, the line of his hip bones, the bulge in his boxer briefs that made my mouth water. He'd grown into his confidence, no longer self-conscious about being seen.

When he settled between my legs, his mouth found my inner thigh. Soft kisses working higher, deliberately avoiding where I wanted him most.

"Alex..."

"Patience." His breath ghosted over sensitive skin. "I'm celebrating."

"By torturing me?"

"By savoring my fiancée." He finally locked his mouth on me.

I gasped, my hands fisting in his hair. Two years of learning exactly what I liked, and he applied that knowledge mercilessly. His tongue moved in slow, deliberate circles before he added his fingers. The combination made my hips lift off the bed.

"That's it." The words murmured against me. "Let me hear you."

I didn't hold back. We'd learned each other's sounds, what worked, what didn't. He adjusted based on my responses, reading my body like one of his pharmaceutical journals.

When he crooked his fingers just right while his tongue worked that perfect spot, the pressure built fast. My thighs trembled.

"Alex, I'm going to—"

"Good." He didn't let up, steady and relentless until I shattered, crying out his name.

He kissed his way back up my body while I caught my breath. When he reached my mouth, I tasted myself on his lips.

"Show off."

"Just thorough." He kissed me again, slow and deep.

I reached between us, wrapping my hand around him through his boxers. He groaned into my mouth, his hips pressing into my palm.

"These need to go." I tugged at the waistband.

He helped me push them down, then pressed against me. The slide of bare skin made us both gasp.

"Condom." He reached for the nightstand.

I caught his wrist. "Actually... what if we didn't?"

He froze. "Kate..."

"I'm on the pill. I have been for months." I'd switched for cycle regulation, but the secondary benefit hadn't escaped my notice. "And we're getting married. Moving to Maine. Building a life together."

"We haven't talked about this." Not saying no, but not saying yes.

"I'm not saying we have to. I'm saying we could." I traced the line of his jaw. "If you want to."

He studied my face. "Are you sure?"

"I'm sure I want you. However you want this."

Heat and tenderness and want all mixed together crossed his face. "Then yes. I want to feel all of you."

He positioned himself and pressed in slowly. The difference was subtle but profound—warmth and friction and nothing between us. We both made soft sounds, foreheads pressed together.

"Okay?"

"So okay." I wrapped my legs around his waist, pulling him deeper. "Move."

His mouth found my neck as he did, teeth scraping gently. I arched into him, meeting each thrust. One of his hands slid between us, fingers finding that bundle of nerves.

"Again." The word rumbled against my throat. "I want to feel you come around me."

His words combined with his touch and the perfect angle pushed me over the edge again. I clenched around him, gasping his name.

He followed minutes later, his rhythm faltering as he buried himself deep. Warmth spread through me as he pulsed inside me. His face pressed into my neck, breathing hard.

We stayed like that for a long moment, tangled together, hearts racing in tandem.

"Well," I said eventually. "That was quite a celebration."

He laughed, the sound muffled against my skin. "I should propose more often."

"Me too."

Later, much later, we called Gemma. Who screamed so loud Alex had to hold the phone away from his ear. Then Isa, who demanded to see the ring immediately via FaceTime. Then my siblings, who were suspiciously unsurprised. Then my parents, who confessed to spilling the beans to the rest of the Westfield clan. And last, his parents, who were uncharacteristically warm.

But through all of it, Alex's hand stayed wrapped around mine. Our fingers intertwined, the ring's smooth band warm against my skin. A tangible reminder that love didn't follow spreadsheets or careful plans, it followed its own path, shaped by two people brave enough to meet in the middle.

Also by Angelica Eling

Afterword

In college, I made the same choice Kate almost makes: I took the safe path.

Business school meant a stable career, financial security, the kind of future that made sense on paper. Art, writing, music? Beautiful dreams, not practical ones. So those passions got tucked away.

The career worked out. Success came. A comfortable living followed. By every conventional measure, it was the right choice.

But somewhere along the way came the feeling of being lost at sea. The financial security was real. The professional accomplishments were real. But no promotion or paycheck filled what was missing. Late at night: *What if the path had been different? What if there'd been courage to follow those creative passions?*

That question nagged me for twenty years.

Then, at forty, enough was enough. The wondering had become its own prison.

I started my exploration of Waverly Cove. And with it, my own return to the dreams I'd set aside.

Kate changes course at twenty. I waited until forty. But the struggle is the same: family expectations, disappointing people you love, choosing what you want instead of what's expected.

This story is for everyone who chose the safe path and wondered about the other one. For the dreamers, the artists, the creative souls who got quiet.

You can still change course. You can pursue what you've kept quiet. You can choose yourself.

With gratitude,

Angelica

Acknowledgments

Bringing Kate and Alex's story to life wouldn't have been possible without the incredible support system that surrounds me.

To my family: your unwavering support means everything. Ryan, thank you for never questioning why I was glued to my laptop, for listening to me talk through plot problems, and for believing in my dreams even when I doubted them myself.

To my friends who've become chosen family: thank you for celebrating every milestone, for understanding when I disappeared into revision caves, and for reminding me that there's a world outside my laptop screen.

To my beta readers and critique partners, DR, RE, EL, JC and AC: you are absolute treasures. Thank you for your honest feedback, for catching my plot holes, and for cheering me on through every draft.

Finally, to my readers: thank you for returning to Waverly Cove with me. Thank you for believing in slow-burn romance, for cheering on characters who struggle to reconcile duty with desire, and for understanding that the best love stories support us in becoming who we're meant to be.

About the Author

Angelica lives in Southern Maine with her husband, Ryan, and two step-sons. She writes the stories she has always wanted to read: ones where women's experiences are portrayed with honesty, complexity, and respect.

The Waverly Cove series allows her to explore the rich tapestry of small-town life while celebrating authentic love stories. Sign up for exclusive access to bonus chapters and learn what's next in Waverly Cove at www.angelicaeling.com.

www.ingramcontent.com/pod-product-compliance
Lightning Source LLC
LaVergne TN
LVHW040037080526
838202LV00045B/3379